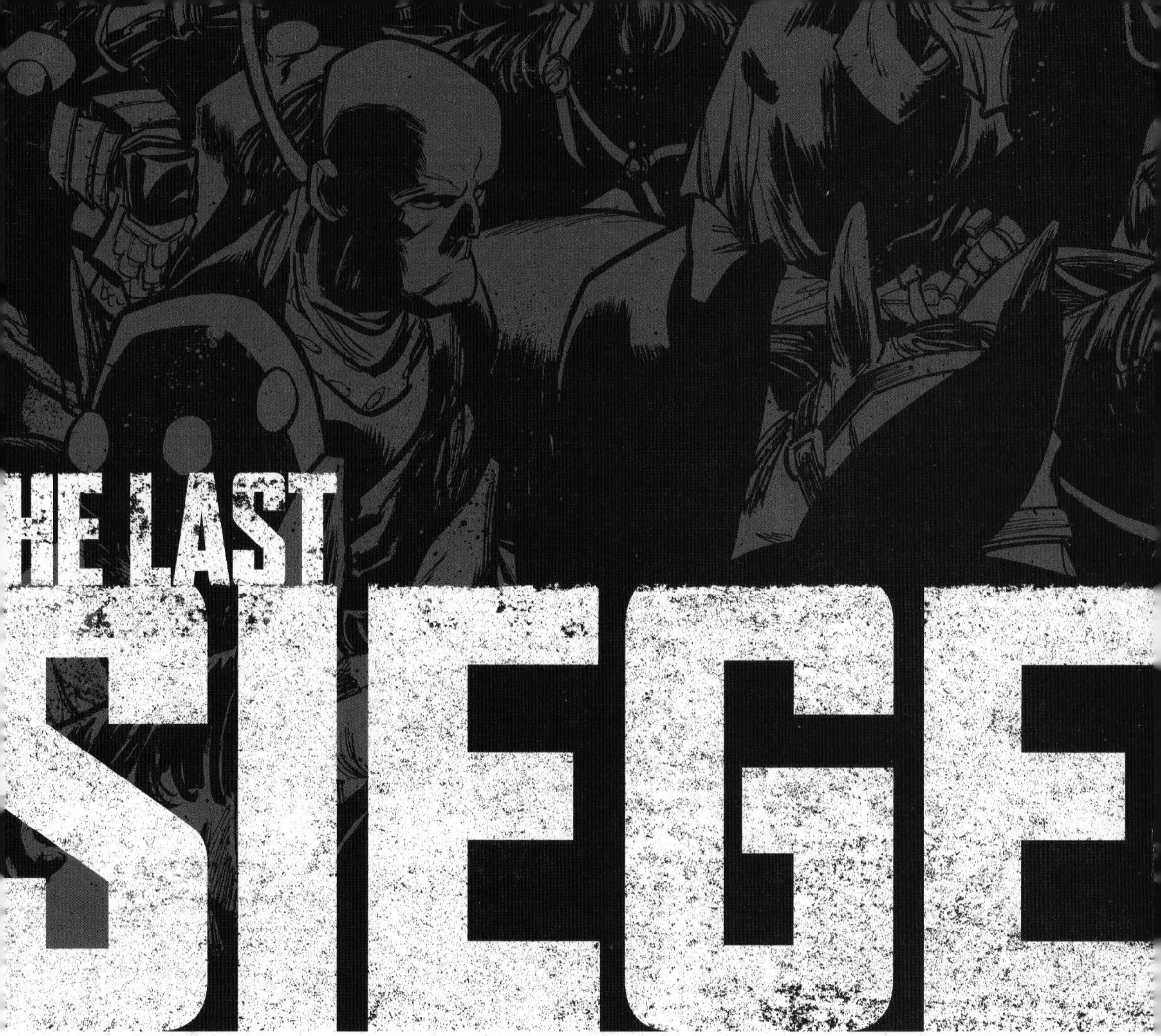
HE LAST
SIEGE

WRITTEN BY
× LANDRY Q. WALKER

ARTWORK BY
× JUSTIN GREENWOOD

CHAPTERS 1-4 COLORED BY
× ERIC JONES

CHAPTERS 5-8 COLORED BY
× BRAD SIMPSON

LETTERED BY
× PATRICK BROSSEAU

DESIGNED BY
× KEITH WOOD

COVER BY
× JUSTIN GREENWOOD

COVER COLORED BY
× BRAD SIMPSON

PRODUCED BY
× JON GUHL

EDITED
× BRA

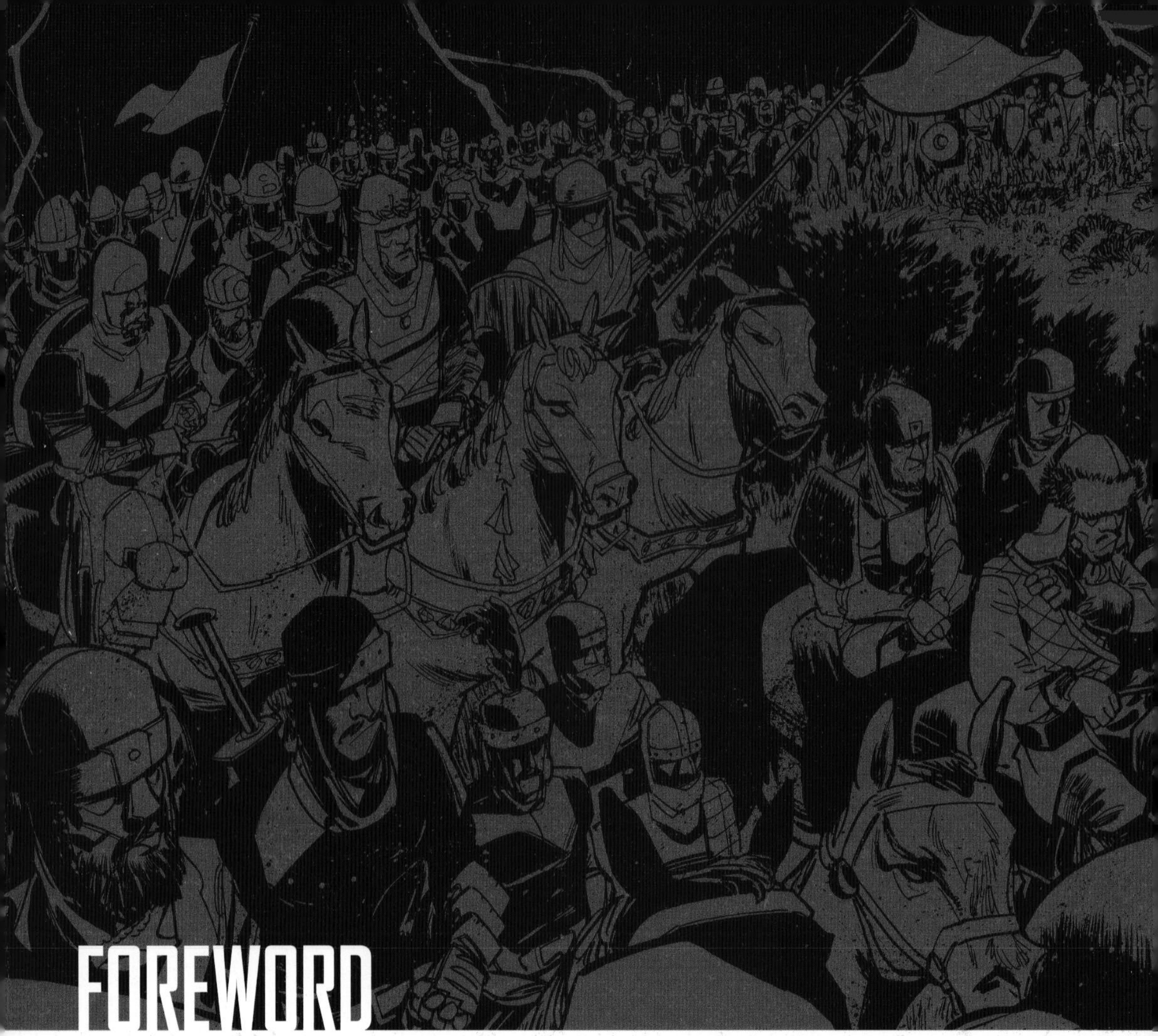

FOREWORD

"THEY FILLED THE LAND WITH CASTLES, AND THEY FILLED THE CASTLES WITH DEVILS."

I wrote these words in a notebook back around 2002, when I first started working on the book you have in your hands now. It's a quote I pulled from *The Anglo-Saxon Chronicle*, a history largely written a thousand years ago. Medieval warfare has always held a high place of interest for me. Steel blades striking armor, siege engines tearing down castle walls. That sort of thing. I'm a big fan of that era of history.

But as a casual student of the past you quickly discover something. Popular interpretations of history are almost always a human invention. Or more to the point, the versions that rise to the collective consciousness are often simply a collection of perspectives masquerading as facts. Much of what we assume as absolute truth, even regarding recent events, is filtered through a flawed system. Propaganda, bias, misconceptions — they all affect our understanding of the past.

So... it should go without saying that this book is NOT historically accurate. When constructing this story, I certainly kept my eye out for historical anachronisms and contradictions, but when they worked for the overall narrative, I left them in and moved on, comforted in my conviction that they were not important. Because, first and foremost, what a fictional story must do is entertain; that's always enough of a challenge without worrying about what styles of haircut were worn in Saxon England, or whether a wooden fortification would be more appropriate than a stone one.

Let's just say that if medieval period films portrayed stone castles accurately, they would all be smoothly constructed and often plastered with limestone and painted so that they appeared a garish pink or yellow or some other bright color. Drop that historically-accurate look into a movie and many people will wonder why you failed to depict castles accurately, and why you failed to showcase the gray, crumbling stone walls, covered in moss and mold.

Right out of the gate, we cheat the details.

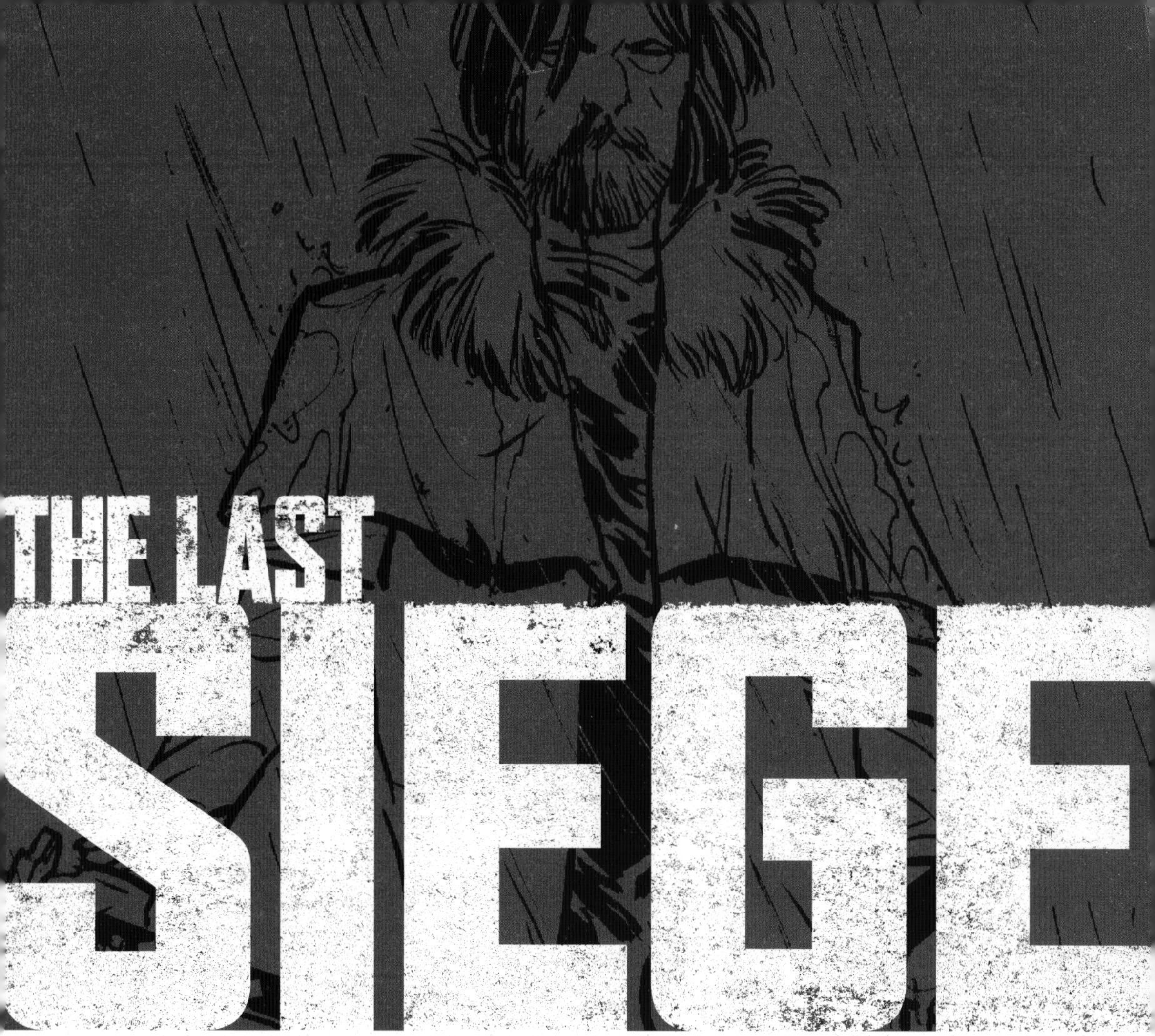

THE LAST SIEGE

image

IMAGE COMICS, INC.

ROBERT KIRKMAN
Chief Operating Officer

ERIK LARSEN
Chief Financial Officer

TODD MCFARLANE
President

MARC SILVESTRI
Chief Executive Officer

JIM VALENTINO
Vice President

ERIC STEPHENSON
Publisher / Chief Creative Officer

COREY HART
Director of Sales

JEFF BOISON
Director of Publishing Planning
& Book Trade Sales

CHRIS ROSS
Director of Digital Sales

JEFF STANG
Directtor of Specialty Sales

KAT SALAZAR
Director of PR & Marketing

DREW GILL
Art Director

HEATHER DOORNINK
Production Director

NICOLE LAPALME
Controller

IMAGECOMICS.COM

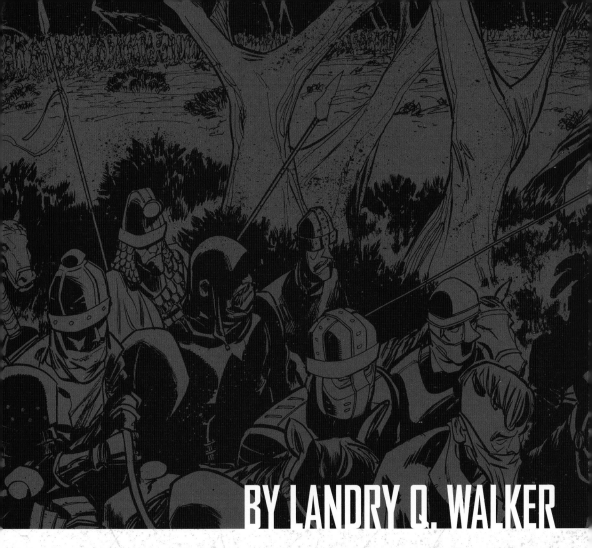

BY LANDRY Q. WALKER

This story doesn't really take place in a specific location and time — though if I were pressed to say otherwise, I would point to England, a few years after the Norman Conquest. That was certainly the primary point of inspiration, anyway. William the Conqueror defeated the Saxon King Harold at the Battle of Hastings, but that doesn't mean he was instantly handed the keys to the country. The next several years were spent with the new king consolidating his power, extending his reach to every corner of the country — and people fought back. Most relevant to this story, Hereward the Wake returned home to find the Normans had butchered his family. The DNA of his legend is encoded within the pages of this comic, but there are many other sources, and it's probably fair to say that *The Last Siege*'s invading king has more in common, tactics-wise, with Genghis Khan than he does with William the Conqueror.

Back to the quote at the top of the previous page. That version is inaccurate. I've paraphrased it (or to put it another way, I cheated the details but delivered the gist).

"EVERY RICH MAN BUILT HIS CASTLES AND DEFENDED THEM, AND THEY FILLED THE LAND FULL OF CASTLES. AND THEY GREATLY OPPRESSED THE WRETCHED PEOPLE, BY MAKING THEM WORK AT THESE CASTLES; AND WHEN THE CASTLES WERE FINISHED, THEY FILLED THEM WITH DEVILS AND EVIL MEN."

The Norman method of government revolved around the idea that all land belongs to the king — a vassal system where those trusted by the ruling Lord would be placed in powerful positions, governing his land — holding it for the one true king, as it were. William the Conqueror overthrew the many Saxon lords, seized their territories, and sent loyal subordinates to govern them in his name.

It was a brutal moment in history for those on the losing end of the equation. The story in this comic may not depict this moment in a historically accurate manner — the fashions might be off; the architecture, the titles, and yes, even the hairstyles — but the strategy employed by the conquering army, and the fear and violence that accompanied it, are of more interest to myself, Justin, and the entire team. And we believe, of greater import to the story.

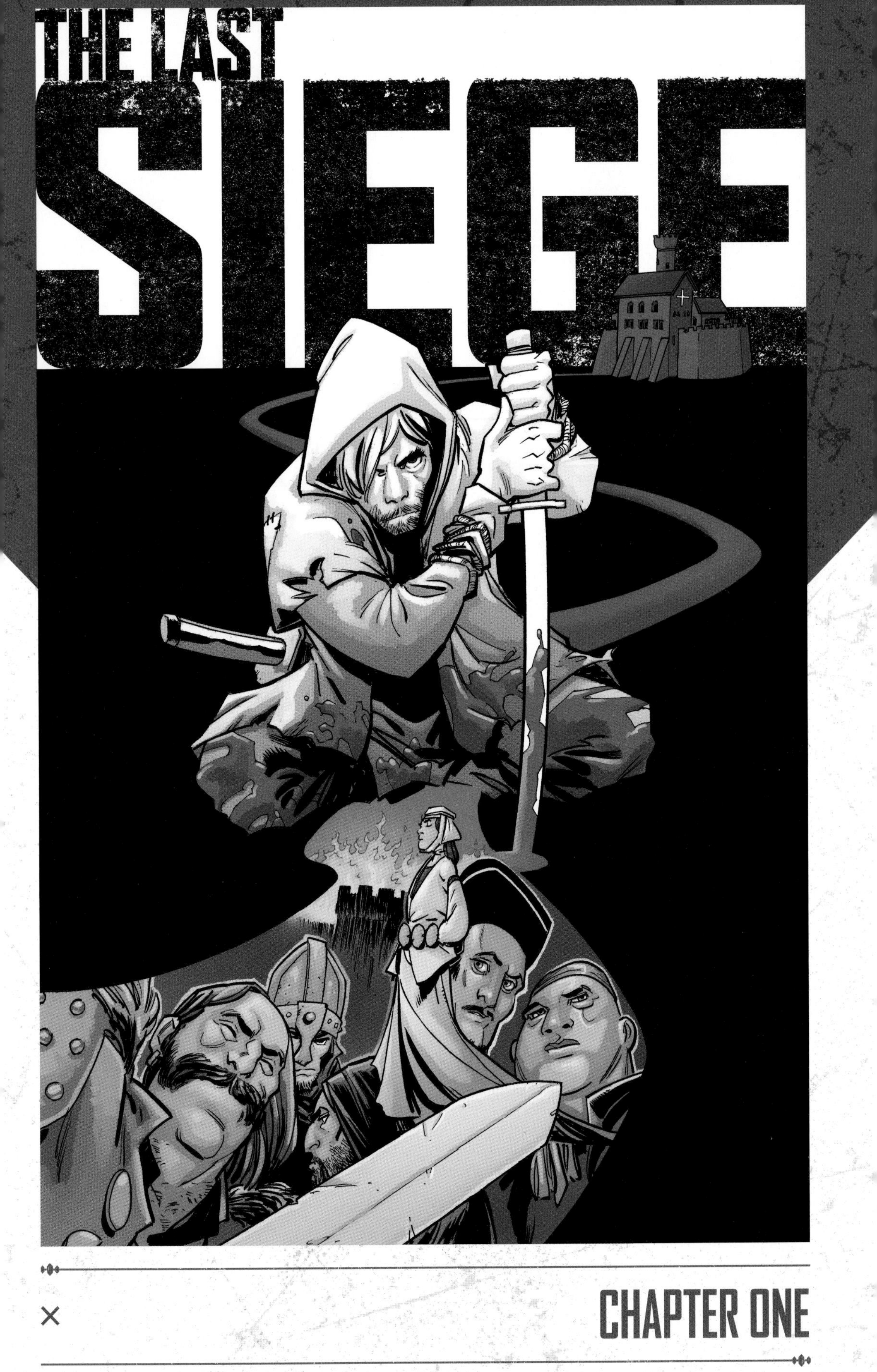
THE LAST
SIEGE

× CHAPTER ONE

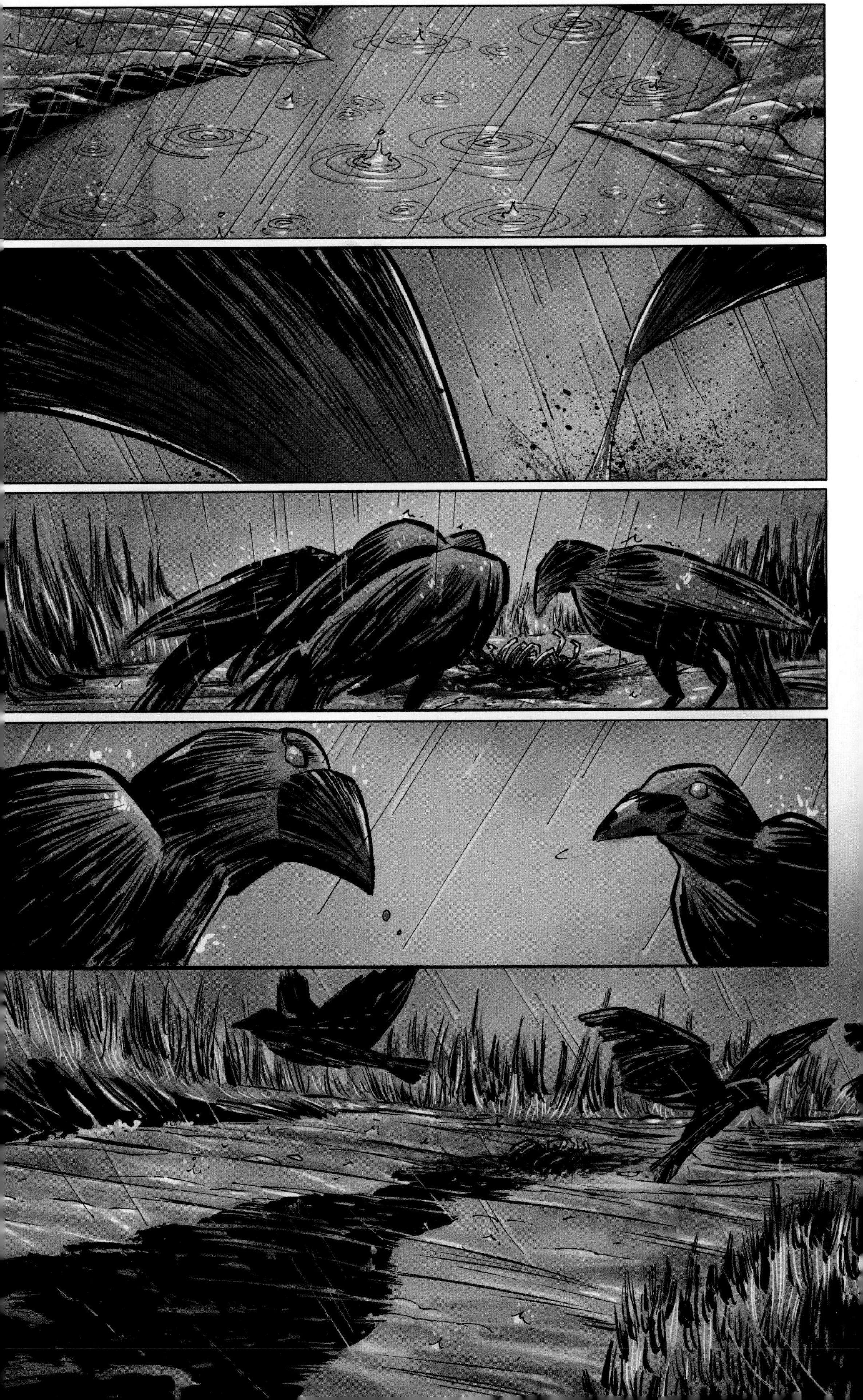

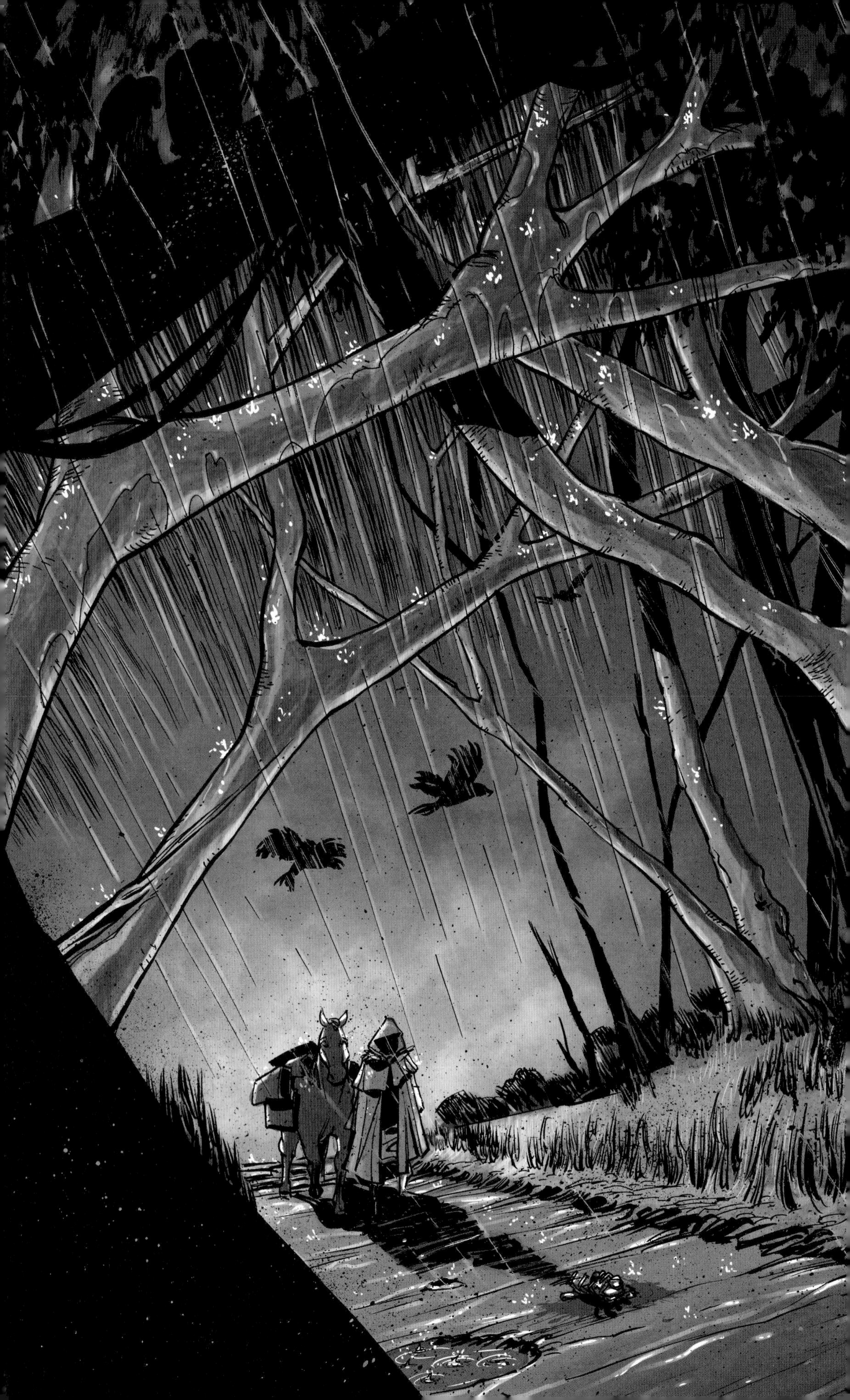

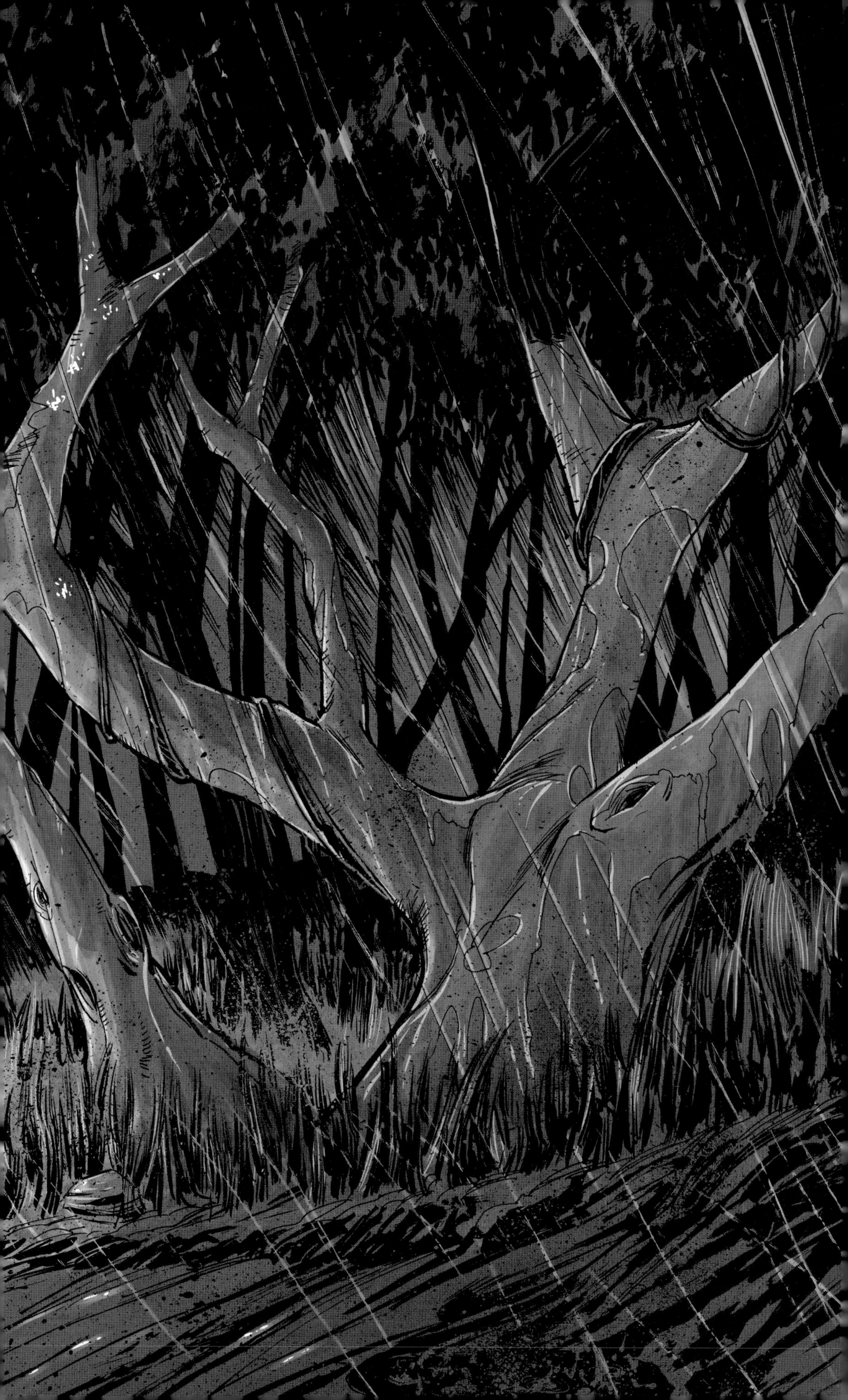

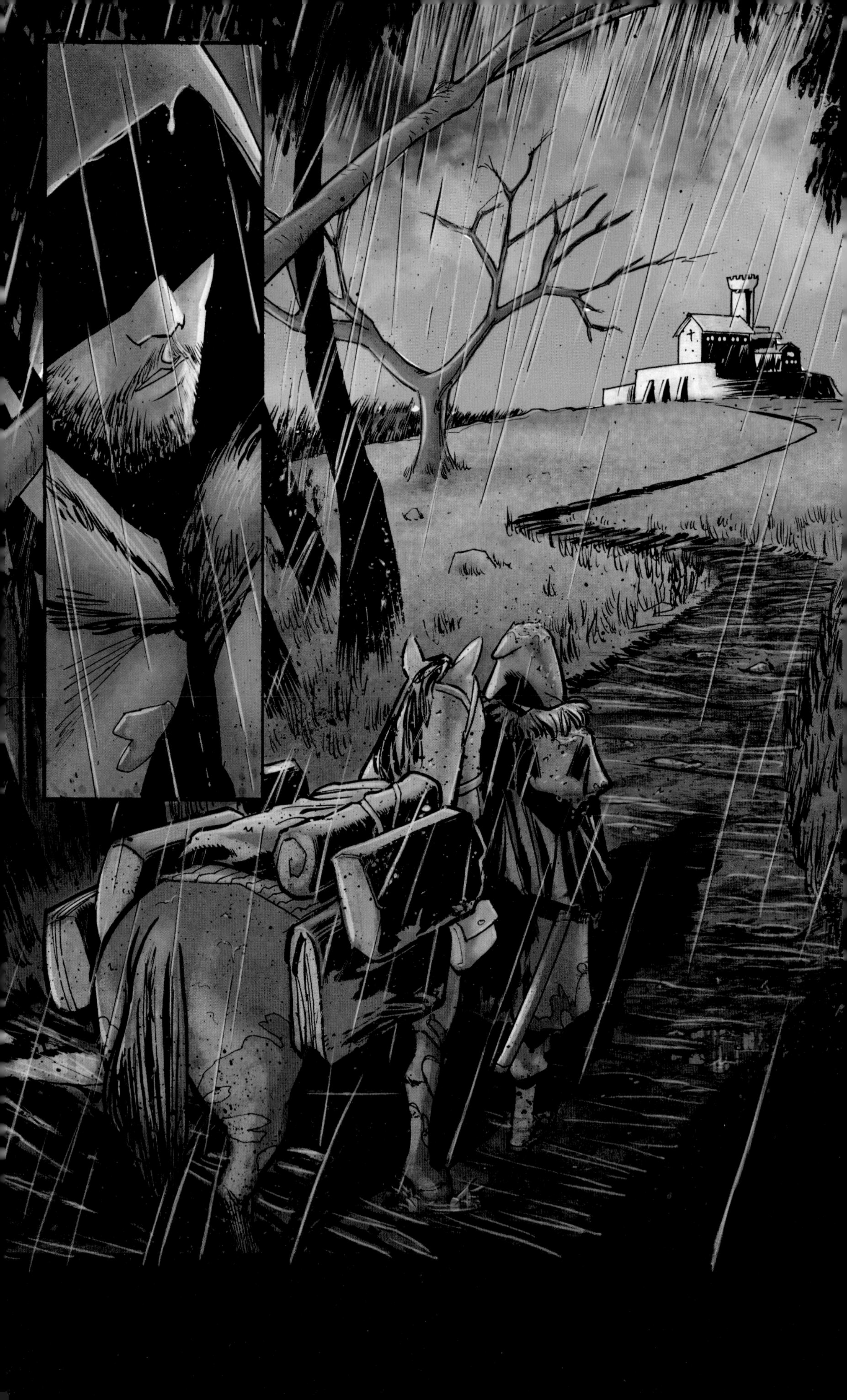

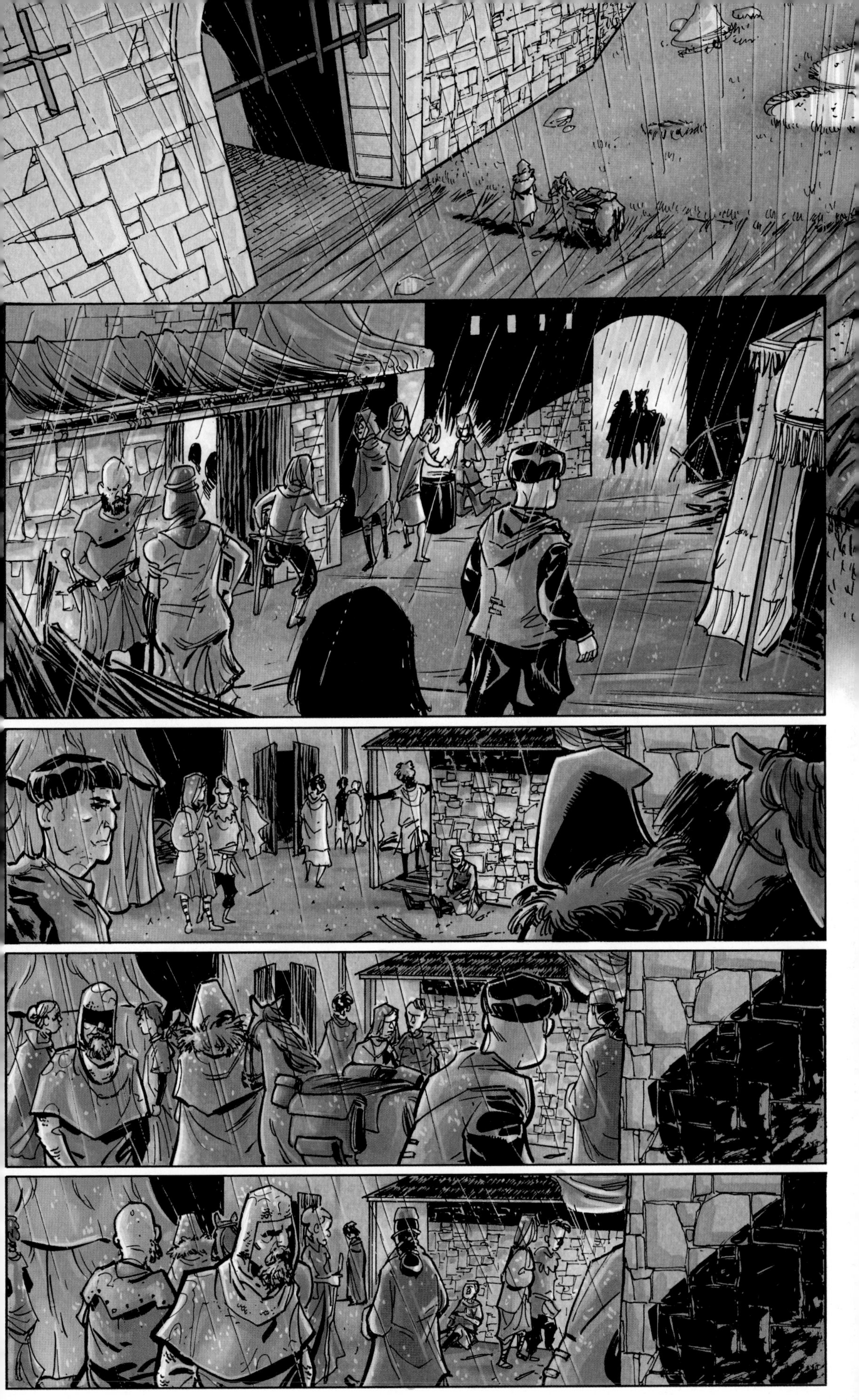

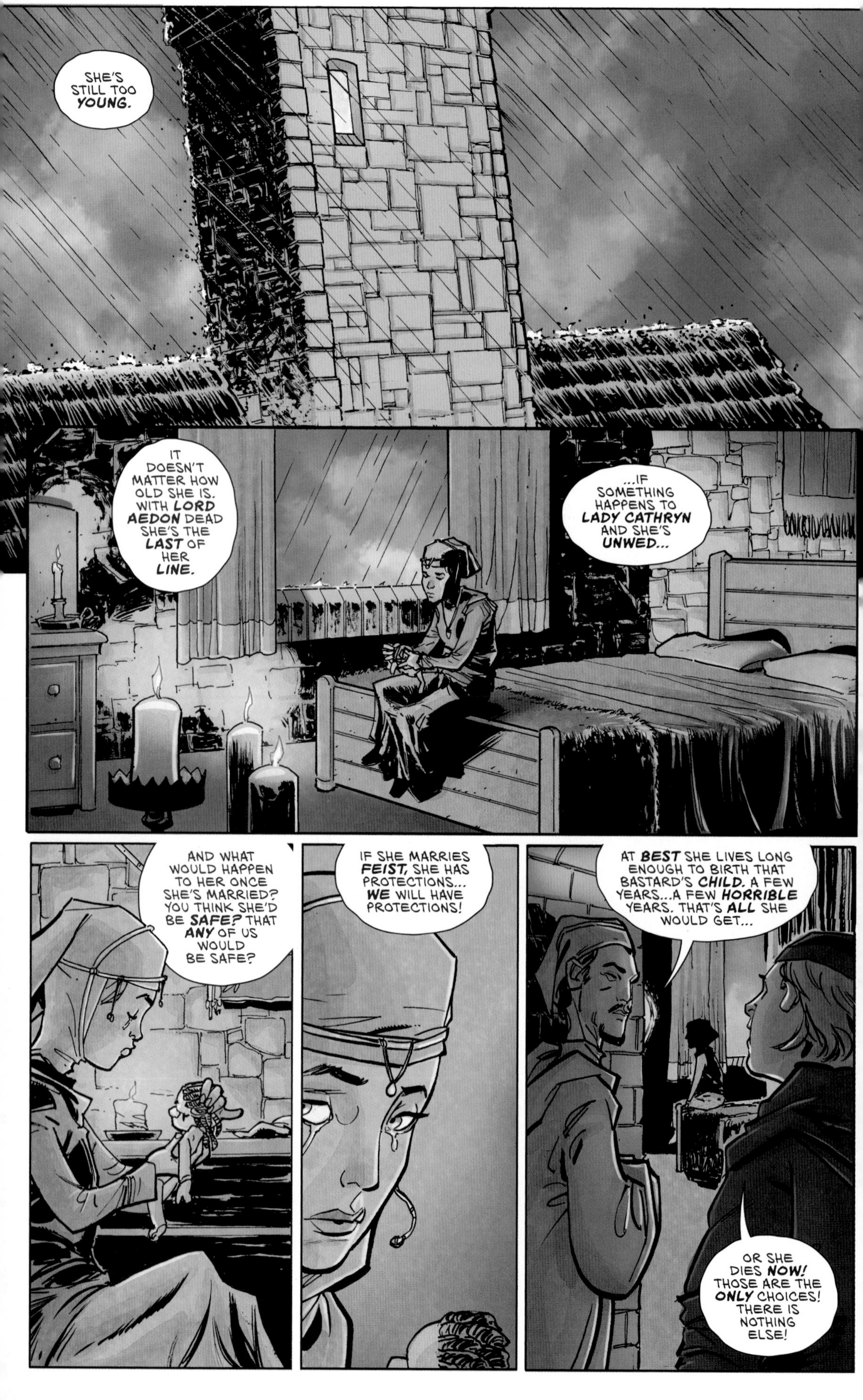
SHE'S STILL TOO YOUNG.
IT DOESN'T MATTER HOW OLD SHE IS. WITH LORD AEDON DEAD SHE'S THE LAST OF HER LINE.
...IF SOMETHING HAPPENS TO LADY CATHRYN AND SHE'S UNWED...
AND WHAT WOULD HAPPEN TO HER ONCE SHE'S MARRIED? YOU THINK SHE'D BE SAFE? THAT ANY OF US WOULD BE SAFE?
IF SHE MARRIES FEIST, SHE HAS PROTECTIONS... WE WILL HAVE PROTECTIONS!
AT BEST SHE LIVES LONG ENOUGH TO BIRTH THAT BASTARD'S CHILD. A FEW YEARS...A FEW HORRIBLE YEARS. THAT'S ALL SHE WOULD GET...
OR SHE DIES NOW! THOSE ARE THE ONLY CHOICES! THERE IS NOTHING ELSE!

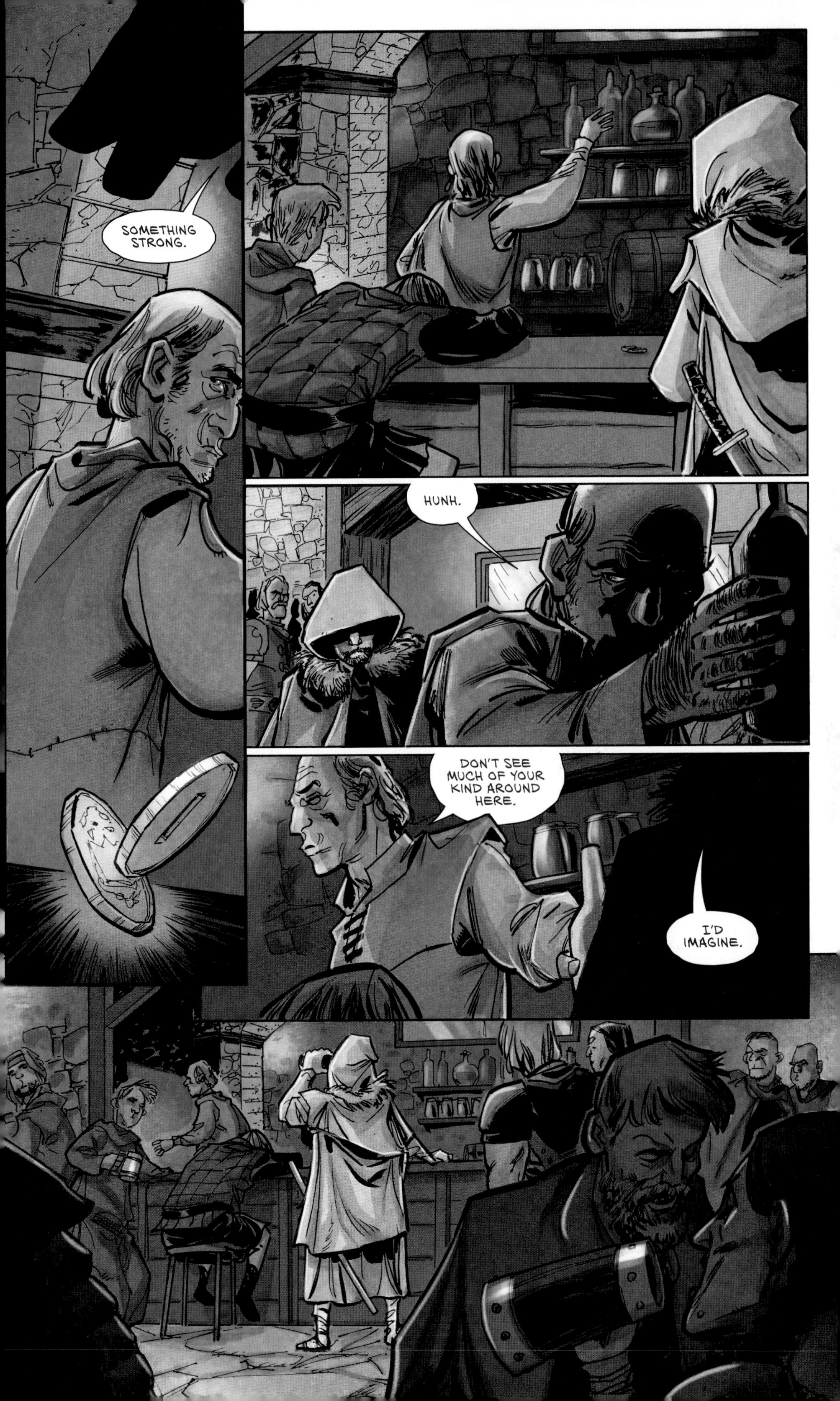
SOMETHING STRONG.
HUNH.
DON'T SEE MUCH OF YOUR KIND AROUND HERE.
I'D IMAGINE.

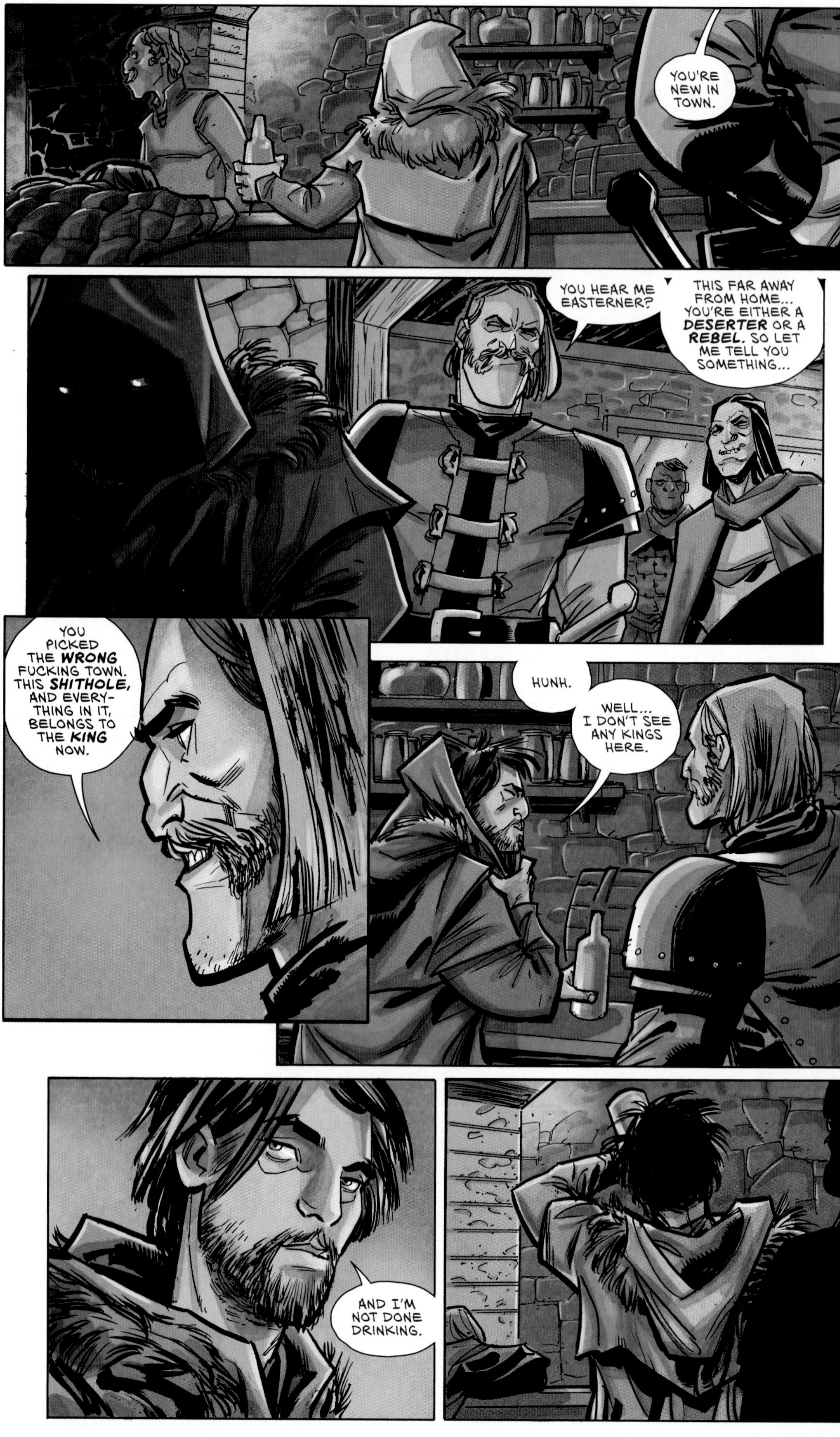
YOU'RE NEW IN TOWN.
YOU HEAR ME EASTERNER?
THIS FAR AWAY FROM HOME... YOU'RE EITHER A **DESERTER** OR A **REBEL.** SO LET ME TELL YOU SOMETHING...
YOU PICKED THE **WRONG** FUCKING TOWN. THIS **SHITHOLE,** AND EVERY-THING IN IT, BELONGS TO THE **KING** NOW.
HUNH.
WELL... I DON'T SEE ANY KINGS HERE.
AND I'M NOT DONE DRINKING.

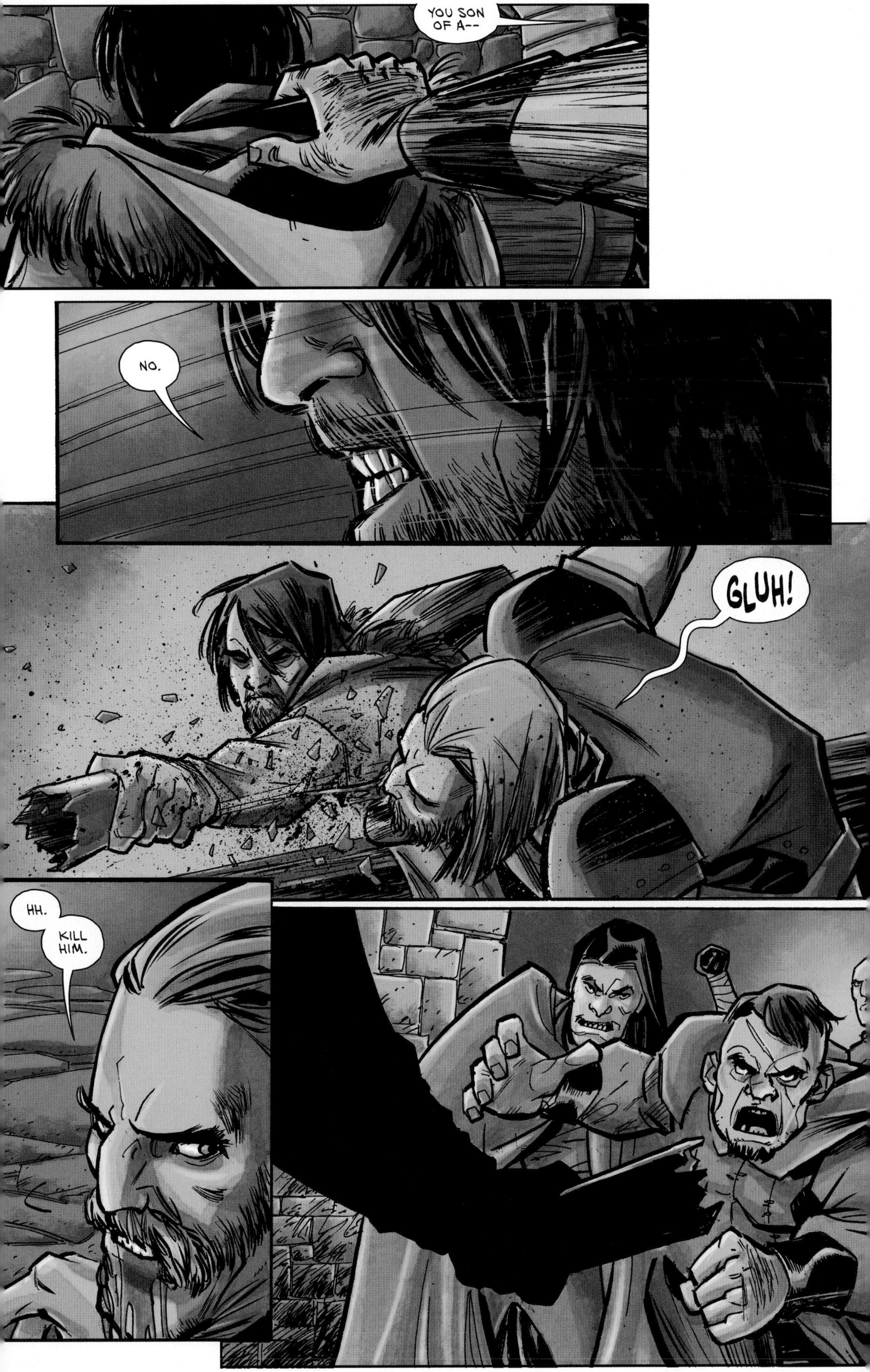
YOU SON OF A--
NO.
GLUH!
HH.
KILL HIM.

THE ARGUMENT IS *POINTLESS.* SIR FEIST IS *HERE,* AND HE WILL *NOT* BE EASILY DENIED.

WE STILL OUTNUMBER THE KNIGHT AND HIS MEN...

LADY CATHRYN SHOULD HAVE A *SAY* IN THIS...SHE *IS* HER FATHER'S DAUGHTER.

SHE'S A *CHILD.* AND A *WOMAN.* SHE NEEDS *US* TO GUIDE HER...

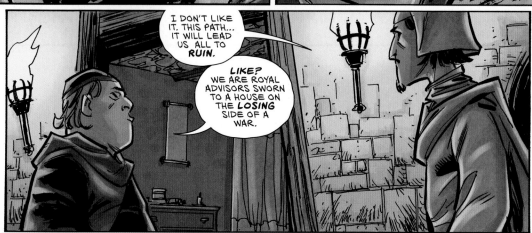

I DON'T LIKE IT. THIS PATH... IT WILL LEAD US ALL TO *RUIN.*

LIKE? WE ARE ROYAL ADVISORS SWORN TO A HOUSE ON THE *LOSING* SIDE OF A WAR.

WE *OUTLIVED* OUR LORD. A LORD WHO HAD *NO* SONS.

YOU THINK WHAT YOU LIKE OR DISLIKE *MATTERS* IN THE *LEAST?*

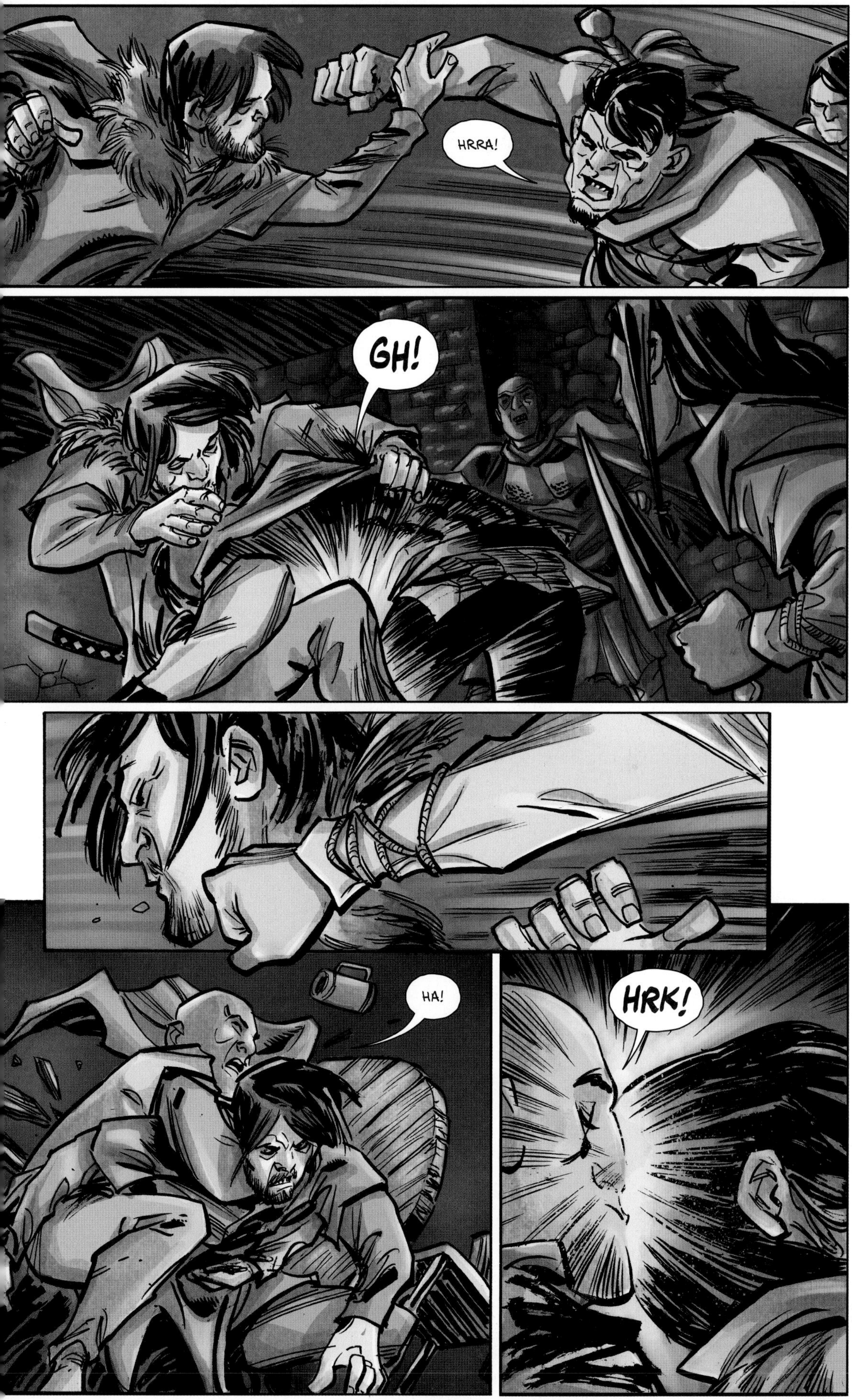
HRRA!
GH!
HA!
HRK!

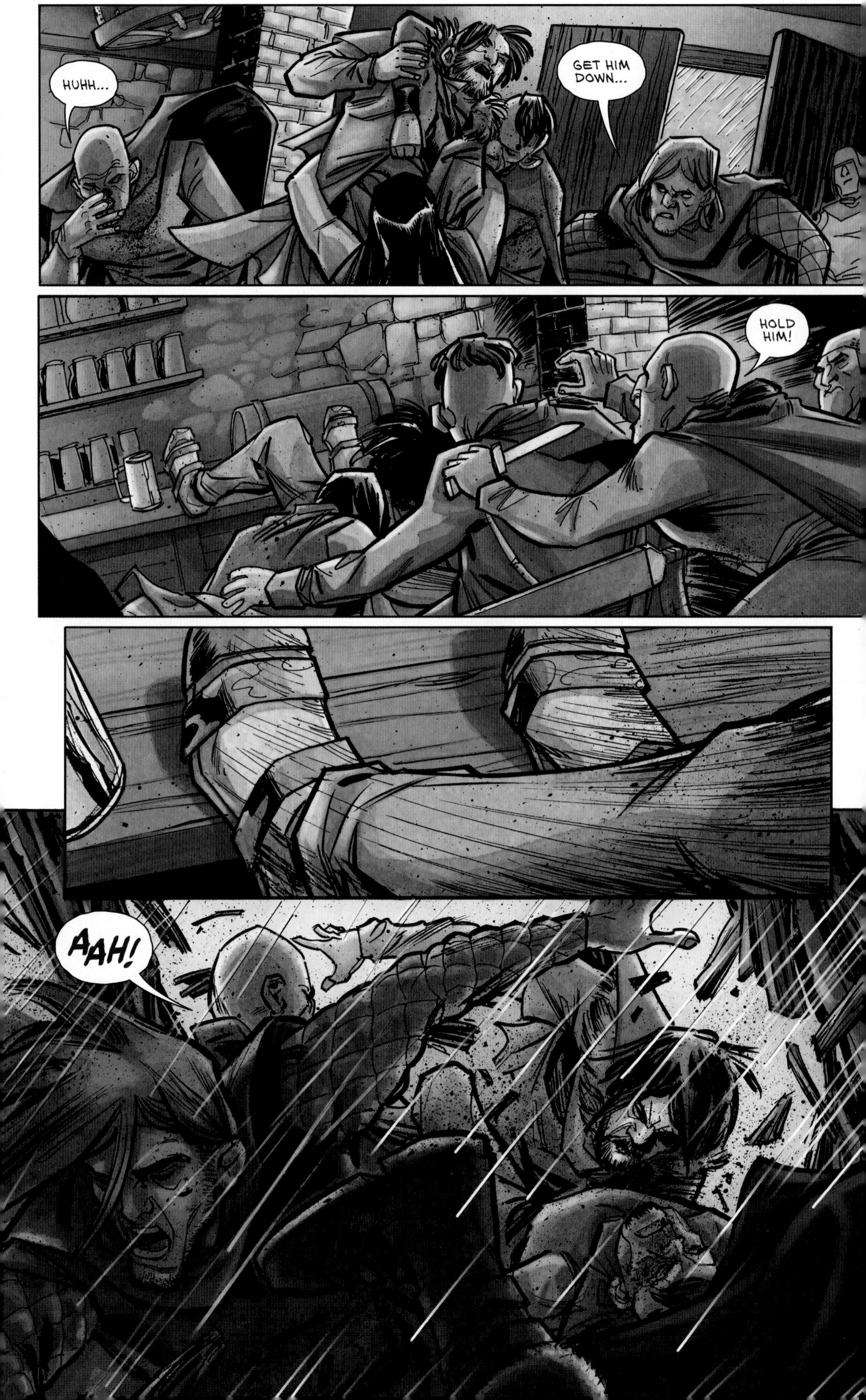
HUHH...
GET HIM DOWN...
HOLD HIM!
AAH!

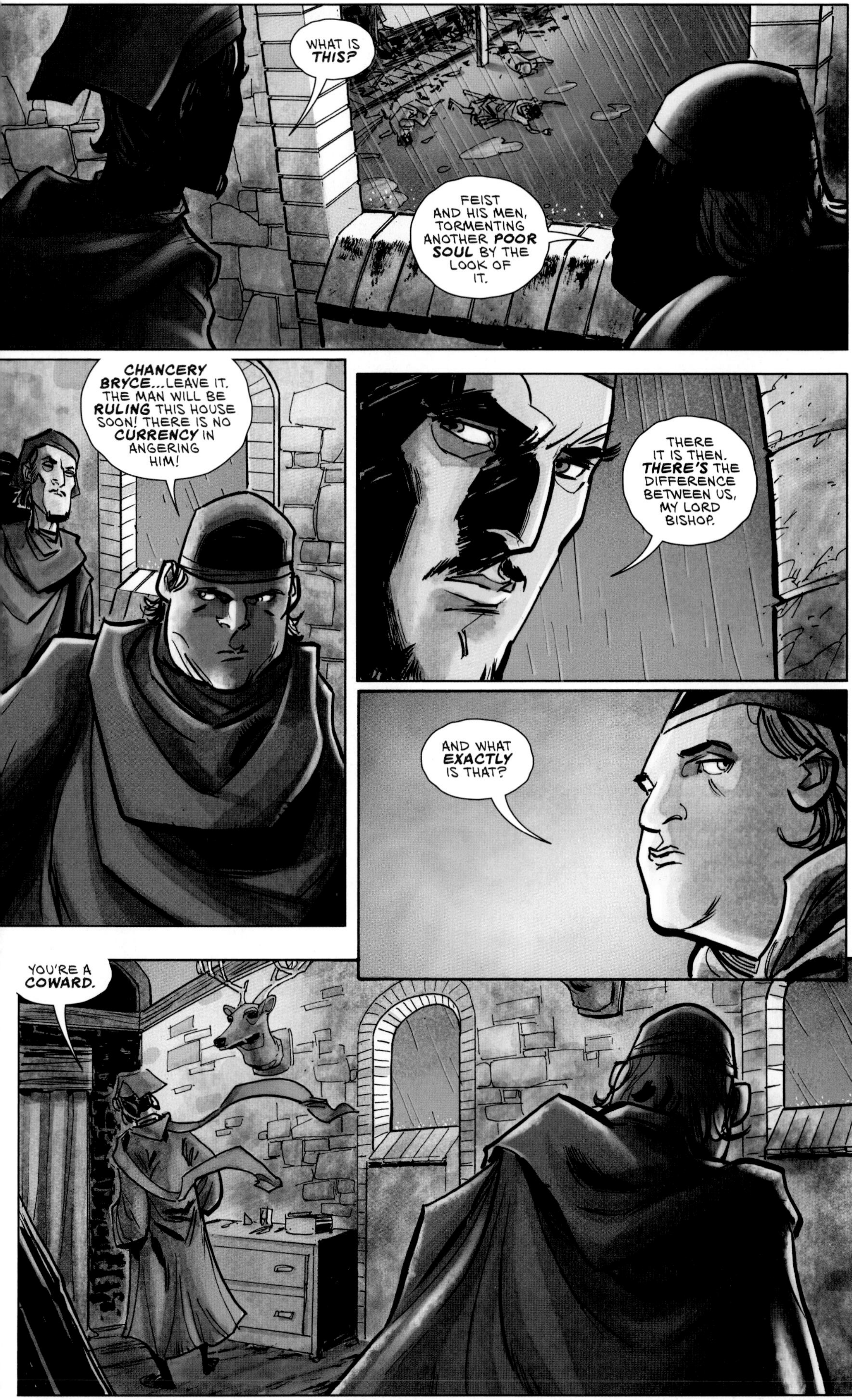
WHAT IS THIS?
FEIST AND HIS MEN, TORMENTING ANOTHER POOR SOUL BY THE LOOK OF IT.
CHANCERY BRYCE...LEAVE IT. THE MAN WILL BE RULING THIS HOUSE SOON! THERE IS NO CURRENCY IN ANGERING HIM!
THERE IT IS THEN. THERE'S THE DIFFERENCE BETWEEN US, MY LORD BISHOP.
AND WHAT EXACTLY IS THAT?
YOU'RE A COWARD.

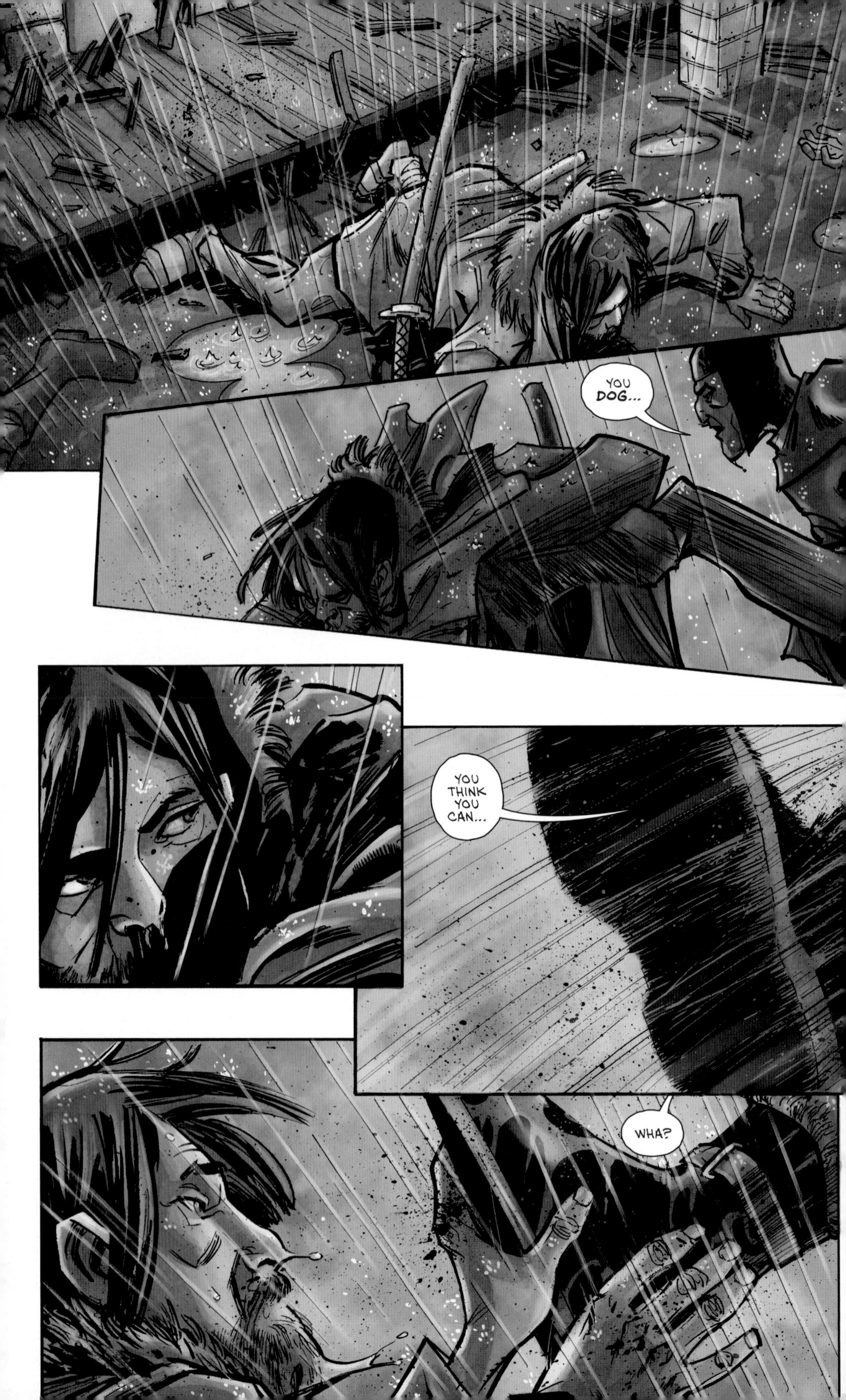
YOU DOG...
YOU THINK YOU CAN...
WHA?

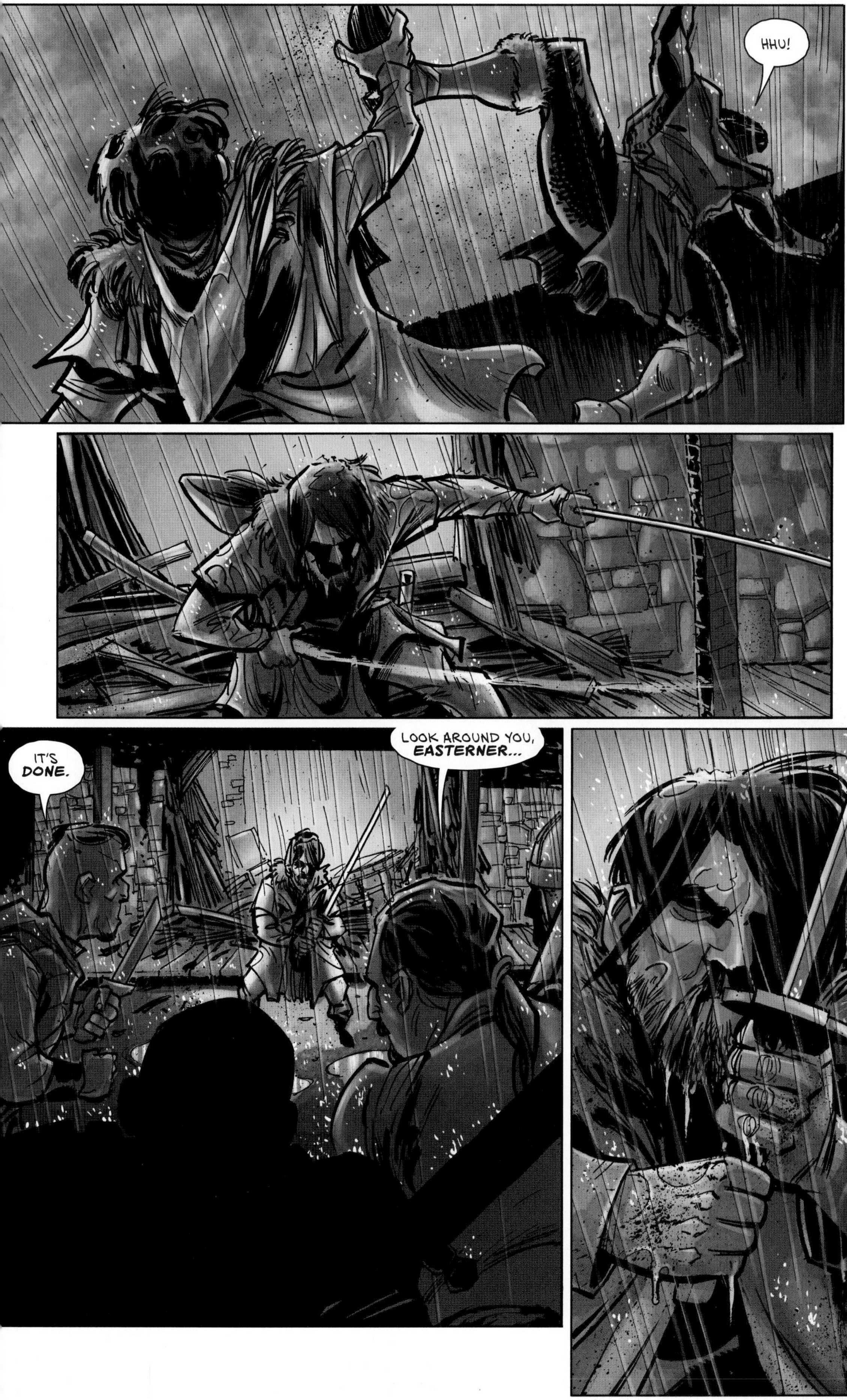
HHU!
IT'S DONE.
LOOK AROUND YOU, EASTERNER...

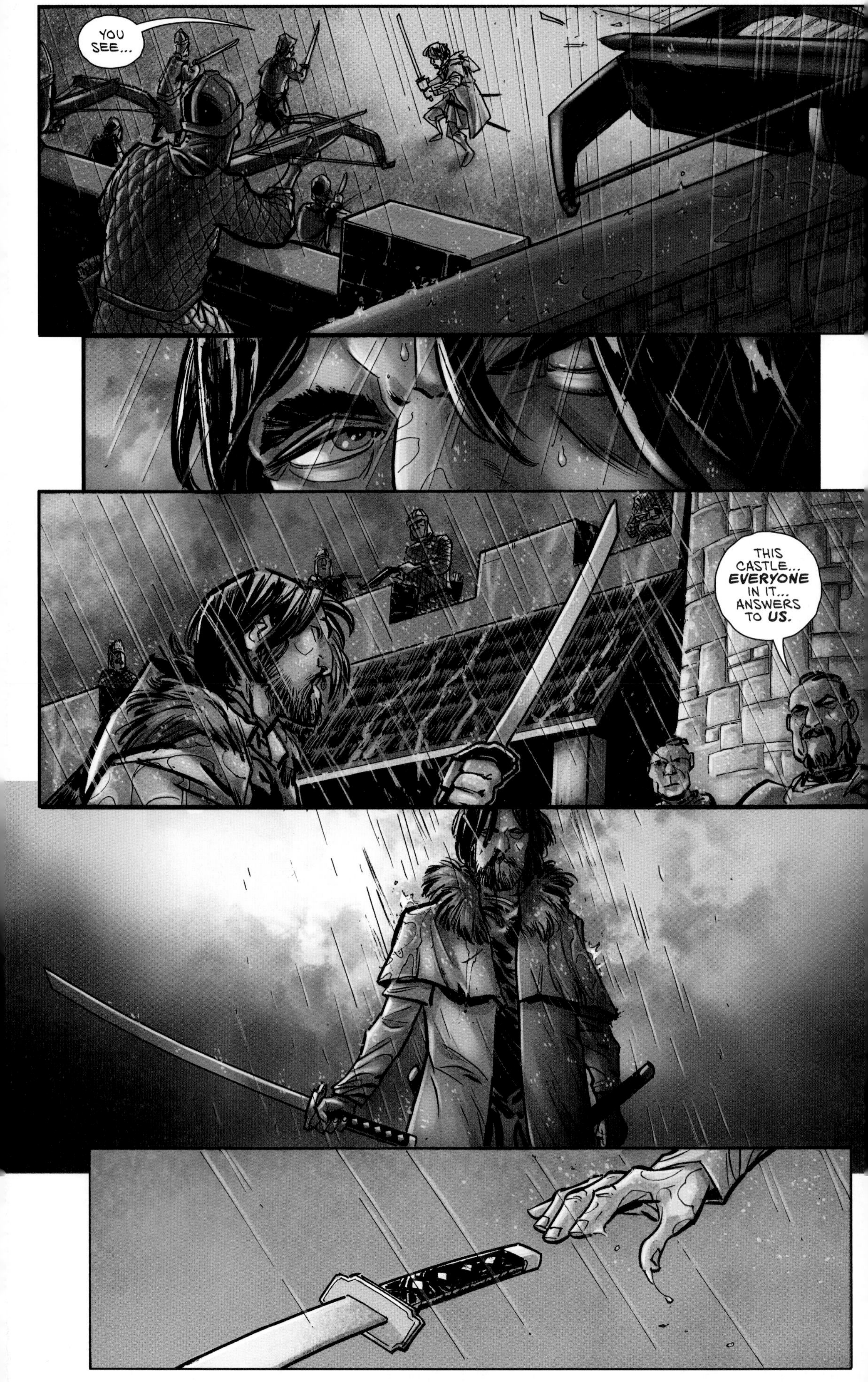
YOU SEE...
THIS CASTLE... EVERYONE IN IT... ANSWERS TO US.

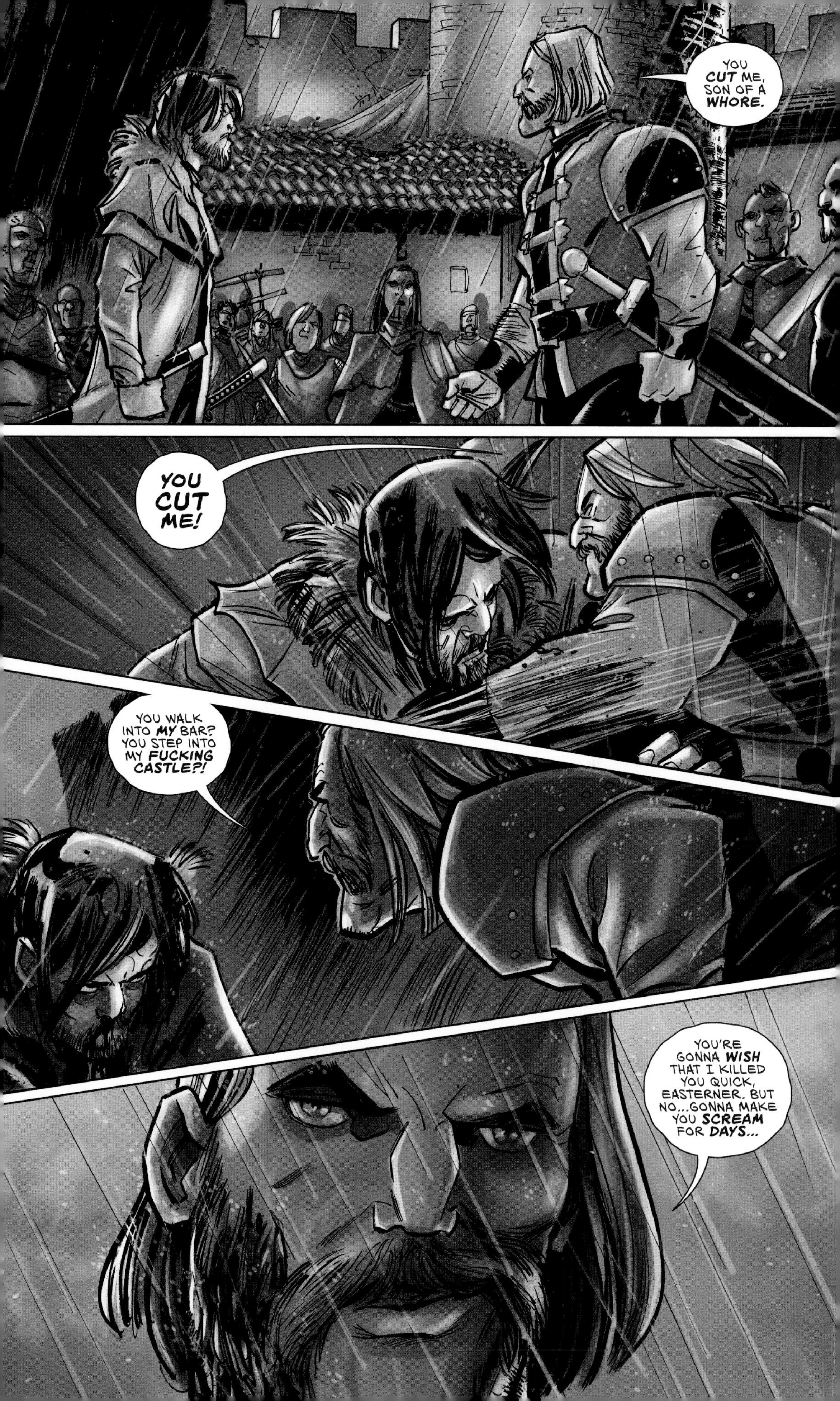
YOU CUT ME, SON OF A WHORE.
YOU CUT ME!
YOU WALK INTO MY BAR? YOU STEP INTO MY FUCKING CASTLE?!
YOU'RE GONNA WISH THAT I KILLED YOU QUICK, EASTERNER. BUT NO...GONNA MAKE YOU SCREAM FOR DAYS...

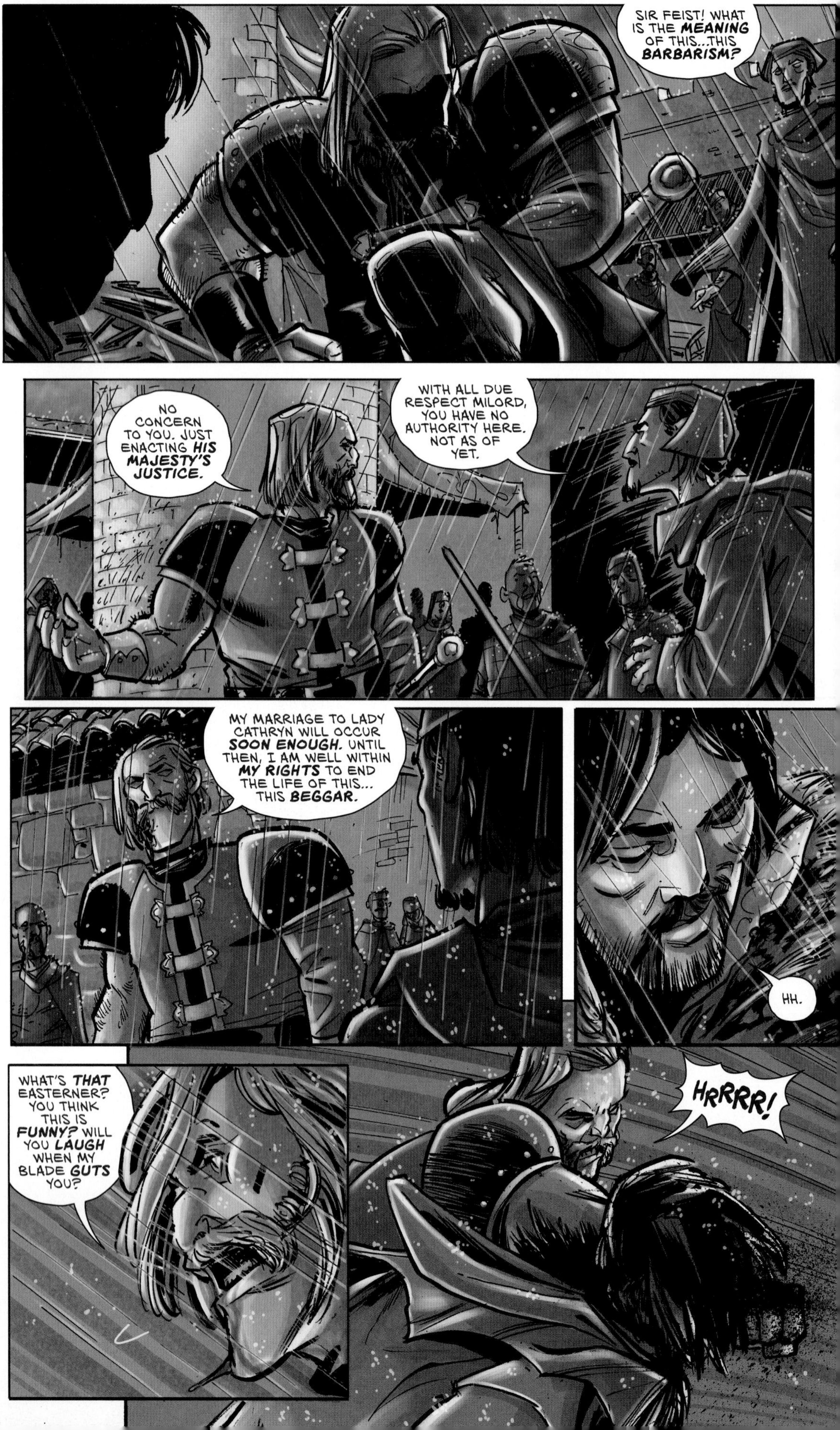
SIR FEIST! WHAT IS THE MEANING OF THIS...THIS BARBARISM?
NO CONCERN TO YOU. JUST ENACTING HIS MAJESTY'S JUSTICE.
WITH ALL DUE RESPECT MILORD, YOU HAVE NO AUTHORITY HERE. NOT AS OF YET.
MY MARRIAGE TO LADY CATHRYN WILL OCCUR SOON ENOUGH. UNTIL THEN, I AM WELL WITHIN MY RIGHTS TO END THE LIFE OF THIS... THIS BEGGAR.
HH.
WHAT'S THAT EASTERNER? YOU THINK THIS IS FUNNY? WILL YOU LAUGH WHEN MY BLADE GUTS YOU?
HRRRR!

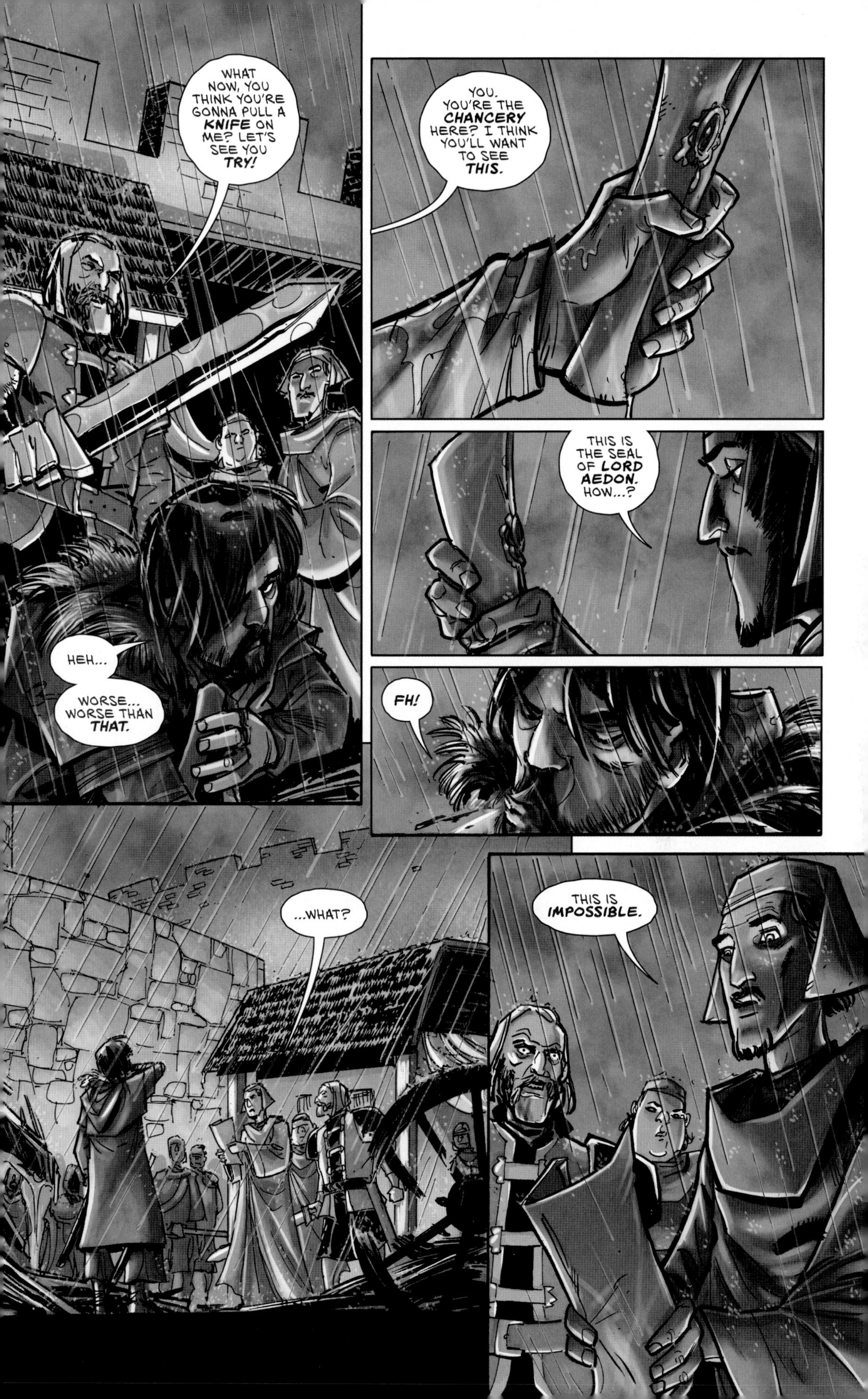
WHAT NOW, YOU THINK YOU'RE GONNA PULL A KNIFE ON ME? LET'S SEE YOU TRY!
HEH...
WORSE... WORSE THAN THAT.
YOU. YOU'RE THE CHANCERY HERE? I THINK YOU'LL WANT TO SEE THIS.
THIS IS THE SEAL OF LORD AEDON. HOW...?
FH!
...WHAT?
THIS IS IMPOSSIBLE.

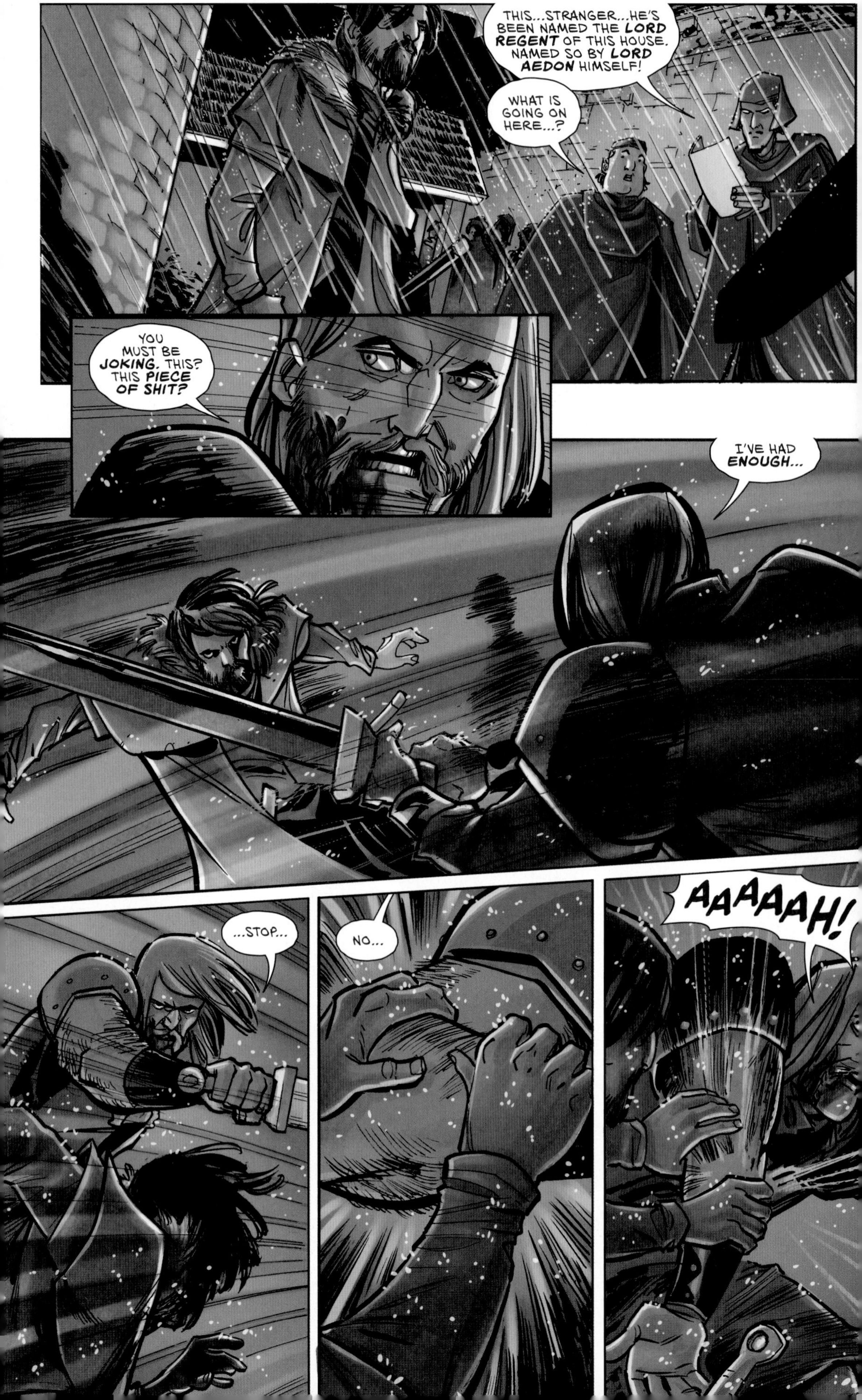
THIS...STRANGER...HE'S BEEN NAMED THE **LORD REGENT** OF THIS HOUSE. NAMED SO BY **LORD AEDON** HIMSELF!
WHAT IS GOING ON HERE...?
YOU MUST BE **JOKING.** THIS? THIS **PIECE OF SHIT?**
I'VE HAD **ENOUGH...**
...STOP...
NO...
AAAAAH!

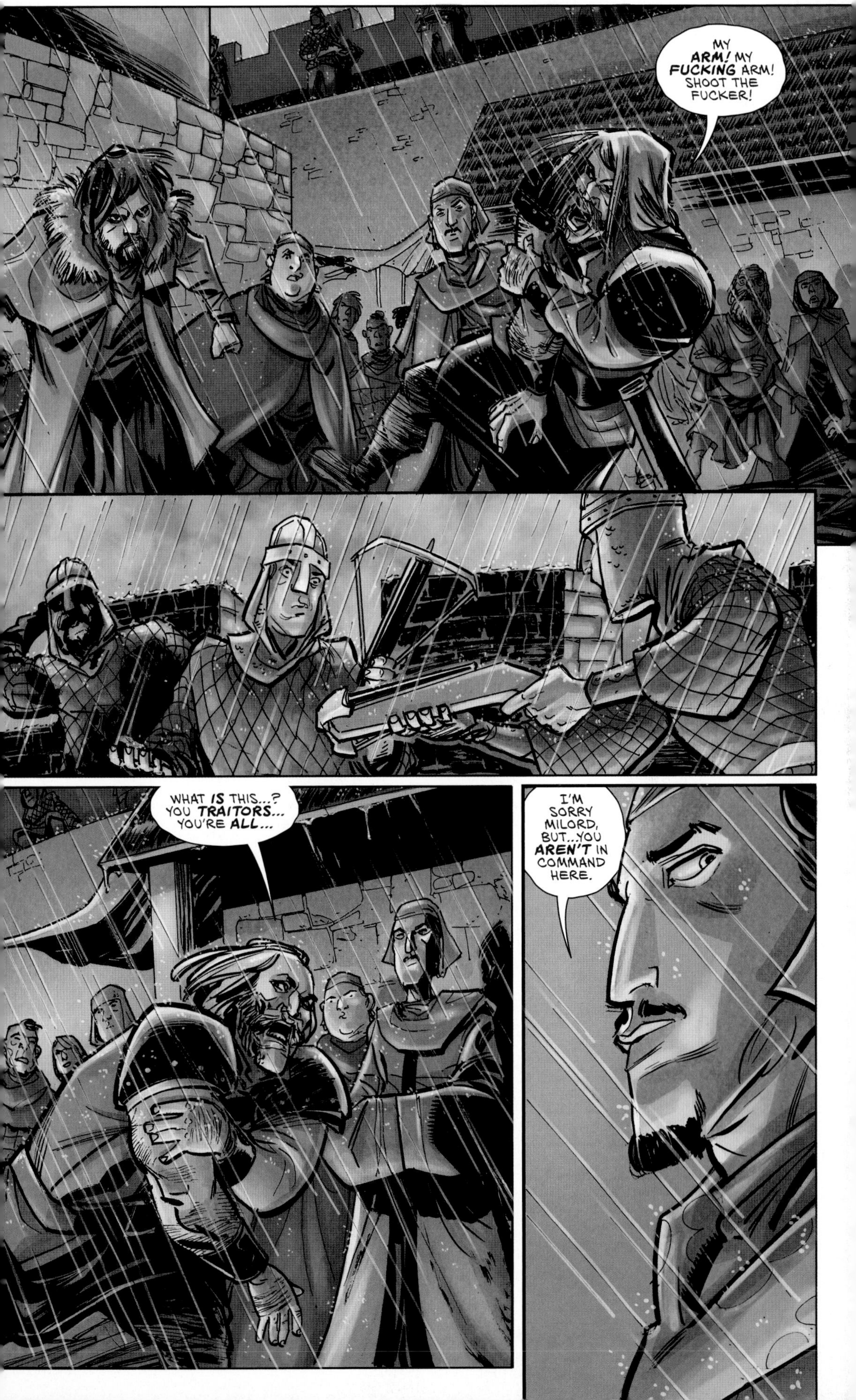
MY ARM! MY FUCKING ARM! SHOOT THE FUCKER!
WHAT IS THIS...? YOU TRAITORS... YOU'RE ALL...
I'M SORRY MILORD, BUT...YOU AREN'T IN COMMAND HERE.

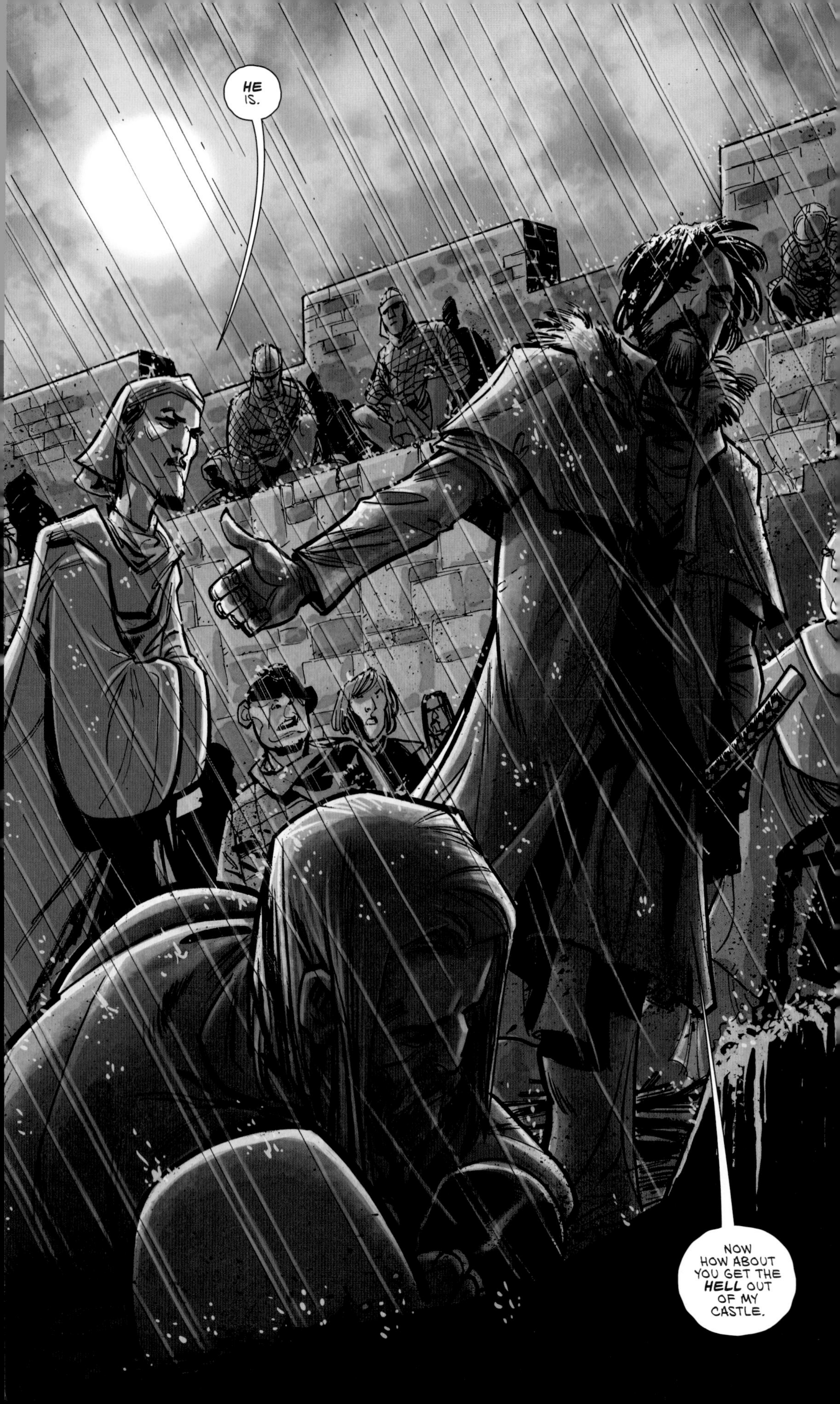
HE IS.
NOW HOW ABOUT YOU GET THE **HELL** OUT OF MY CASTLE.

THE KING RISES

~chapter 1~

By the time he arrived at the battle it was already too late.

Istvan was ten years old. Stout and broad chested for his age, the boy was the only son of Jarmill, a minor lord of an impoverished manor, sworn ally of the newly crowned King Grigorii.

Too late.

The young boy looked down at his fingers. He could still feel the weight of the golden circlet, freshly forged and gleaming with polished brilliance. He had been in attendance at the ceremony, held at the dawn of the last day of the harvest. It had been a magical experience. Never before had Istvan witnessed such grandeur: hundreds of knights stood as witness, a testament to the strength of the new regime that promised to unite all people under one banner. The celebrations had lasted throughout the day, into the night, and only ended with the next dawn. For the first time in his short life, Istvan had felt true joy; a sense of hope that he had never believed possible. A belief in a future that held promise and reward.

Now everyone that had delivered that promise lay dead on an open field, their blood staining the dry grass of late summer.

In his hands he held his father's sword, a heavy two-handed blade with a dull edge designed for breaking bones. The edge was notched in several places — nothing that couldn't be repaired, Istvan considered. He ran his finger on the edge, absently. The blade was sturdy, reliable and true — or so the boy had been taught. But now it was marred by the failures of his father and the king he had entrusted.

They were all dead.

In the distance, Istvan could see the army of murderers marching towards the manor he called home. Led by the old lords against whom King Grigorii had rallied, the soldiery would be busy for days, killing and raping their way through the families huddled behind the wooden walls of the palisade.

Istvan dropped the battered sword near the corpse of his father, stopping only to pry the broken crown from Grigorii's cracked skull. Why something of such value had been left behind on the battlefield he could not imagine. Perhaps it had been missed among the carnage. Maybe it was an ill omen to take the crown of a fallen king. It didn't matter. It belonged to Istvan now.

With that, the boy turned his back on the field of dead men, and began marching away from the village he had called home. In the distance, he could hear the screams of the wives and children that had been left behind. It didn't matter, he told himself. They were the families of the fallen, and they had allied themselves with a failure.

All that mattered was the future.

✕

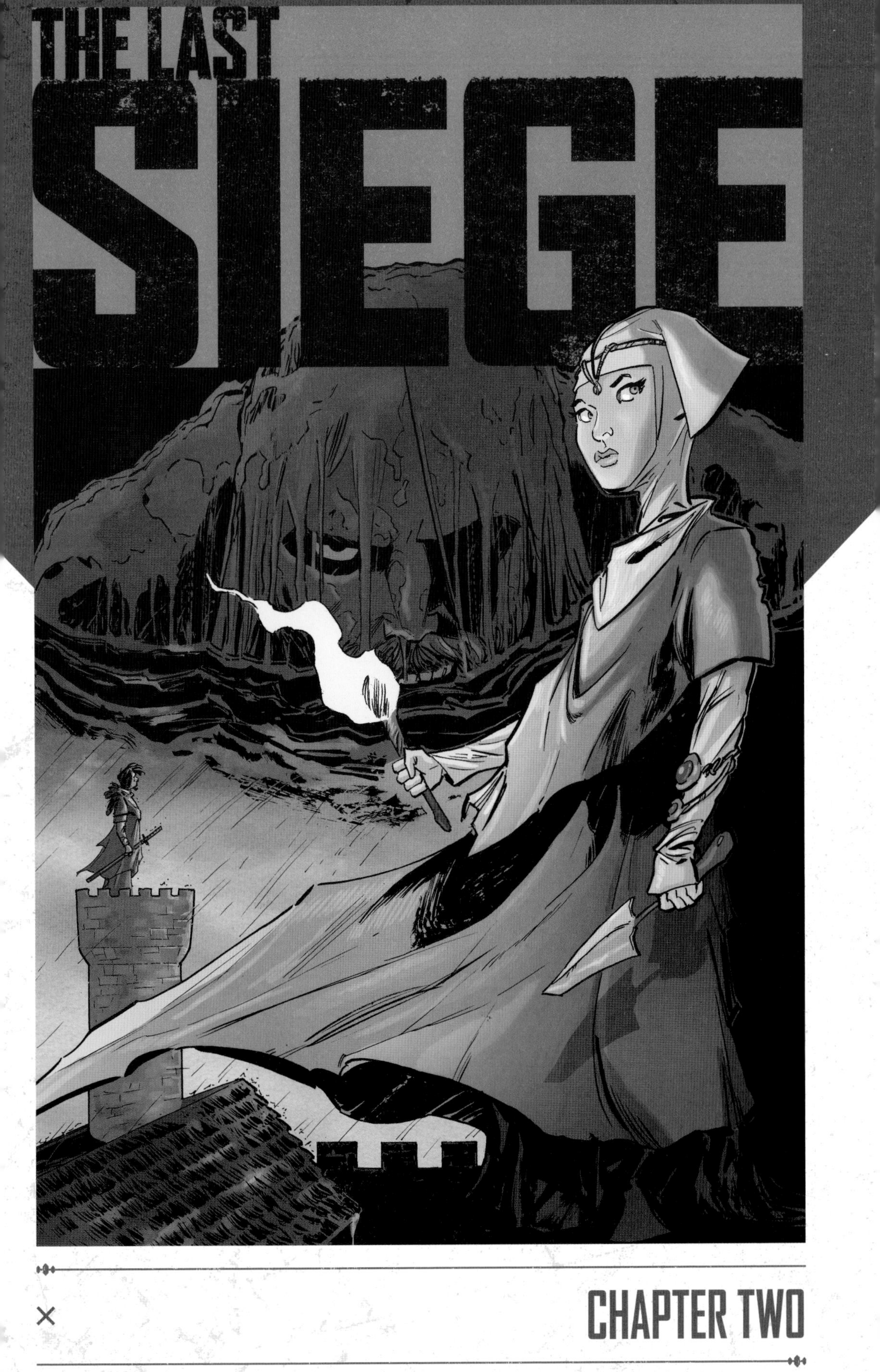
THE LAST
SIEGE

CHAPTER TWO

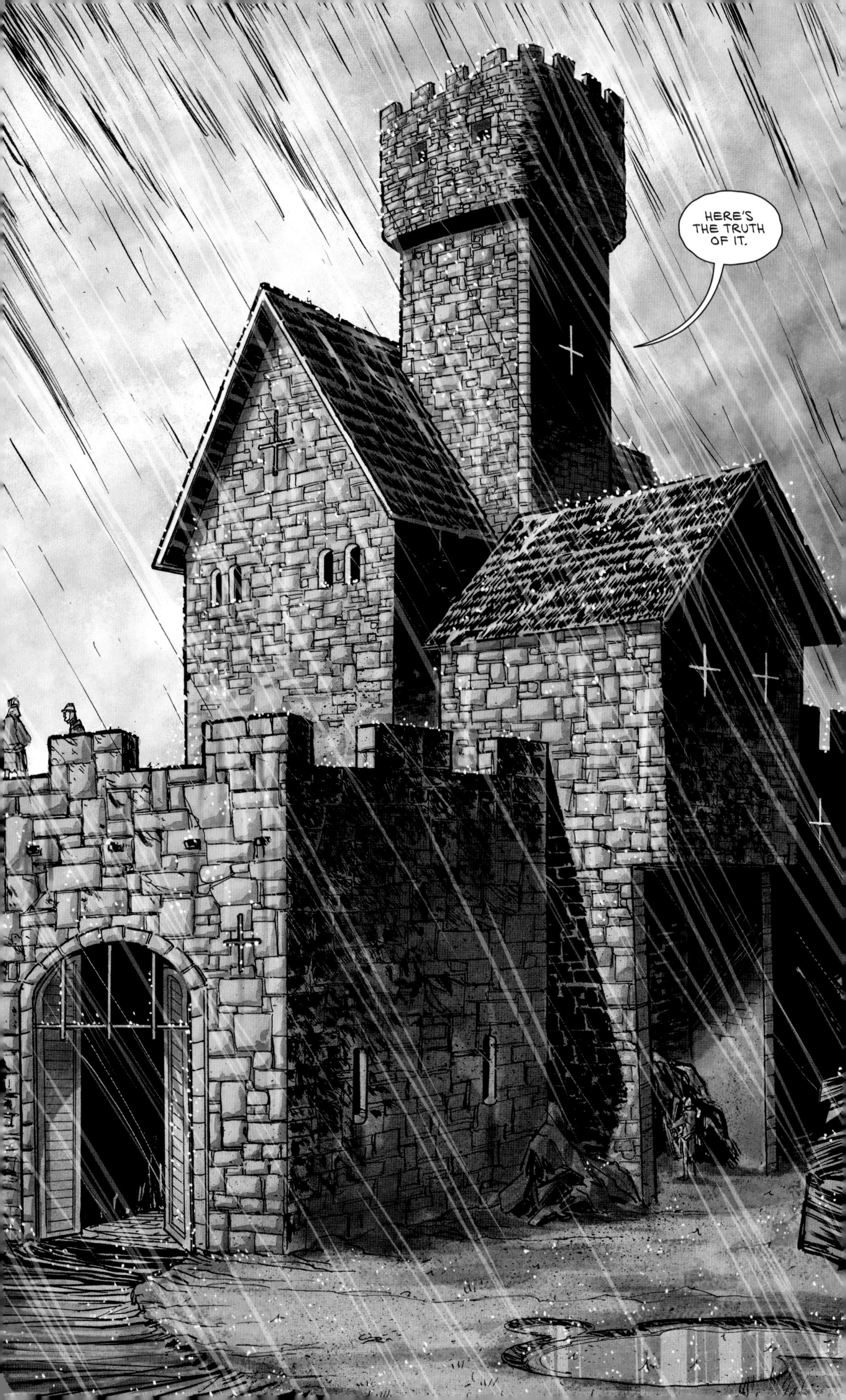
HERE'S THE TRUTH OF IT.

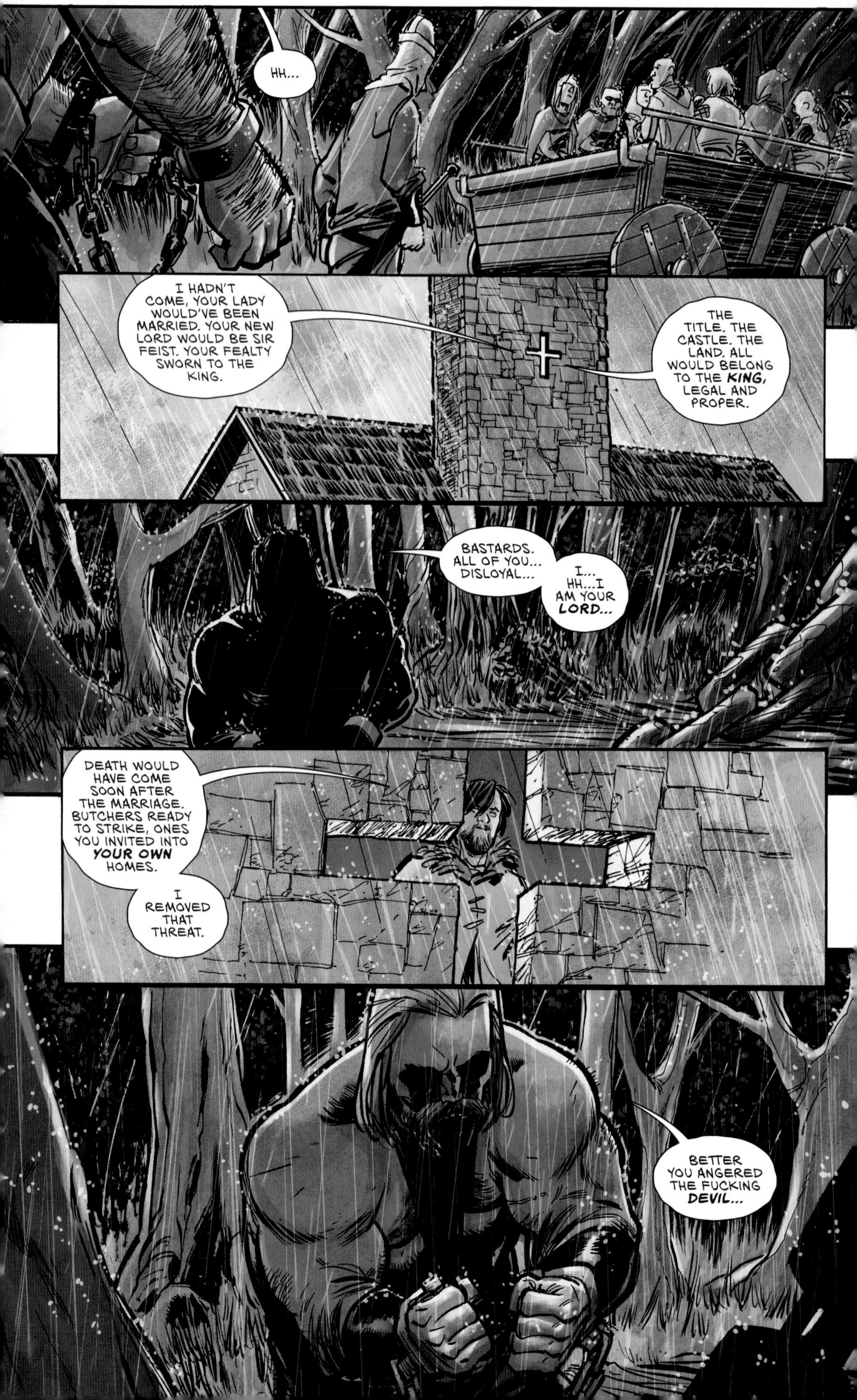
HH...
I HADN'T COME, YOUR LADY WOULD'VE BEEN MARRIED. YOUR NEW LORD WOULD BE SIR FEIST. YOUR FEALTY SWORN TO THE KING.
THE TITLE. THE CASTLE. THE LAND. ALL WOULD BELONG TO THE **KING**, LEGAL AND PROPER.
BASTARDS. ALL OF YOU... DISLOYAL...
I... HH...I AM YOUR **LORD...**
DEATH WOULD HAVE COME SOON AFTER THE MARRIAGE. BUTCHERS READY TO STRIKE, ONES YOU INVITED INTO ***YOUR OWN*** HOMES.
I REMOVED THAT THREAT.
BETTER YOU ANGERED THE FUCKING **DEVIL...**

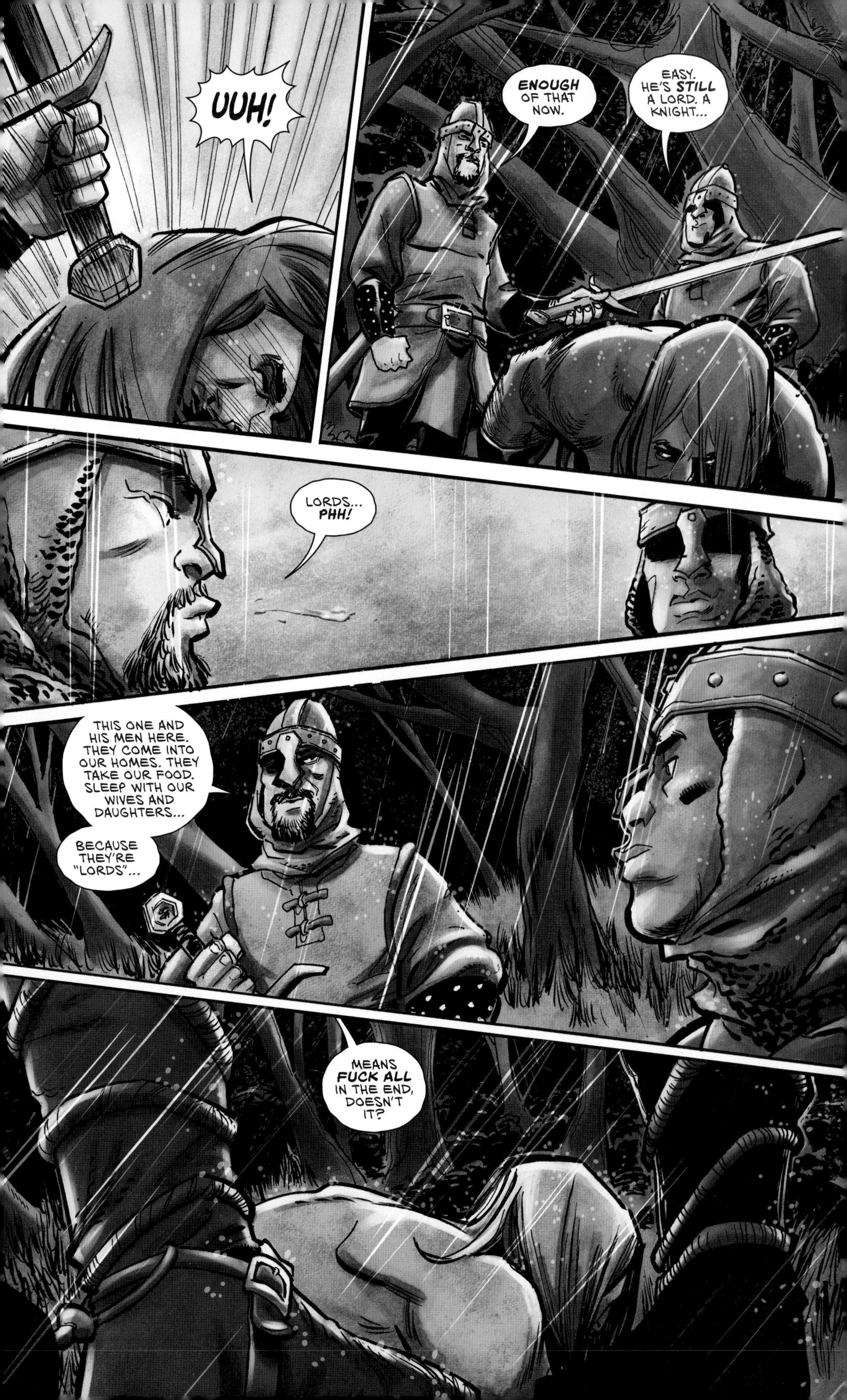
UUH!
ENOUGH OF THAT NOW.
EASY. HE'S STILL A LORD. A KNIGHT...
LORDS... PHH!
THIS ONE AND HIS MEN HERE. THEY COME INTO OUR HOMES. THEY TAKE OUR FOOD. SLEEP WITH OUR WIVES AND DAUGHTERS...
BECAUSE THEY'RE "LORDS"...
MEANS FUCK ALL IN THE END, DOESN'T IT?

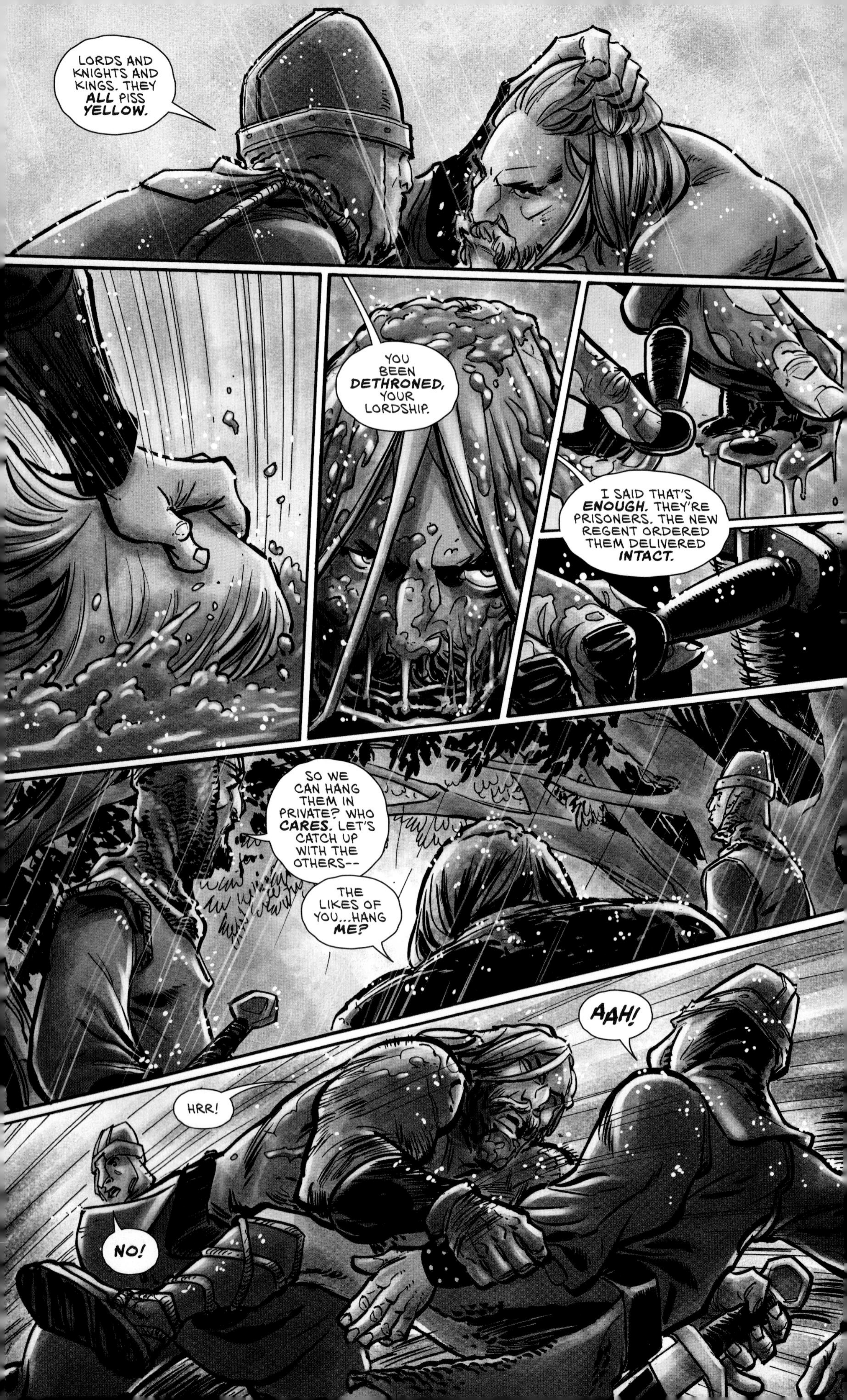
LORDS AND KNIGHTS AND KINGS. THEY ALL PISS YELLOW.
YOU BEEN DETHRONED, YOUR LORDSHIP.
I SAID THAT'S ENOUGH. THEY'RE PRISONERS. THE NEW REGENT ORDERED THEM DELIVERED INTACT.
SO WE CAN HANG THEM IN PRIVATE? WHO CARES. LET'S CATCH UP WITH THE OTHERS--
THE LIKES OF YOU...HANG ME?
AAH!
HRR!
NO!

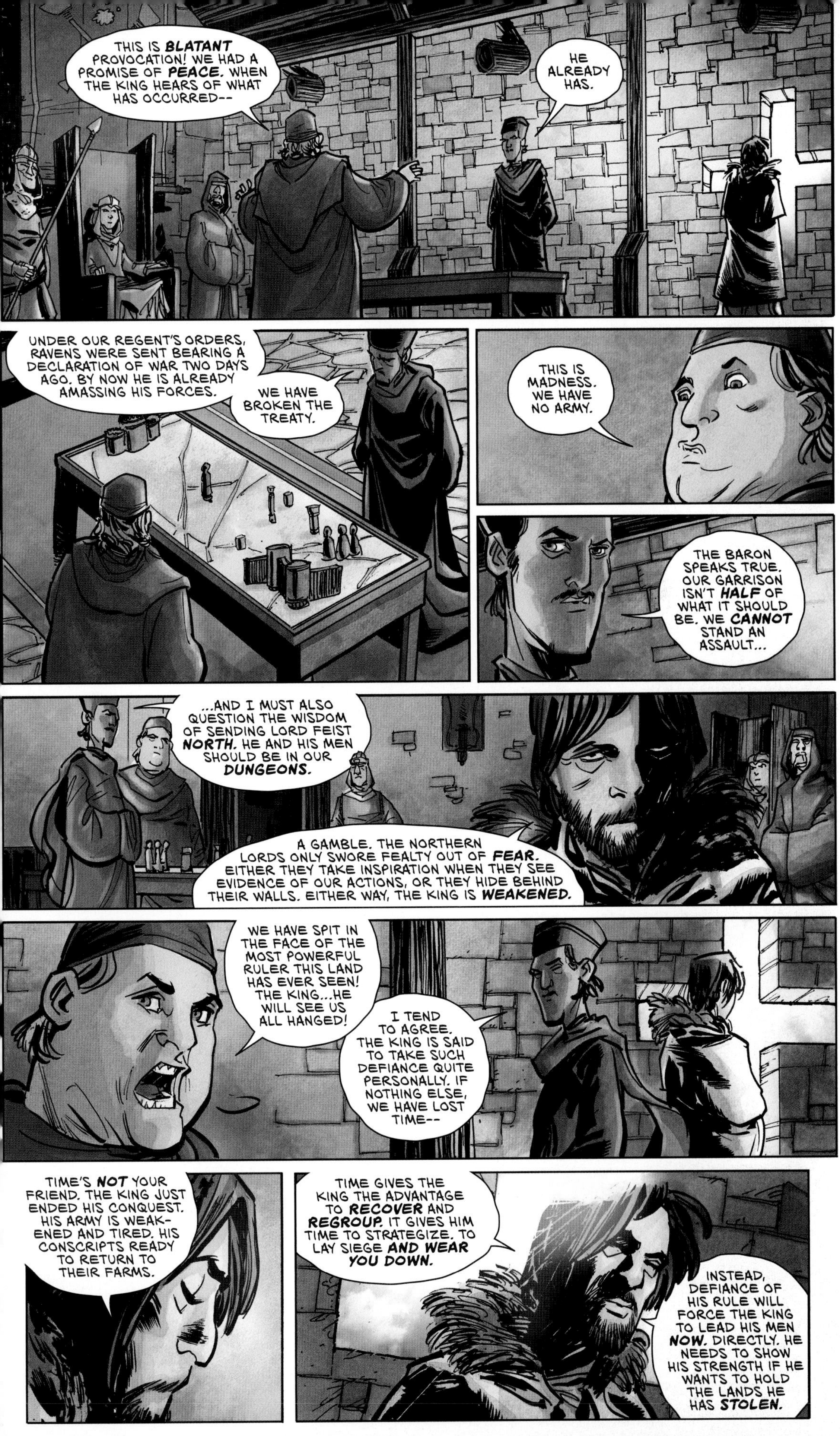
THIS IS BLATANT PROVOCATION! WE HAD A PROMISE OF PEACE. WHEN THE KING HEARS OF WHAT HAS OCCURRED--
HE ALREADY HAS.
UNDER OUR REGENT'S ORDERS, RAVENS WERE SENT BEARING A DECLARATION OF WAR TWO DAYS AGO. BY NOW HE IS ALREADY AMASSING HIS FORCES.
WE HAVE BROKEN THE TREATY.
THIS IS MADNESS. WE HAVE NO ARMY.
THE BARON SPEAKS TRUE. OUR GARRISON ISN'T HALF OF WHAT IT SHOULD BE. WE CANNOT STAND AN ASSAULT...
...AND I MUST ALSO QUESTION THE WISDOM OF SENDING LORD FEIST NORTH. HE AND HIS MEN SHOULD BE IN OUR DUNGEONS.
A GAMBLE. THE NORTHERN LORDS ONLY SWORE FEALTY OUT OF FEAR. EITHER THEY TAKE INSPIRATION WHEN THEY SEE EVIDENCE OF OUR ACTIONS, OR THEY HIDE BEHIND THEIR WALLS. EITHER WAY, THE KING IS WEAKENED.
WE HAVE SPIT IN THE FACE OF THE MOST POWERFUL RULER THIS LAND HAS EVER SEEN! THE KING...HE WILL SEE US ALL HANGED!
I TEND TO AGREE. THE KING IS SAID TO TAKE SUCH DEFIANCE QUITE PERSONALLY. IF NOTHING ELSE, WE HAVE LOST TIME--
TIME'S NOT YOUR FRIEND. THE KING JUST ENDED HIS CONQUEST. HIS ARMY IS WEAK-ENED AND TIRED. HIS CONSCRIPTS READY TO RETURN TO THEIR FARMS.
TIME GIVES THE KING THE ADVANTAGE TO RECOVER AND REGROUP. IT GIVES HIM TIME TO STRATEGIZE. TO LAY SIEGE AND WEAR YOU DOWN.
INSTEAD, DEFIANCE OF HIS RULE WILL FORCE THE KING TO LEAD HIS MEN NOW. DIRECTLY. HE NEEDS TO SHOW HIS STRENGTH IF HE WANTS TO HOLD THE LANDS HE HAS STOLEN.

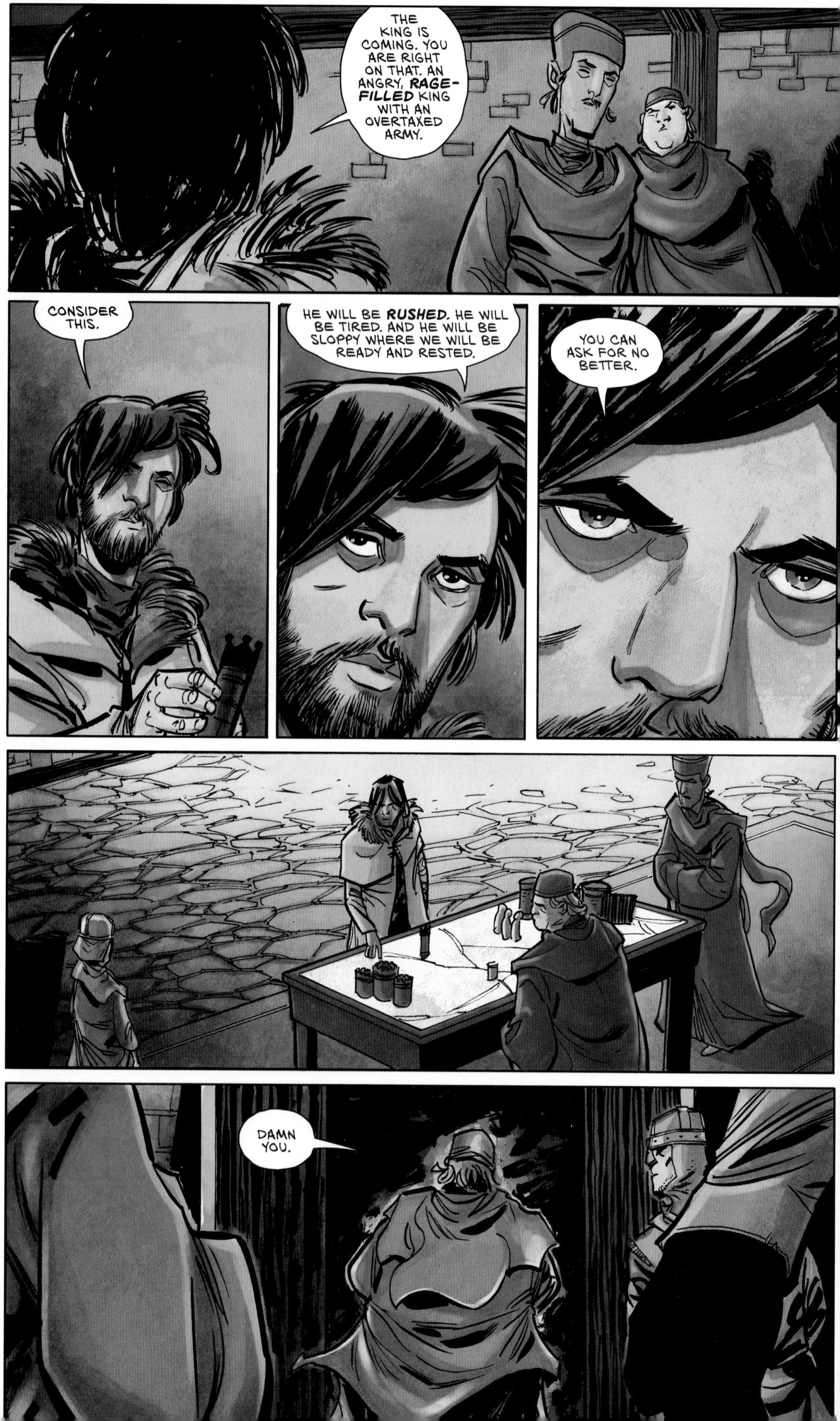
THE KING IS COMING. YOU ARE RIGHT ON THAT. AN ANGRY, **RAGE-FILLED** KING WITH AN OVERTAXED ARMY.
CONSIDER THIS.
HE WILL BE **RUSHED.** HE WILL BE TIRED. AND HE WILL BE SLOPPY WHERE WE WILL BE READY AND RESTED.
YOU CAN ASK FOR NO BETTER.
DAMN YOU.

THERE IS MUCH TO SEE DONE THEN. AND YOU HAVE ENSURED WE HAVE *LITTLE* CHOICE.

YOU NEVER HAD A CHOICE AT ALL. I'M JUST MAKING YOU SEE IT.

REGARDLESS, THE KING WILL MARCH ON US WITH NO LESS THAN *FIVE HUNDRED MEN.*

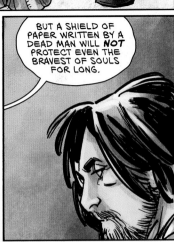

THEY WILL BE HIS MOST LOYAL, AND HIS MOST *BRUTAL.*

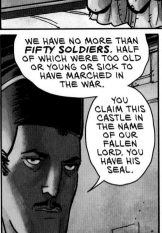

WE HAVE NO MORE THAN *FIFTY SOLDIERS.* HALF OF WHICH WERE TOO OLD OR YOUNG OR SICK TO HAVE MARCHED IN THE WAR.

YOU CLAIM THIS CASTLE IN THE NAME OF OUR FALLEN LORD. YOU HAVE HIS SEAL.

BUT A SHIELD OF PAPER WRITTEN BY A DEAD MAN WILL *NOT* PROTECT EVEN THE BRAVEST OF SOULS FOR LONG.

YOU HAVE MY SERVICE. YOU HAVE THE SWORDS OF THOSE FEW SOLDIERS THAT REMAIN HERE.

DO *NOT* SQUANDER THEIR LIVES OR THEIR TRUST.

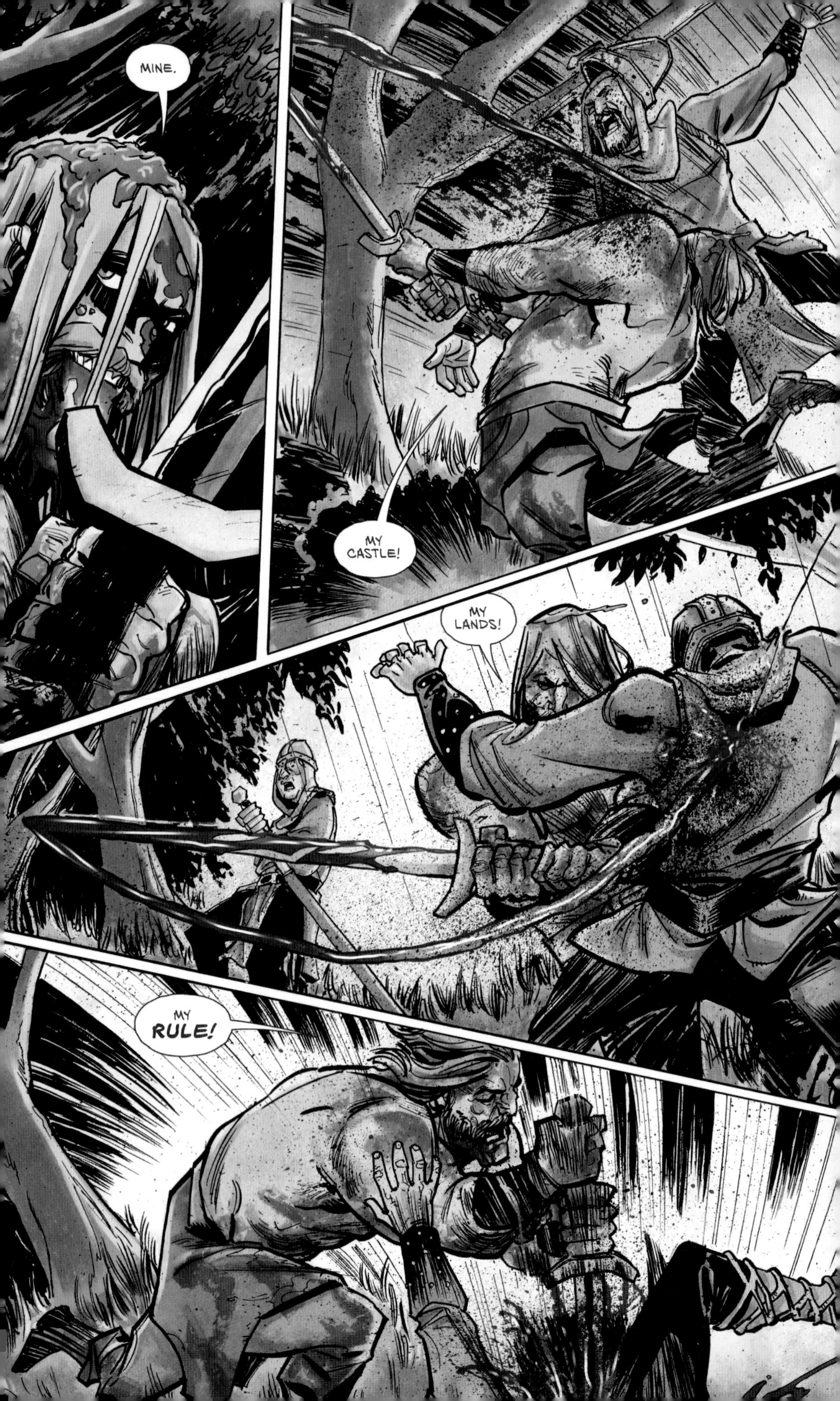
MINE.
MY CASTLE!
MY LANDS!
MY RULE!

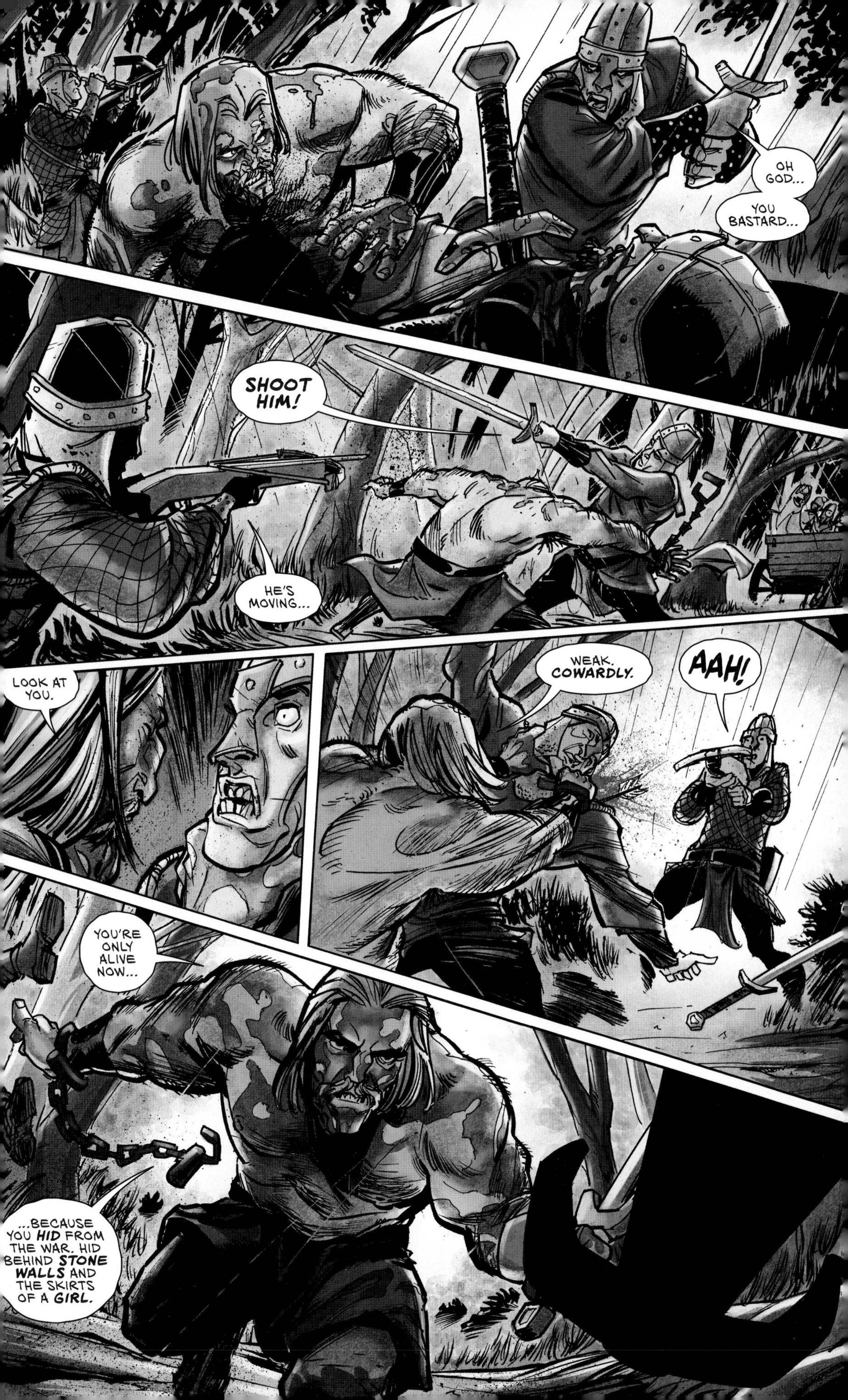
OH GOD...
YOU BASTARD...
SHOOT HIM!
HE'S MOVING...
LOOK AT YOU.
WEAK. COWARDLY.
AAH!
YOU'RE ONLY ALIVE NOW...
...BECAUSE YOU HID FROM THE WAR. HID BEHIND STONE WALLS AND THE SKIRTS OF A GIRL.

LADY CATHRYN.

YOU'RE WONDERING *WHY* YOUR FATHER SENT ME?

I FOUGHT WITH HIM. WHEN I THOUGHT I HAD LOST *EVERYTHING*, HE SHOWED ME ANOTHER PATH.

WHAT YOUR ADVISOR SAYS IS TRUE ENOUGH. WE *CANNOT* HOLD AGAINST THE KING'S MEN.

EVEN IF WE COULD DEFEAT HIS ARMY, HE WOULD SIMPLY SEND ANOTHER. AND *ANOTHER*. ALL FROM THE COMFORT OF HIS *DISTANT* THRONE.

IT WAS YOUR FATHER'S WAY TO *LEAD* THE CHARGE. HE COMMANDED MEN THROUGH STRENGTH OF WILL AND SHEER *BRAVERY*.

BUT IF HE HAD LED FROM BEHIND THE LINES, *HE* WOULD BE HERE TODAY TO GUIDE YOU AND COMFORT YOU.

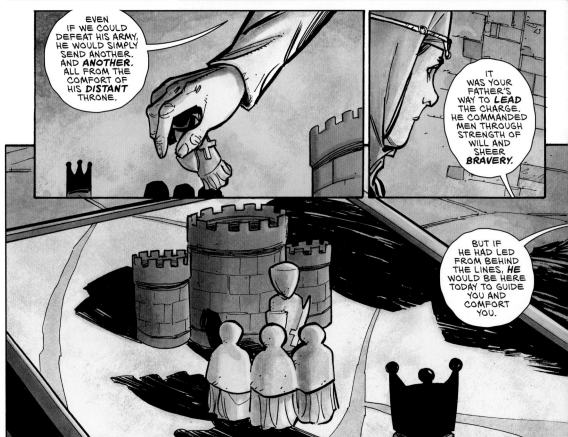

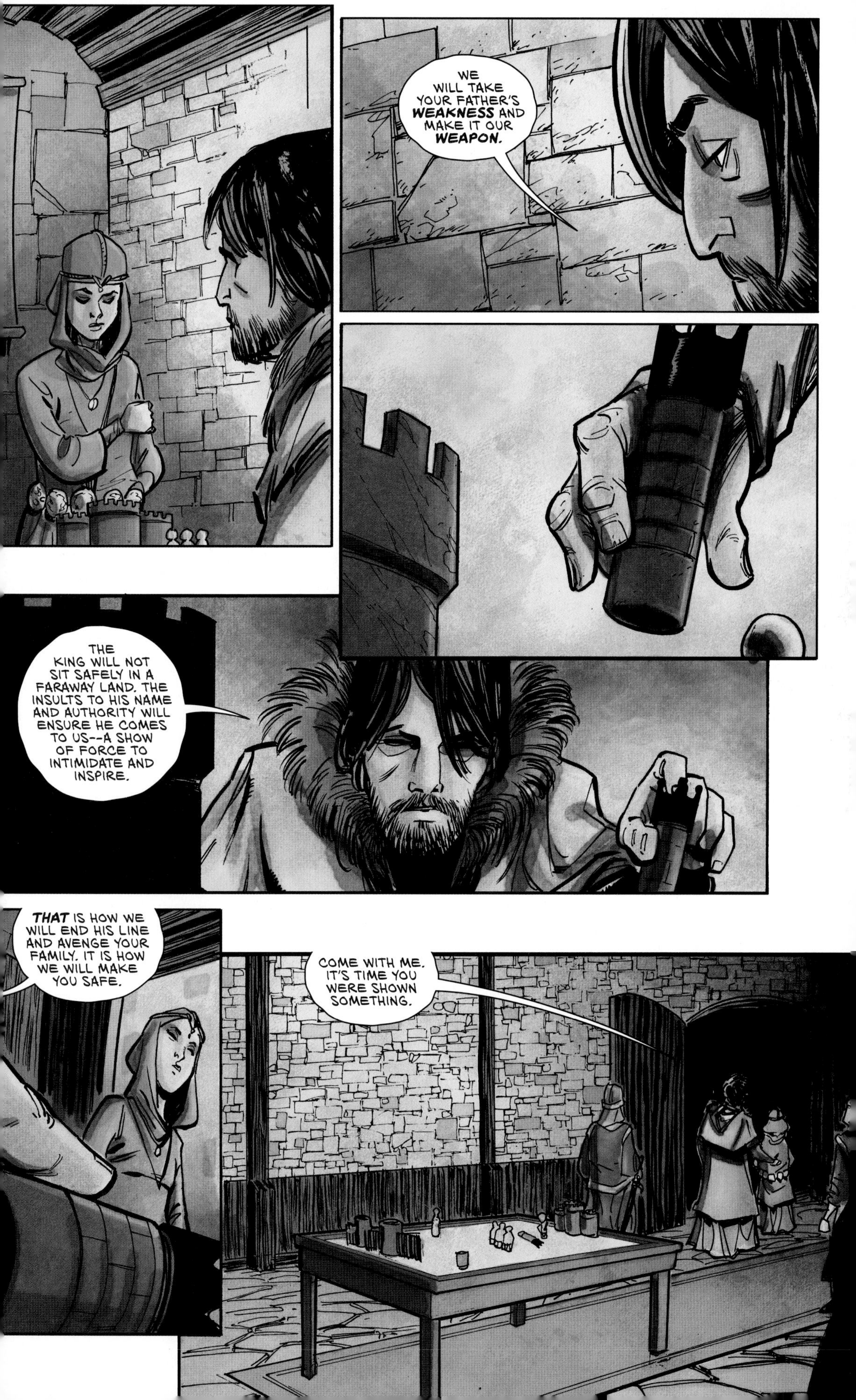
WE WILL TAKE YOUR FATHER'S WEAKNESS AND MAKE IT OUR WEAPON.
THE KING WILL NOT SIT SAFELY IN A FARAWAY LAND. THE INSULTS TO HIS NAME AND AUTHORITY WILL ENSURE HE COMES TO US--A SHOW OF FORCE TO INTIMIDATE AND INSPIRE.
THAT IS HOW WE WILL END HIS LINE AND AVENGE YOUR FAMILY. IT IS HOW WE WILL MAKE YOU SAFE.
COME WITH ME. IT'S TIME YOU WERE SHOWN SOMETHING.

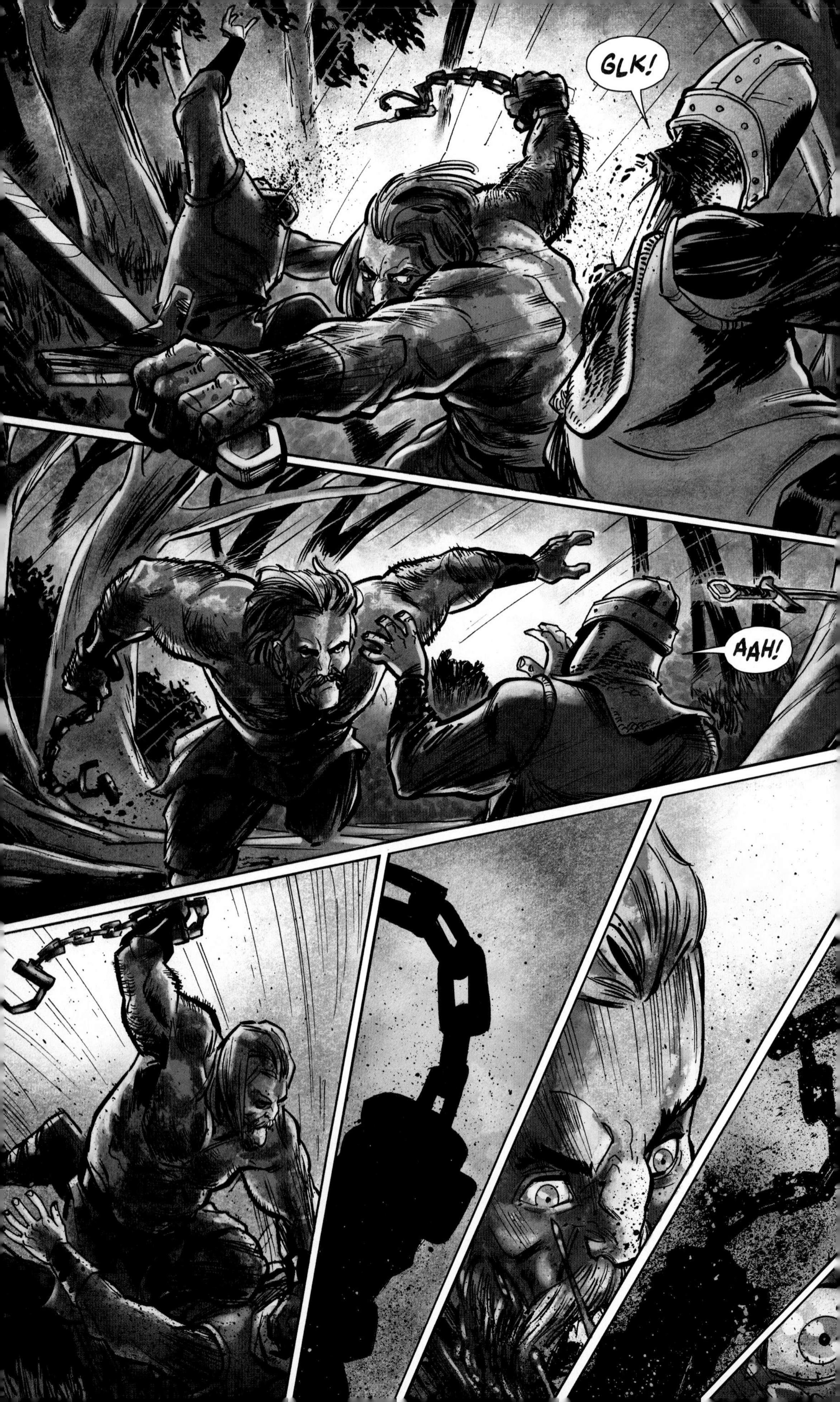
GLK!
AAH!

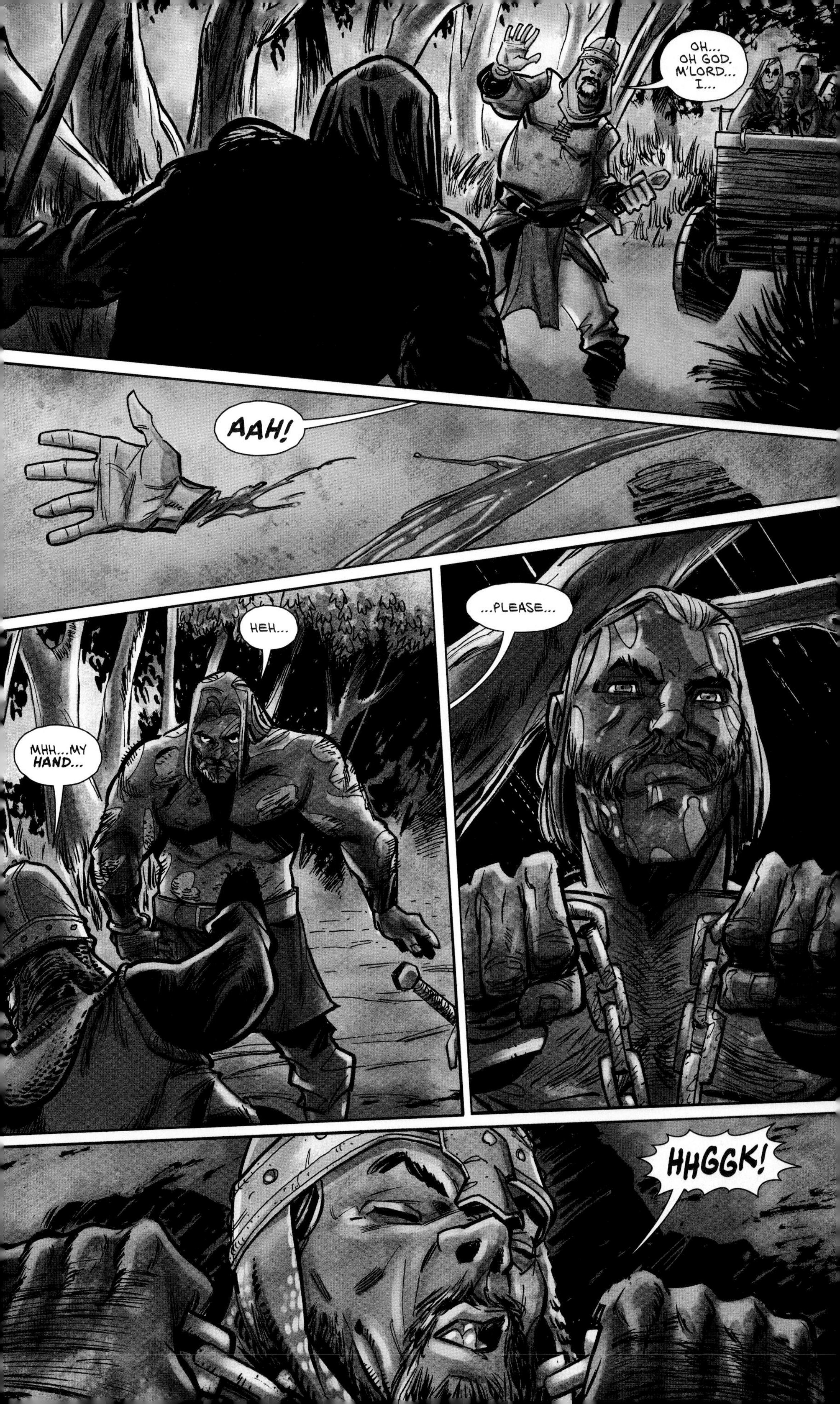
OH... OH GOD. M'LORD... I...
AAH!
HEH...
MHH...MY HAND...
...PLEASE...
HHGGK!

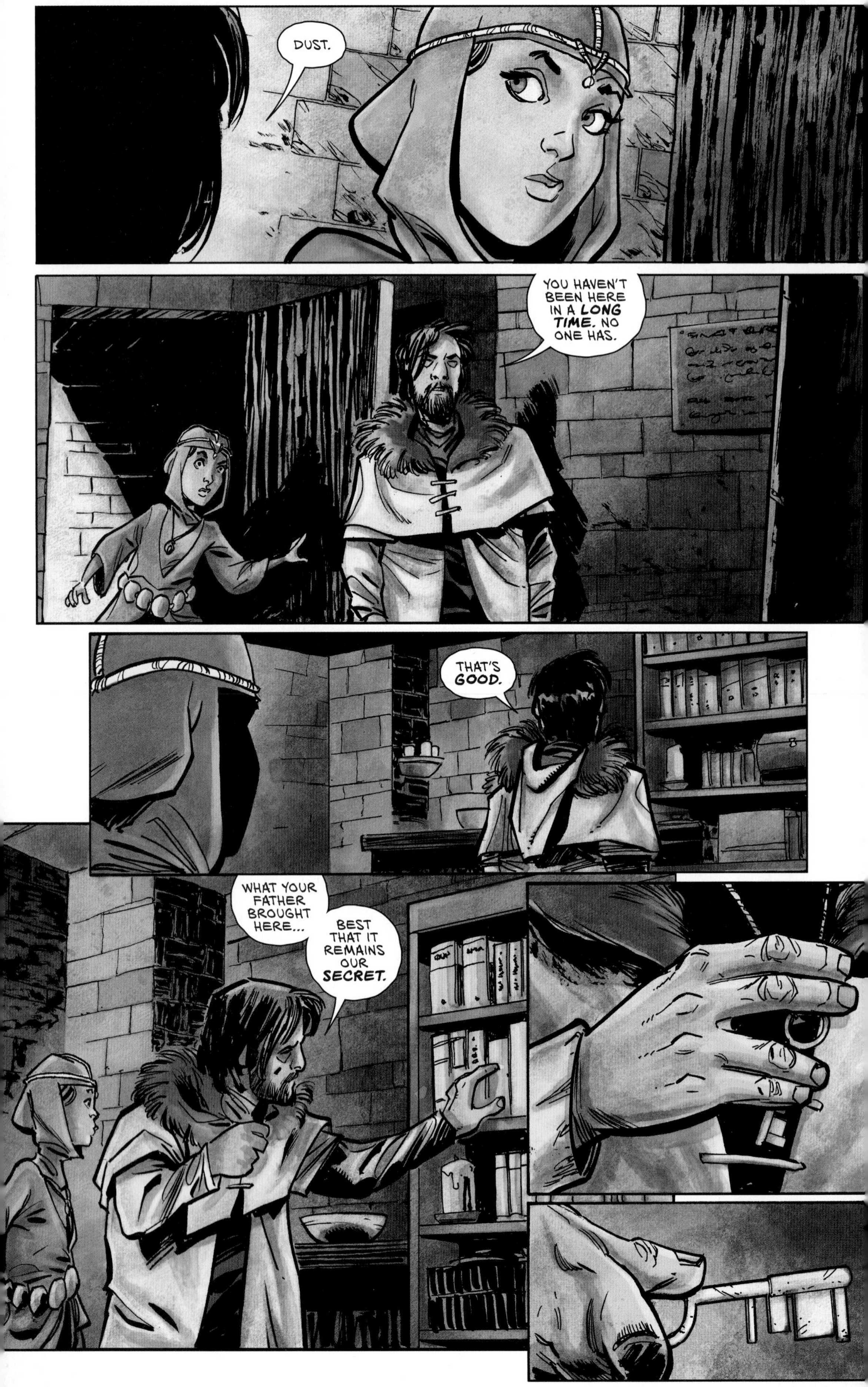
DUST.
YOU HAVEN'T BEEN HERE IN A **LONG TIME.** NO ONE HAS.
THAT'S **GOOD.**
WHAT YOUR FATHER BROUGHT HERE...
BEST THAT IT REMAINS OUR **SECRET.**

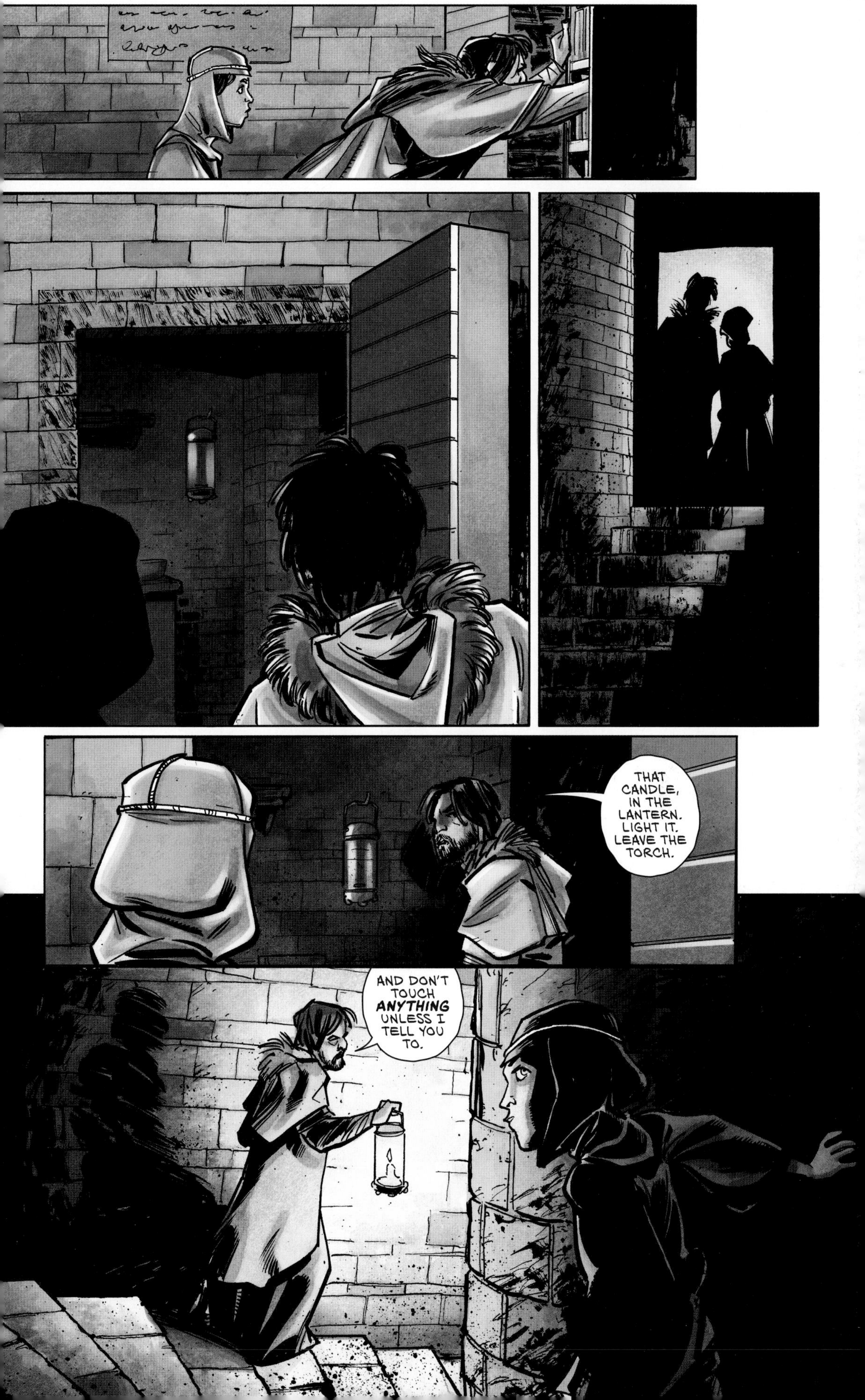
THAT CANDLE, IN THE LANTERN. LIGHT IT. LEAVE THE TORCH.
AND DON'T TOUCH **ANYTHING** UNLESS I TELL YOU TO.

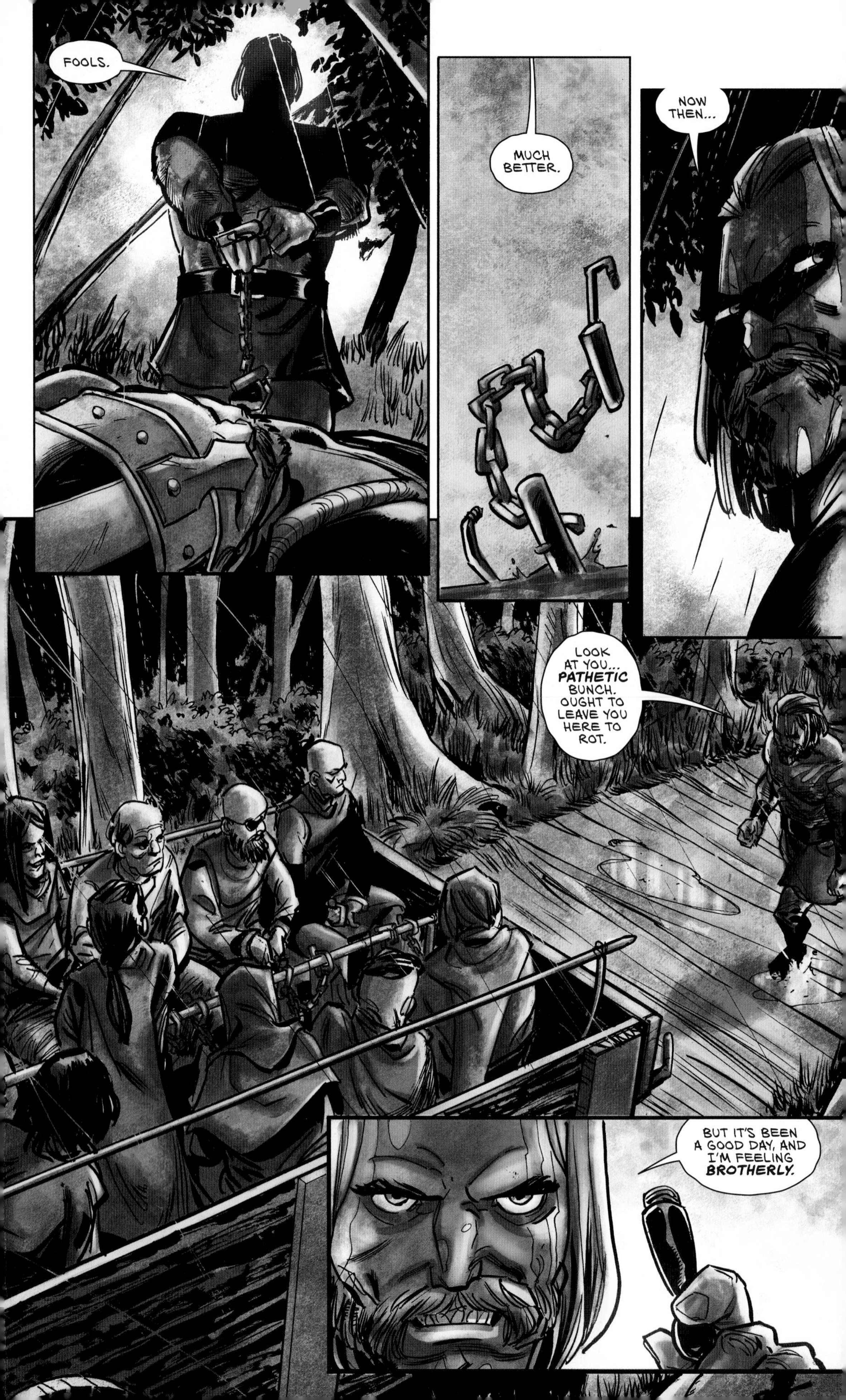
FOOLS.
MUCH BETTER.
NOW THEN...
LOOK AT YOU... PATHETIC BUNCH. OUGHT TO LEAVE YOU HERE TO ROT.
BUT IT'S BEEN A GOOD DAY, AND I'M FEELING BROTHERLY.

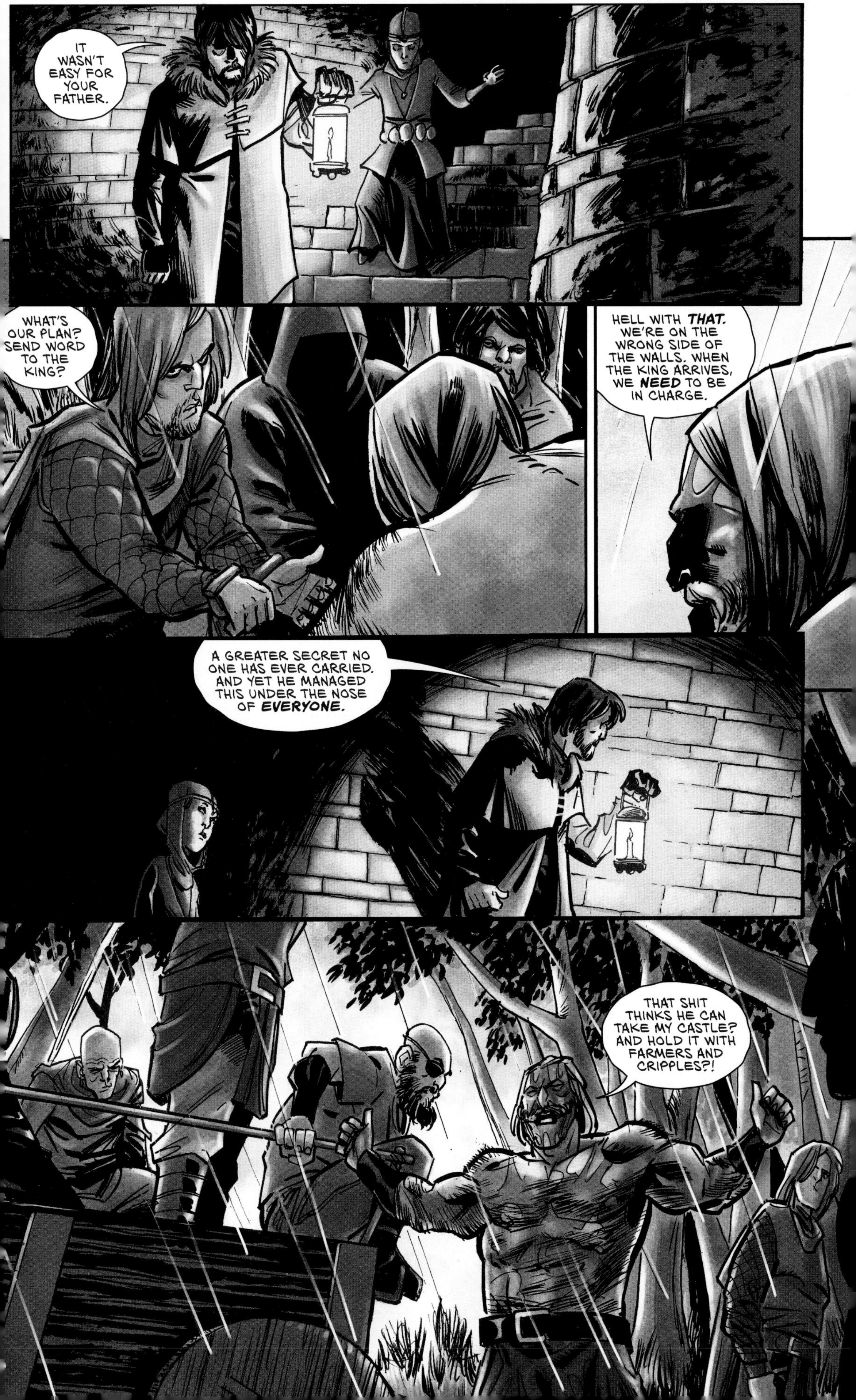
IT WASN'T EASY FOR YOUR FATHER.
WHAT'S OUR PLAN? SEND WORD TO THE KING?
HELL WITH THAT. WE'RE ON THE WRONG SIDE OF THE WALLS. WHEN THE KING ARRIVES, WE NEED TO BE IN CHARGE.
A GREATER SECRET NO ONE HAS EVER CARRIED. AND YET HE MANAGED THIS UNDER THE NOSE OF EVERYONE.
THAT SHIT THINKS HE CAN TAKE MY CASTLE? AND HOLD IT WITH FARMERS AND CRIPPLES?!

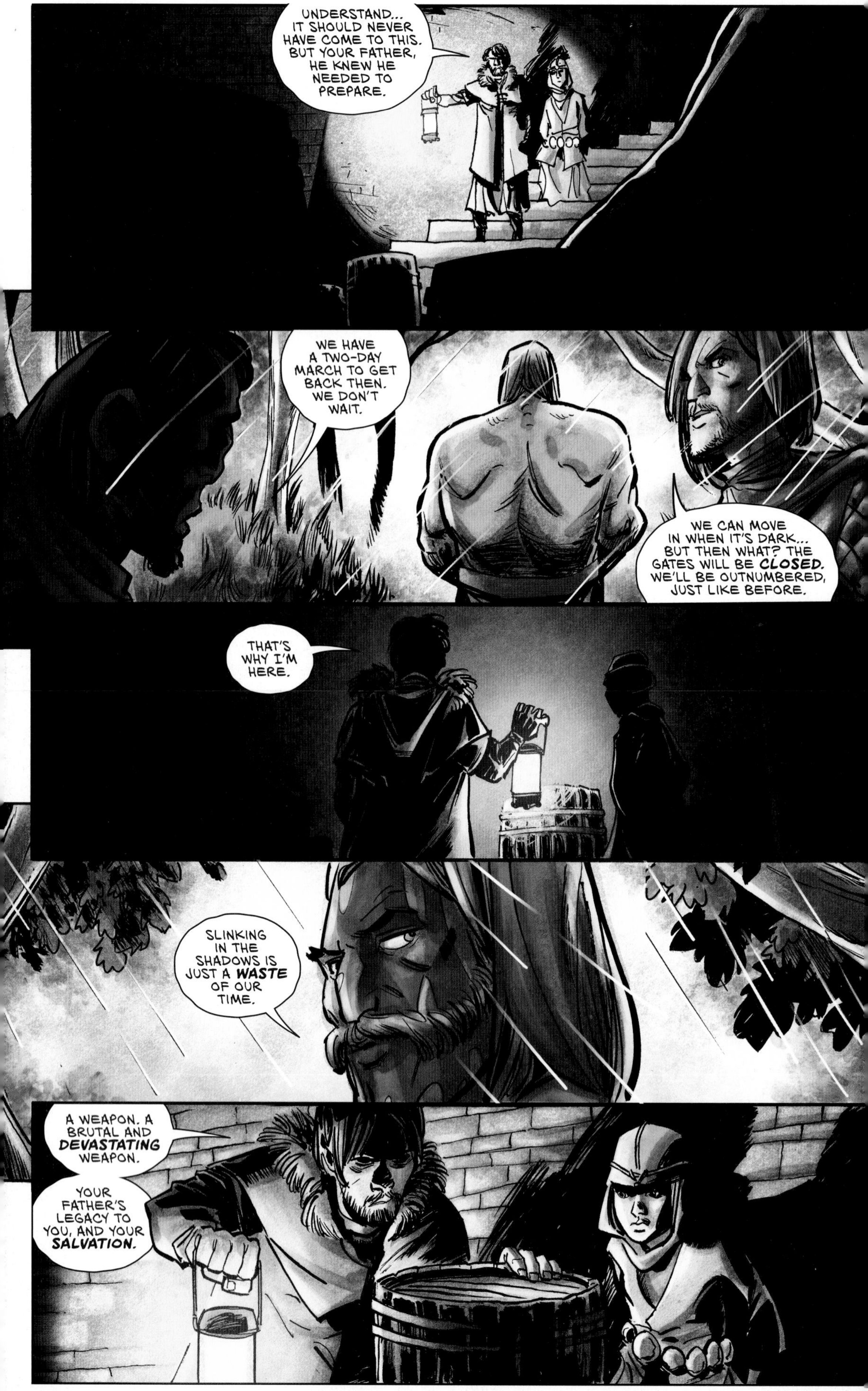
UNDERSTAND... IT SHOULD NEVER HAVE COME TO THIS. BUT YOUR FATHER, HE KNEW HE NEEDED TO PREPARE.
WE HAVE A TWO-DAY MARCH TO GET BACK THEN. WE DON'T WAIT.
WE CAN MOVE IN WHEN IT'S DARK... BUT THEN WHAT? THE GATES WILL BE **CLOSED.** WE'LL BE OUTNUMBERED, JUST LIKE BEFORE.
THAT'S WHY I'M HERE.
SLINKING IN THE SHADOWS IS JUST A **WASTE** OF OUR TIME.
A WEAPON. A BRUTAL AND **DEVASTATING** WEAPON.
YOUR FATHER'S LEGACY TO YOU, AND YOUR **SALVATION.**

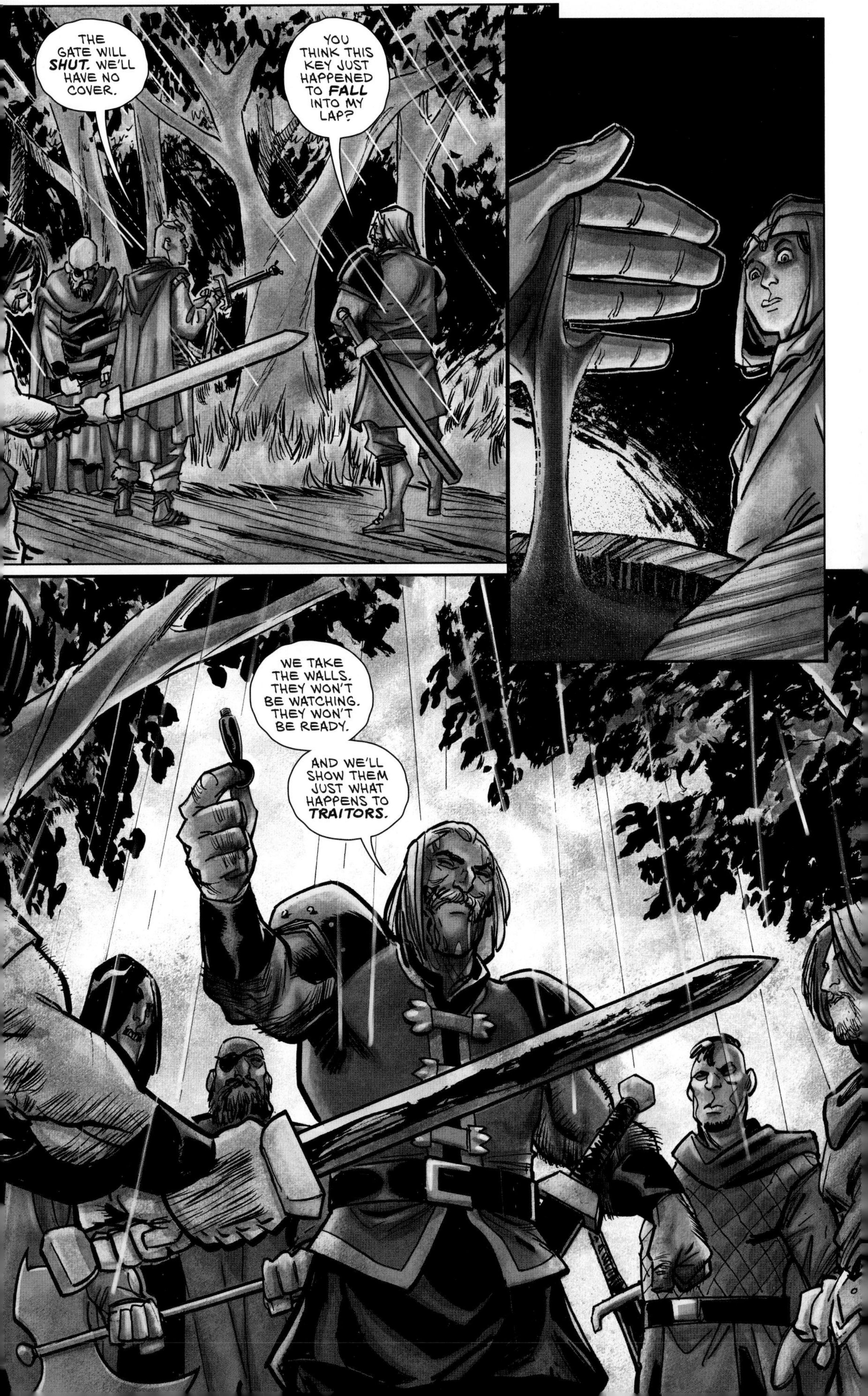

THE GATE WILL **SHUT.** WE'LL HAVE NO COVER.
YOU THINK THIS KEY JUST HAPPENED TO **FALL** INTO MY LAP?
WE TAKE THE WALLS. THEY WON'T BE WATCHING. THEY WON'T BE READY.
AND WE'LL SHOW THEM JUST WHAT HAPPENS TO **TRAITORS.**

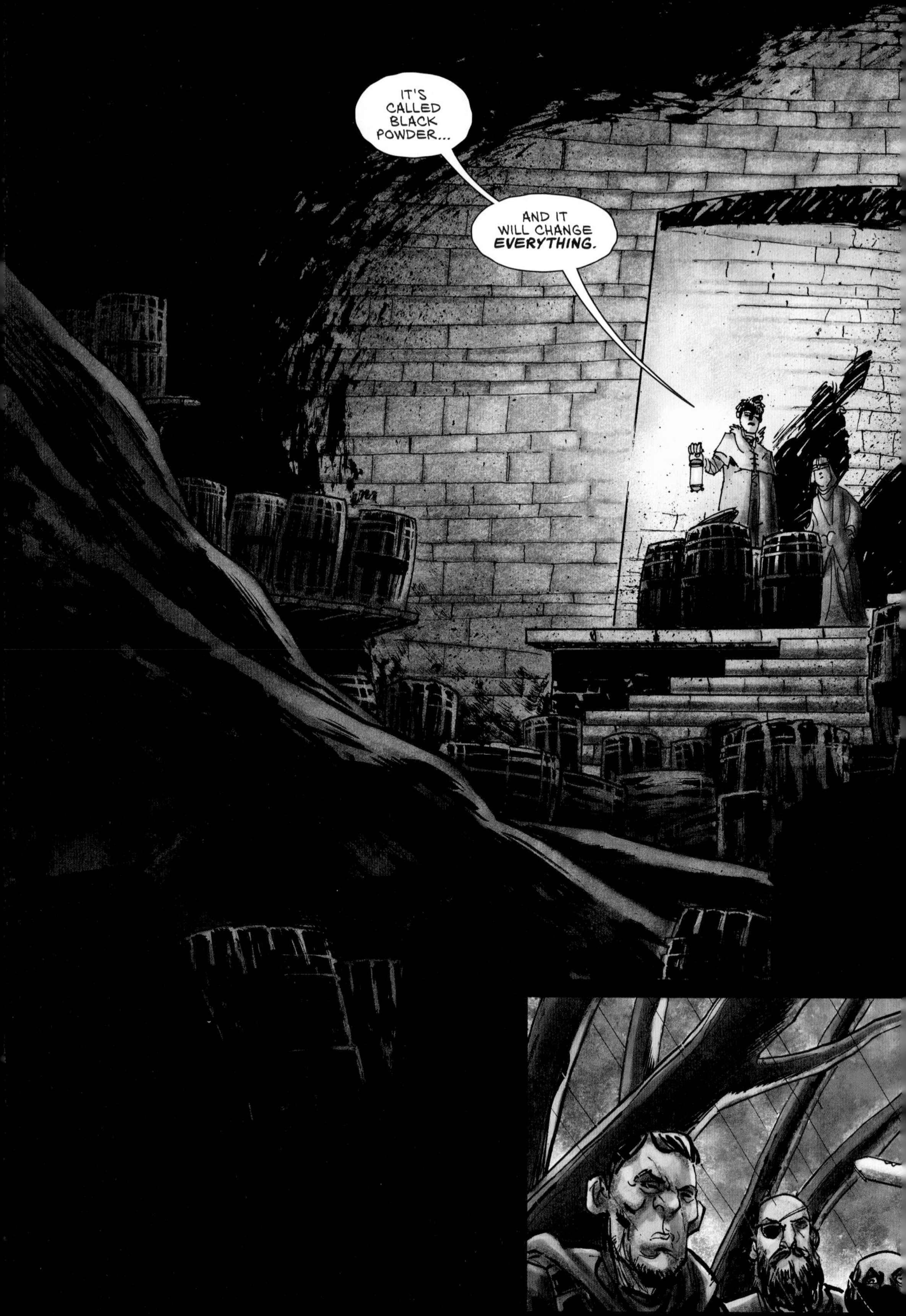
IT'S CALLED BLACK POWDER...
AND IT WILL CHANGE EVERYTHING.

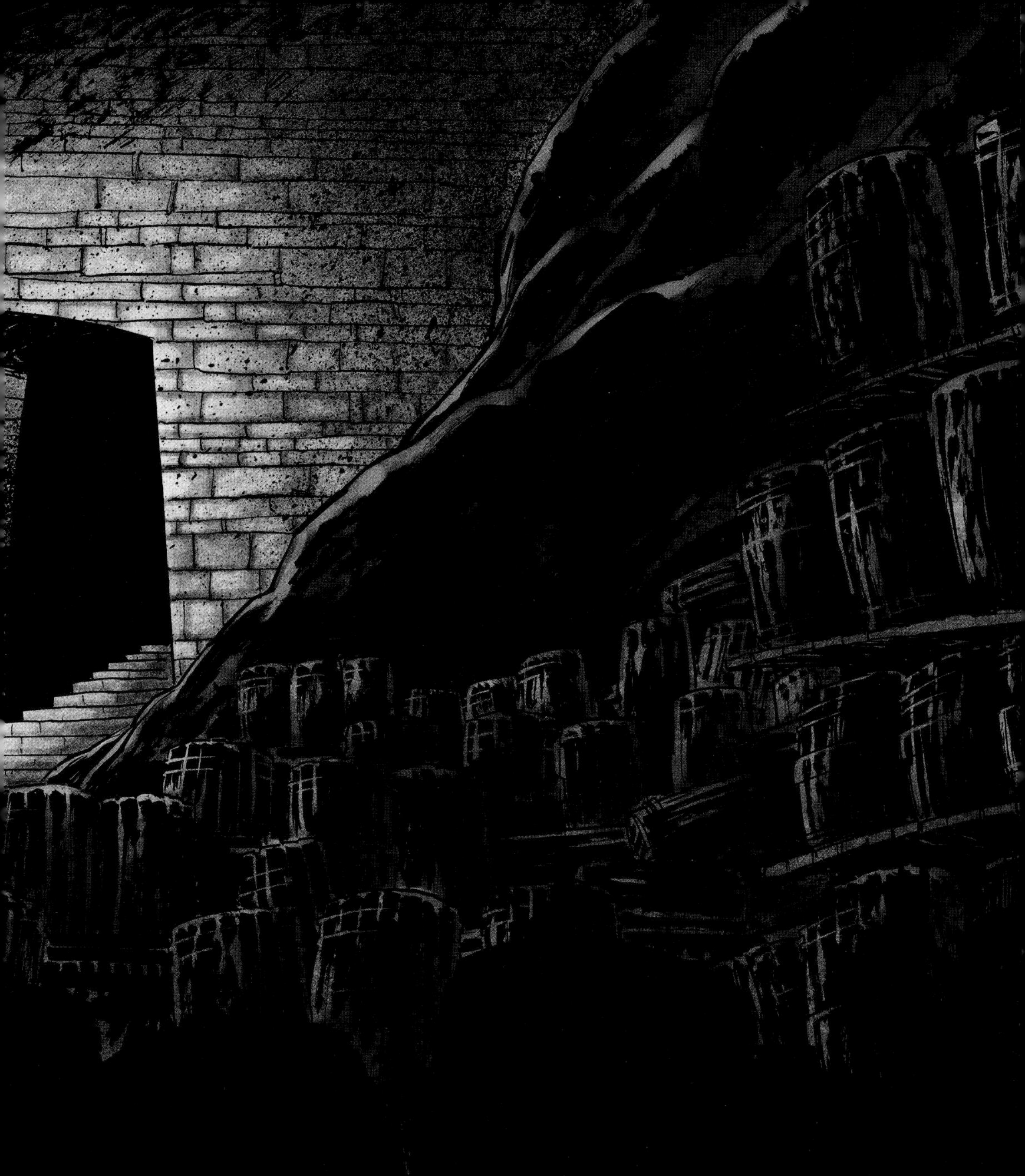

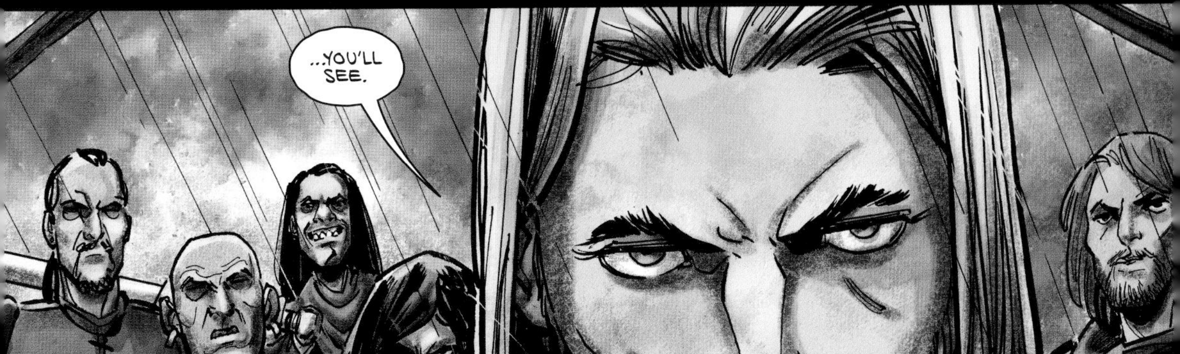
...YOU'LL SEE.

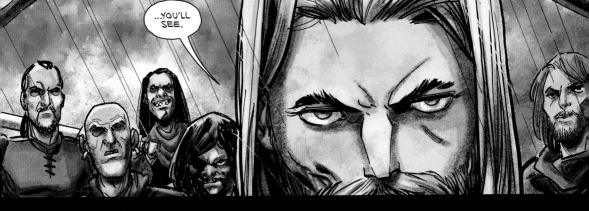

THE KING RISES
~chapter 2~

The stench of the stables made Istvan's head spin.

It had been five years since the fall of the false king, Grigorii. The self-proclaimed monarch was now a forgotten footnote in the histories of the eastern provinces; the families that had allied with his ill-fated dream of a united nation broken, their lands divided up among the powerful lords that ruled in their stead.

Penniless and without a name, Istvan had wandered from village to village, working in every stable and field between his forgotten hometown and the steep plateaus of the eastern borders. It was a harsh existence, one that would have broken many a man, but Istvan knew that every step he took was one that bore him closer to the role he had trained for in childhood.

He was meant to be a ruler. A commander of men. And one day, he would be.

"You're lazy," teased a voice.

Though Tomislav was almost of an age with Istvan, the younger man was tall and willowy, with thick black hair hanging down into his eyes. He was proud and easy to laugh. A young lord, in all but title — and even that would one day be his.

"Your father is happy enough with the work I do," countered Istvan. "He pays me, anyway."

Tomislav shrugged. "Well, finish it already. We could be drinking, you know?"

Istvan didn't have to ask — he could smell the sour wine on his friend. "You've been drinking already, more than you should have been, I'd say."

"You probably would," the younger man agreed, "but it's no good alone. Drink with me and tell me more stories of the lands you have visited. Come on…"

"You could just visit them yourself."

"Pff. My father… as if he would allow me to wander the countryside like… well, like you have. He is…"

Istvan grabbed the arm of his taller friend, steadying him as he staggered. "Fine. Help me finish, and I'll drink with you. I'll tell you all you want to hear."

With that, he shoved a pitchfork into the hands of Tomislav, who looked at the tool as if he had never seen such a thing before.

"But you…" Istvan continued, "you will do something for me in return. You're going to go with me and see something of this land you're supposed to rule with your own eyes. Fair?"

Tomislav shrugged, and the two friends went to work.

THE LAST SIEGE

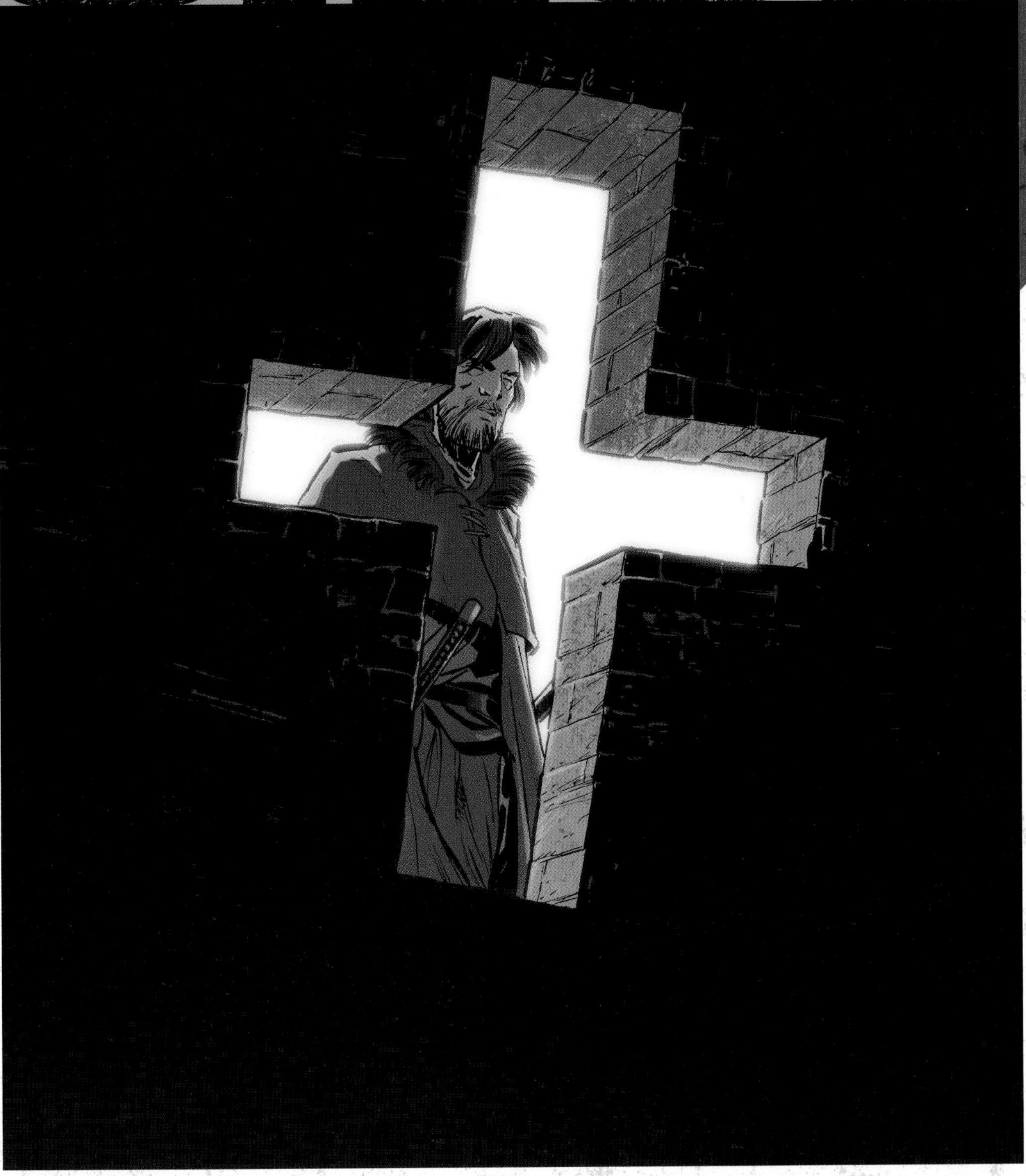

CHAPTER THREE

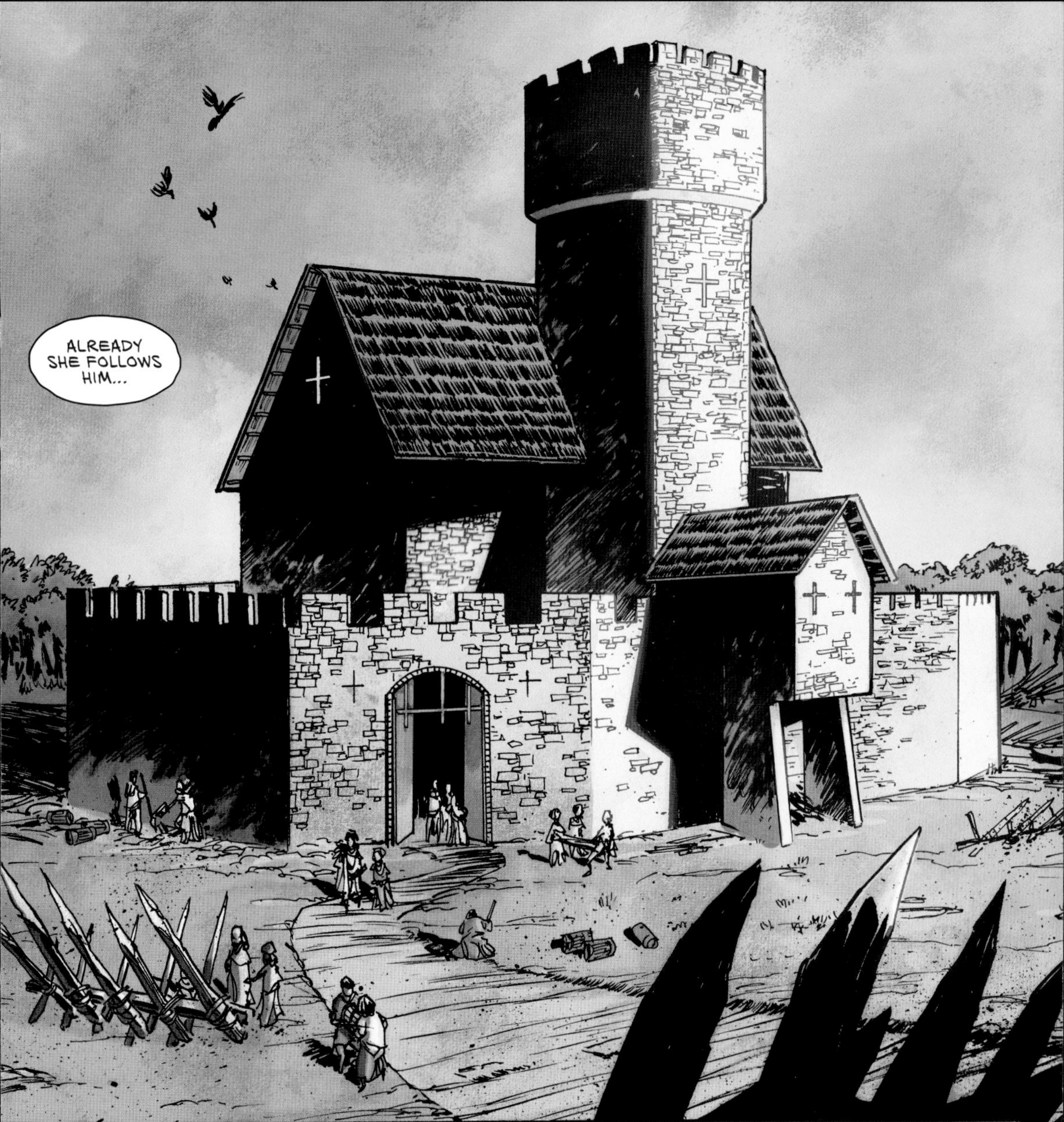
ALREADY SHE FOLLOWS HIM...

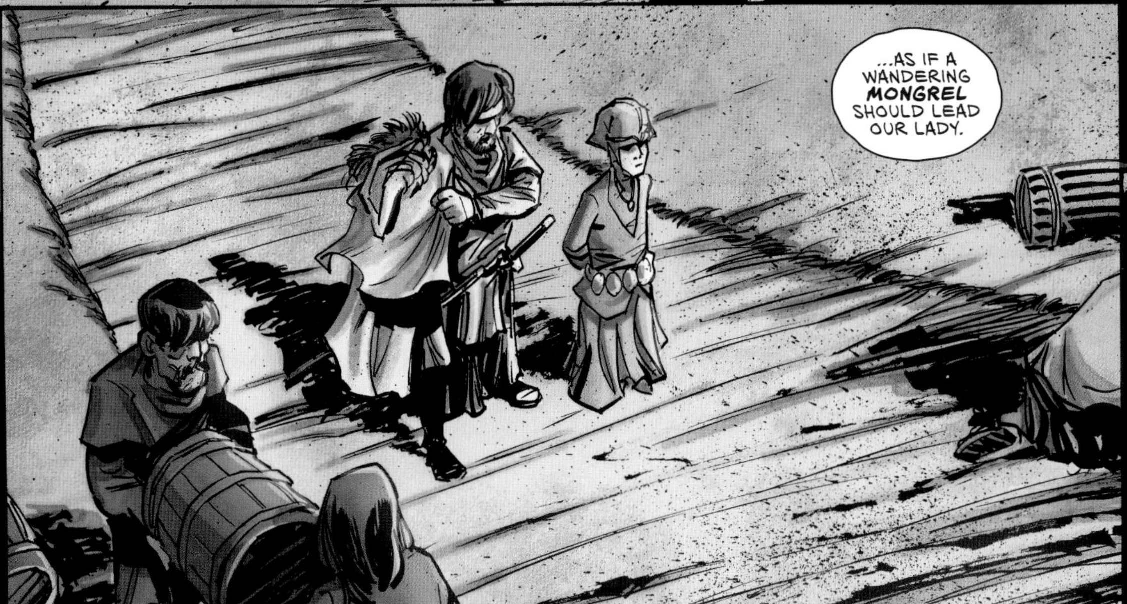
...AS IF A WANDERING MONGREL SHOULD LEAD OUR LADY.

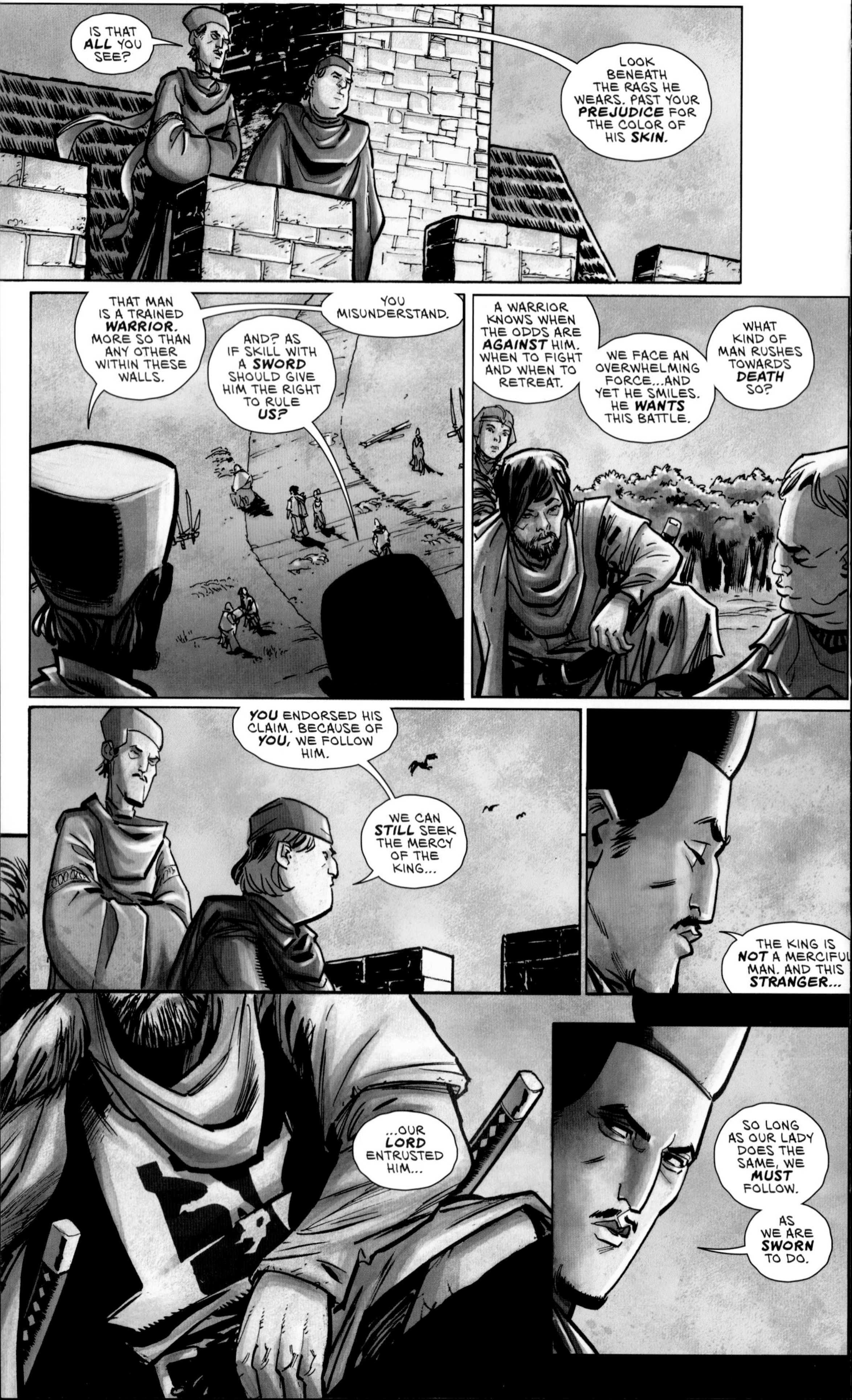
IS THAT ALL YOU SEE?
LOOK BENEATH THE RAGS HE WEARS. PAST YOUR PREJUDICE FOR THE COLOR OF HIS SKIN.
THAT MAN IS A TRAINED WARRIOR. MORE SO THAN ANY OTHER WITHIN THESE WALLS.
AND? AS IF SKILL WITH A SWORD SHOULD GIVE HIM THE RIGHT TO RULE US?
YOU MISUNDERSTAND.
A WARRIOR KNOWS WHEN THE ODDS ARE AGAINST HIM. WHEN TO FIGHT AND WHEN TO RETREAT.
WE FACE AN OVERWHELMING FORCE...AND YET HE SMILES. HE WANTS THIS BATTLE.
WHAT KIND OF MAN RUSHES TOWARDS DEATH SO?
YOU ENDORSED HIS CLAIM. BECAUSE OF YOU, WE FOLLOW HIM.
WE CAN STILL SEEK THE MERCY OF THE KING...
THE KING IS NOT A MERCIFUL MAN. AND THIS STRANGER...
...OUR LORD ENTRUSTED HIM...
SO LONG AS OUR LADY DOES THE SAME, WE MUST FOLLOW.
AS WE ARE SWORN TO DO.

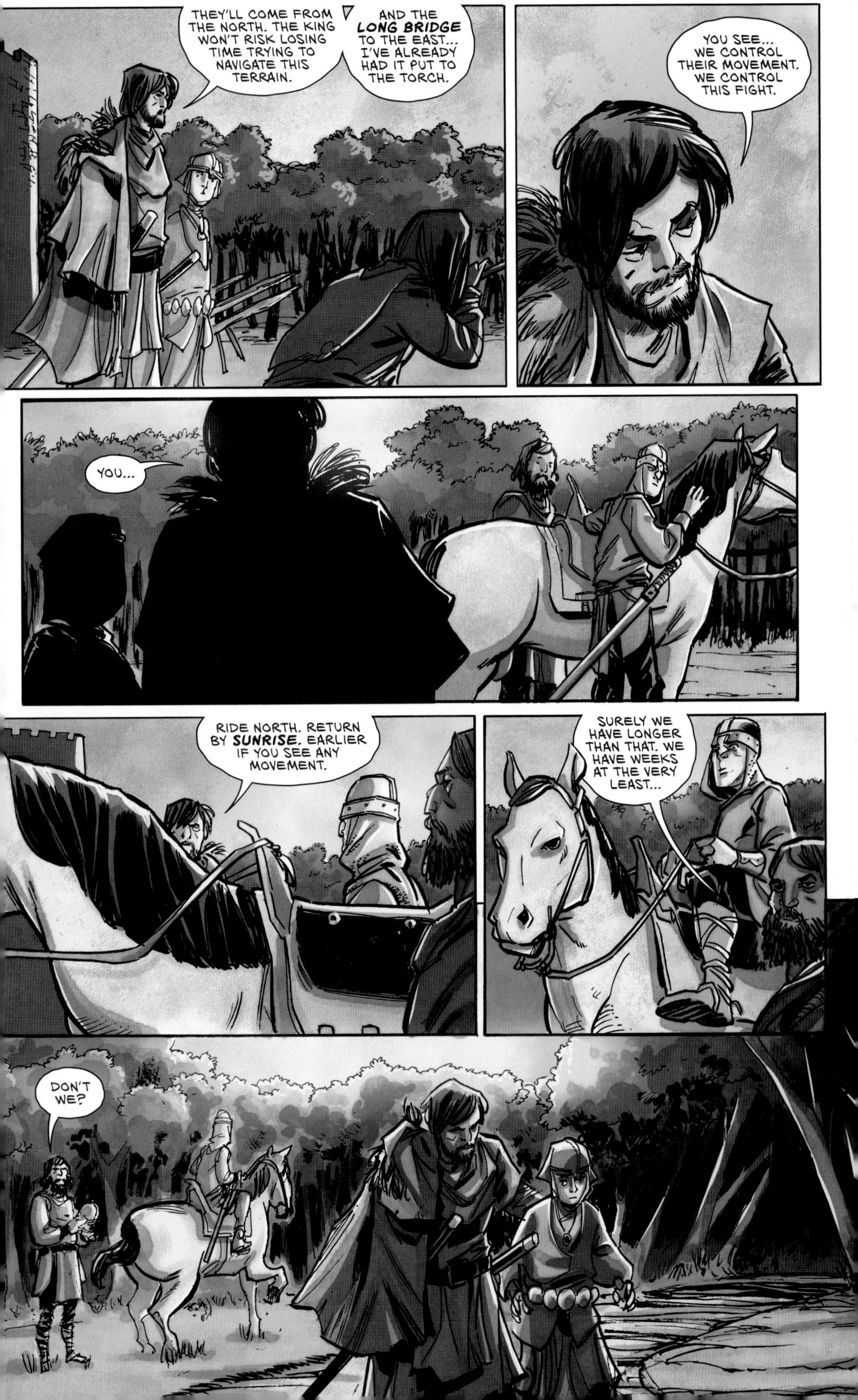
THEY'LL COME FROM THE NORTH. THE KING WON'T RISK LOSING TIME TRYING TO NAVIGATE THIS TERRAIN.
AND THE **LONG BRIDGE** TO THE EAST... I'VE ALREADY HAD IT PUT TO THE TORCH.
YOU SEE... WE CONTROL THEIR MOVEMENT. WE CONTROL THIS FIGHT.
YOU...
RIDE NORTH. RETURN BY **SUNRISE.** EARLIER IF YOU SEE ANY MOVEMENT.
SURELY WE HAVE LONGER THAN THAT. WE HAVE WEEKS AT THE VERY LEAST...
DON'T WE?

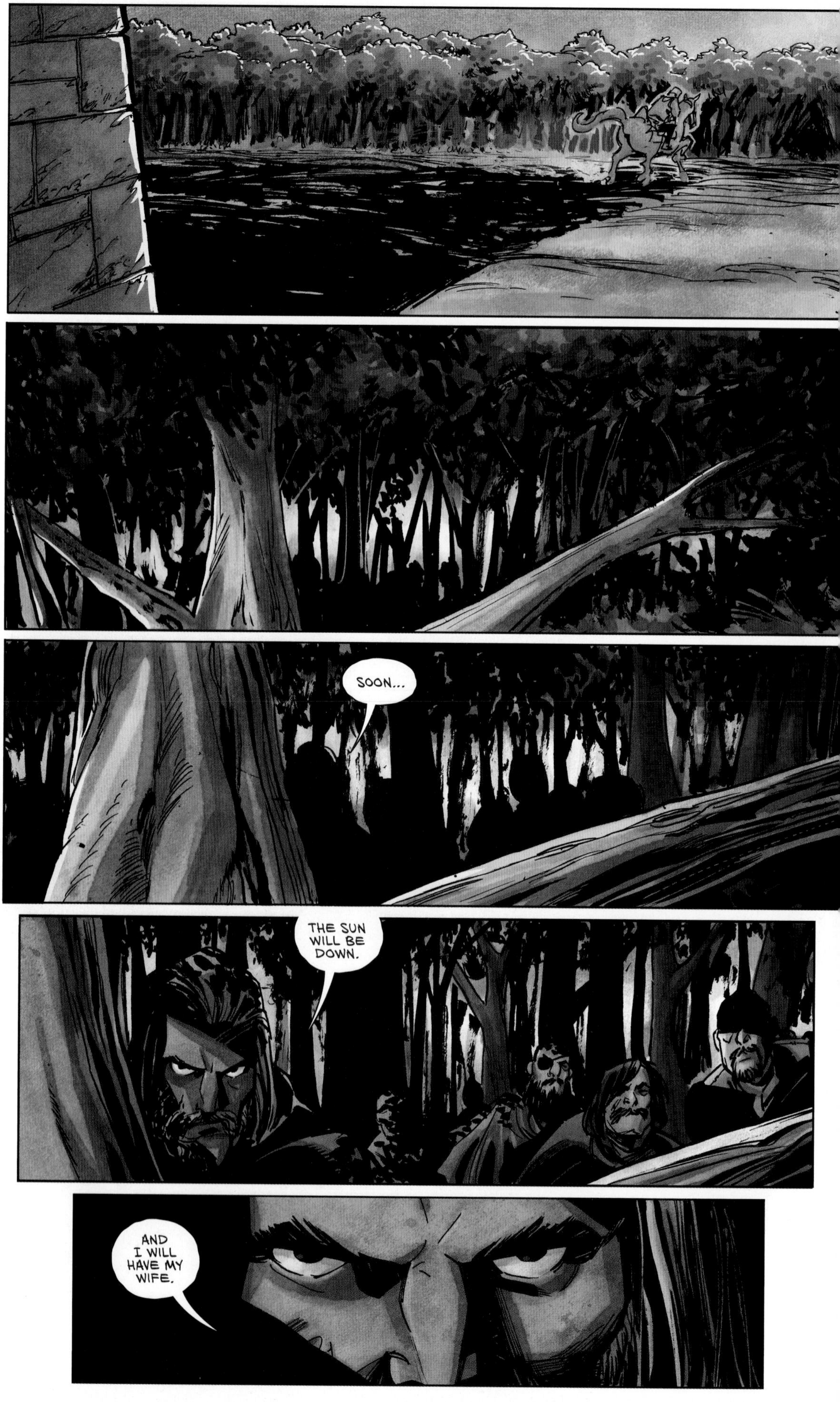
SOON...
THE SUN WILL BE DOWN.
AND I WILL HAVE MY WIFE.

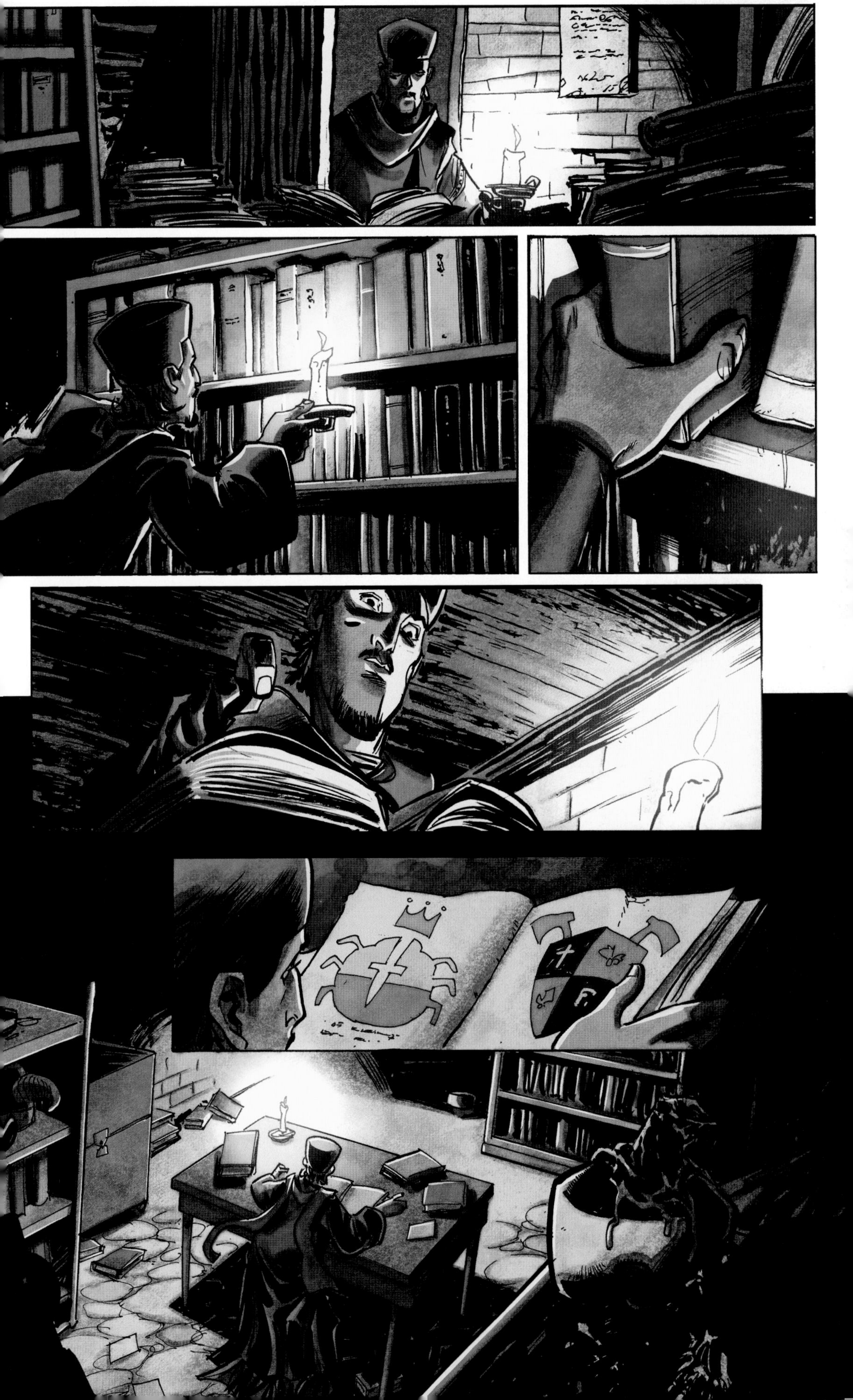

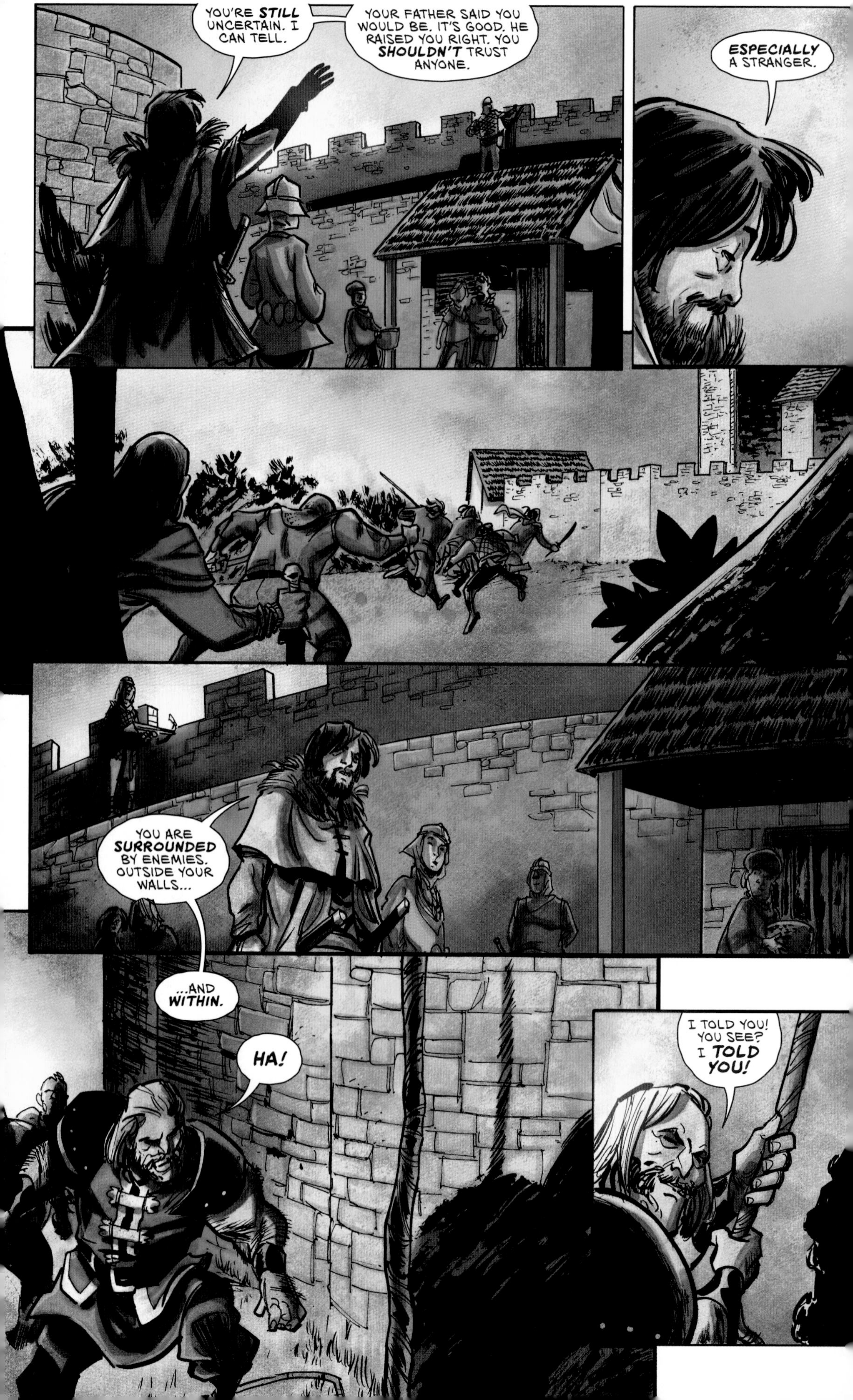
YOU'RE STILL UNCERTAIN. I CAN TELL.
YOUR FATHER SAID YOU WOULD BE. IT'S GOOD. HE RAISED YOU RIGHT. YOU SHOULDN'T TRUST ANYONE.
ESPECIALLY A STRANGER.
YOU ARE SURROUNDED BY ENEMIES. OUTSIDE YOUR WALLS...
...AND WITHIN.
HA!
I TOLD YOU! YOU SEE? I TOLD YOU!

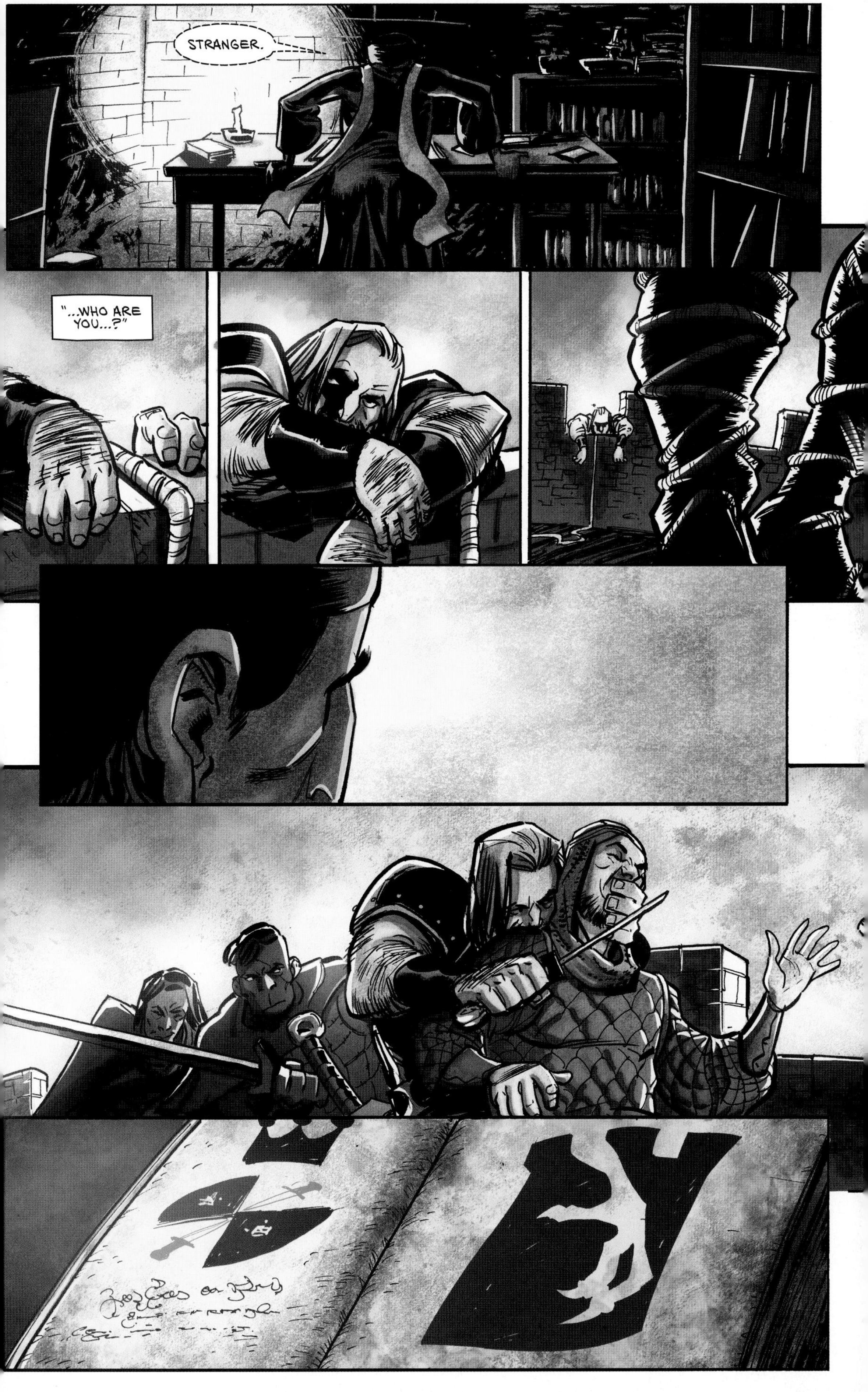
STRANGER.
"...WHO ARE YOU...?"

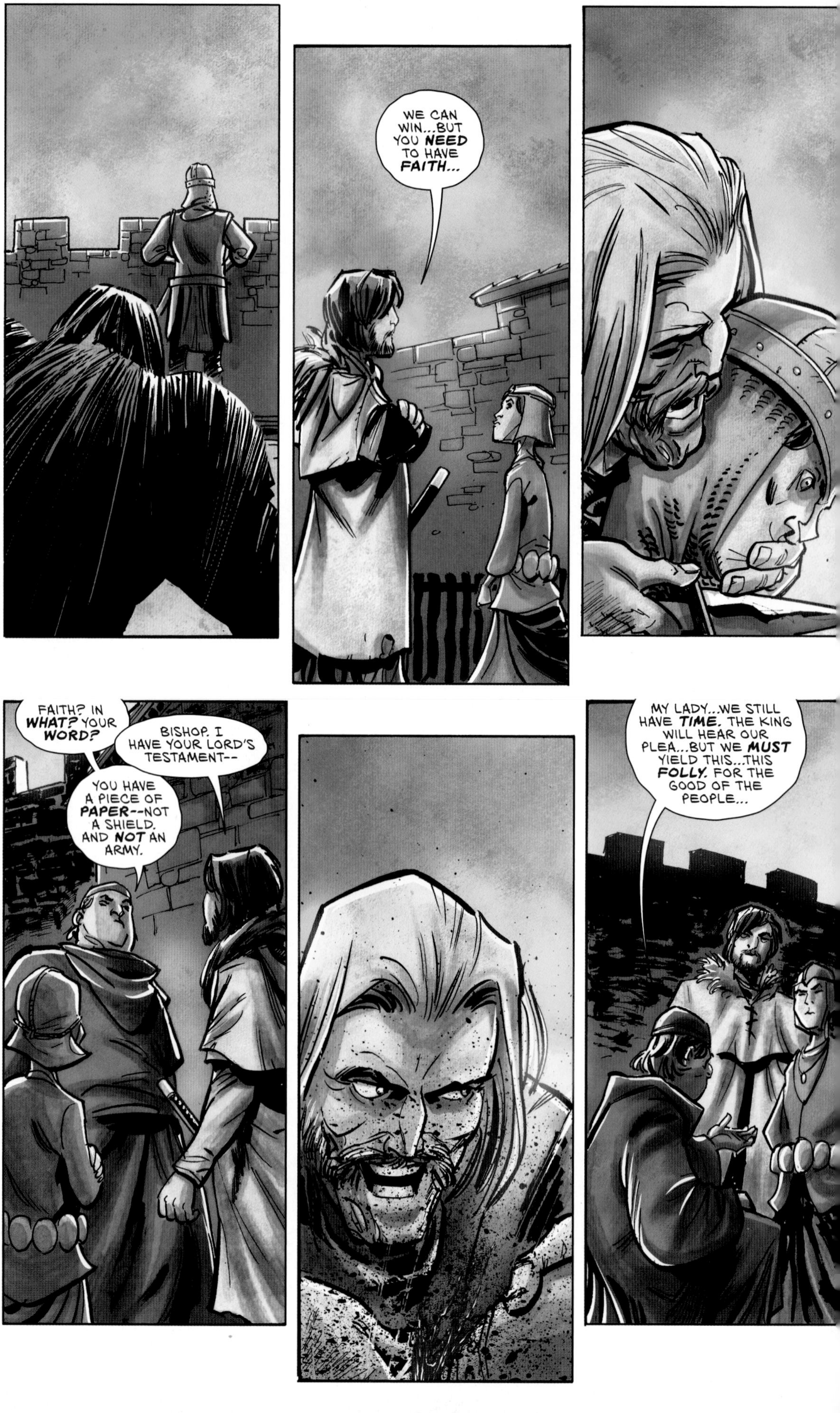
WE CAN WIN...BUT YOU NEED TO HAVE FAITH...
FAITH? IN WHAT? YOUR WORD?
BISHOP. I HAVE YOUR LORD'S TESTAMENT--
YOU HAVE A PIECE OF PAPER--NOT A SHIELD. AND NOT AN ARMY.
MY LADY...WE STILL HAVE TIME. THE KING WILL HEAR OUR PLEA...BUT WE MUST YIELD THIS...THIS FOLLY. FOR THE GOOD OF THE PEOPLE...

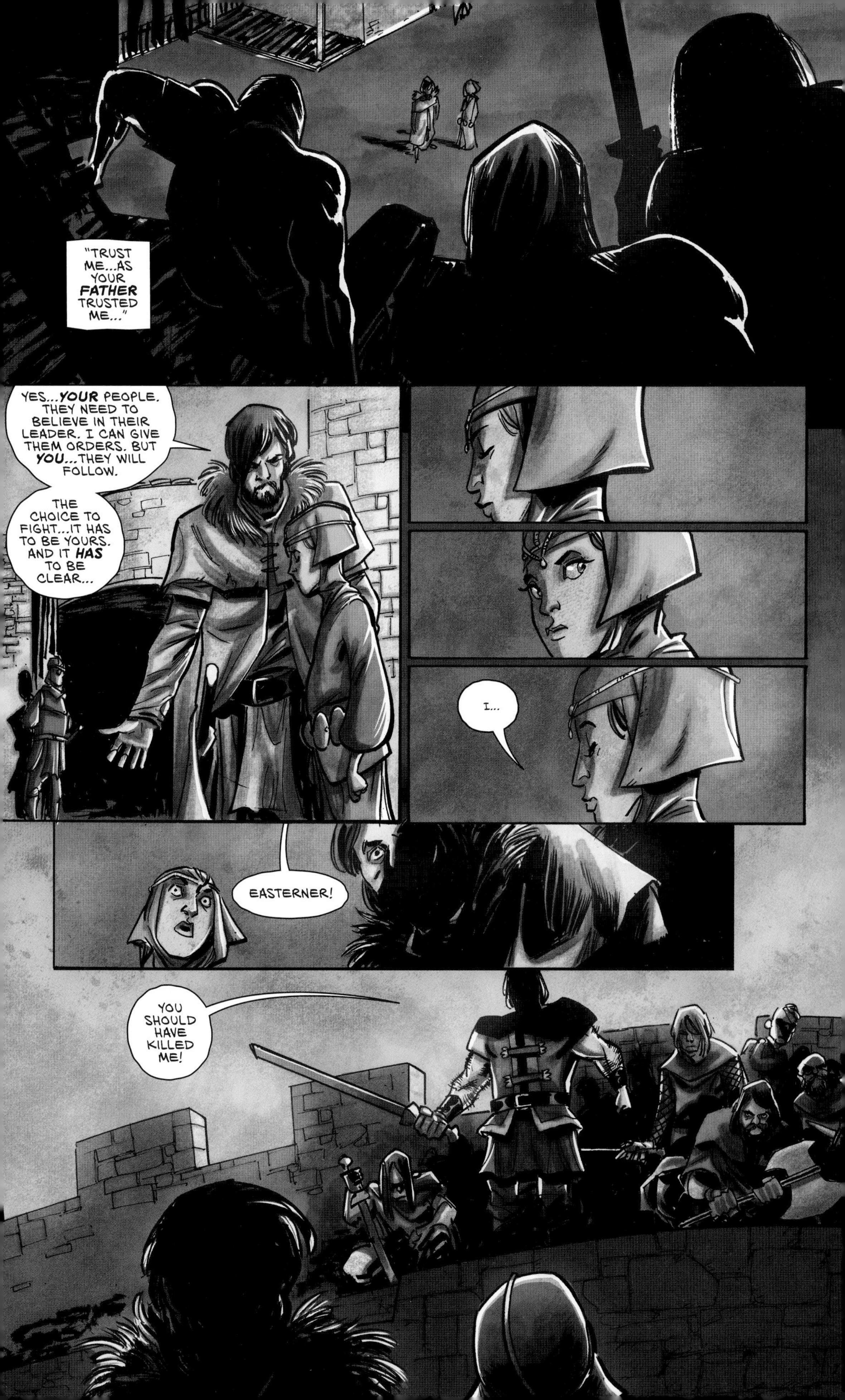
"TRUST ME...AS YOUR FATHER TRUSTED ME..."
YES...YOUR PEOPLE. THEY NEED TO BELIEVE IN THEIR LEADER. I CAN GIVE THEM ORDERS. BUT YOU...THEY WILL FOLLOW.
THE CHOICE TO FIGHT...IT HAS TO BE YOURS. AND IT HAS TO BE CLEAR...
I...
EASTERNER!
YOU SHOULD HAVE KILLED ME!

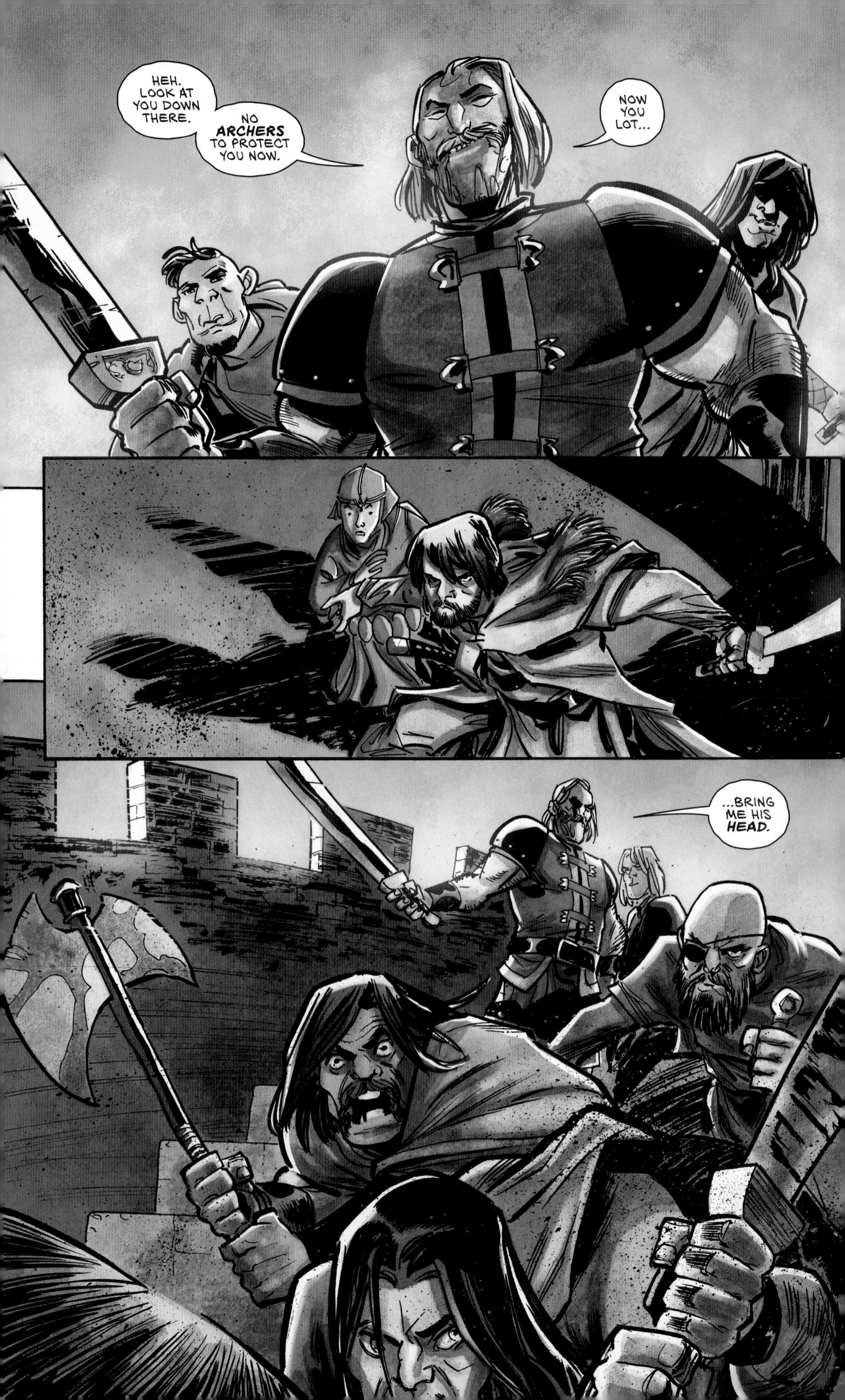
HEH. LOOK AT YOU DOWN THERE.
NO **ARCHERS** TO PROTECT YOU NOW.
NOW YOU LOT...
...BRING ME HIS **HEAD.**

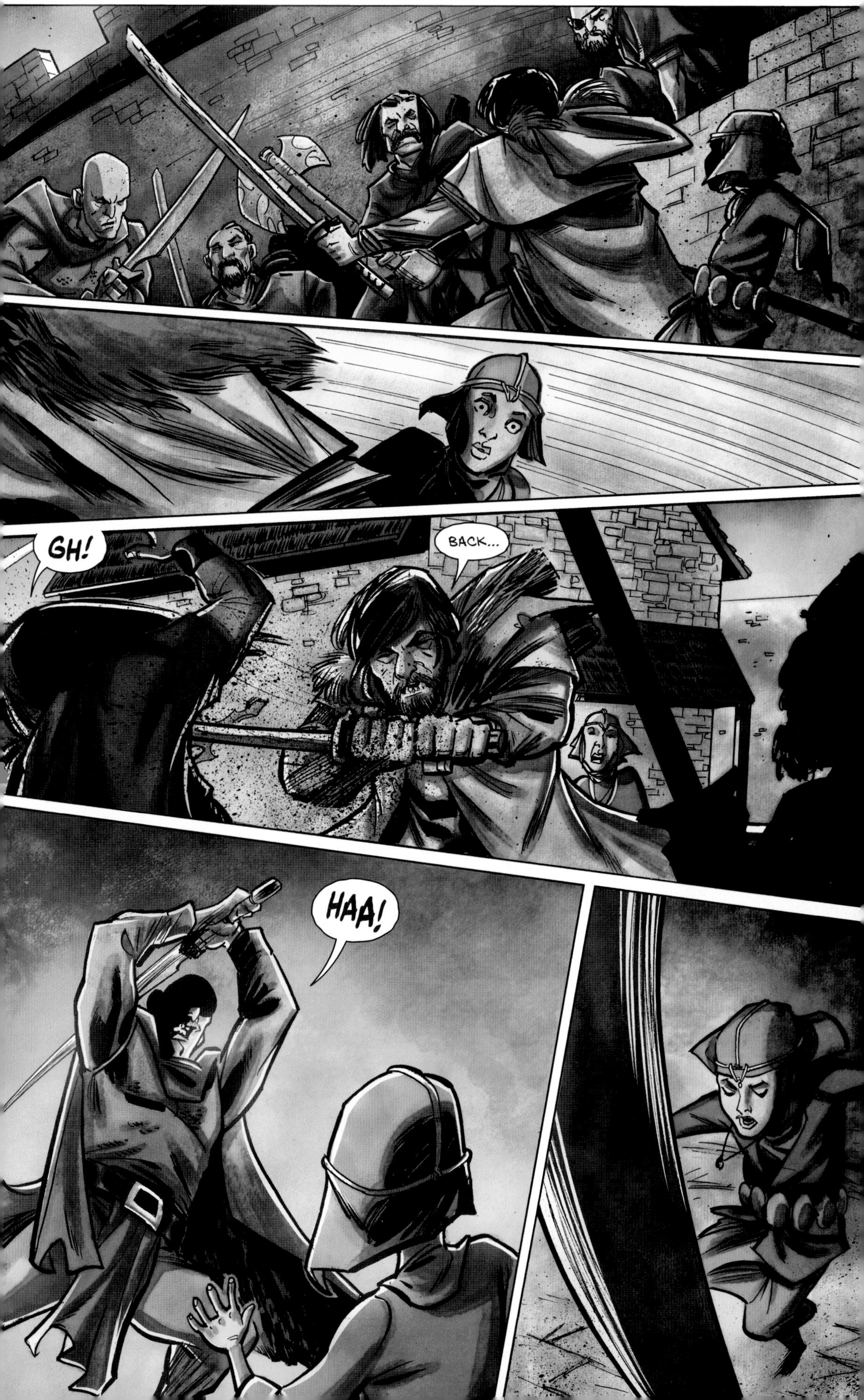
GH!
BACK...
HAA!

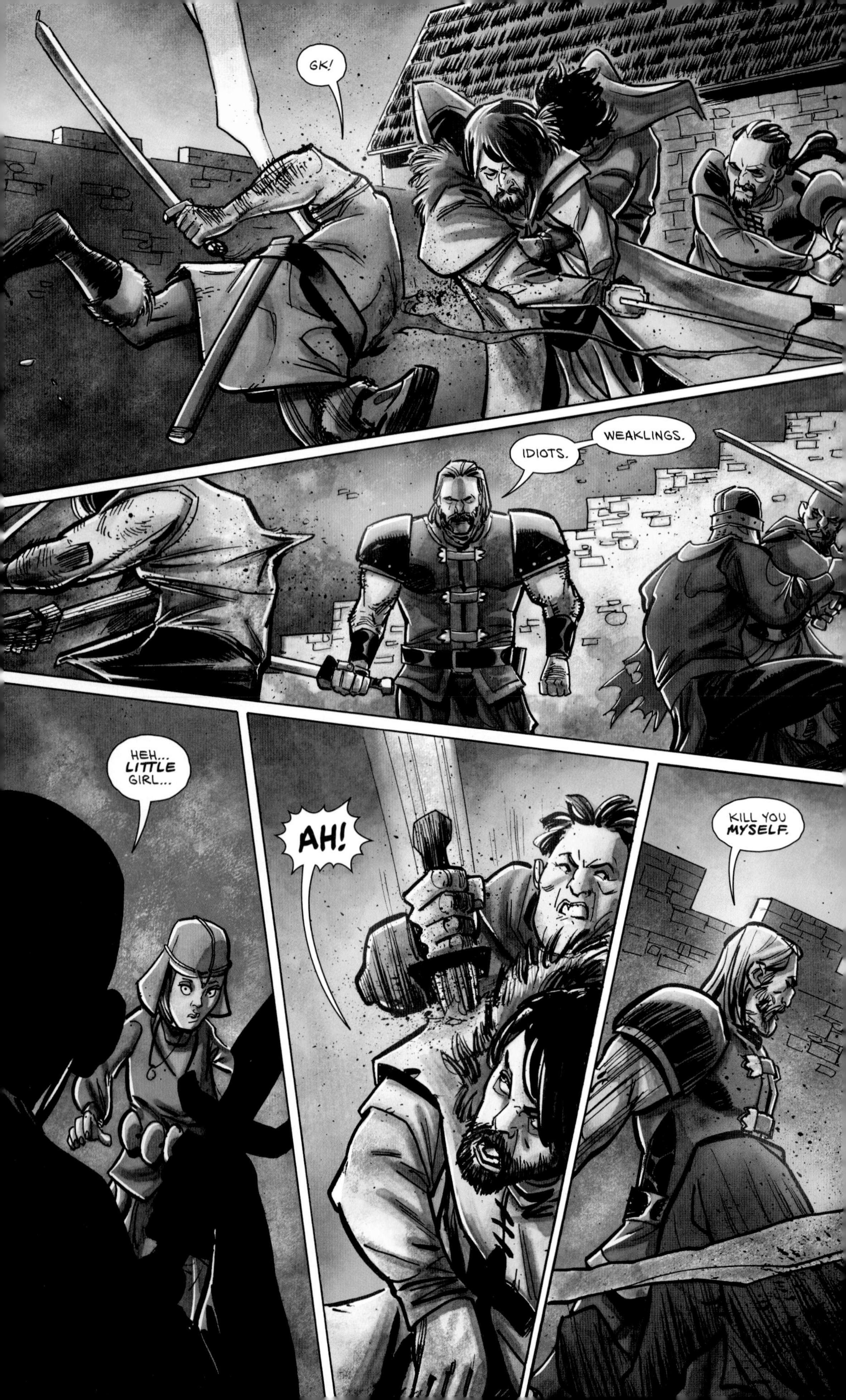
GK!
IDIOTS.
WEAKLINGS.
HEH... LITTLE GIRL...
AH!
KILL YOU MYSELF.

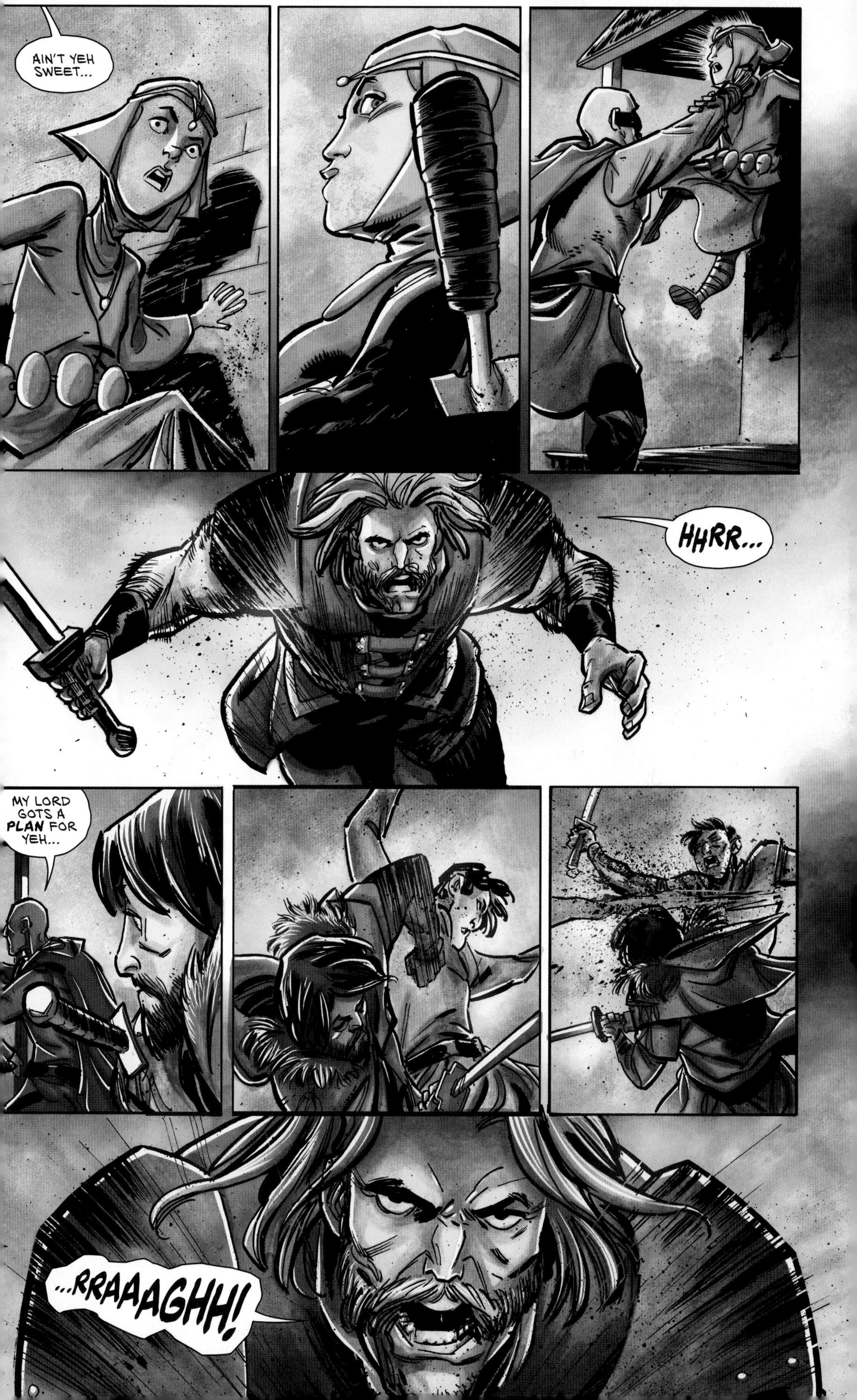
AIN'T YEH SWEET...
HHRR...
MY LORD GOTS A **PLAN** FOR YEH...
...RRAAAGHH!

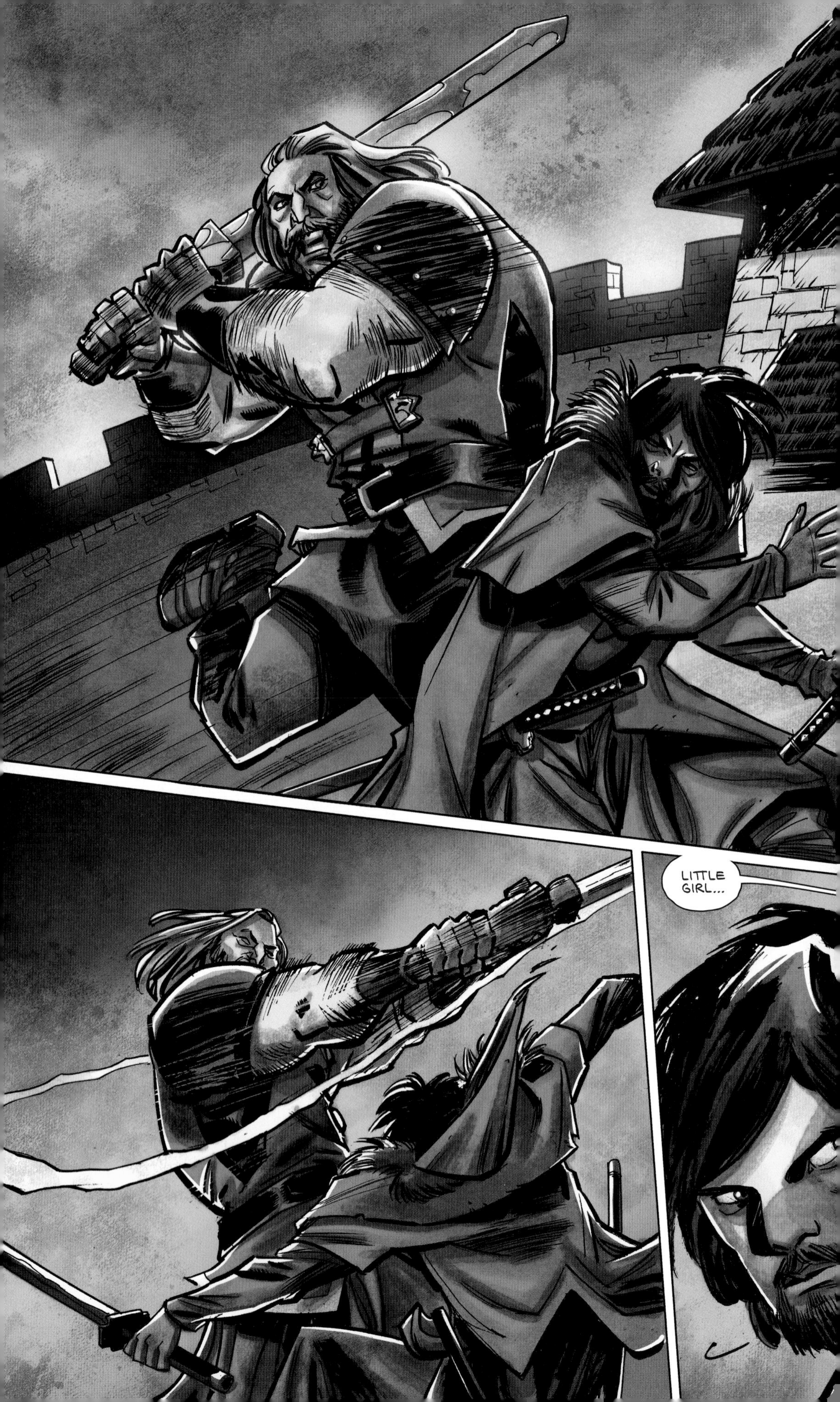
LITTLE GIRL...

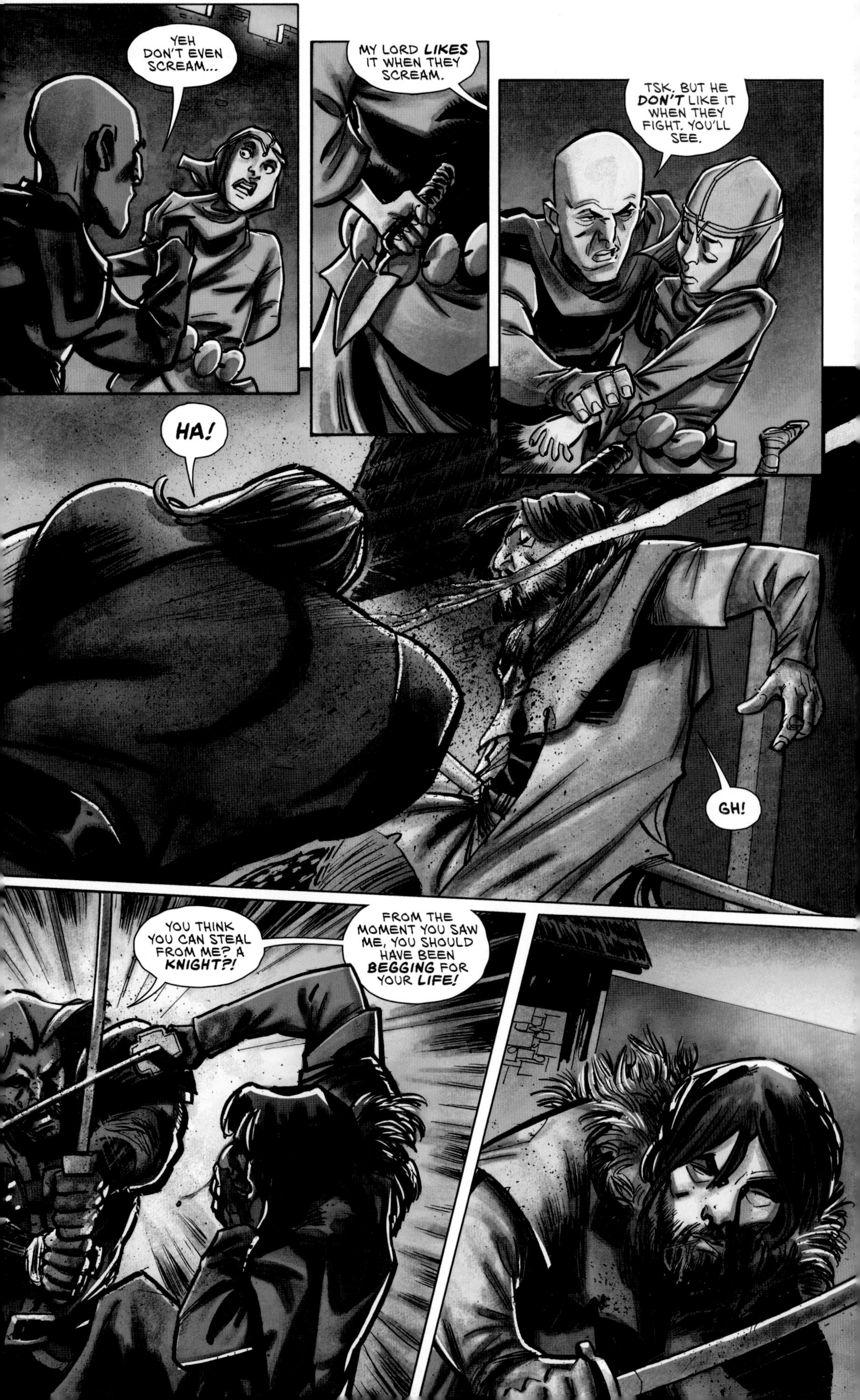
YEH DON'T EVEN SCREAM...
MY LORD **LIKES** IT WHEN THEY SCREAM.
TSK. BUT HE **DON'T** LIKE IT WHEN THEY FIGHT. YOU'LL SEE.
HA!
GH!
YOU THINK YOU CAN STEAL FROM ME? A **KNIGHT**?!
FROM THE MOMENT YOU SAW ME, YOU SHOULD HAVE BEEN **BEGGING** FOR YOUR **LIFE**!

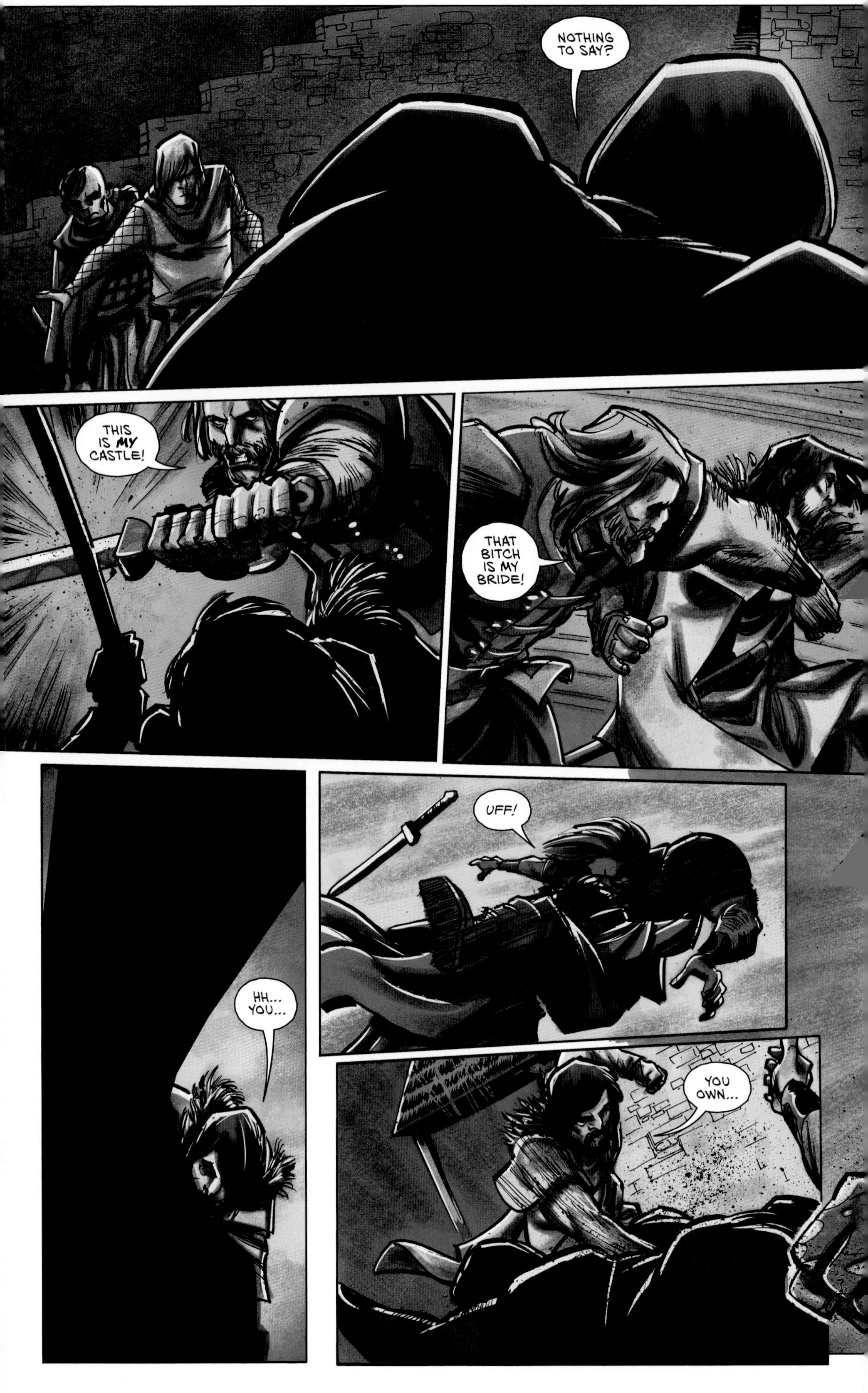
NOTHING TO SAY?
THIS IS MY CASTLE!
THAT BITCH IS MY BRIDE!
HH... YOU...
UFF!
YOU OWN...

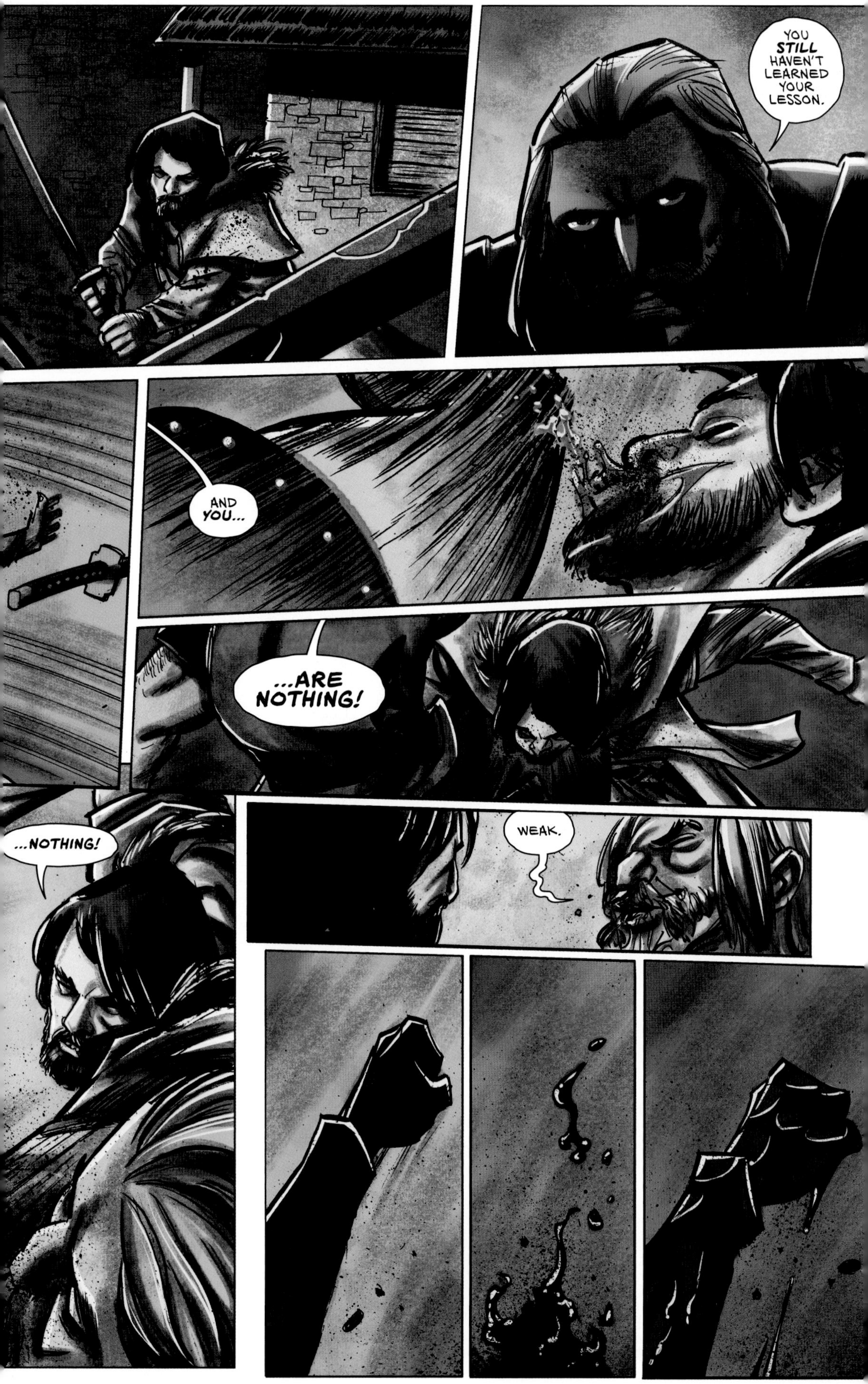
YOU STILL HAVEN'T LEARNED YOUR LESSON.
AND YOU...
...ARE NOTHING!
...NOTHING!
WEAK.

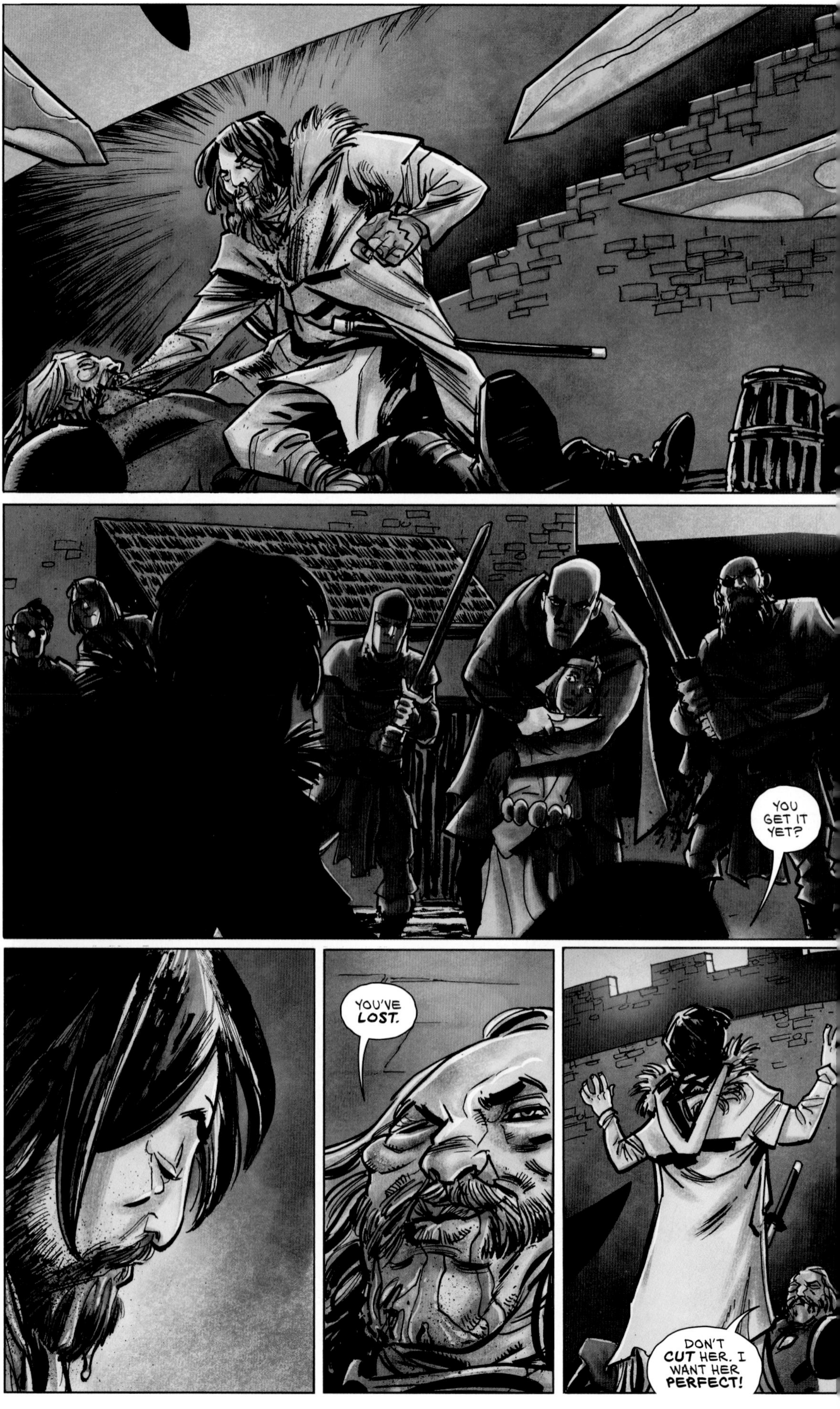
YOU GET IT YET?
YOU'VE LOST.
DON'T CUT HER. I WANT HER PERFECT!

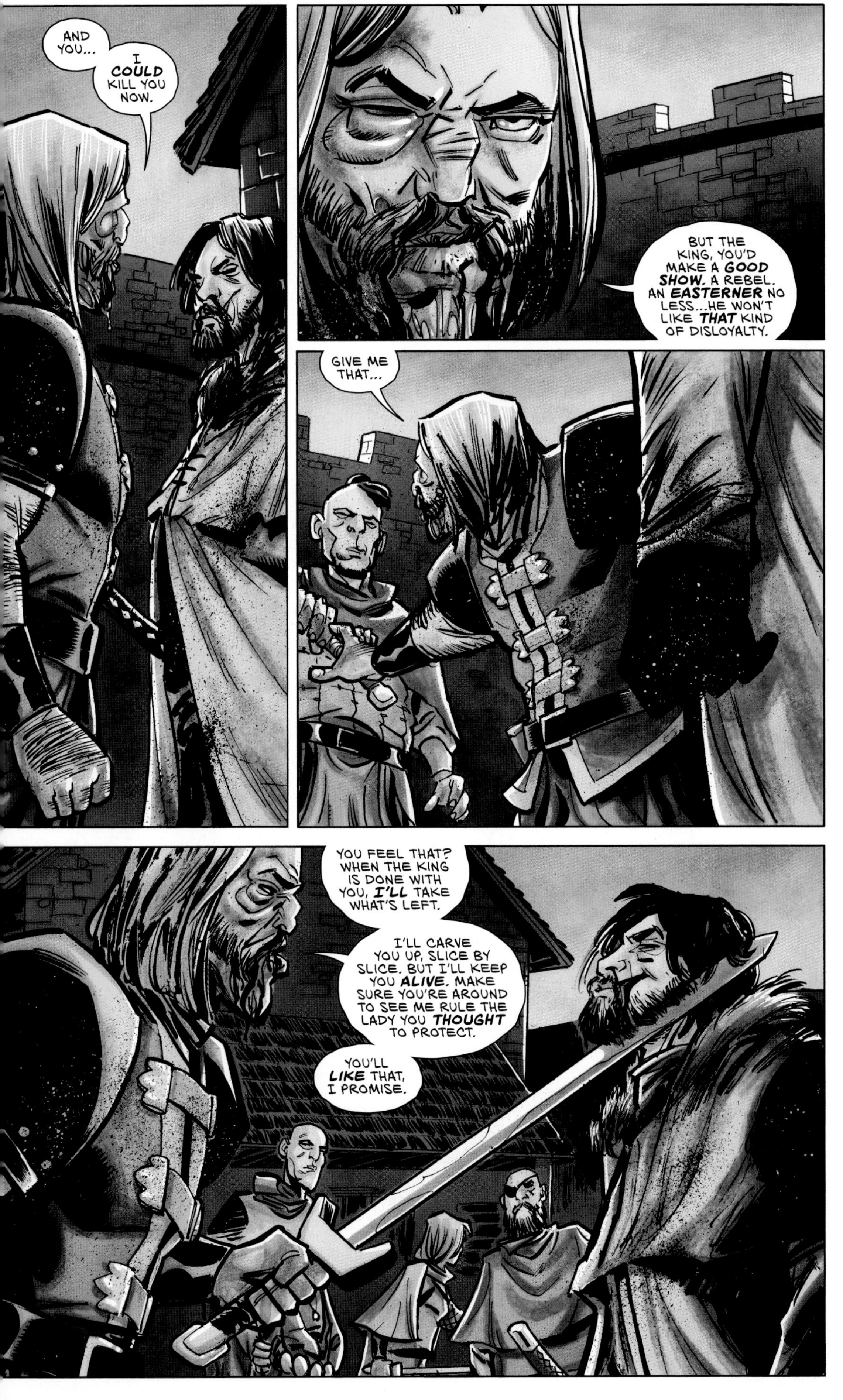
AND YOU...
I COULD KILL YOU NOW.
BUT THE KING, YOU'D MAKE A GOOD SHOW. A REBEL. AN EASTERNER NO LESS...HE WON'T LIKE THAT KIND OF DISLOYALTY.
GIVE ME THAT...
YOU FEEL THAT? WHEN THE KING IS DONE WITH YOU, I'LL TAKE WHAT'S LEFT.
I'LL CARVE YOU UP, SLICE BY SLICE. BUT I'LL KEEP YOU ALIVE. MAKE SURE YOU'RE AROUND TO SEE ME RULE THE LADY YOU THOUGHT TO PROTECT.
YOU'LL LIKE THAT, I PROMISE.

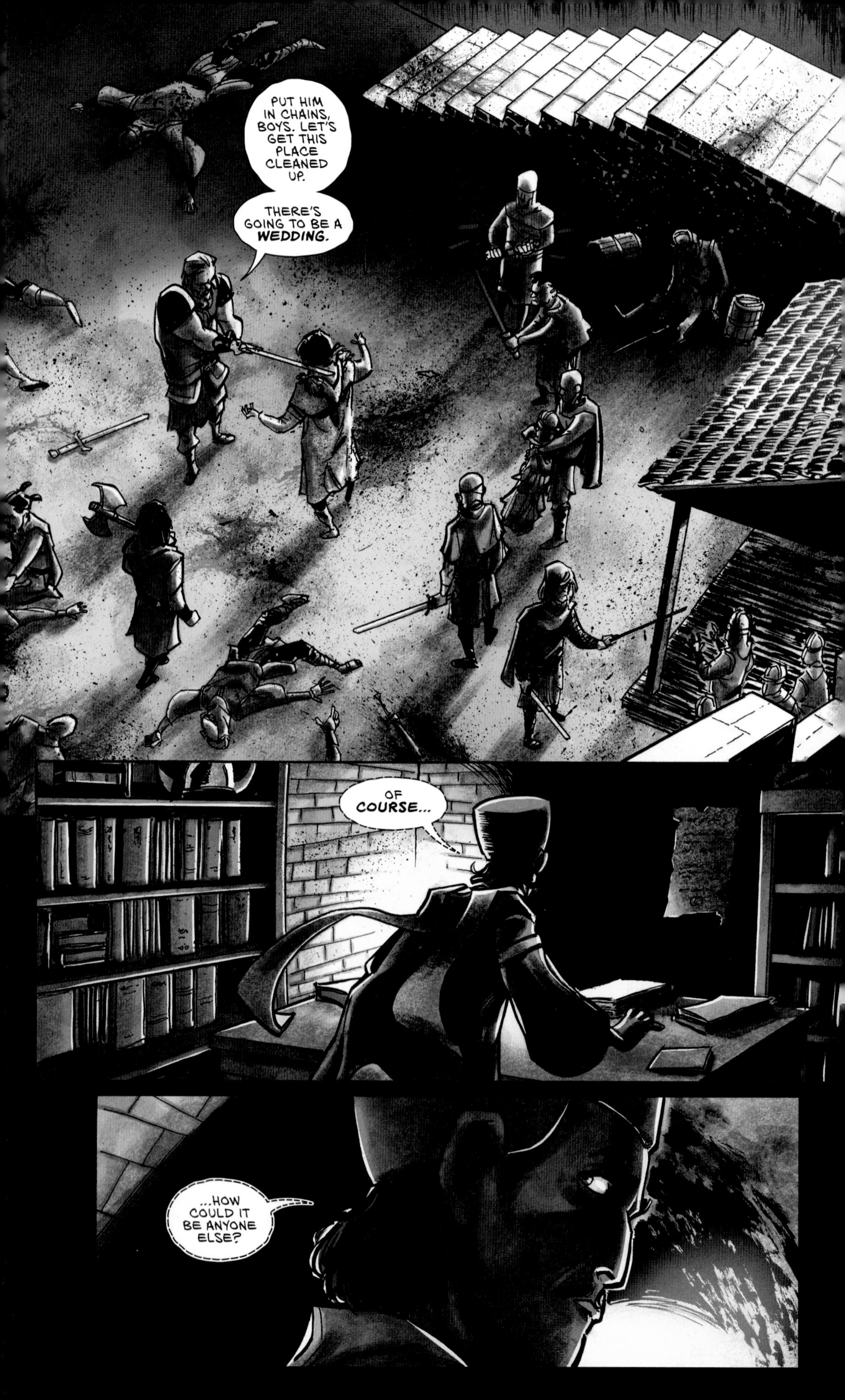
PUT HIM IN CHAINS, BOYS. LET'S GET THIS PLACE CLEANED UP.
THERE'S GOING TO BE A **WEDDING.**
OF **COURSE...**
...HOW COULD IT BE ANYONE ELSE?

The King Rises

— Chapter 3 —

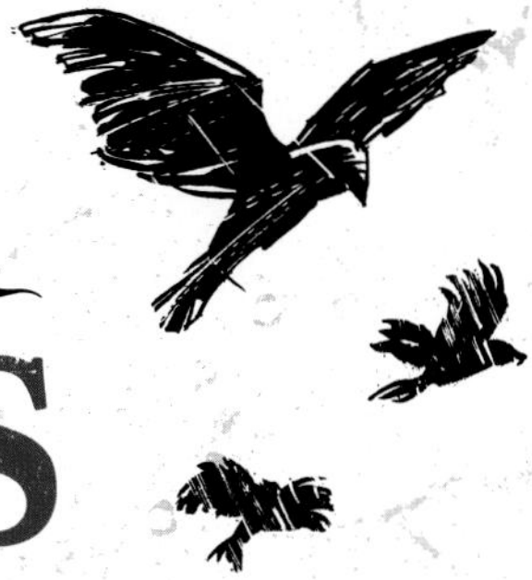

Deep in the lawless regions of the plateaus, Istvan and Tomislav drank at the fire pit, surrounded by their hosts — a nomadic tribe that had set up camp just outside the borders of the land Tomislav's father ruled.

It had been a year since Istvan had convinced his younger friend to step outside the shadow of his family and witness what the larger world had to offer. A year of exploring the poverty-stricken manors, a year of dancing on the edge of territories deemed too uncivilized for one born to rule.

"You drink like a baby," the woman draped across Tomislav's lap said with a laugh and a wide smile. She was older — probably older than both young men combined, but she was still beautiful, and raw and wild.

Tomislav frowned, holding up the flask he had been nursing. "It's strong," he complained, taking a small sip.

The woman pulled the flask from Tomislav's hands and raised it to her lips. Moments later, it was empty. She leaned in close, and whispered loud enough for everyone to hear. "...Like a baby."

The campfire was engulfed in howling laughter.

This tribe was only a small band from a much larger camp — one that stretched for miles across the flat mountain territories. Most of the people were bred from diverse cultures — a product of generations of migration. The current camp only existed as close as it did to the provinces due to the machinations of the two young travelers — Tomislav, largely at the suggestion of Istvan, had arranged for his father's scouts to "miss" the region of the encampment, and had even routed a small number of wagons to the tribe. As a result, the pair had found themselves guests of honor on more than one night.

Tomislav frowned, his mood turning sour. "You need to relax," Istvan pushed quietly as the revelry continued around them. "This... it's not the place for one of your moods. It's rude to our hosts."

Tomislav pushed the woman off to the side. "It's not... this," the younger man said. "Or it is. Look at this world. These people. They live on the edge, traveling from place to place while we..."

"You're telling me this? Tomislav, you really are a little lord, aren't you?"

Tomislav glowered at his friend. "Don't call me that."

Istvan waved away Tomislav's irritation. "You would do well to listen to me. You think the sickness in the world started the day you decided to open your eyes?"

"I'm helping them."

"You tolerate them. You send them your leftovers." Istvan took another drink. "But you're still going to go home to your rich palisade, waited on by servants, following the orders of your family. And these people, ultimately they will be driven away."

"What would you have me do?" Tomislav growled. "We live in the world we live in."

Istvan smiled. "Every day brings change, little lord. You'll see." ✕

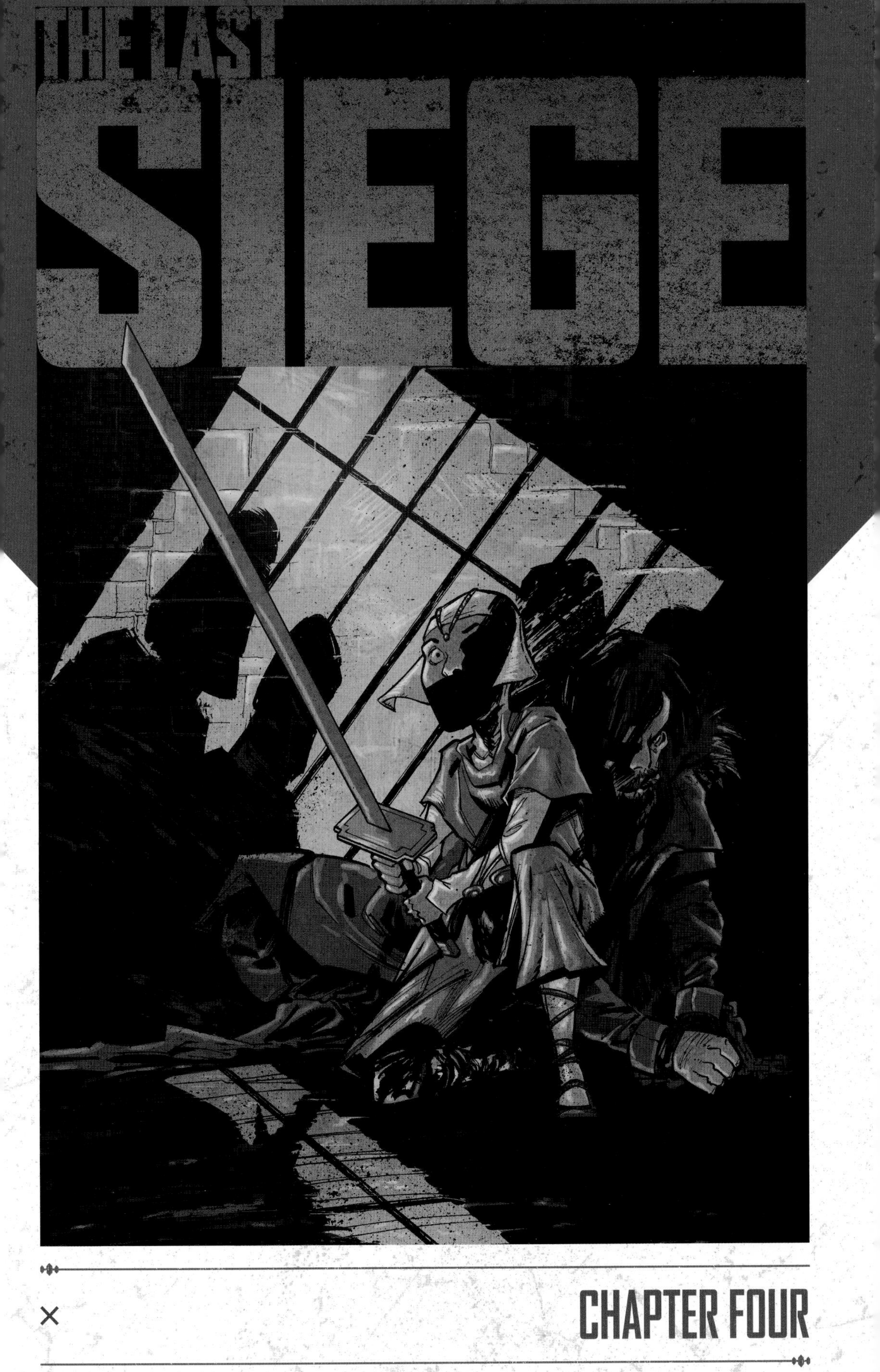
THE LAST
SIEGE

CHAPTER FOUR

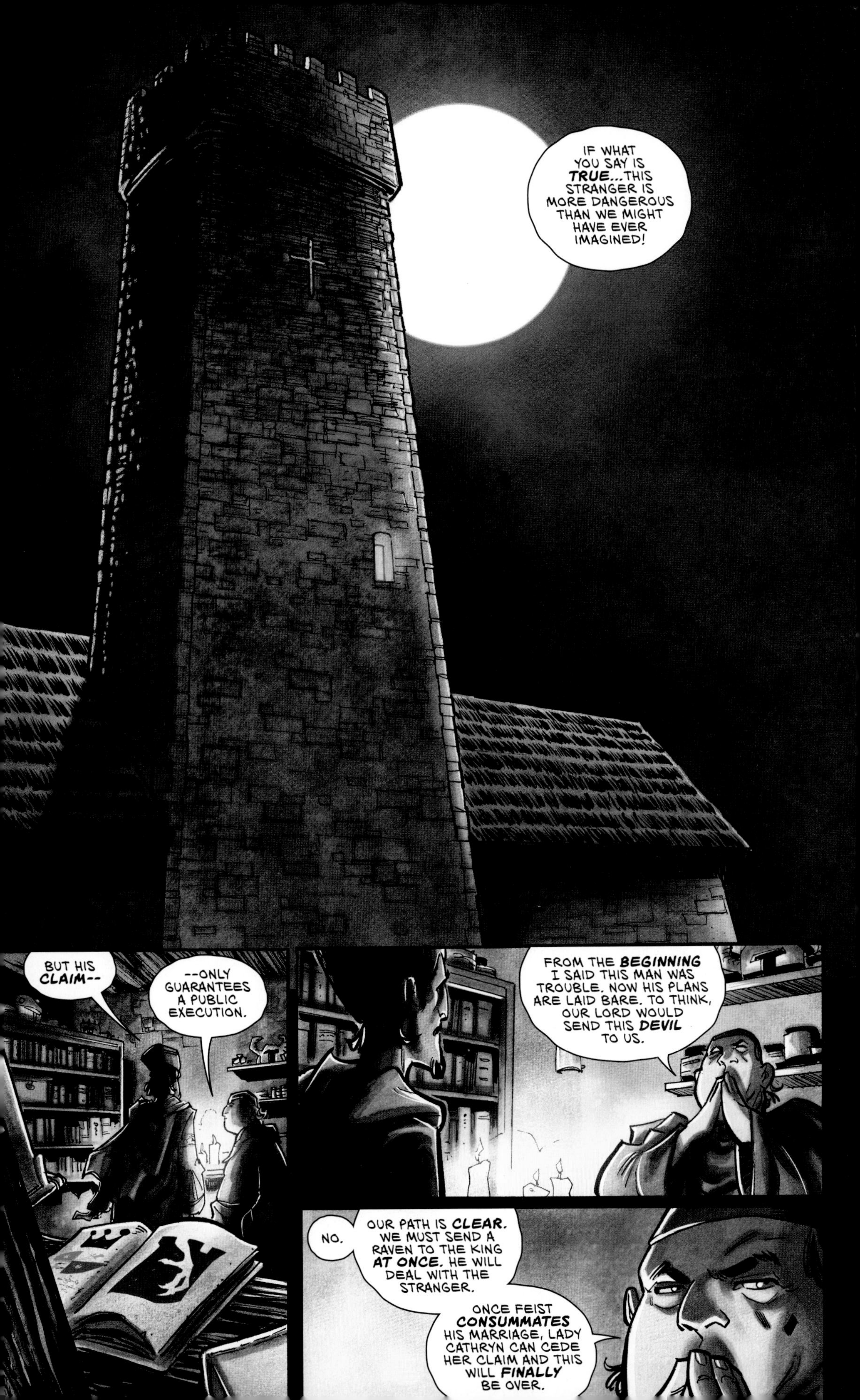
IF WHAT YOU SAY IS **TRUE**... THIS STRANGER IS MORE DANGEROUS THAN WE MIGHT HAVE EVER IMAGINED!
BUT HIS **CLAIM**--
--ONLY GUARANTEES A PUBLIC EXECUTION.
FROM THE **BEGINNING** I SAID THIS MAN WAS TROUBLE. NOW HIS PLANS ARE LAID BARE. TO THINK, OUR LORD WOULD SEND THIS **DEVIL** TO US.
NO.
OUR PATH IS **CLEAR.** WE MUST SEND A RAVEN TO THE KING **AT ONCE.** HE WILL DEAL WITH THE STRANGER.
ONCE FEIST **CONSUMMATES** HIS MARRIAGE, LADY CATHRYN CAN CEDE HER CLAIM AND THIS WILL **FINALLY** BE OVER.

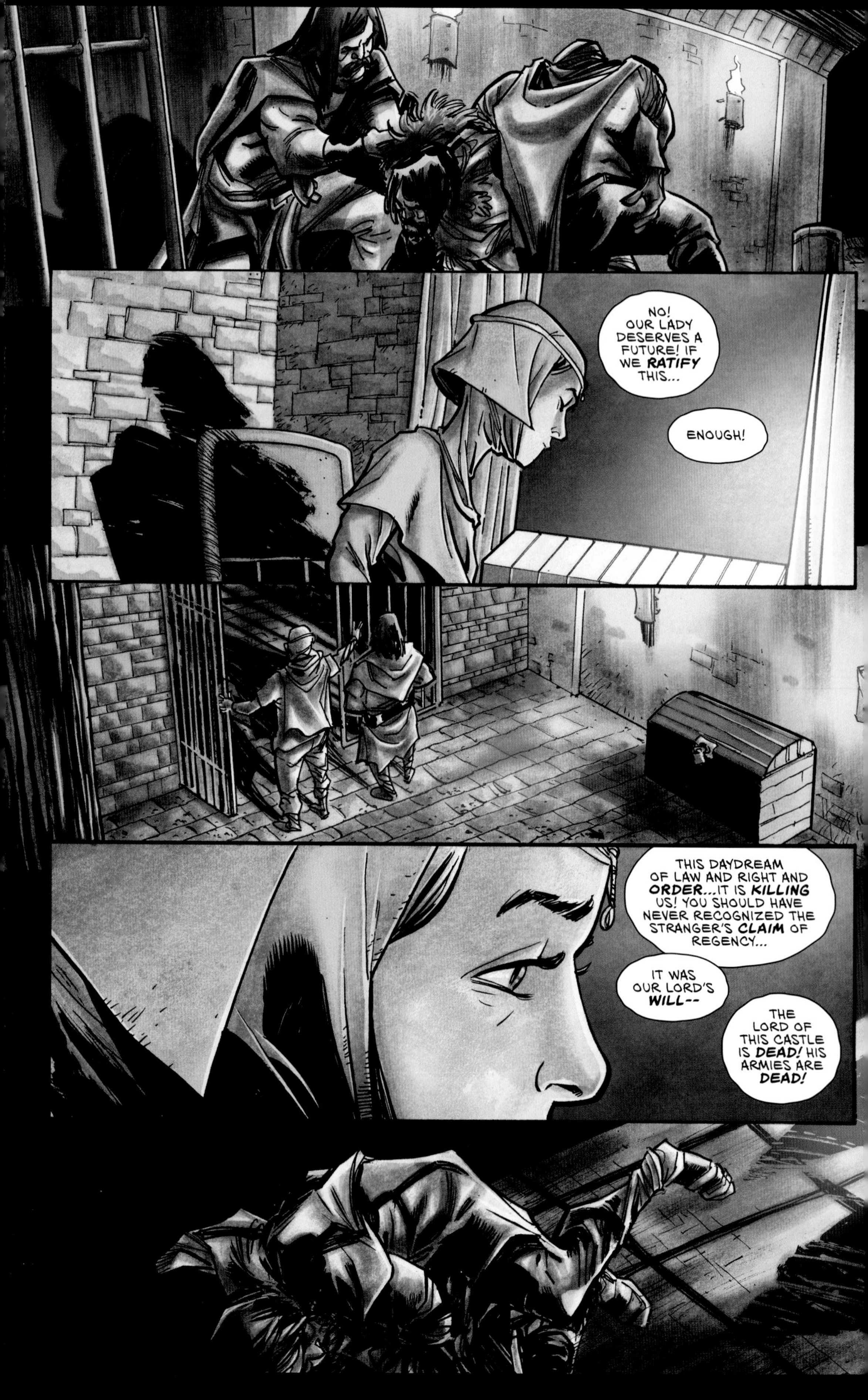
NO! OUR LADY DESERVES A FUTURE! IF WE **RATIFY** THIS...
ENOUGH!
THIS DAYDREAM OF LAW AND RIGHT AND **ORDER**... IT IS **KILLING** US! YOU SHOULD HAVE NEVER RECOGNIZED THE STRANGER'S **CLAIM** OF REGENCY...
IT WAS OUR LORD'S **WILL**--
THE LORD OF THIS CASTLE IS **DEAD!** HIS ARMIES ARE **DEAD!**

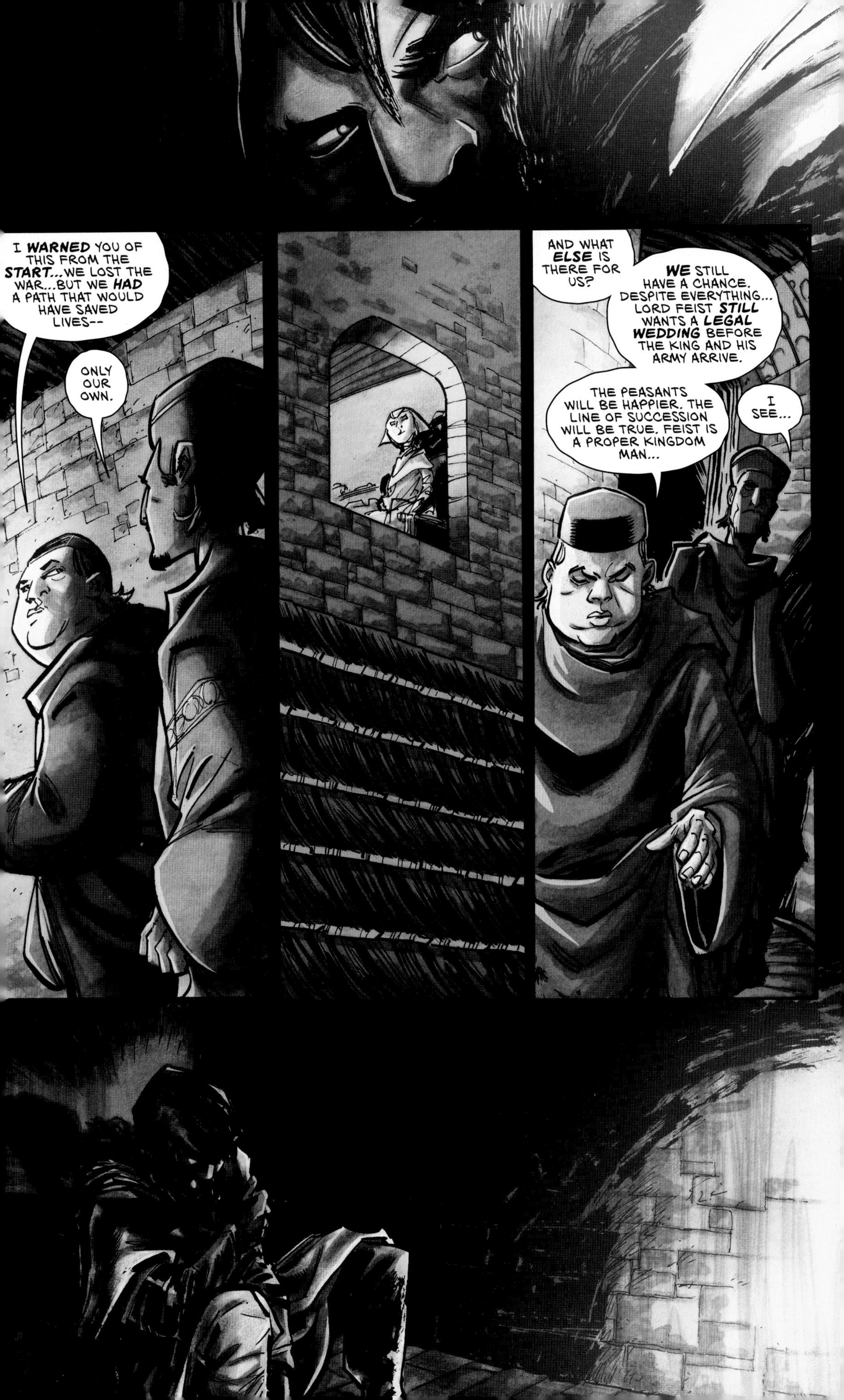

I WARNED YOU OF THIS FROM THE START...WE LOST THE WAR...BUT WE HAD A PATH THAT WOULD HAVE SAVED LIVES--
ONLY OUR OWN.
AND WHAT ELSE IS THERE FOR US?
WE STILL HAVE A CHANCE. DESPITE EVERYTHING... LORD FEIST STILL WANTS A LEGAL WEDDING BEFORE THE KING AND HIS ARMY ARRIVE.
THE PEASANTS WILL BE HAPPIER. THE LINE OF SUCCESSION WILL BE TRUE. FEIST IS A PROPER KINGDOM MAN...
I SEE...

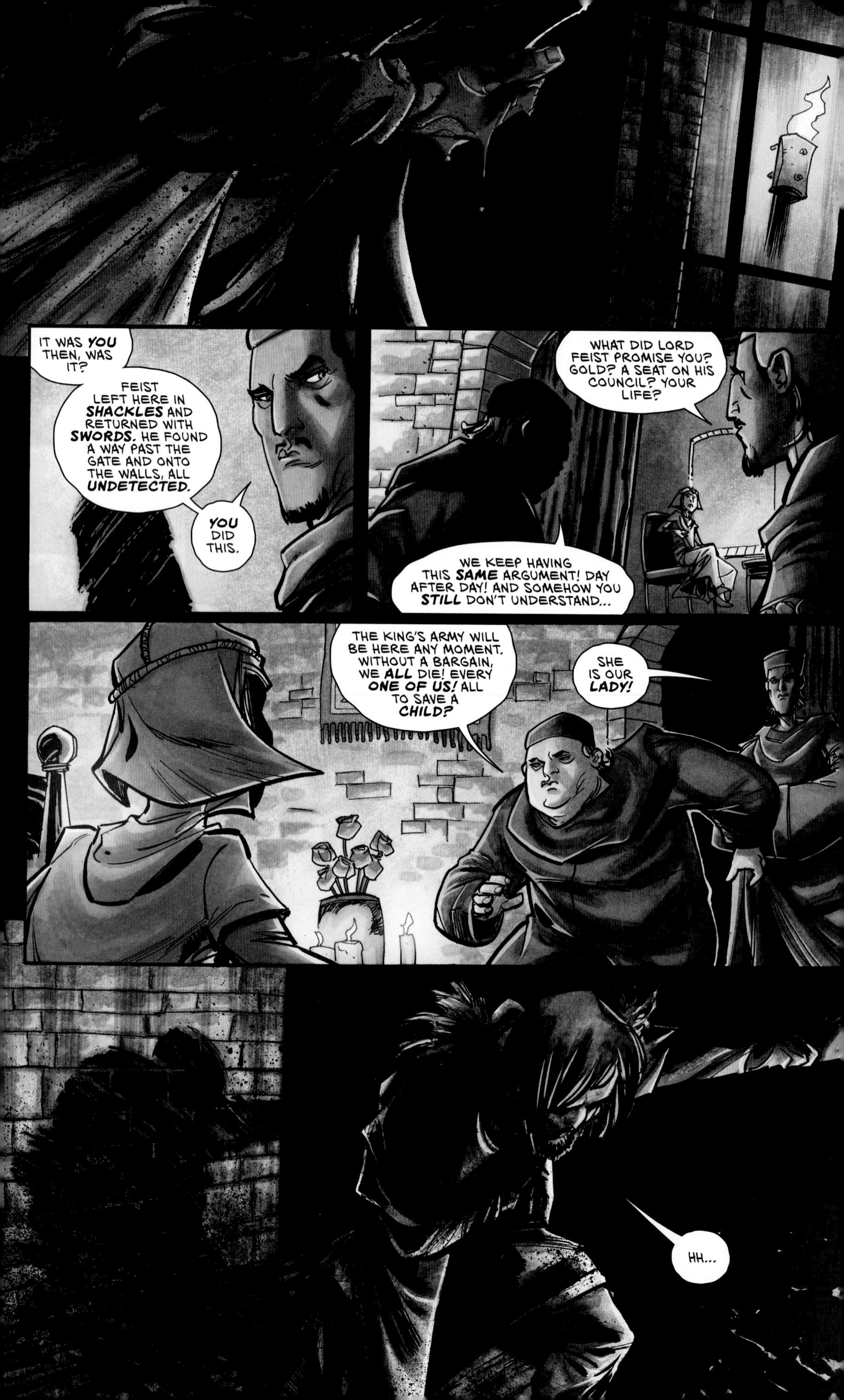
IT WAS **YOU** THEN, WAS IT?
FEIST LEFT HERE IN **SHACKLES** AND RETURNED WITH **SWORDS.** HE FOUND A WAY PAST THE GATE AND ONTO THE WALLS, ALL **UNDETECTED.**
YOU DID THIS.
WHAT DID LORD FEIST PROMISE YOU? GOLD? A SEAT ON HIS COUNCIL? YOUR LIFE?
WE KEEP HAVING THIS **SAME** ARGUMENT! DAY AFTER DAY! AND SOMEHOW YOU **STILL** DON'T UNDERSTAND...
THE KING'S ARMY WILL BE HERE ANY MOMENT. WITHOUT A BARGAIN, WE **ALL** DIE! EVERY **ONE OF US!** ALL TO SAVE A **CHILD?**
SHE IS OUR **LADY!**
HH...

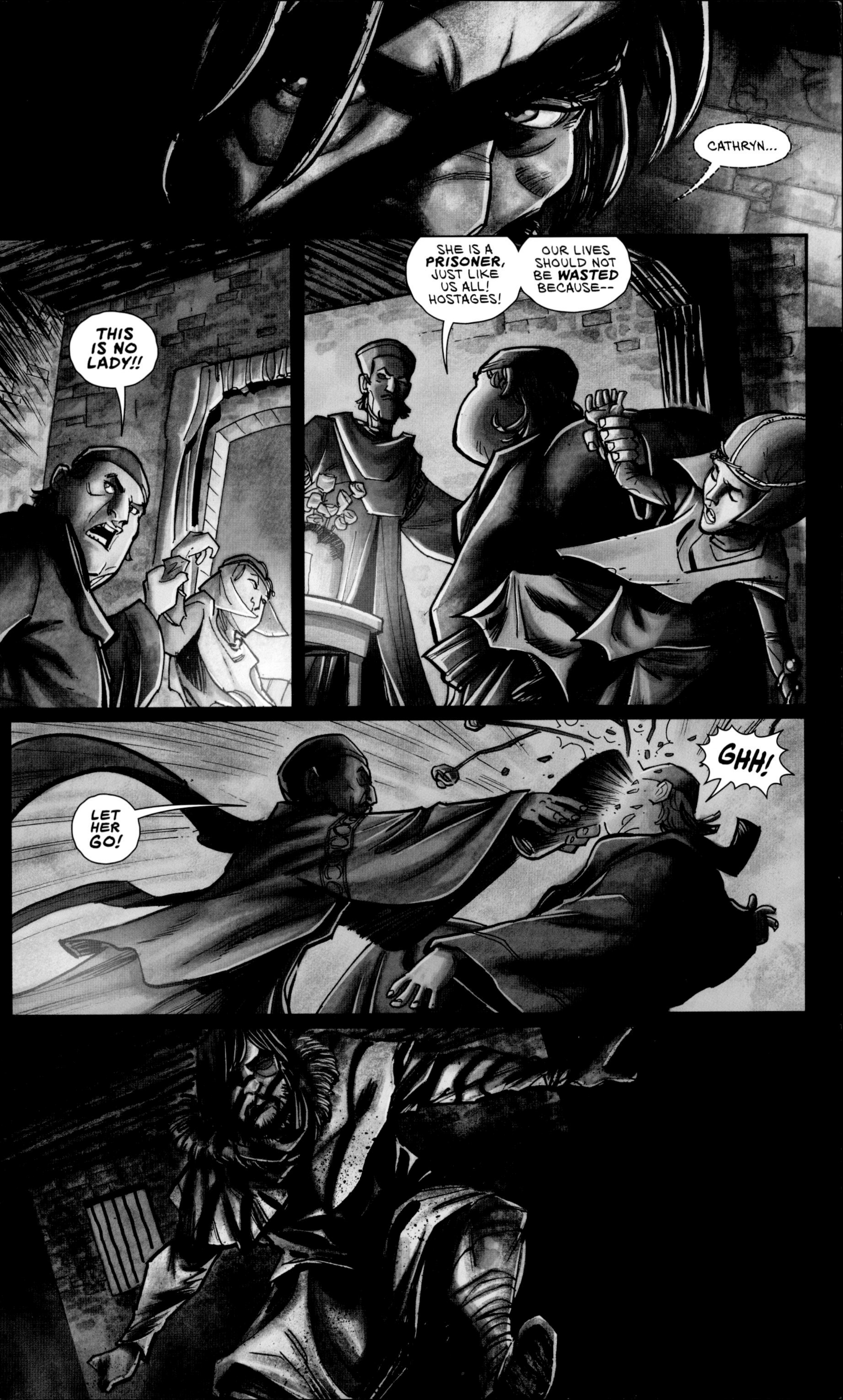
CATHRYN...
THIS IS NO LADY!!
SHE IS A PRISONER, JUST LIKE US ALL! HOSTAGES!
OUR LIVES SHOULD NOT BE WASTED BECAUSE--
LET HER GO!
GHH!

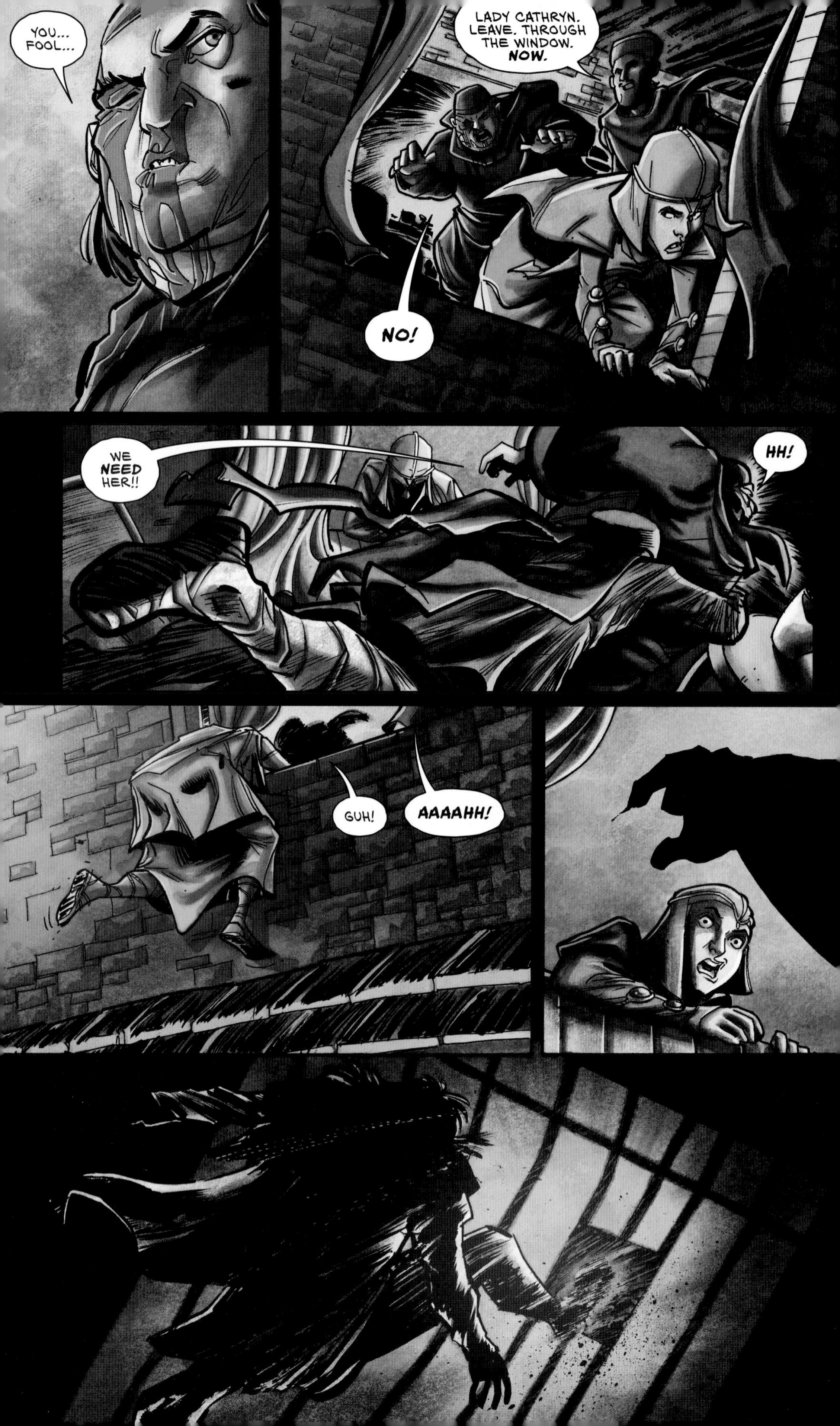
YOU... FOOL...
LADY CATHRYN. LEAVE. THROUGH THE WINDOW. NOW.
NO!
WE NEED HER!!
HH!
GUH!
AAAAHH!

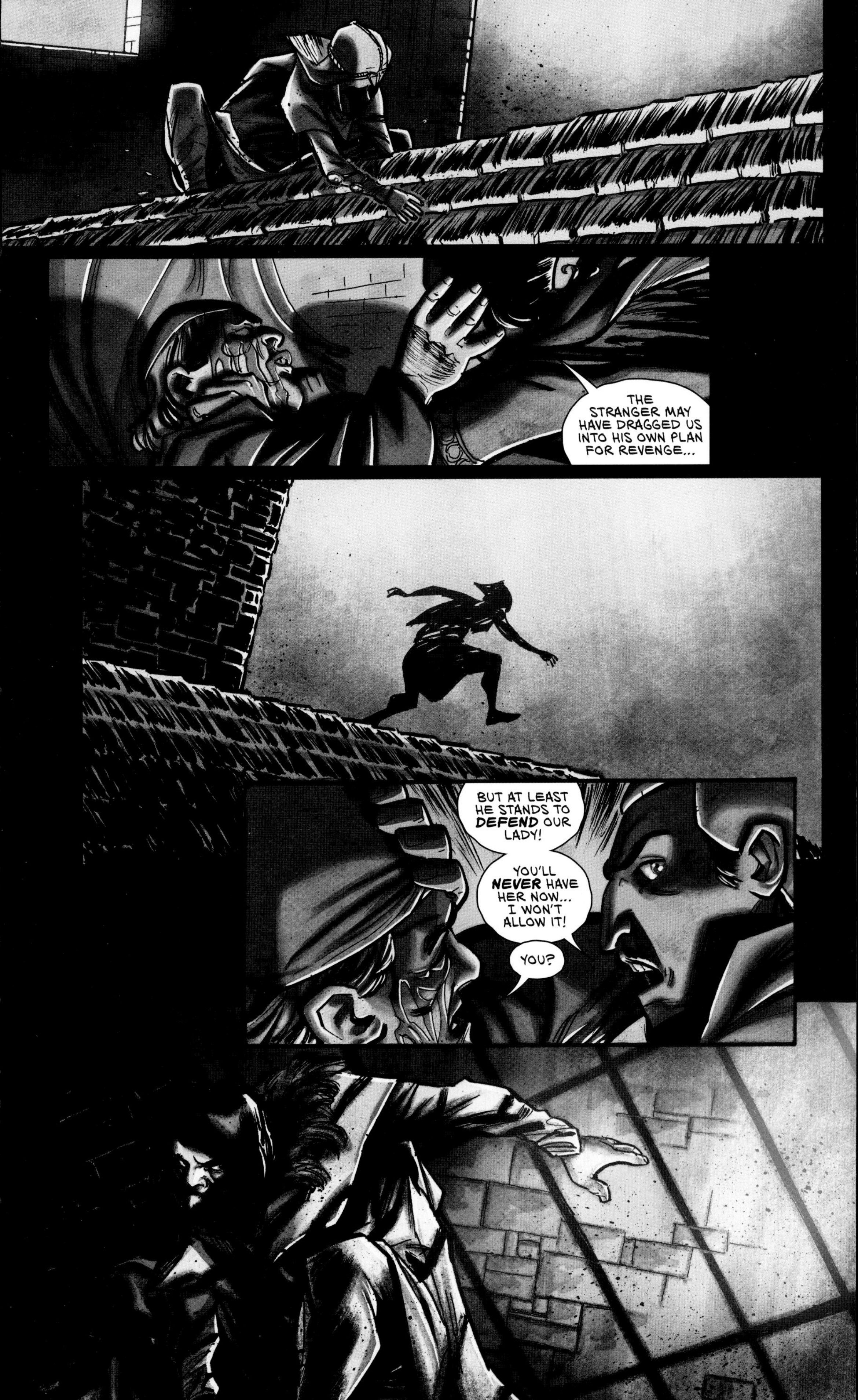
THE STRANGER MAY HAVE DRAGGED US INTO HIS OWN PLAN FOR REVENGE...
BUT AT LEAST HE STANDS TO DEFEND OUR LADY!
YOU'LL NEVER HAVE HER NOW... I WON'T ALLOW IT!
YOU?

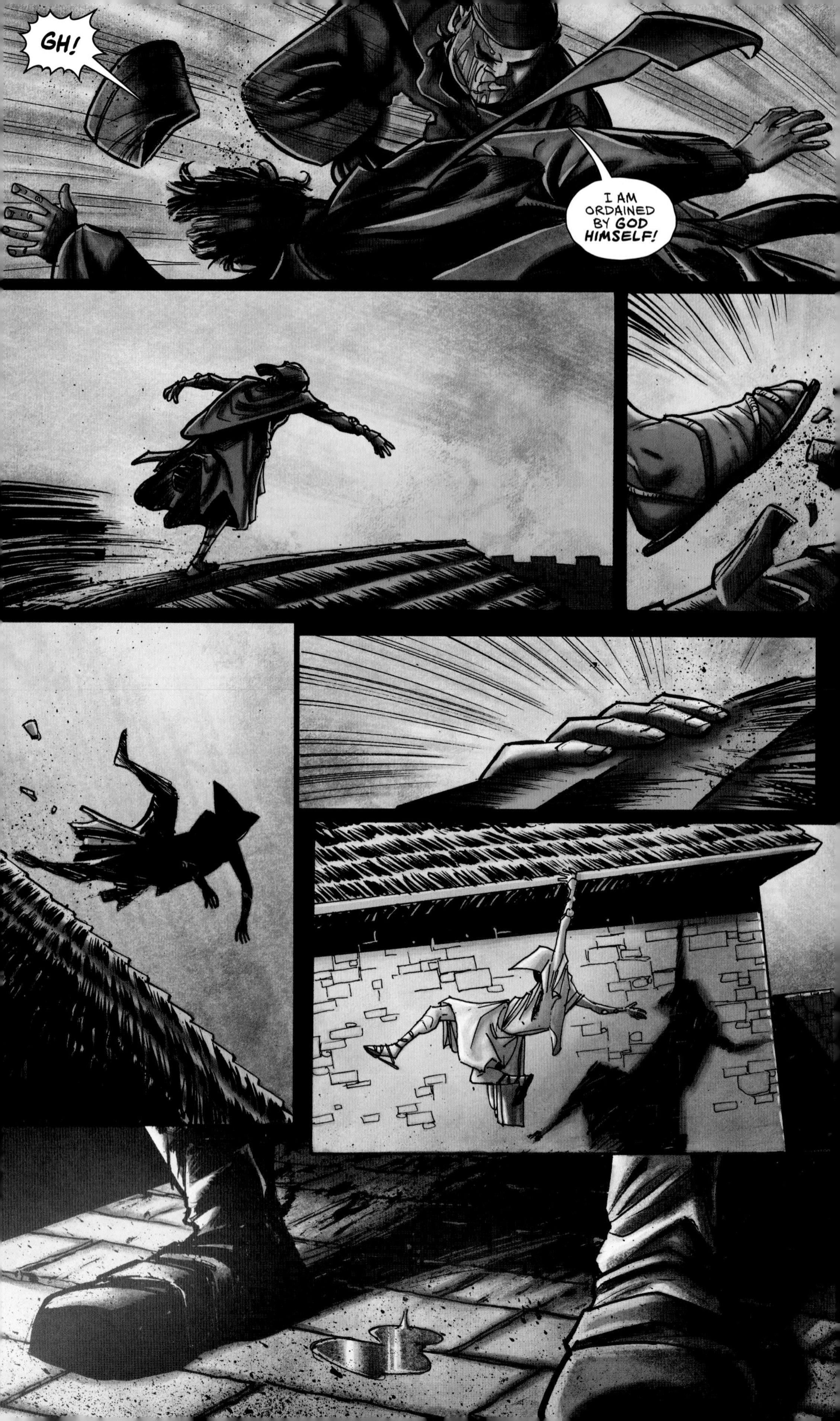
GH!
I AM ORDAINED BY GOD HIMSELF!

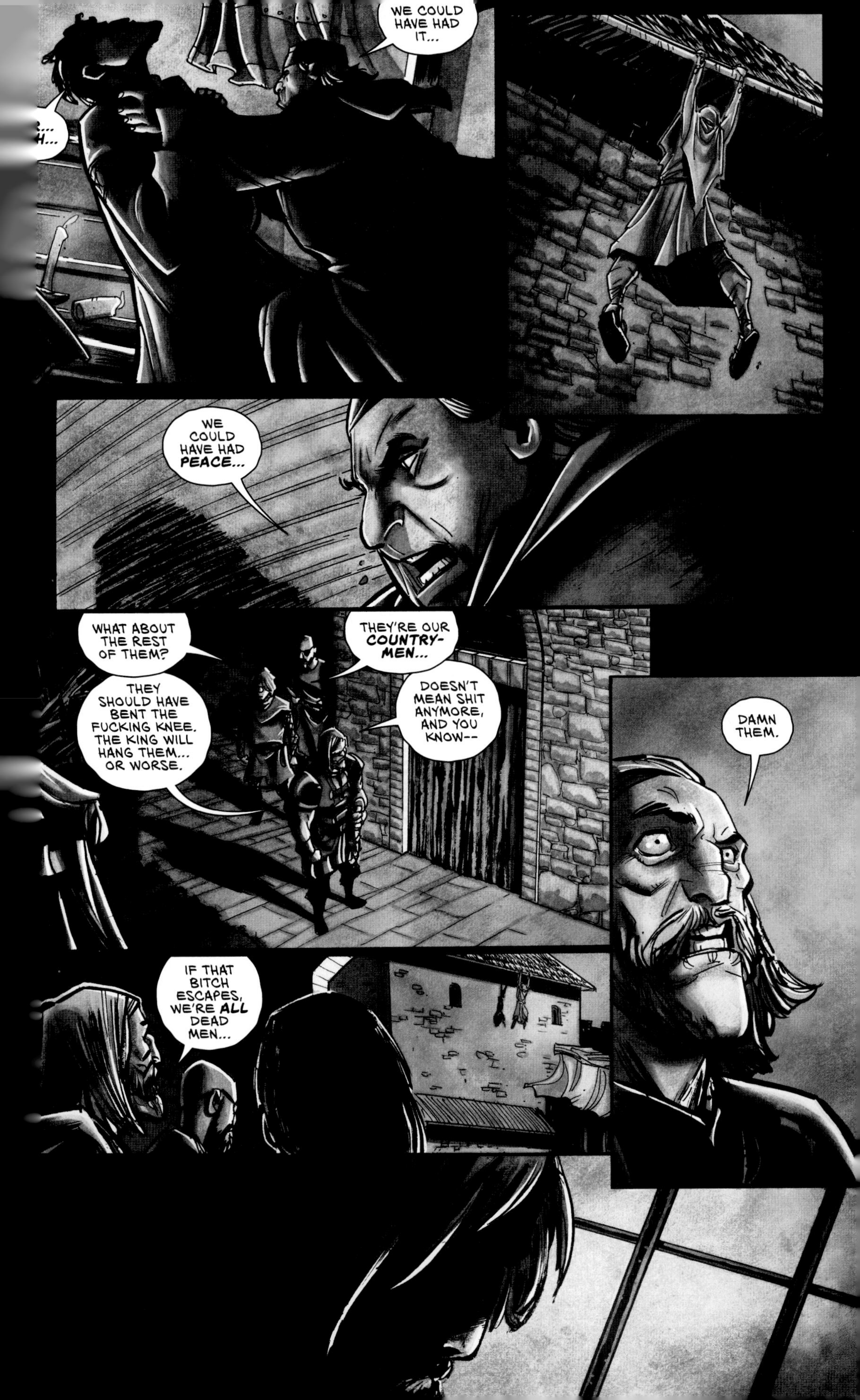
WE COULD HAVE HAD IT...
WE COULD HAVE HAD **PEACE...**
WHAT ABOUT THE REST OF THEM?
THEY SHOULD HAVE BENT THE FUCKING KNEE. THE KING WILL HANG THEM... OR WORSE.
THEY'RE OUR **COUNTRY-MEN...**
DOESN'T MEAN SHIT ANYMORE, AND YOU KNOW--
DAMN THEM.
IF THAT BITCH ESCAPES, WE'RE **ALL** DEAD MEN...

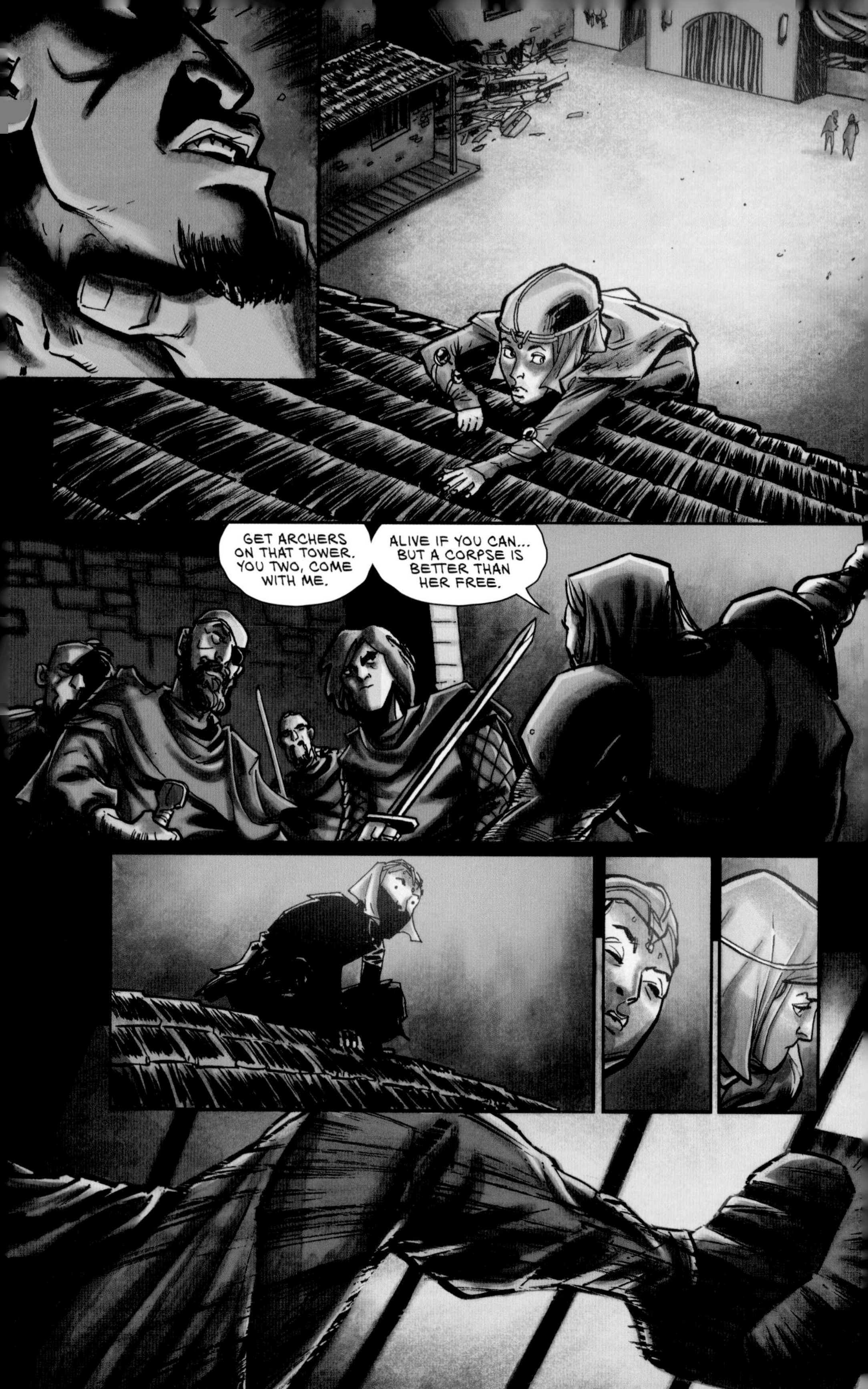
GET ARCHERS ON THAT TOWER. YOU TWO, COME WITH ME.
ALIVE IF YOU CAN... BUT A CORPSE IS BETTER THAN HER FREE.

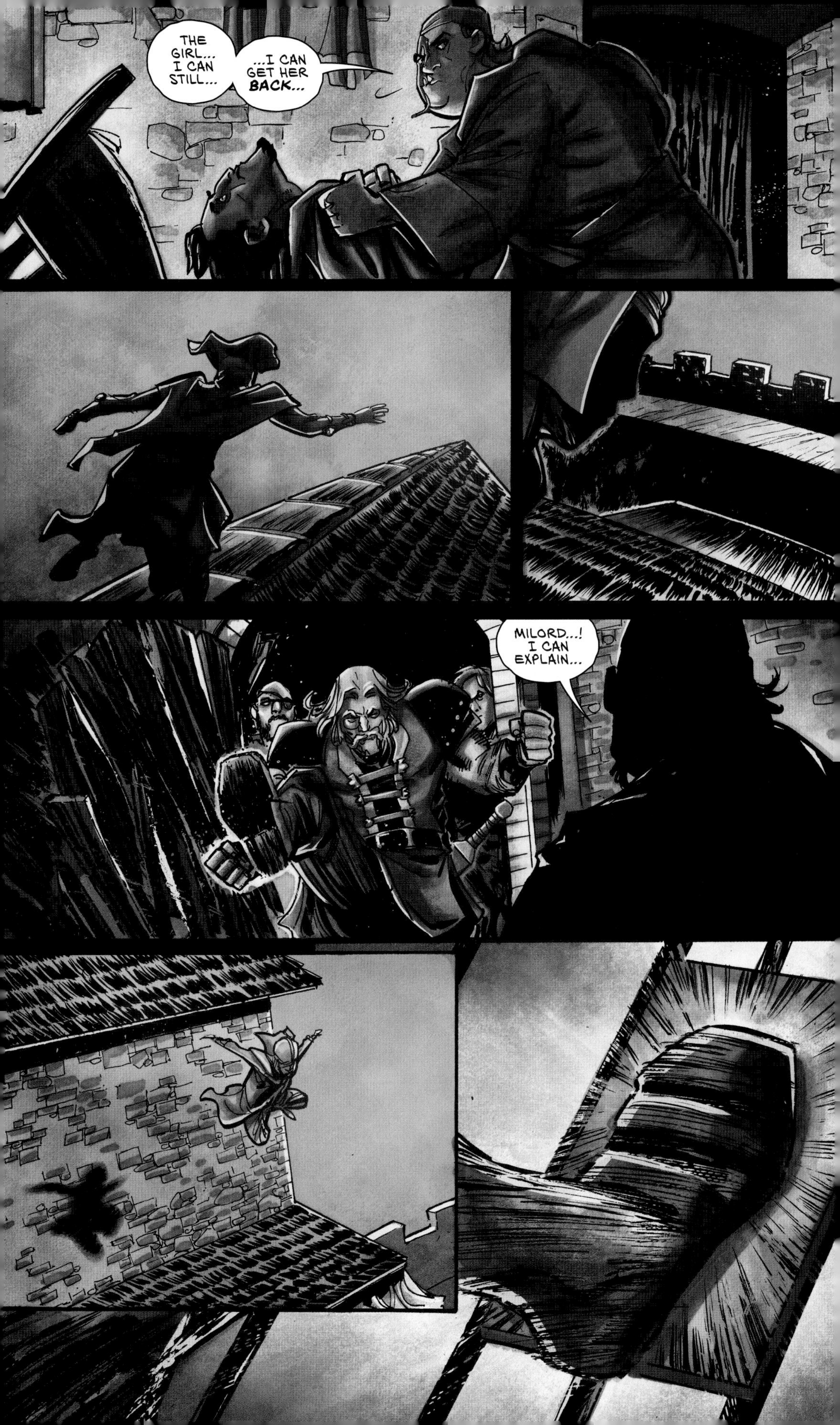
THE GIRL... I CAN STILL...
...I CAN GET HER BACK...
MILORD...! I CAN EXPLAIN...

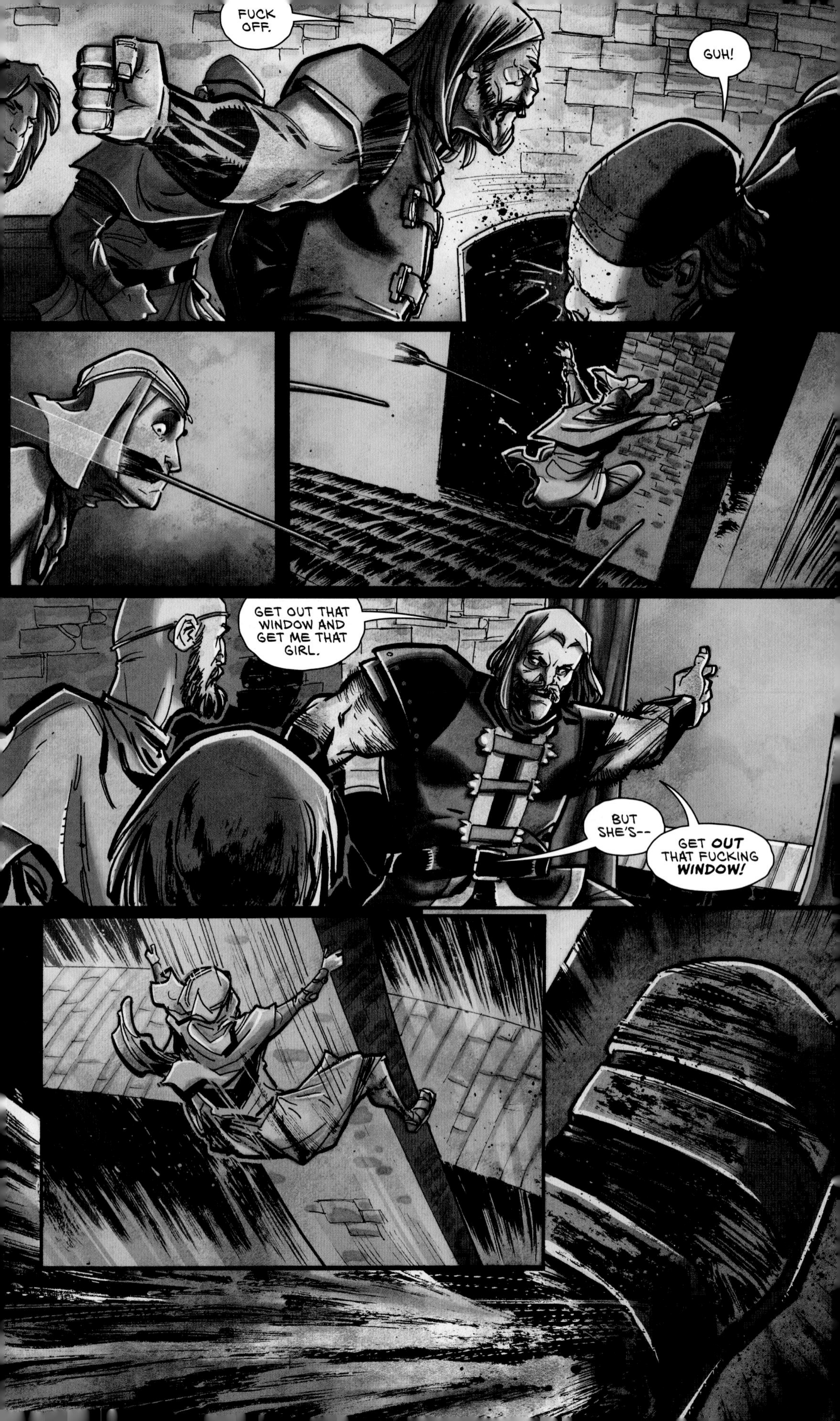
FUCK OFF.
GUH!
GET OUT THAT WINDOW AND GET ME THAT GIRL.
BUT SHE'S--
GET OUT THAT FUCKING WINDOW!

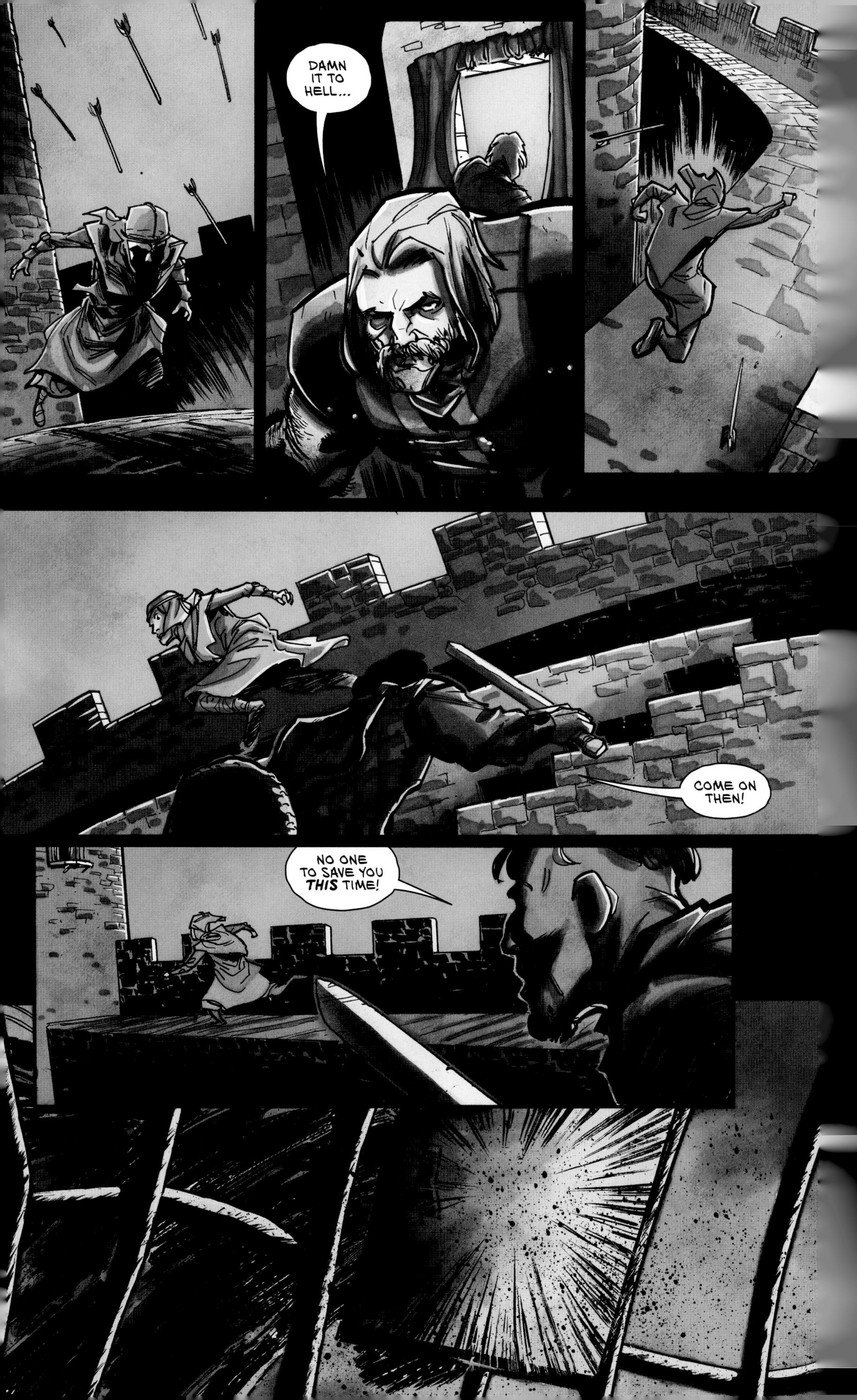
DAMN IT TO HELL...
COME ON THEN!
NO ONE TO SAVE YOU ***THIS*** TIME!

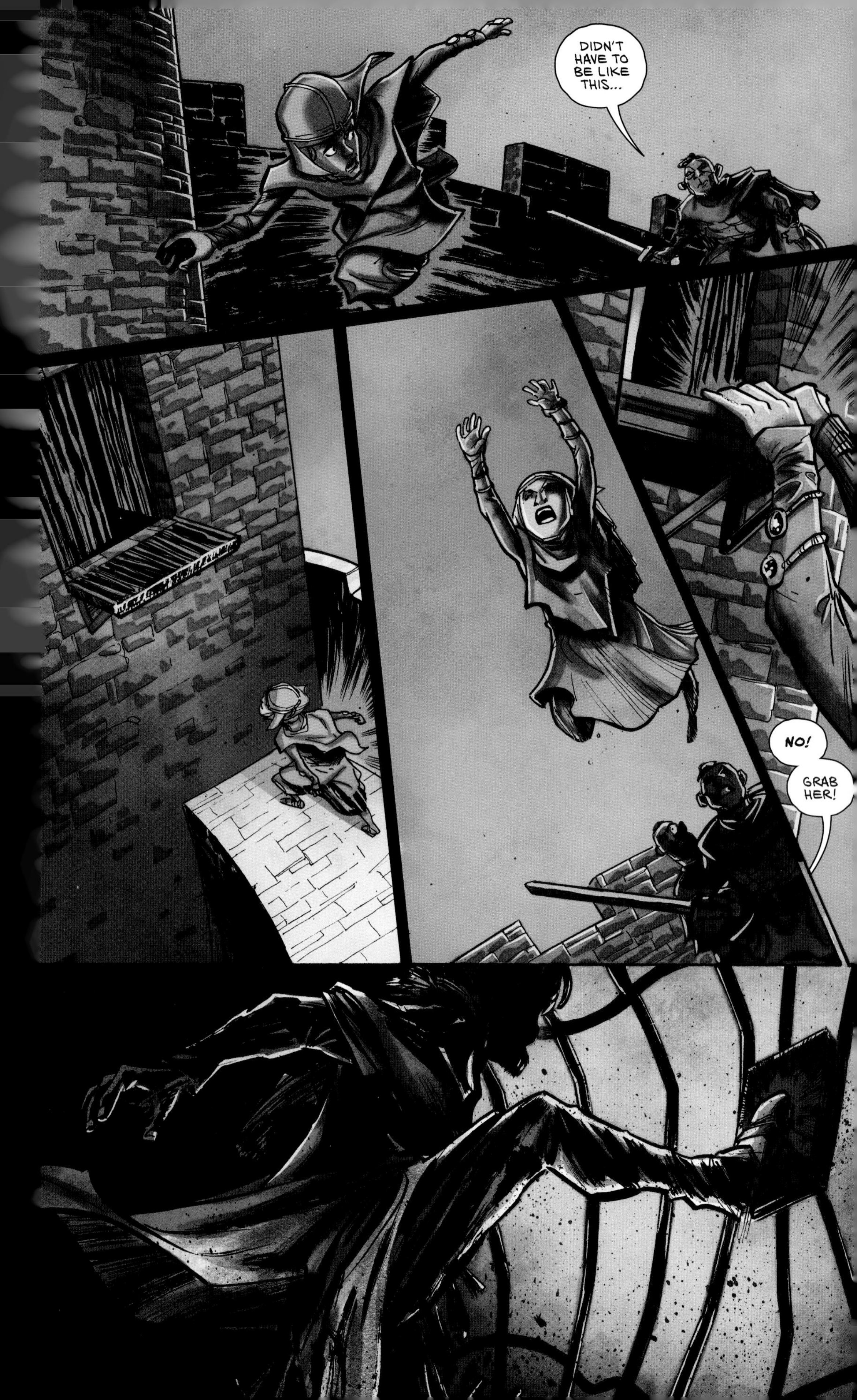
DIDN'T HAVE TO BE LIKE THIS...
NO!
GRAB HER!

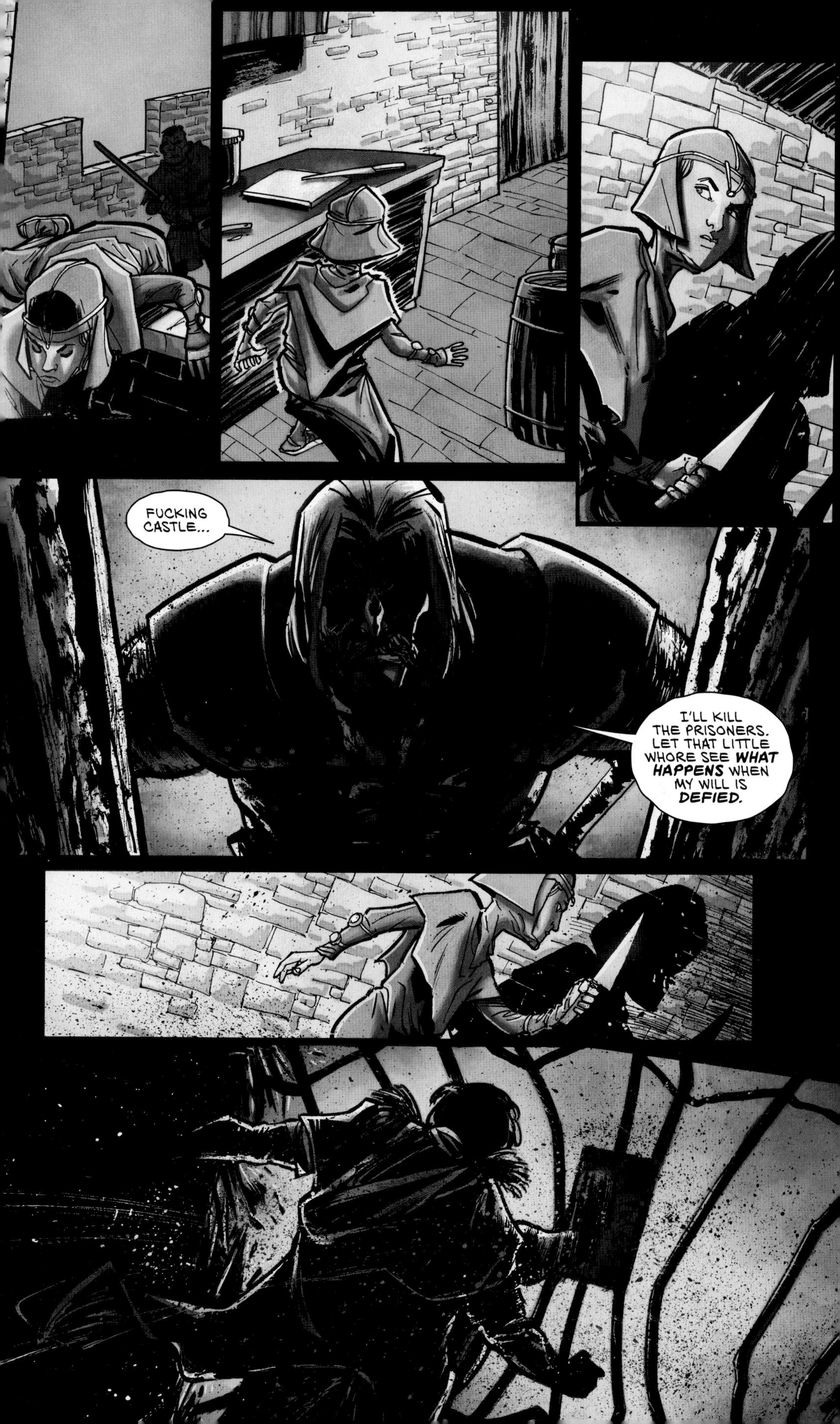
FUCKING CASTLE...
I'LL KILL THE PRISONERS. LET THAT LITTLE WHORE SEE **WHAT HAPPENS** WHEN MY WILL IS **DEFIED.**

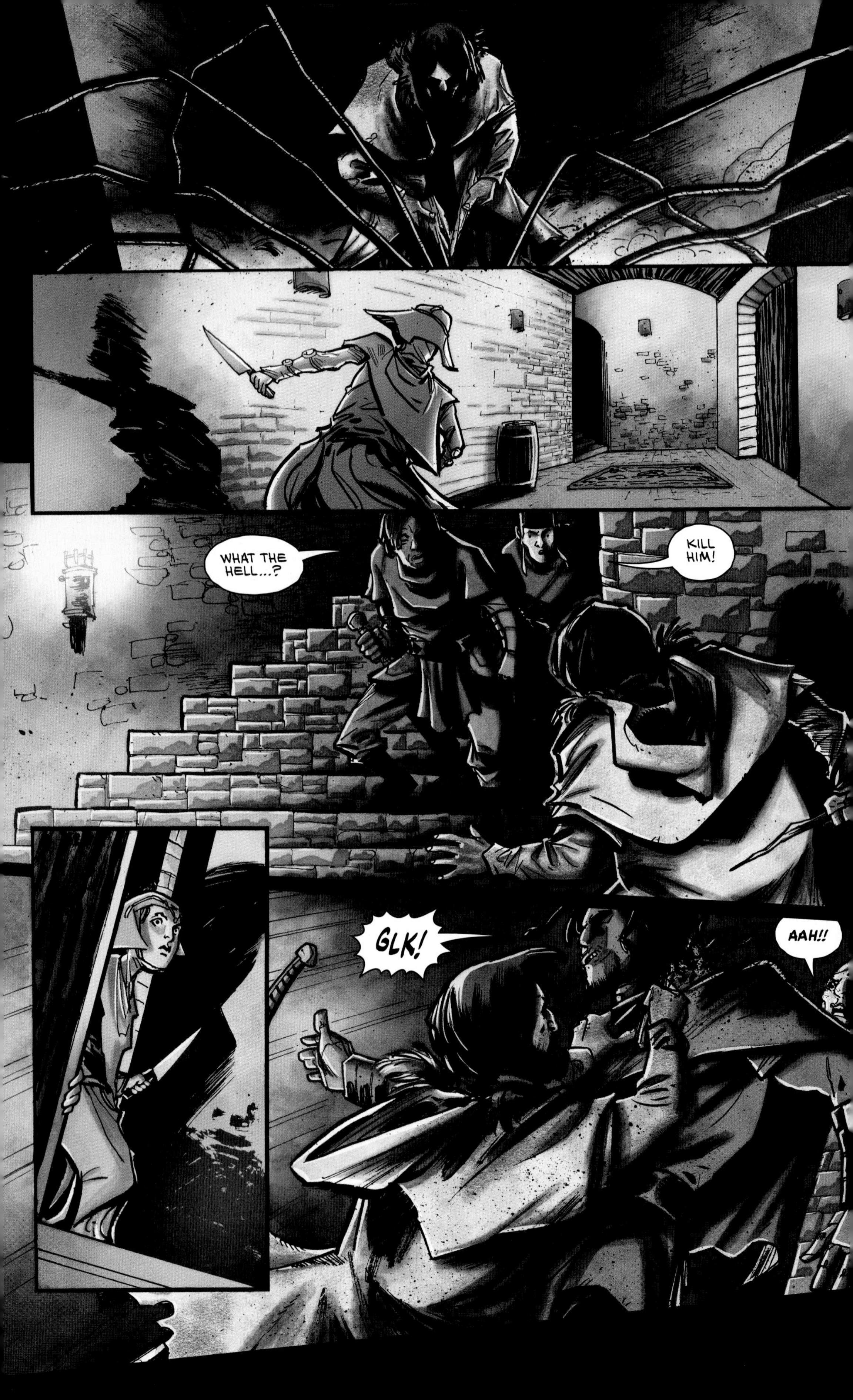
WHAT THE HELL...?
KILL HIM!
GLK!
AAH!!

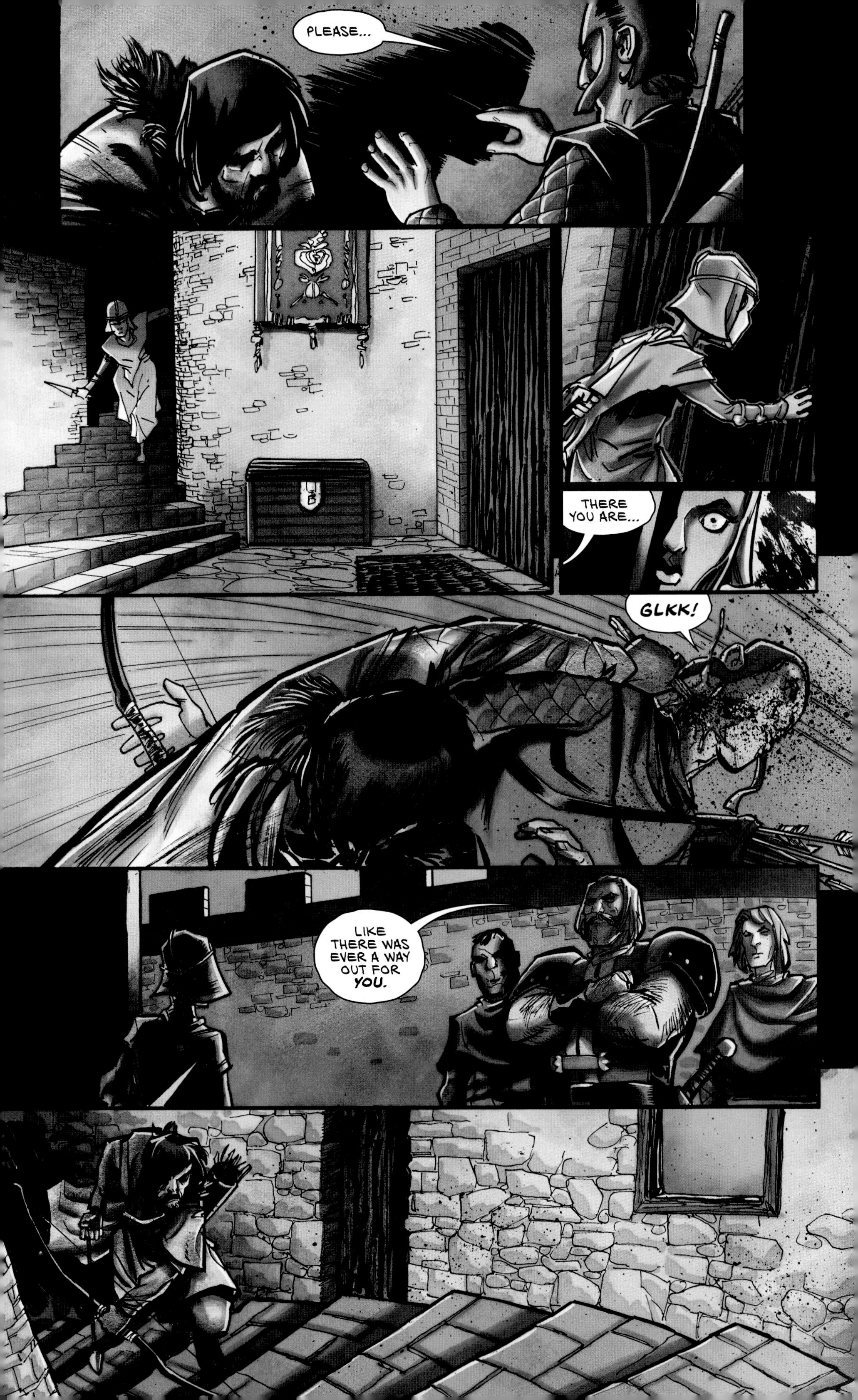
PLEASE...
THERE YOU ARE...
GLKK!
LIKE THERE WAS EVER A WAY OUT FOR YOU.

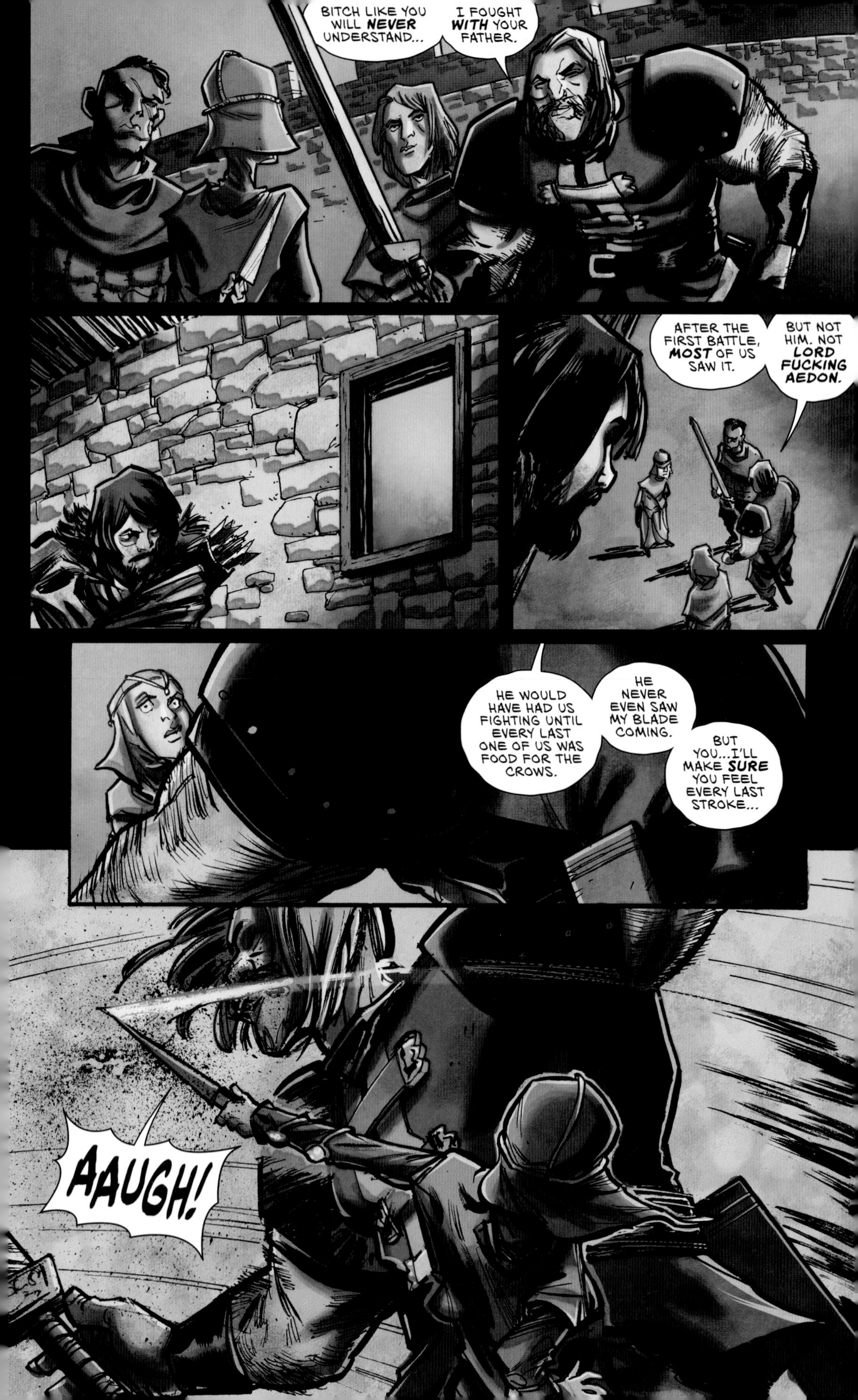
BITCH LIKE YOU WILL NEVER UNDERSTAND...
I FOUGHT WITH YOUR FATHER.
AFTER THE FIRST BATTLE, MOST OF US SAW IT.
BUT NOT HIM. NOT LORD FUCKING AEDON.
HE WOULD HAVE HAD US FIGHTING UNTIL EVERY LAST ONE OF US WAS FOOD FOR THE CROWS.
HE NEVER EVEN SAW MY BLADE COMING.
BUT YOU...I'LL MAKE SURE YOU FEEL EVERY LAST STROKE...
AAUGH!

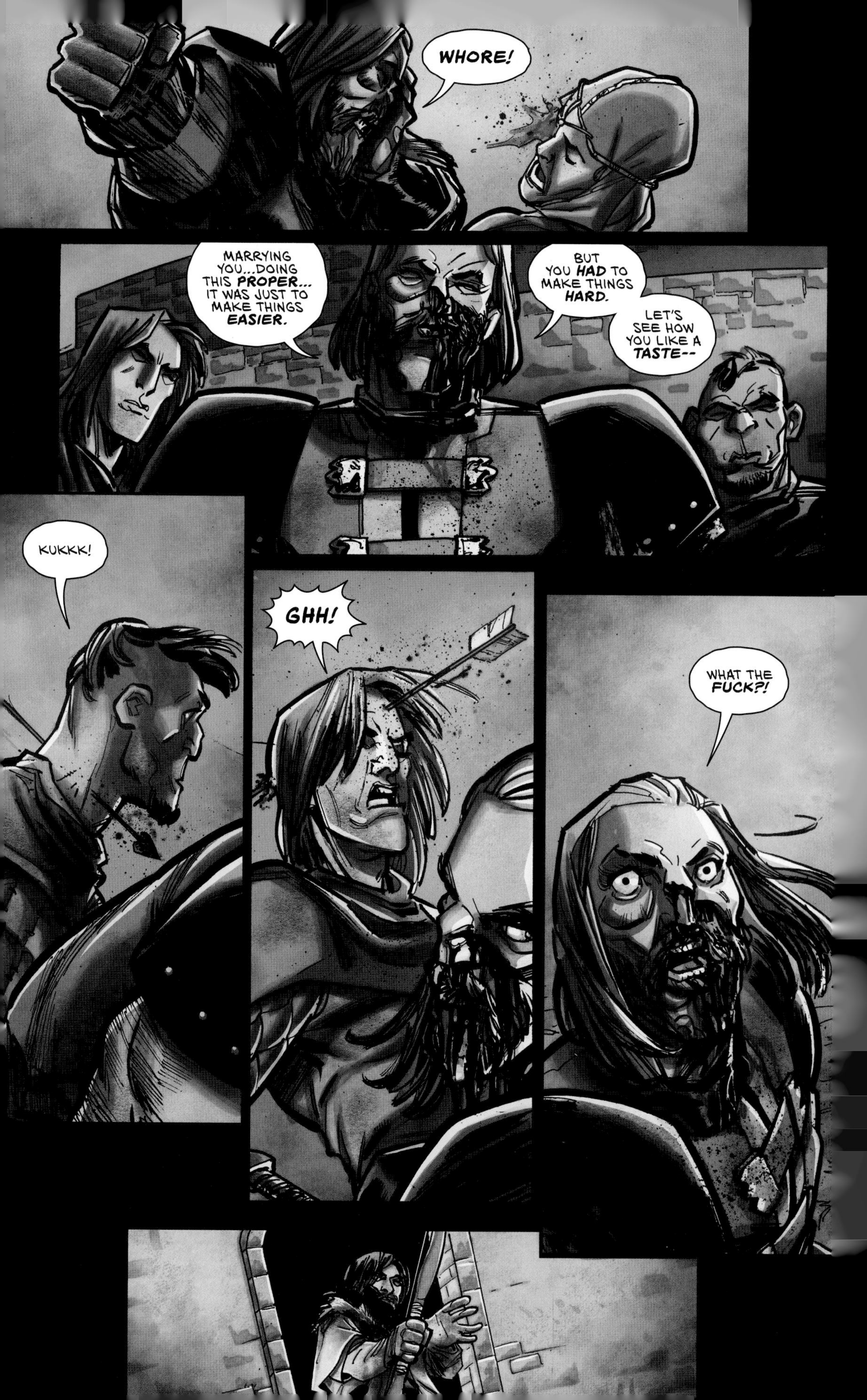
WHORE!
MARRYING YOU...DOING THIS PROPER... IT WAS JUST TO MAKE THINGS EASIER.
BUT YOU HAD TO MAKE THINGS HARD.
LET'S SEE HOW YOU LIKE A TASTE--
KUKKK!
GHH!
WHAT THE FUCK?!

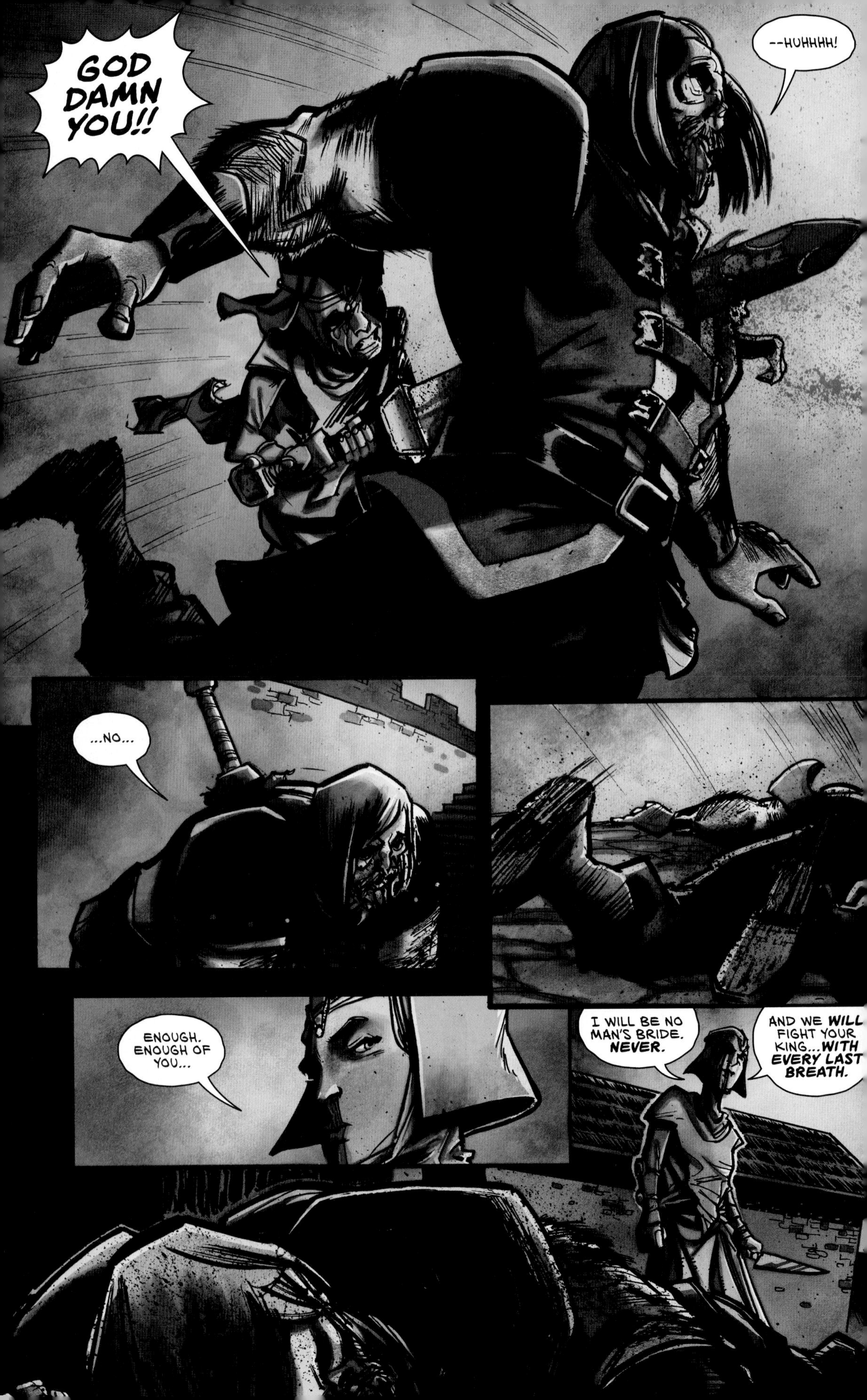
GOD DAMN YOU!!
--HUHHHH!
...NO...
ENOUGH. ENOUGH OF YOU...
I WILL BE NO MAN'S BRIDE. NEVER.
AND WE WILL FIGHT YOUR KING...WITH EVERY LAST BREATH.

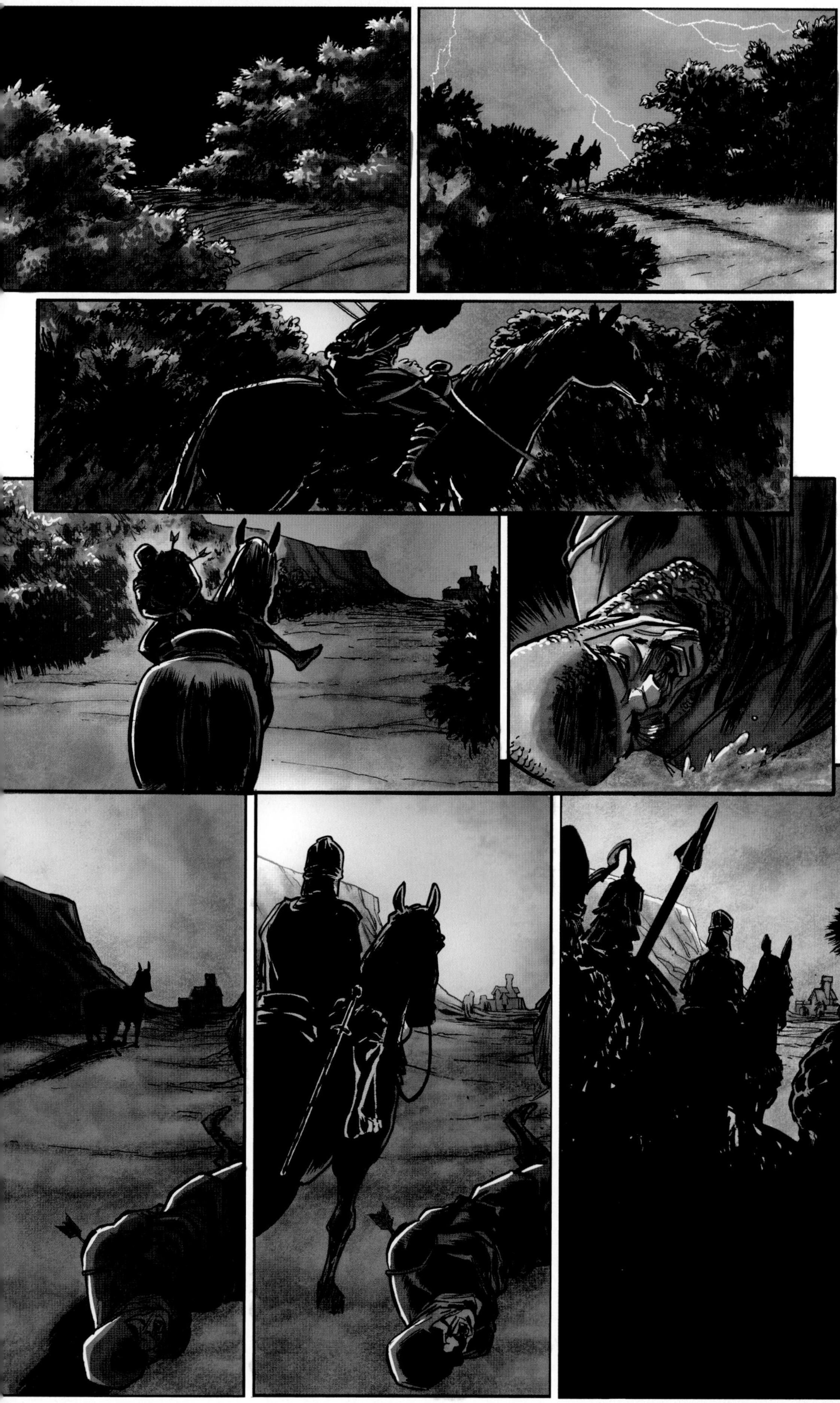

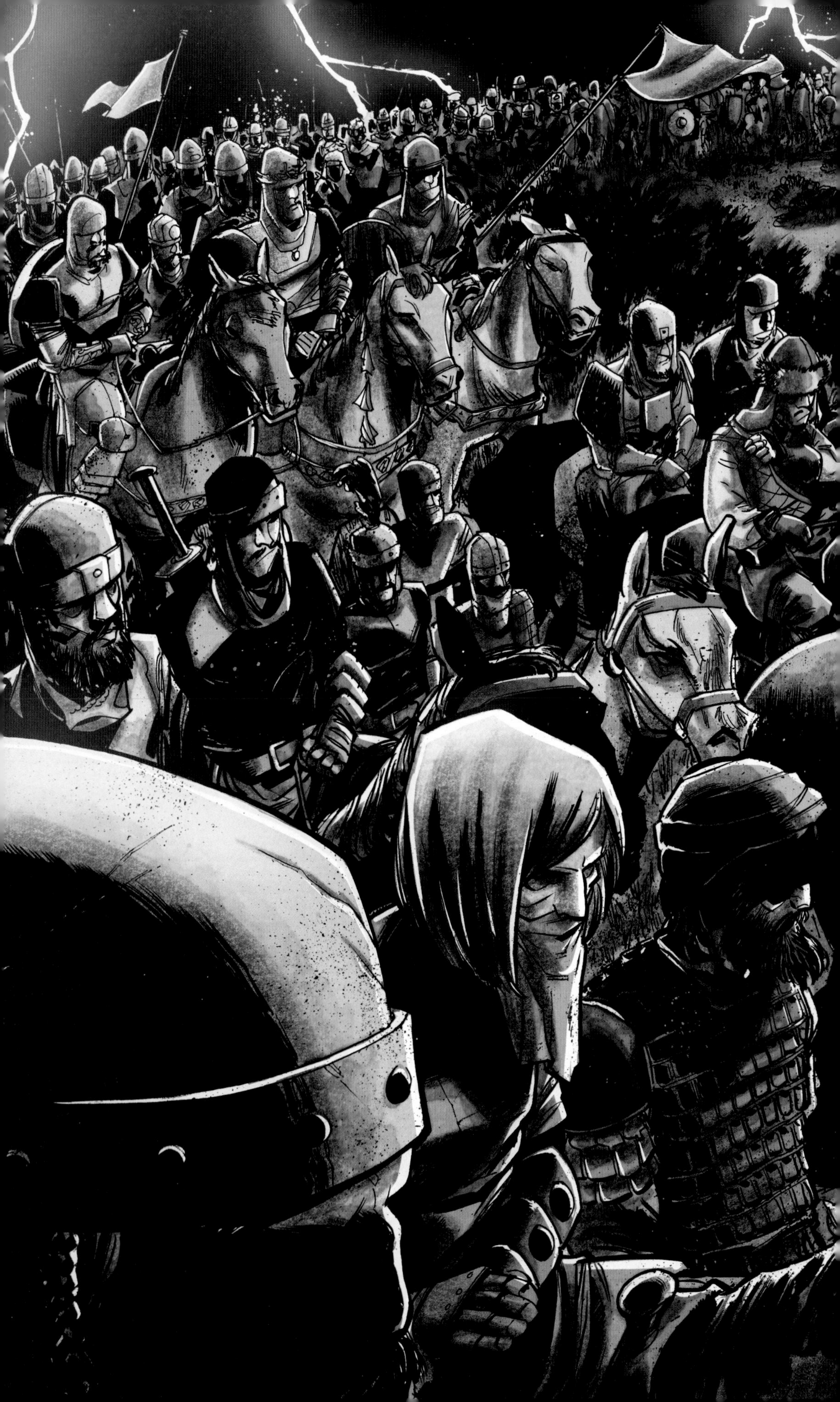

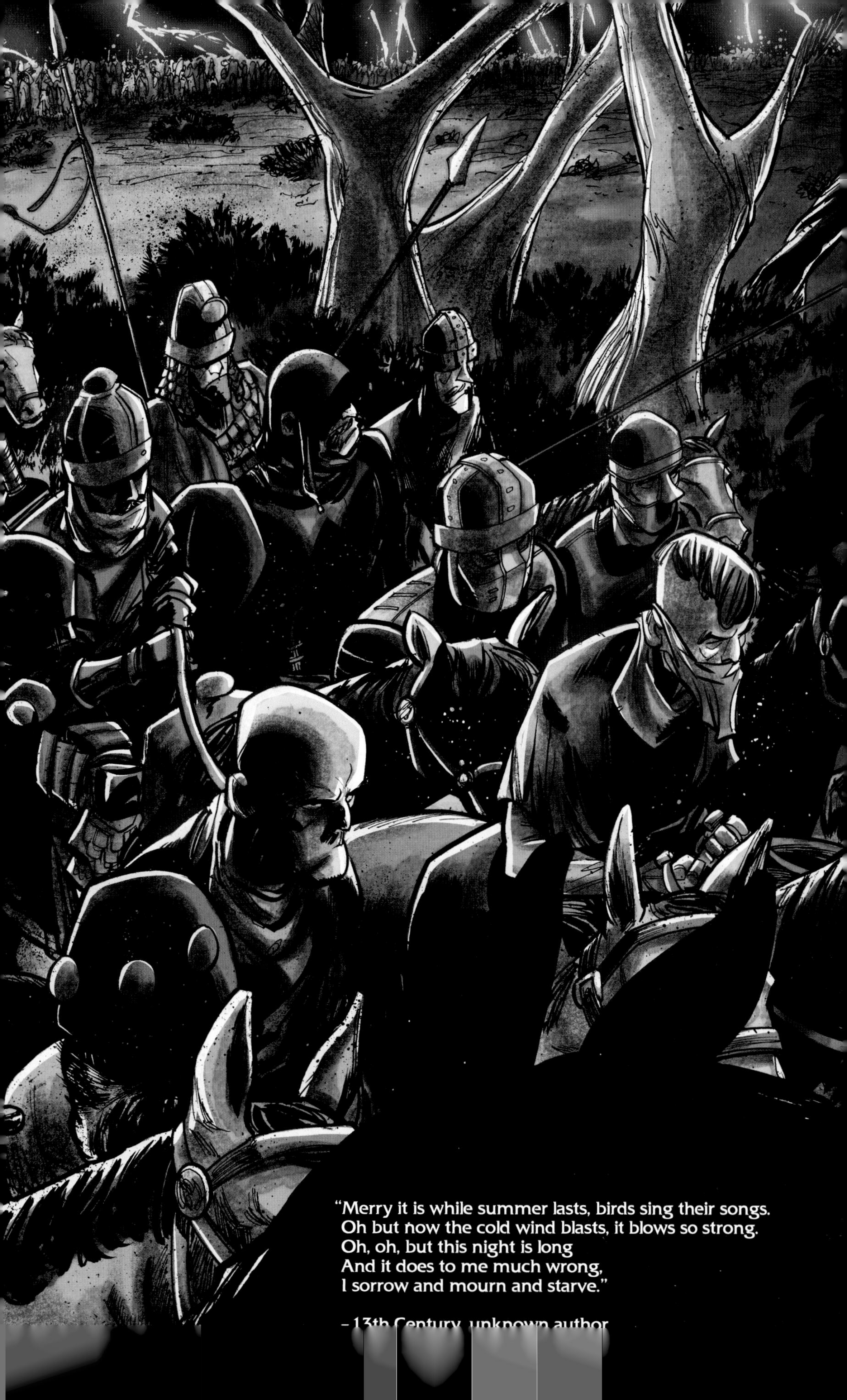
"Merry it is while summer lasts, birds sing their songs.
Oh but now the cold wind blasts, it blows so strong.
Oh, oh, but this night is long
And it does to me much wrong,
I sorrow and mourn and starve."

– 13th Century, unknown author

The King Rises

Chapter 4

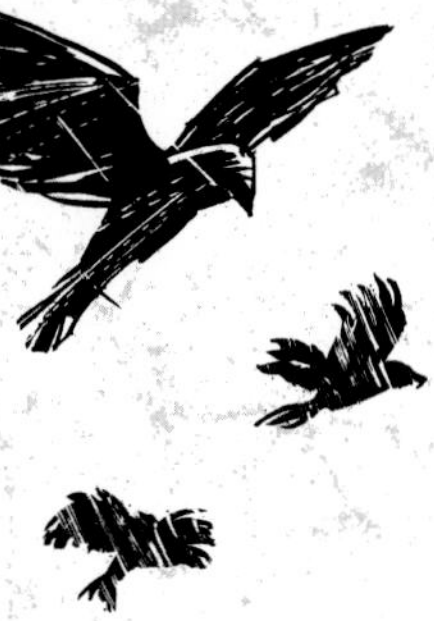

"What have you done?!"

Tomislav stood in the hall of his father, a large house built atop a motte, surrounded by a wooden palisade.

Tomislav winced, rubbing his bruised chin. His father's rage had been fierce, and he had already said so much with his fists long before the first question had escaped his lips.

"I've done what you wouldn't dare," Tomislav spit back. "Helped people who needed help."

The older man roared. "Have you?" Tomislav's father was stocky, his long white hair neatly braided, as was his beard. He picked up a map that had been spread across a large table, and with a quick movement threw it at his son. "Take a look at what your help has cost your family!"

Tomislav unrolled the map. "These encampments... when did they move this far West? They..."

"They what?" his father sneered. "They were supposed to stay in the mountains? Is that what you believed when you drank with them? Oh yes, don't think I don't know where you've been off to. To think my son would lay with the wretched whores —"

Tomislav threw the map back at his father. "We have enough to share," he barked. "So I sent them food? So I helped them survive? So what? All we do is take, the farms and the villages —"

"We stand ready to protect those farms and villages!" his father snapped back.

The older man paced the width of the hall. "You were a child when the lordlings rose up. When they appointed one of their own as king. A king who would unite all the provinces under one banner." He spat as he spoke. "King Grigorii — a peasant in a false crown who thought he could storm our houses. A man who would have murdered you in your sleep had I allowed him the chance."

He reached into a sack sitting on the floor, the contempt in his voice reaching a new level. "And now we see what filth you have brought to my house. We see how you betray your own family."

Upending the bag, Tomislav's father emptied its contents. A dull golden circlet clattered onto the floor, rolling across the rough stonework to stop near Tomislav's feet. It was scratched and cleaved at one side, but it was still unmistakably a crown.

"This..." he whispered. "Where did you —?"

"Your companion. The stable boy? My men failed to capture him, but we did seize the belongings he had hidden here, under my very roof. The depths of this treachery... from my own son..."

"What —? No. Father... let me talk to Istvan. I'm sure... this is a misunderstanding."

Tomislav's father gestured to his guards, two of whom stepped from the shadows, their swords drawn. "The time for talk is over. I will find this treacherous boy and I will have his head. I will send the animals you have invited into our lands back to whatever hell they came from, and you..."

"You will leave my house. You are my son no longer."

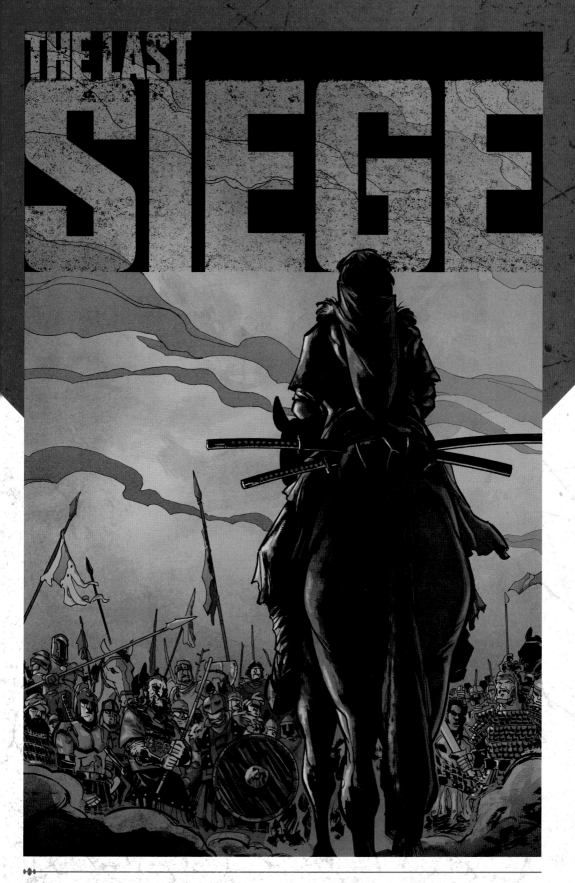

THE LAST SIEGE

CHAPTER FIVE

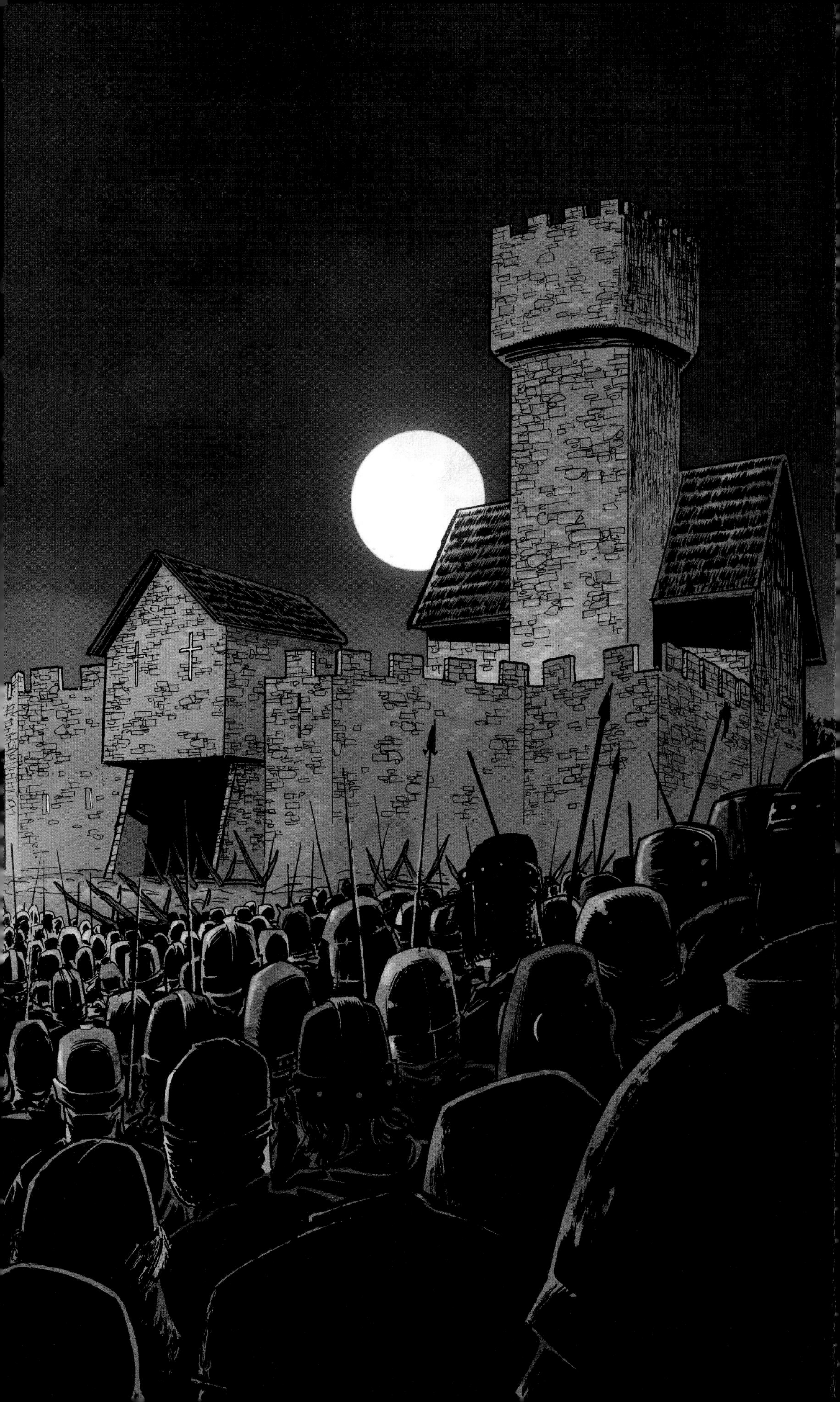

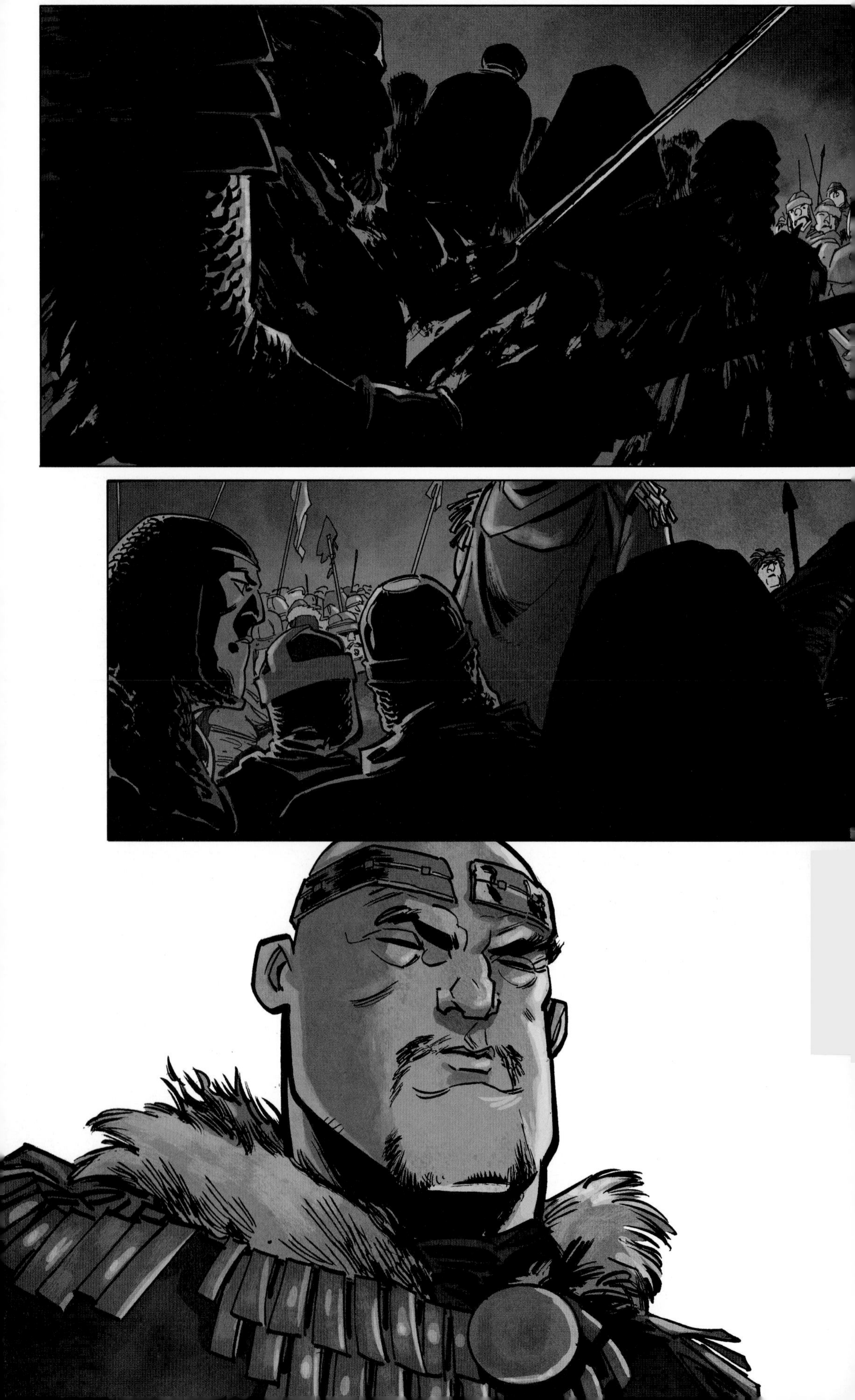

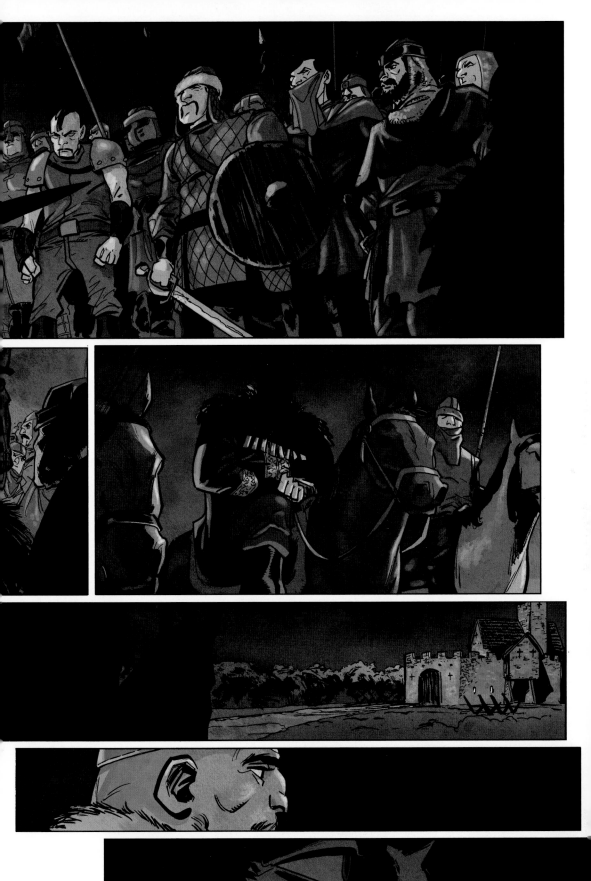

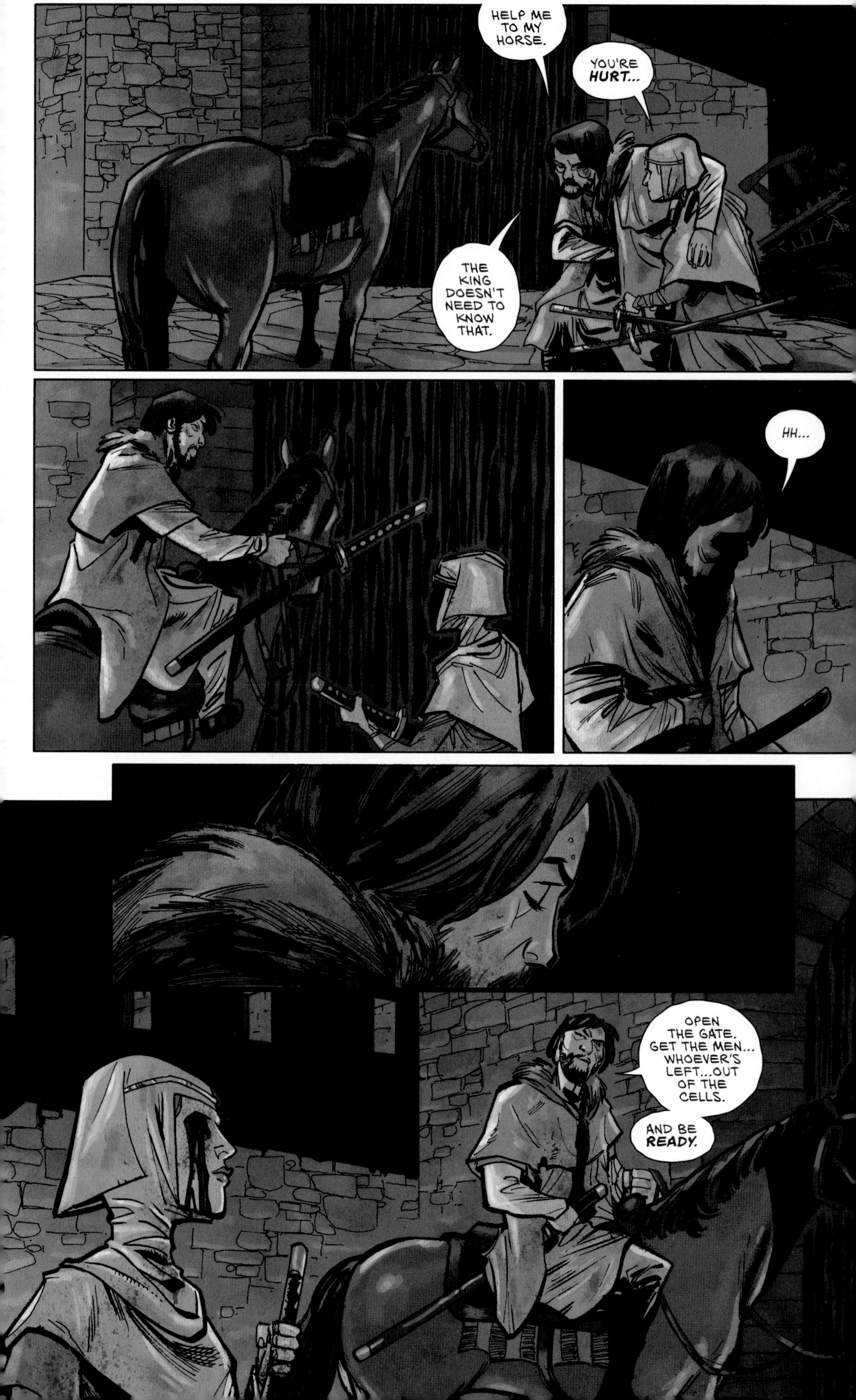
HELP ME TO MY HORSE.
YOU'RE HURT...
THE KING DOESN'T NEED TO KNOW THAT.
HH...
OPEN THE GATE. GET THE MEN... WHOEVER'S LEFT...OUT OF THE CELLS.
AND BE READY.

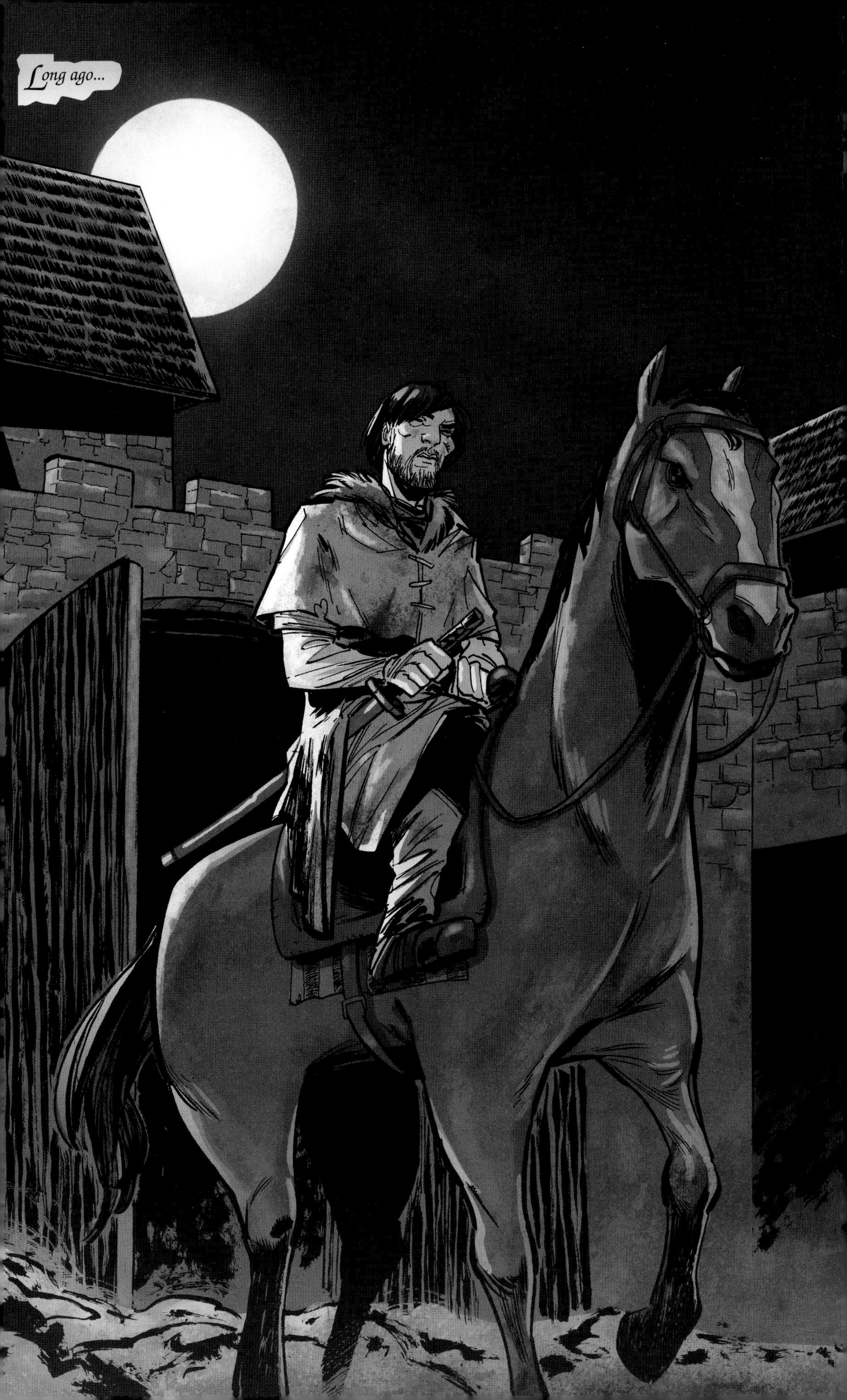
Long ago...

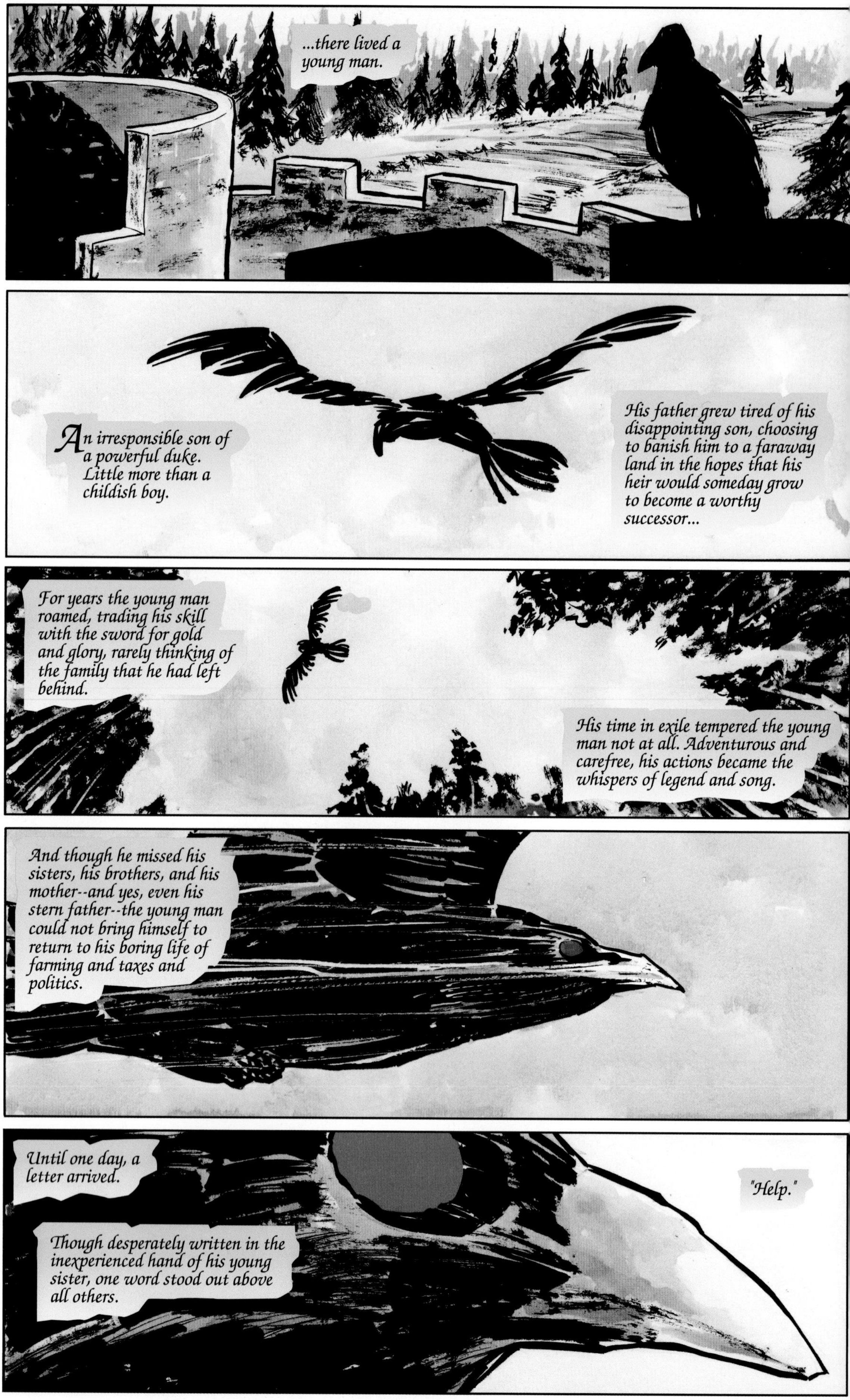
...there lived a young man.
An irresponsible son of a powerful duke. Little more than a childish boy.
His father grew tired of his disappointing son, choosing to banish him to a faraway land in the hopes that his heir would someday grow to become a worthy successor...
For years the young man roamed, trading his skill with the sword for gold and glory, rarely thinking of the family that he had left behind.
His time in exile tempered the young man not at all. Adventurous and carefree, his actions became the whispers of legend and song.
And though he missed his sisters, his brothers, and his mother--and yes, even his stern father--the young man could not bring himself to return to his boring life of farming and taxes and politics.
Until one day, a letter arrived.
Though desperately written in the inexperienced hand of his young sister, one word stood out above all others.
"Help."

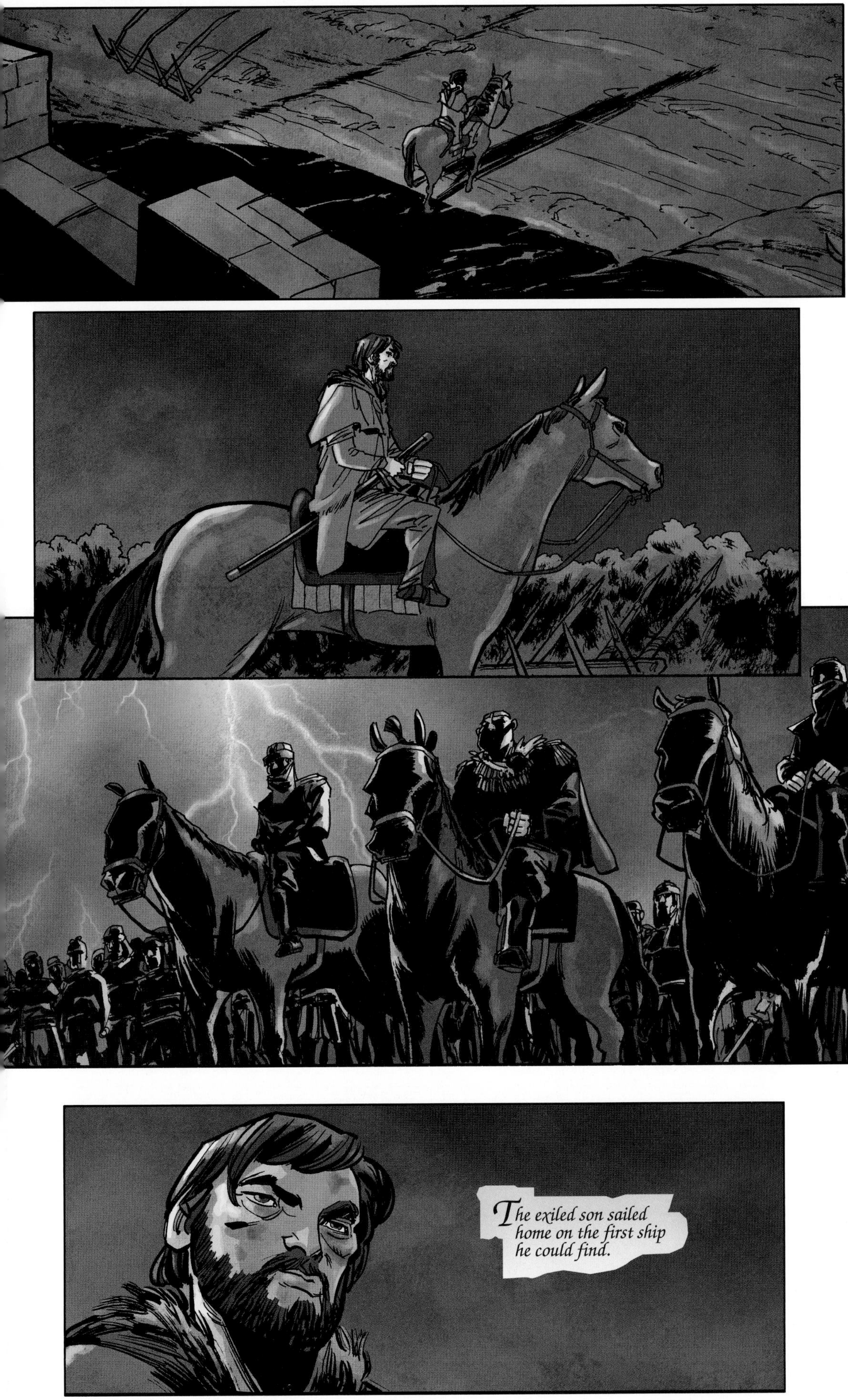
The exiled son sailed home on the first ship he could find.

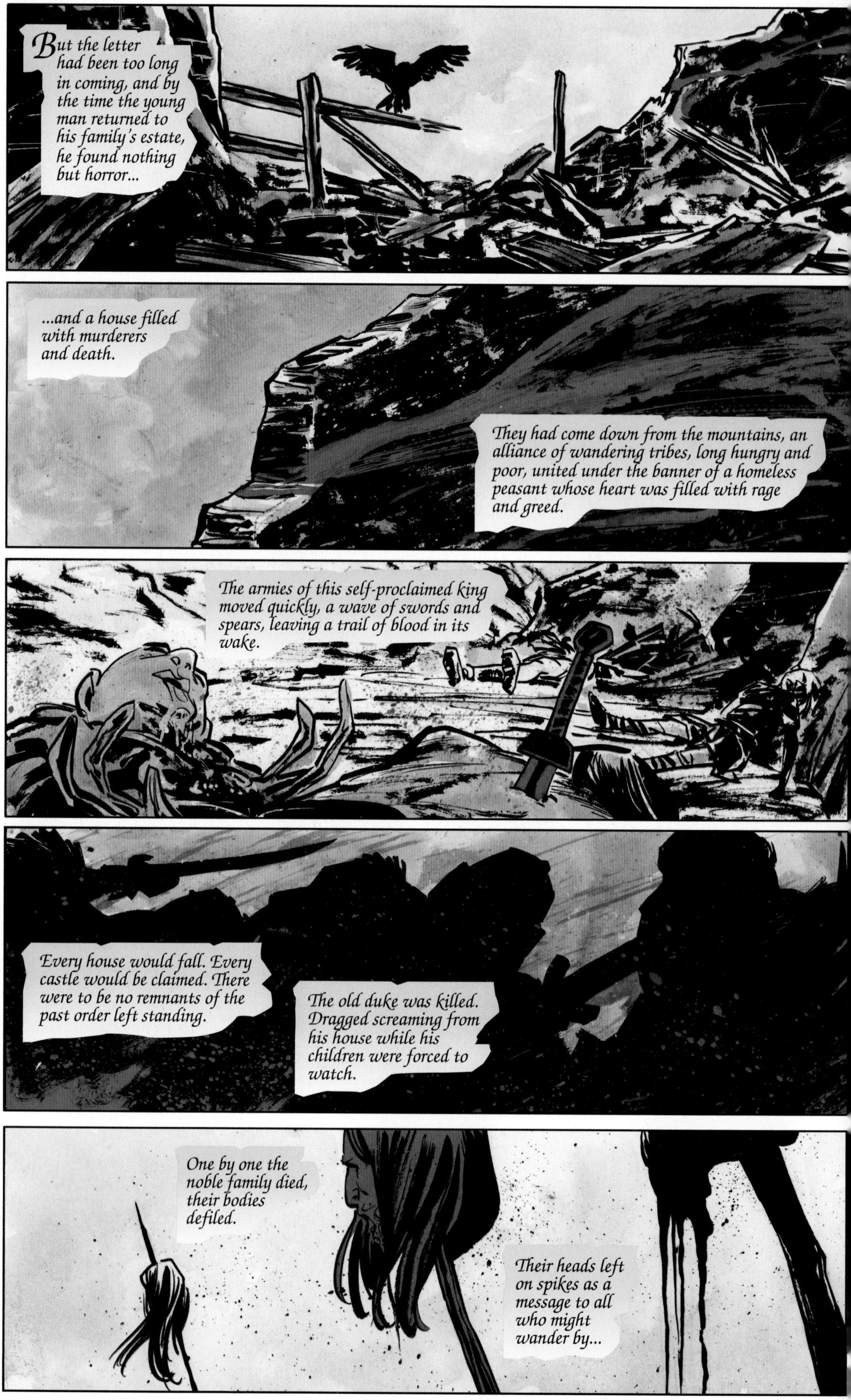
But the letter had been too long in coming, and by the time the young man returned to his family's estate, he found nothing but horror...
...and a house filled with murderers and death.
They had come down from the mountains, an alliance of wandering tribes, long hungry and poor, united under the banner of a homeless peasant whose heart was filled with rage and greed.
The armies of this self-proclaimed king moved quickly, a wave of swords and spears, leaving a trail of blood in its wake.
Every house would fall. Every castle would be claimed. There were to be no remnants of the past order left standing.
The old duke was killed. Dragged screaming from his house while his children were forced to watch.
One by one the noble family died, their bodies defiled.
Their heads left on spikes as a message to all who might wander by...

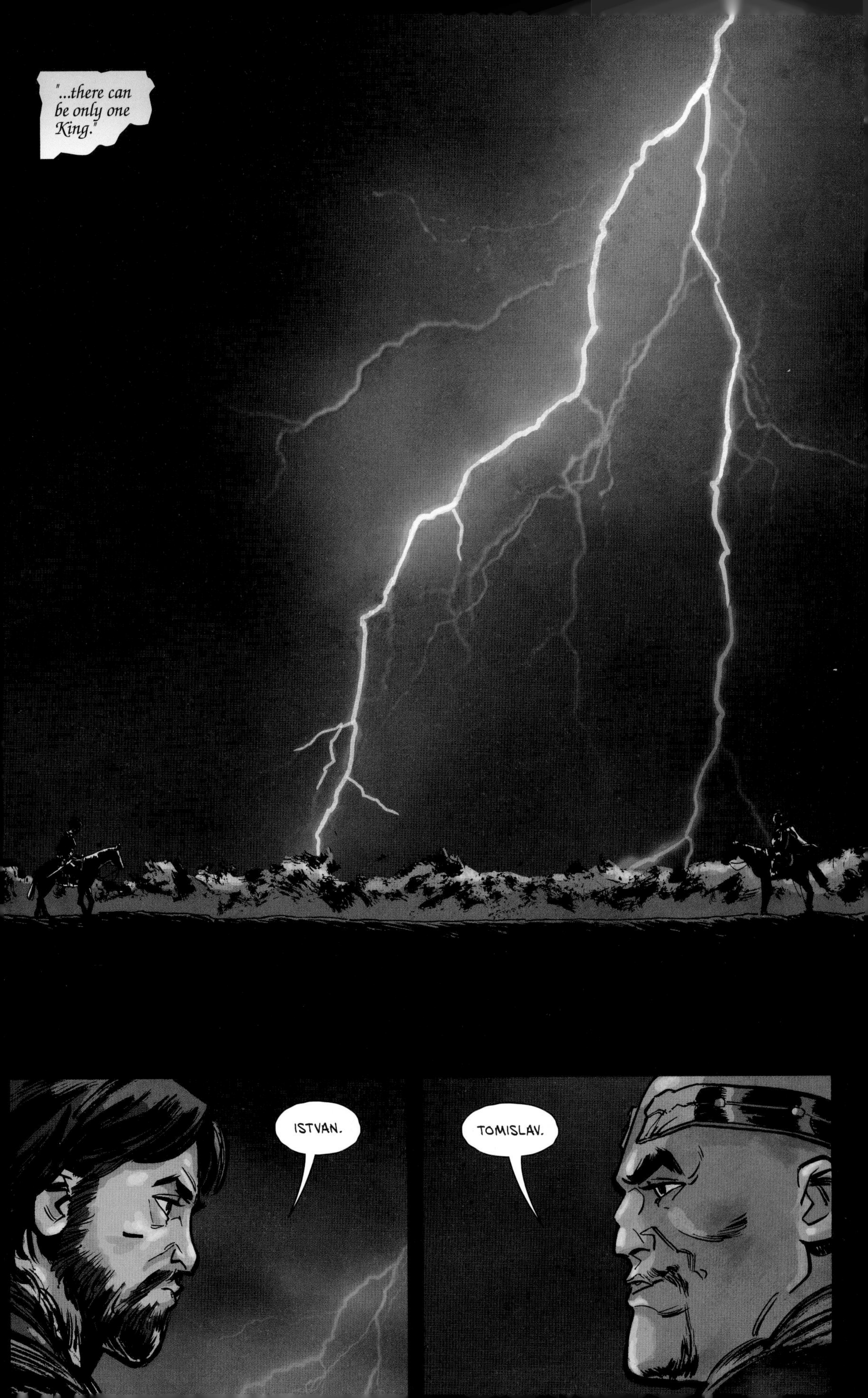
"...there can be only one King."
ISTVAN.
TOMISLAV.

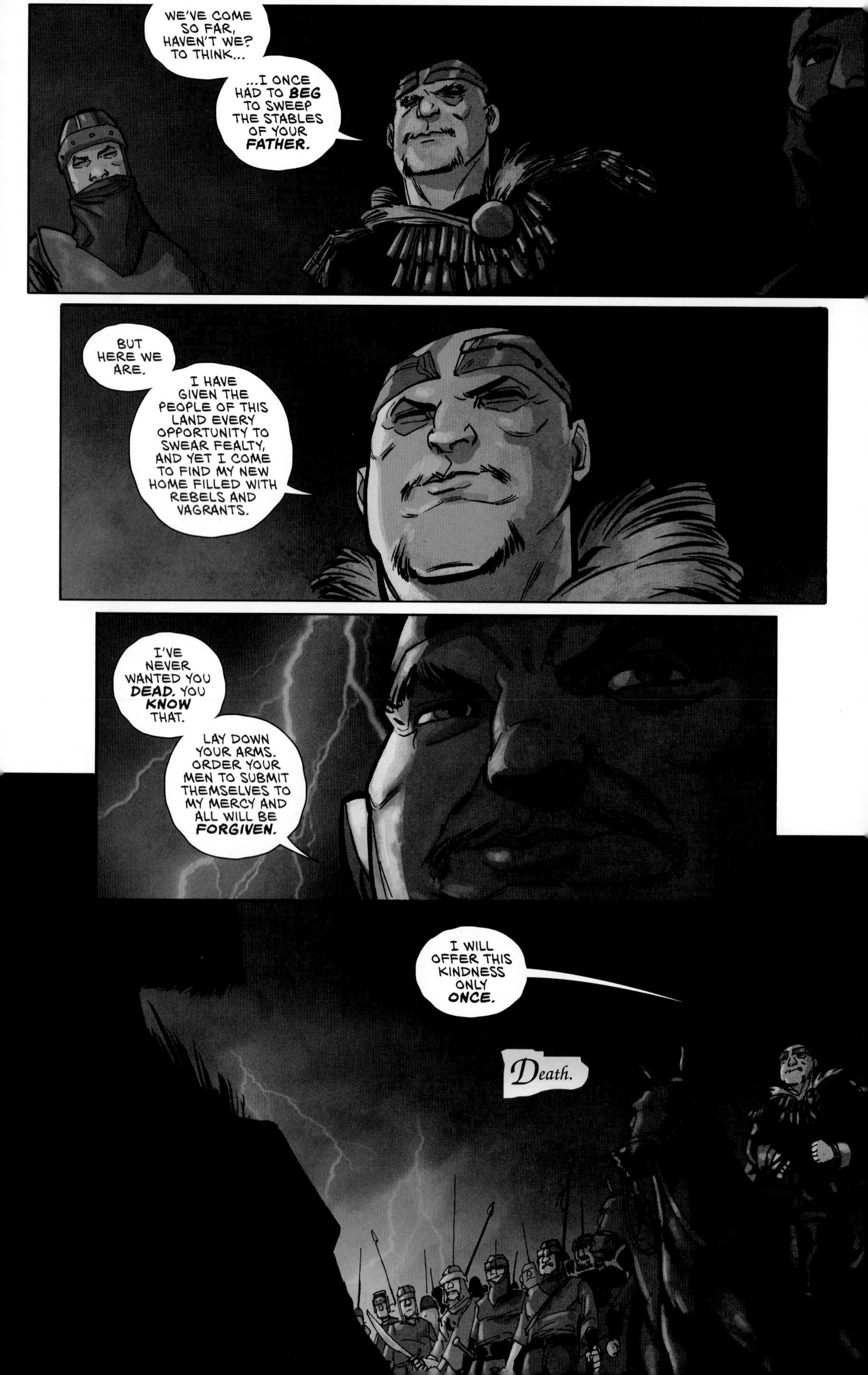
WE'VE COME SO FAR, HAVEN'T WE? TO THINK...
...I ONCE HAD TO BEG TO SWEEP THE STABLES OF YOUR FATHER.
BUT HERE WE ARE.
I HAVE GIVEN THE PEOPLE OF THIS LAND EVERY OPPORTUNITY TO SWEAR FEALTY, AND YET I COME TO FIND MY NEW HOME FILLED WITH REBELS AND VAGRANTS.
I'VE NEVER WANTED YOU DEAD. YOU KNOW THAT.
LAY DOWN YOUR ARMS. ORDER YOUR MEN TO SUBMIT THEMSELVES TO MY MERCY AND ALL WILL BE FORGIVEN.
I WILL OFFER THIS KINDNESS ONLY ONCE.
Death.

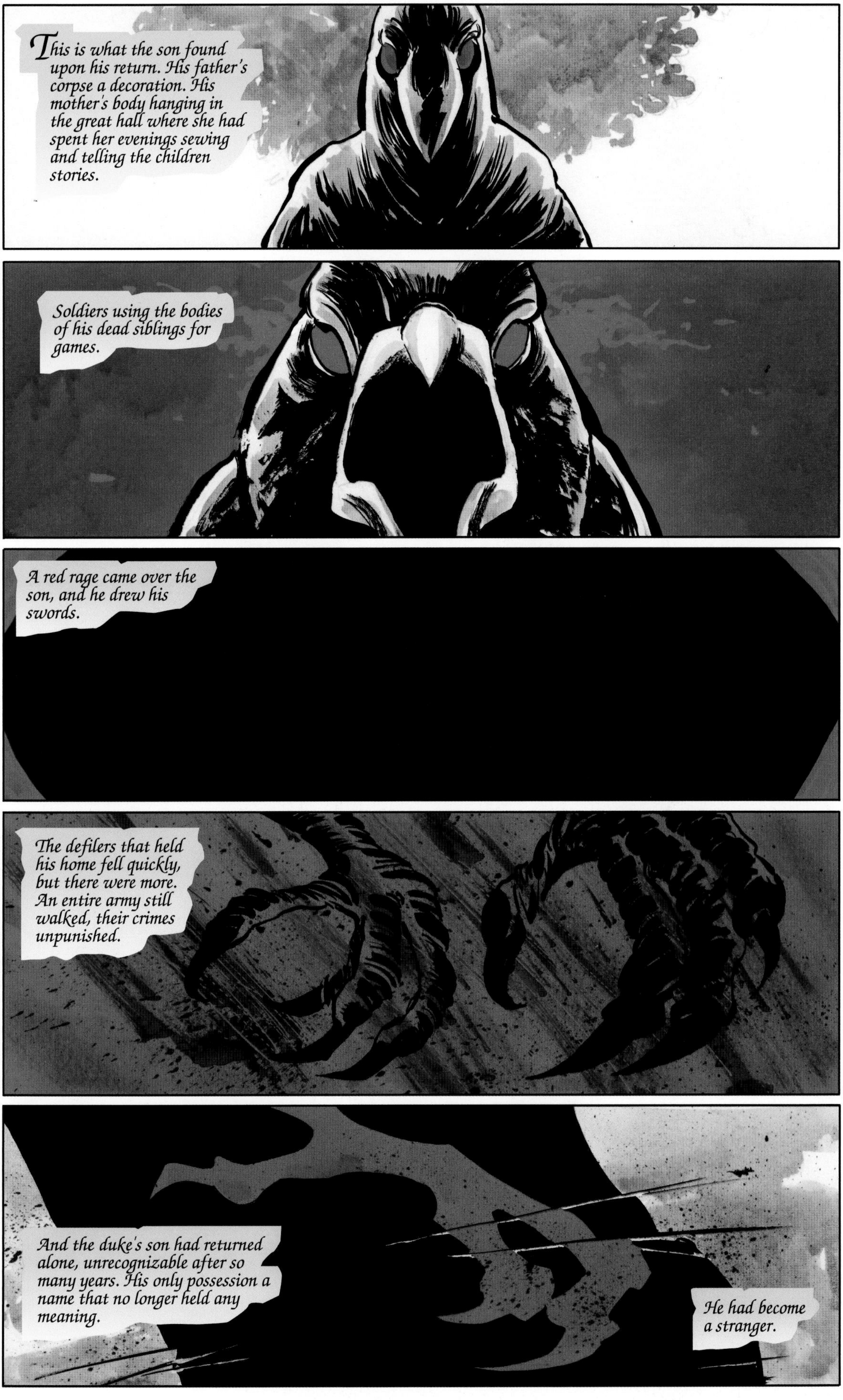
This is what the son found upon his return. His father's corpse a decoration. His mother's body hanging in the great hall where she had spent her evenings sewing and telling the children stories.
Soldiers using the bodies of his dead siblings for games.
A red rage came over the son, and he drew his swords.
The defilers that held his home fell quickly, but there were more. An entire army still walked, their crimes unpunished.
And the duke's son had returned alone, unrecognizable after so many years. His only possession a name that no longer held any meaning.
He had become a stranger.

I'VE SEEN YOUR MERCY. YOUR KINDNESS.

MY FAMILY RECEIVED YOU IN THEIR HALL. THEY TREATED YOU WITH COURTESY.

I WELCOMED YOU LIKE A BROTHER.

YOU'RE A MURDERER. A MONSTER NOT FIT TO WALK THIS WORLD.

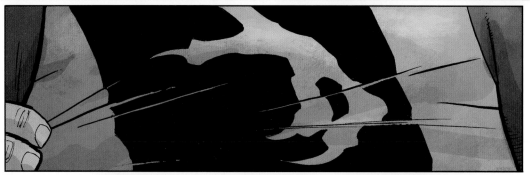

SO I SUGGEST AN ALTERNATE SCENARIO.

YOU WILL DIE TODAY. HERE. WITH MY HANDS AROUND YOUR THROAT AS YOUR MEN LISTEN TO YOU SCREAM.

I WILL OFFER THIS KINDNESS ONLY ONCE.

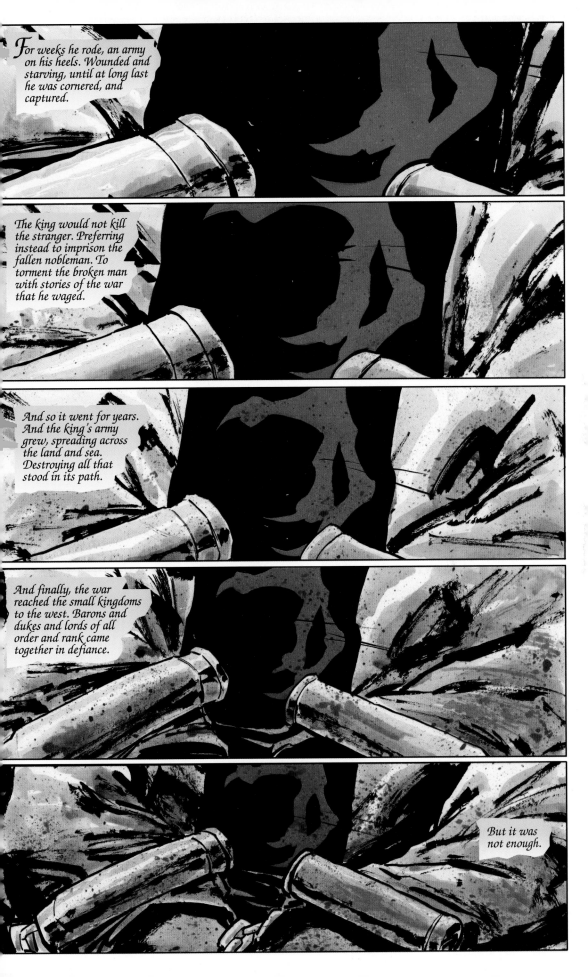

For weeks he rode, an army on his heels. Wounded and starving, until at long last he was cornered, and captured.

The king would not kill the stranger. Preferring instead to imprison the fallen nobleman. To torment the broken man with stories of the war that he waged.

And so it went for years. And the king's army grew, spreading across the land and sea. Destroying all that stood in its path.

And finally, the war reached the small kingdoms to the west. Barons and dukes and lords of all order and rank came together in defiance.

But it was not enough.

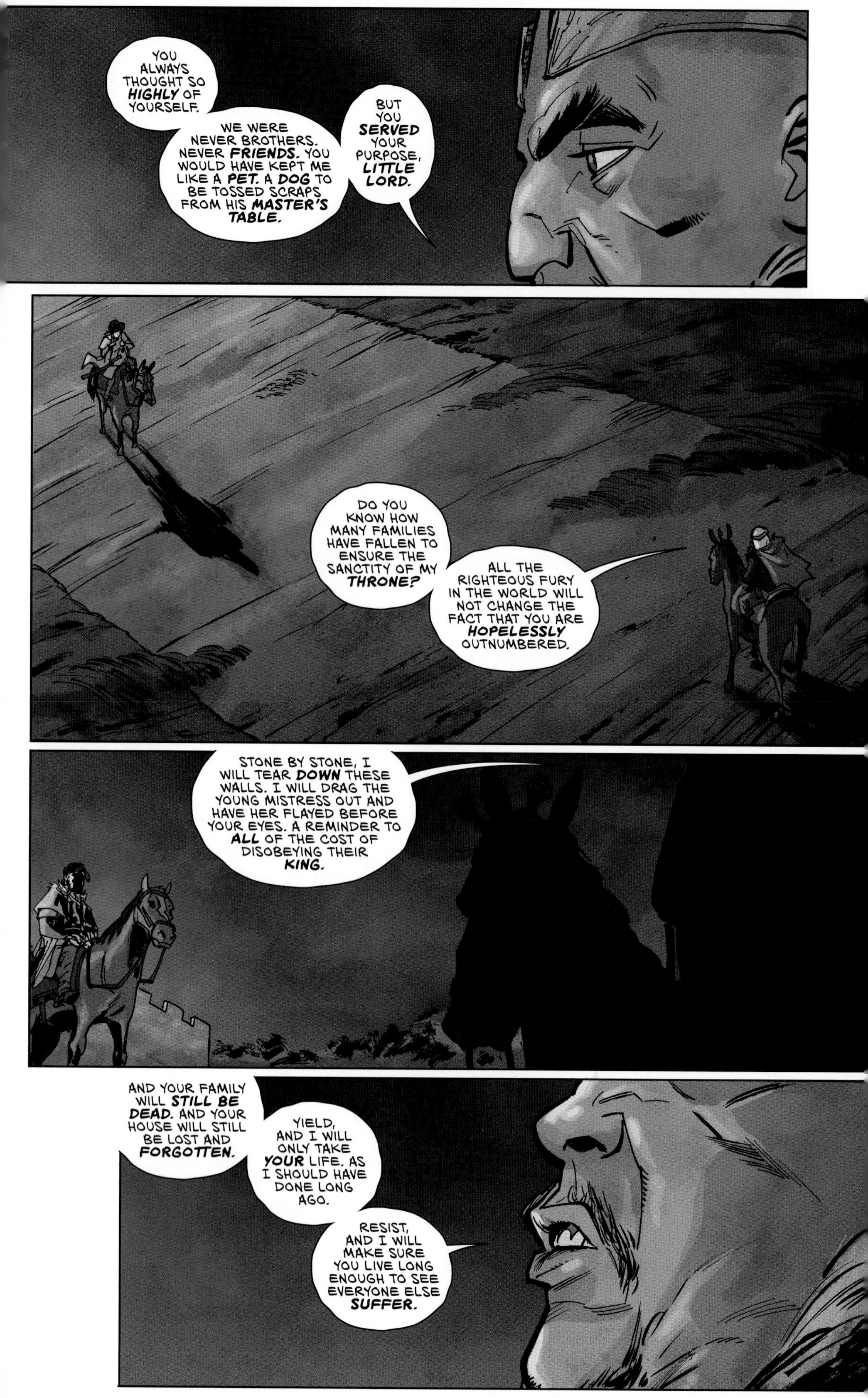
YOU ALWAYS THOUGHT SO HIGHLY OF YOURSELF.
WE WERE NEVER BROTHERS. NEVER FRIENDS. YOU WOULD HAVE KEPT ME LIKE A PET. A DOG TO BE TOSSED SCRAPS FROM HIS MASTER'S TABLE.
BUT YOU SERVED YOUR PURPOSE, LITTLE LORD.
DO YOU KNOW HOW MANY FAMILIES HAVE FALLEN TO ENSURE THE SANCTITY OF MY THRONE?
ALL THE RIGHTEOUS FURY IN THE WORLD WILL NOT CHANGE THE FACT THAT YOU ARE HOPELESSLY OUTNUMBERED.
STONE BY STONE, I WILL TEAR DOWN THESE WALLS. I WILL DRAG THE YOUNG MISTRESS OUT AND HAVE HER FLAYED BEFORE YOUR EYES. A REMINDER TO ALL OF THE COST OF DISOBEYING THEIR KING.
AND YOUR FAMILY WILL STILL BE DEAD. AND YOUR HOUSE WILL STILL BE LOST AND FORGOTTEN.
YIELD, AND I WILL ONLY TAKE YOUR LIFE. AS I SHOULD HAVE DONE LONG AGO.
RESIST, AND I WILL MAKE SURE YOU LIVE LONG ENOUGH TO SEE EVERYONE ELSE SUFFER.

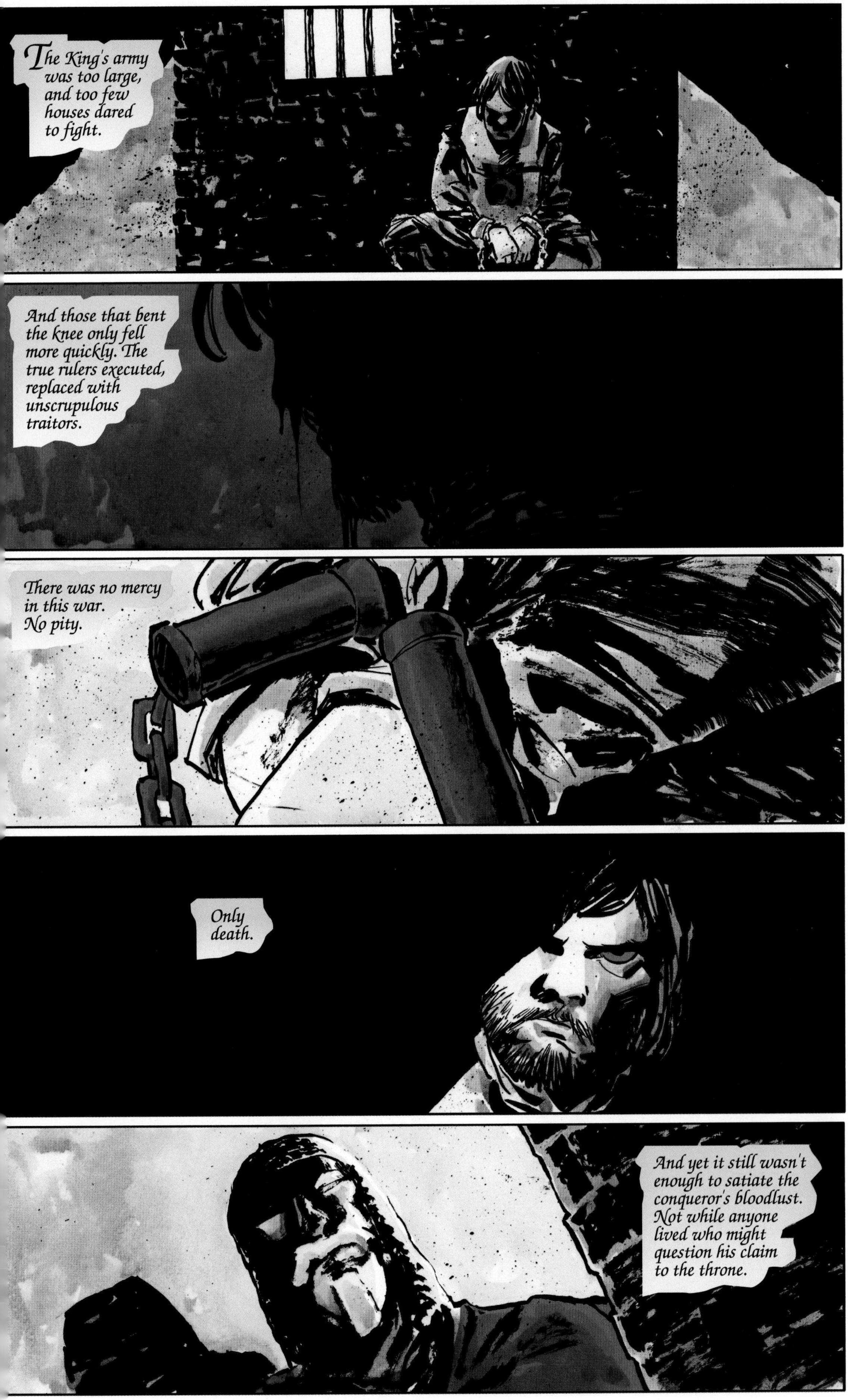
The King's army was too large, and too few houses dared to fight.
And those that bent the knee only fell more quickly. The true rulers executed, replaced with unscrupulous traitors.
There was no mercy in this war. No pity.
Only death.
And yet it still wasn't enough to satiate the conqueror's bloodlust. Not while anyone lived who might question his claim to the throne.

SO SURE OF YOURSELF, WITH THAT ARMY BEHIND YOUR BACK?

HOW LOYAL ARE THEY TO YOU, I WONDER? HOW MANY BENT THE KNEE FROM *FEAR* OR THREAT?

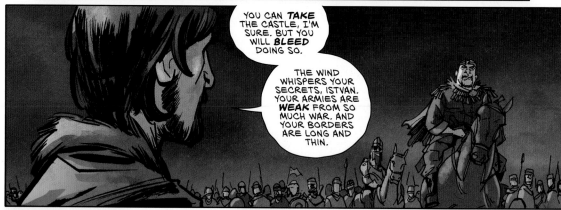

YOU CAN *TAKE* THE CASTLE, I'M SURE. BUT YOU WILL *BLEED* DOING SO.

THE WIND WHISPERS YOUR SECRETS, ISTVAN. YOUR ARMIES ARE *WEAK* FROM SO MUCH WAR. AND YOUR BORDERS ARE LONG AND THIN.

AND A KING WHO CLAIMS A THRONE WITH DAGGERS IN THE NIGHT DOESN'T SLEEP SOUNDLY, I WOULD IMAGINE.

SO *PROVE* YOUR COURAGE. SPARE YOUR MEN.

DEFEAT ME, SINGLE COMBAT. DO THIS AND THE CASTLE IS YOURS.

OR WILL YOU RIDE BACK TO YOUR ARMY AND HIDE BEHIND THEIR SHIELDS AS THEY *DIE?*

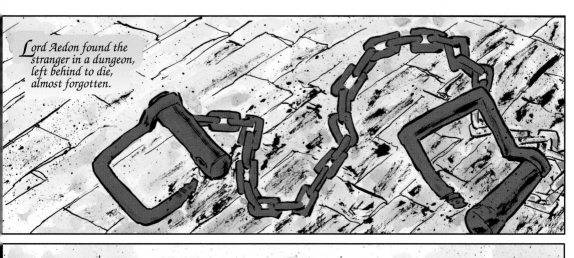

Lord Aedon found the stranger in a dungeon, left behind to die, almost forgotten.

The stranger's fury had not broken during his years in captivity, nor had his imprisonment weakened him.

He hungered for vengeance, but Aedon offered him something more.

A chance for redemption.

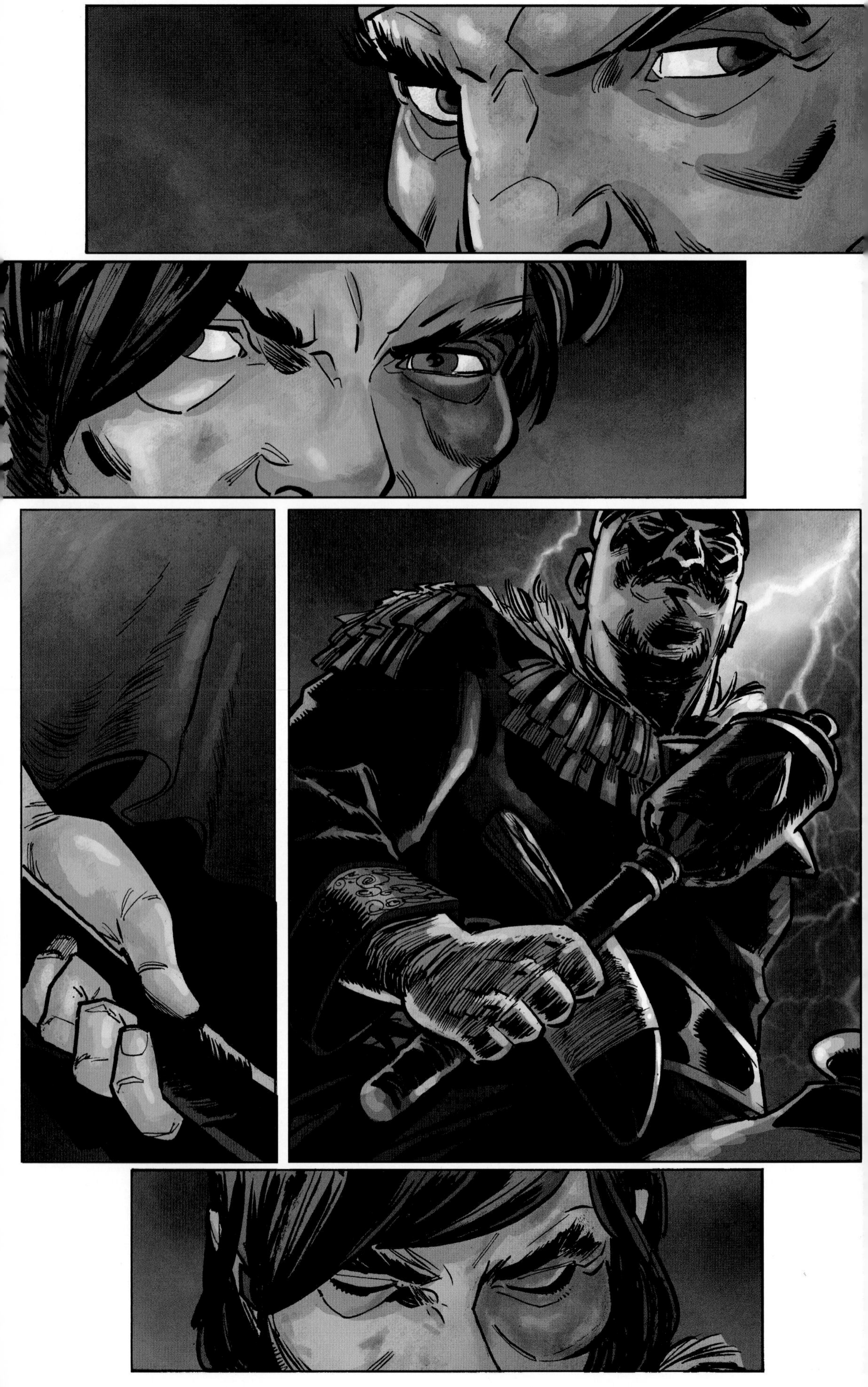

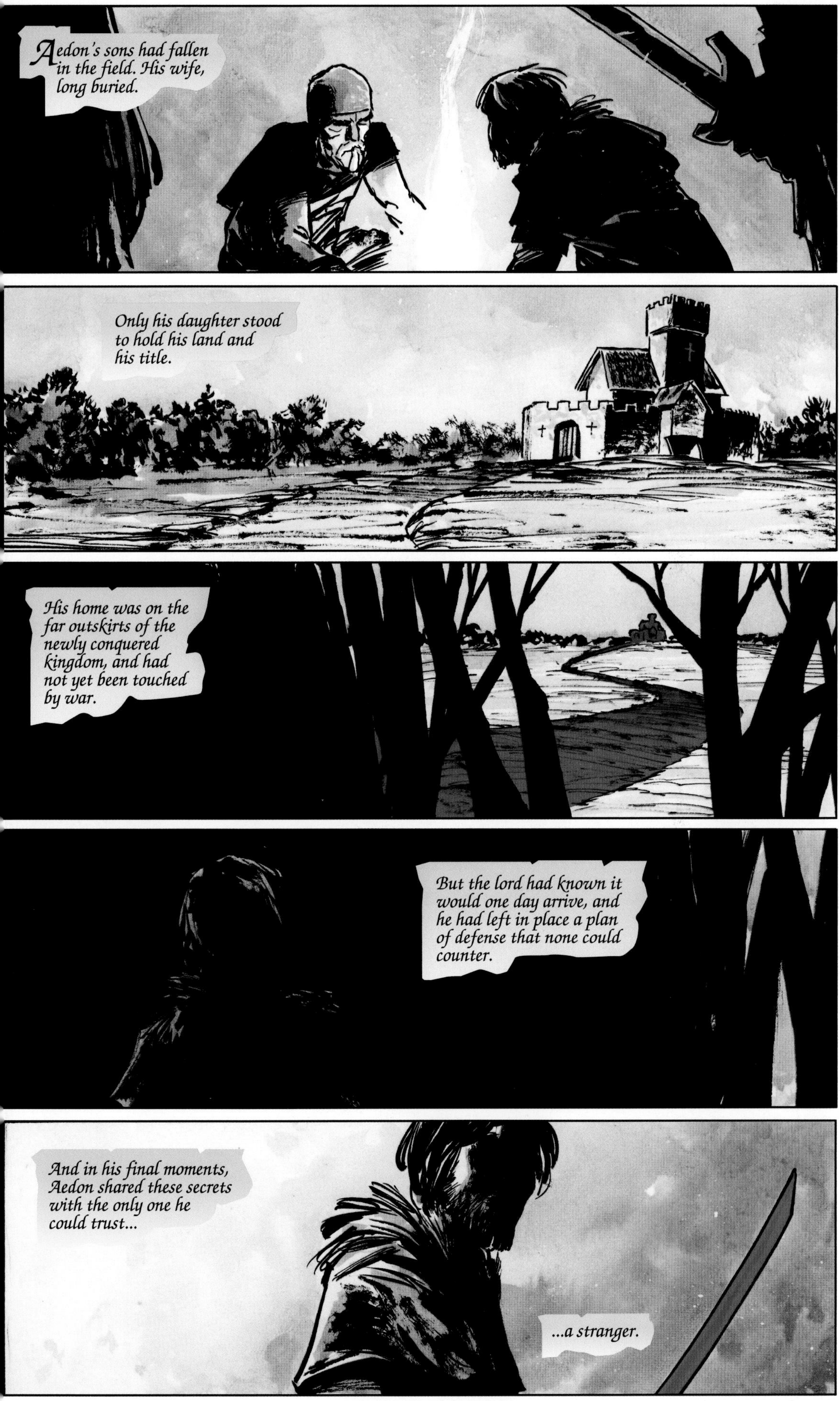
Aedon's sons had fallen in the field. His wife, long buried.
Only his daughter stood to hold his land and his title.
His home was on the far outskirts of the newly conquered kingdom, and had not yet been touched by war.
But the lord had known it would one day arrive, and he had left in place a plan of defense that none could counter.
And in his final moments, Aedon shared these secrets with the only one he could trust...
...a stranger.

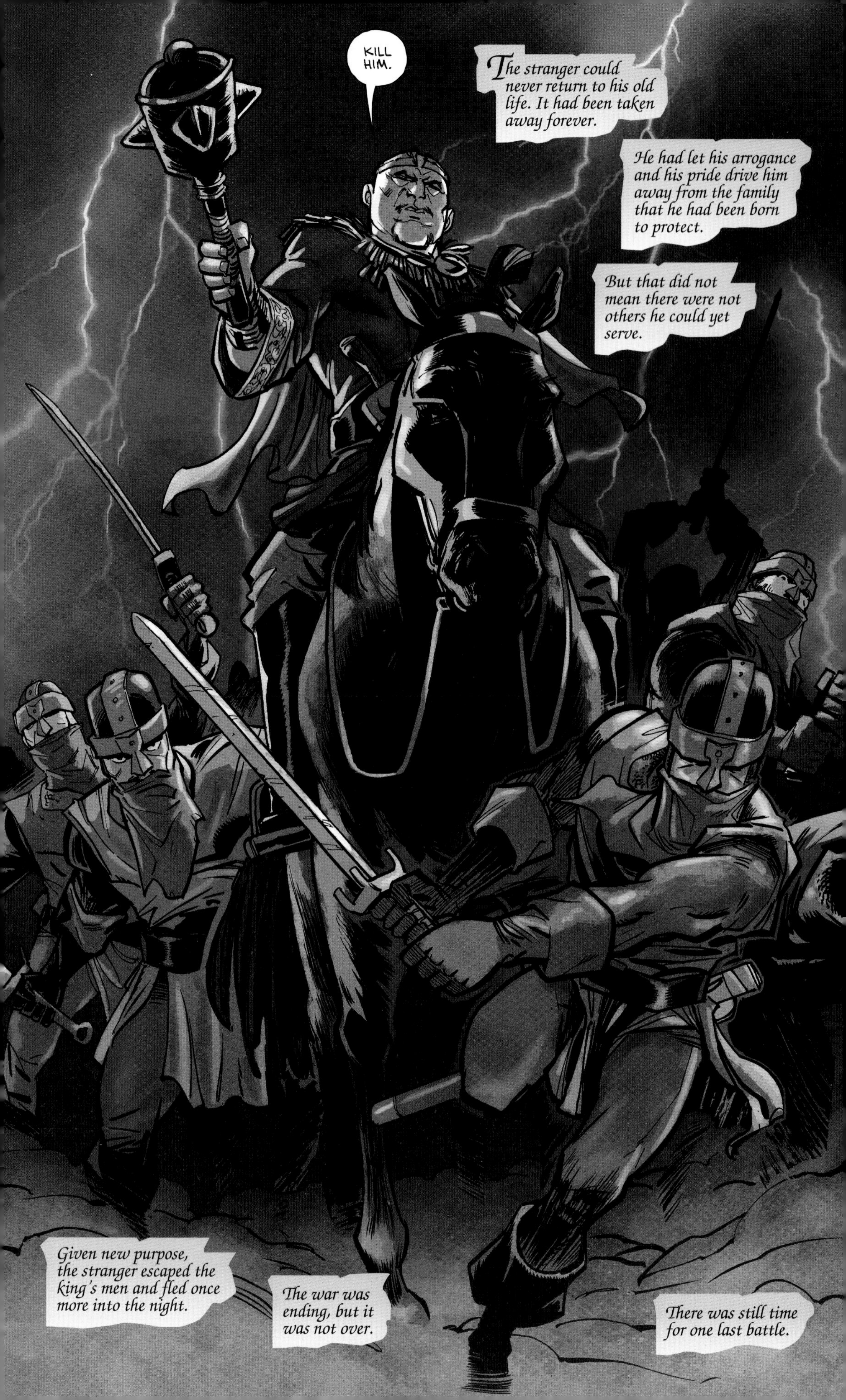
KILL HIM.
The stranger could never return to his old life. It had been taken away forever.
He had let his arrogance and his pride drive him away from the family that he had been born to protect.
But that did not mean there were not others he could yet serve.
Given new purpose, the stranger escaped the king's men and fled once more into the night.
The war was ending, but it was not over.
There was still time for one last battle.

The Two Swords

— Chapter 1 —

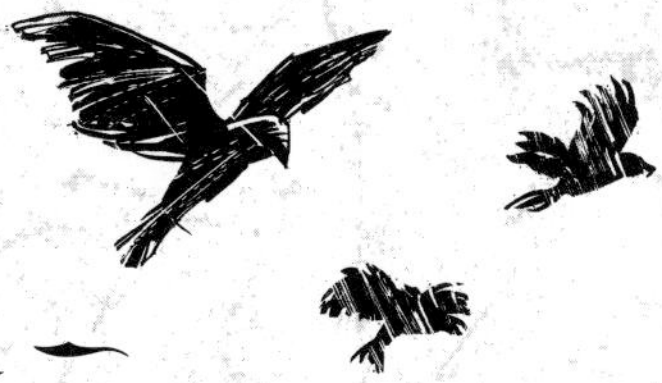

The light burned Tomislav's eyes.

He had been a prisoner for months now. The straw that offered the only comfort and warmth against the cold stone floor was matted and lice ridden. His legs and wrists were chained — a precaution taken after he had broken free of the first two cells in which they had locked him away. Each time, he had murdered more than a dozen of the king's men before being recaptured. The soldiers would beat him and curse him, but never kill him; he was meant to be kept alive. And the soldiers — they were more afraid of the wrath of Istvan than they were of their prisoner.

Istvan.

The name was like a slur on Tomislav's lips. His childhood friend had grown into a monster. The atrocities that the former peasant had committed were too great to count, and it had been Tomislav that had given the man the means to fuel his uprising.

The lock on the door turned. It had been days since anyone had opened that door, and his jailers typically did so only in darkness — another of Istvan's little games. He had visited frequently in the beginning, his vile face made no less hateful under the weight of that broken gold crown he wore, claiming it as a symbol of his heritage.

"We could have been allies," Istvan had said during that first visit, as if such a thing were possible. Tomislav had returned home and witnessed the atrocities that the man who had been his friend had committed. And from that day he began a one-man crusade, all the while tormented by visions of the death of his mother... his father... his sister...

Finally, after killing his way through several of Istvan's chief lieutenants, he had found himself in striking distance of the self-proclaimed king.

But their numbers had been too great, and he was lost. Cast into this pit.

And now... something had changed. The men at the door — they were not his jailers. They were not of Istvan's army.

An older man stepped forward. His bearing was strong, but his eyes looked tired. In his hands he held two swords. Twin blades forged from iron sand, curved, and razor sharp. They were artifacts of a former life that Tomislav never believed he would have a chance to revisit.

They were the swords of his father.

"I am Lord Aedon," the man spoke, "and I believe we can help each other."

THE LAST SIEGE

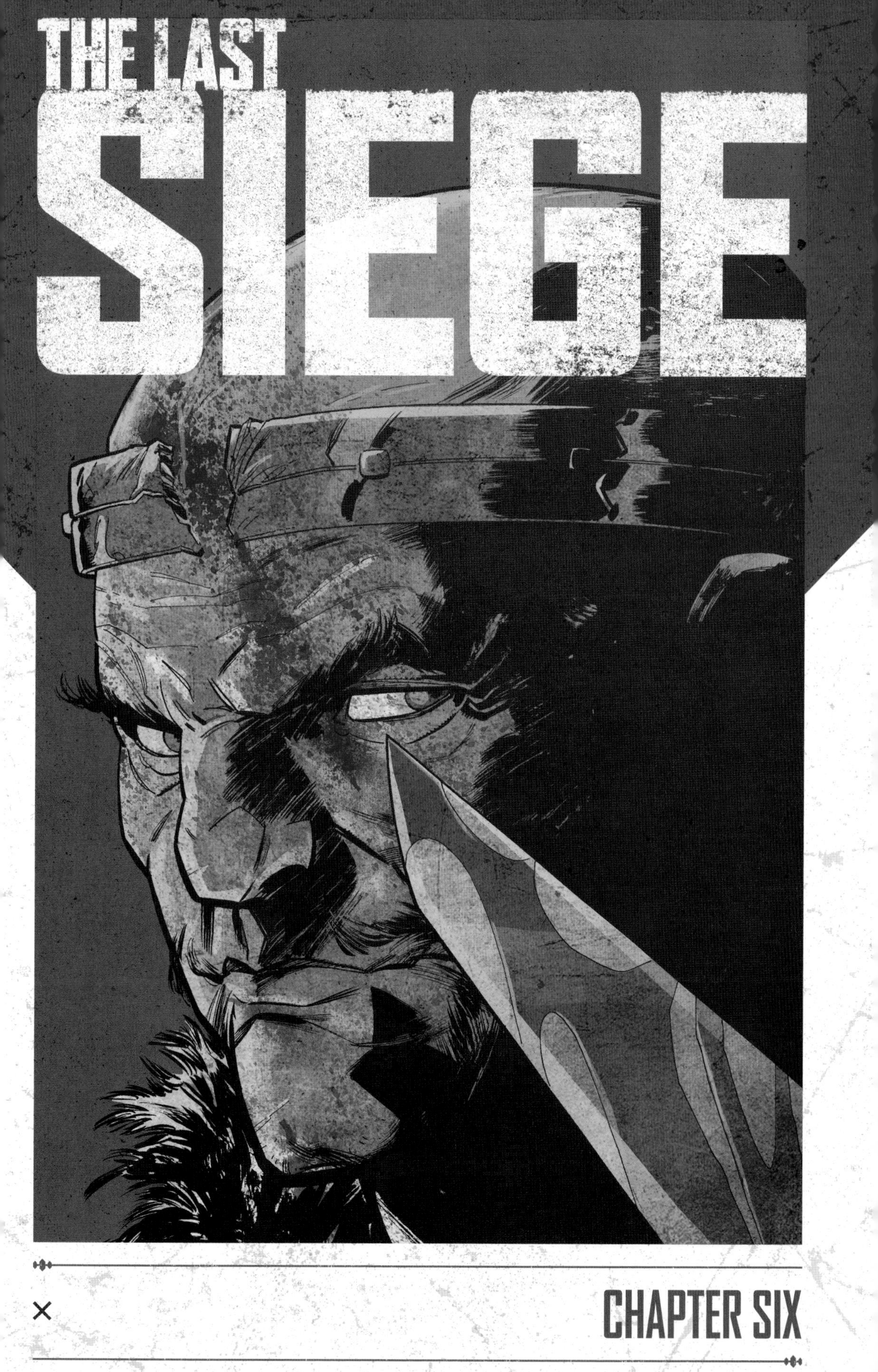

CHAPTER SIX

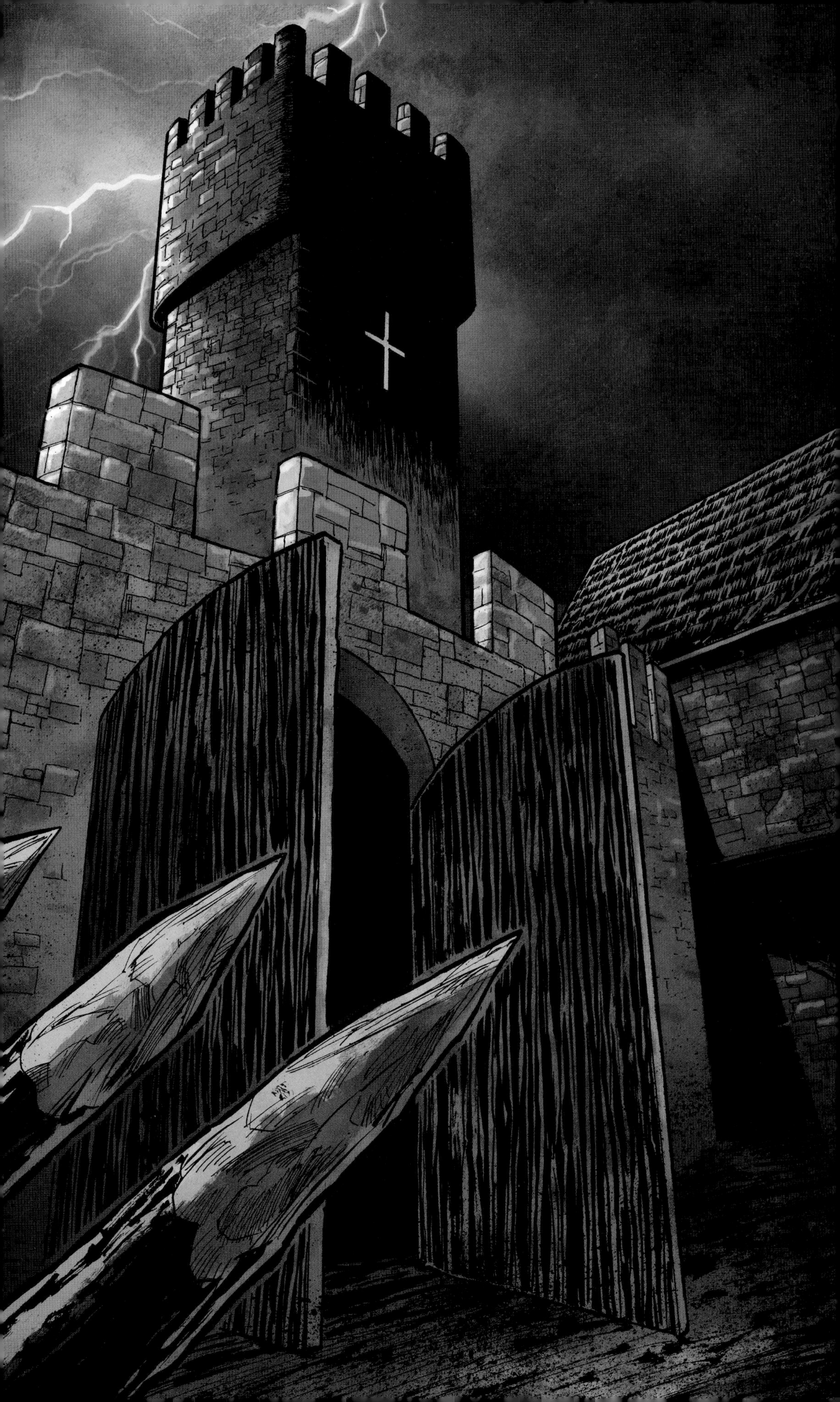

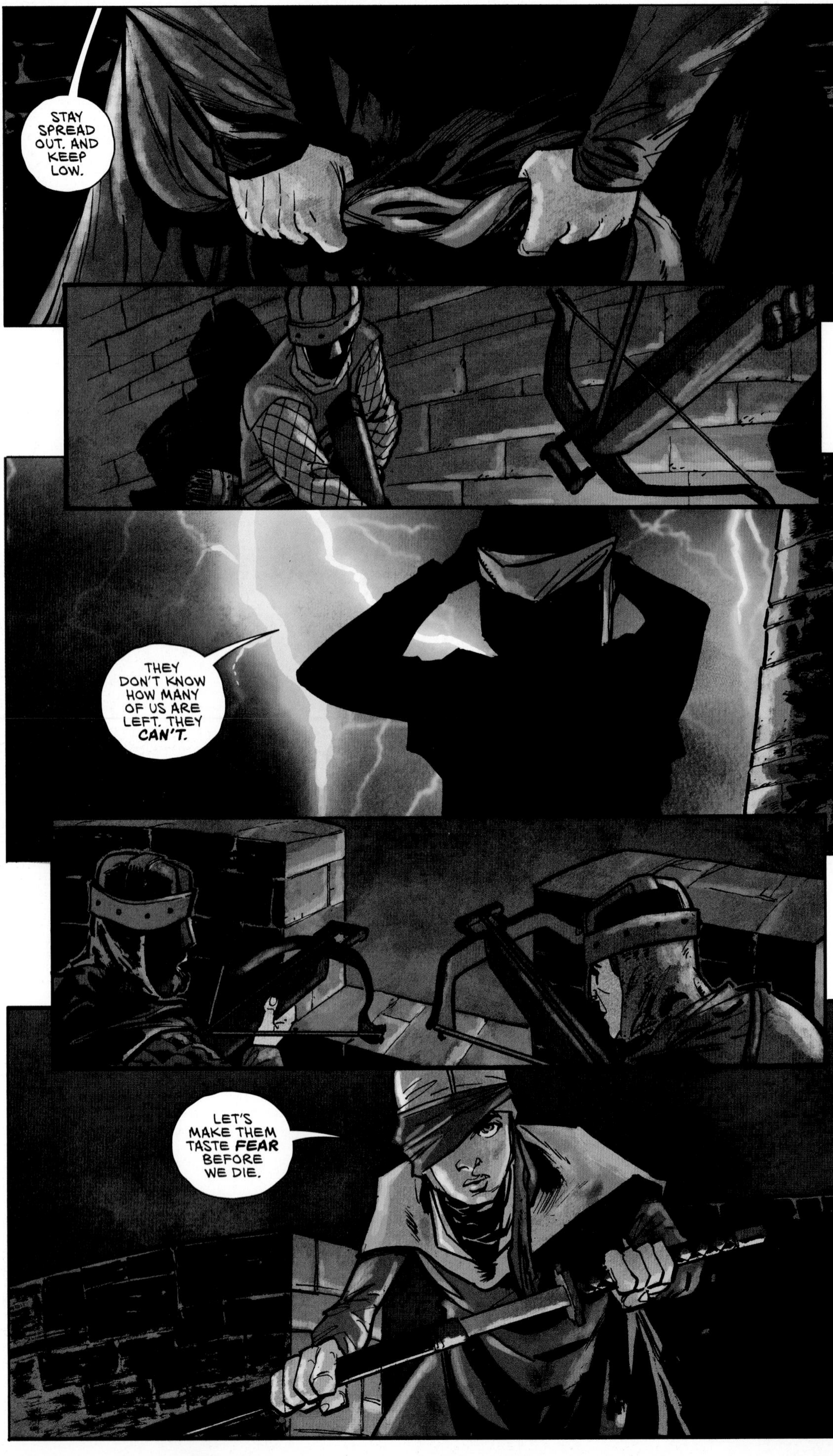

STAY SPREAD OUT. AND KEEP LOW.
THEY DON'T KNOW HOW MANY OF US ARE LEFT. THEY **CAN'T.**
LET'S MAKE THEM TASTE **FEAR** BEFORE WE DIE.

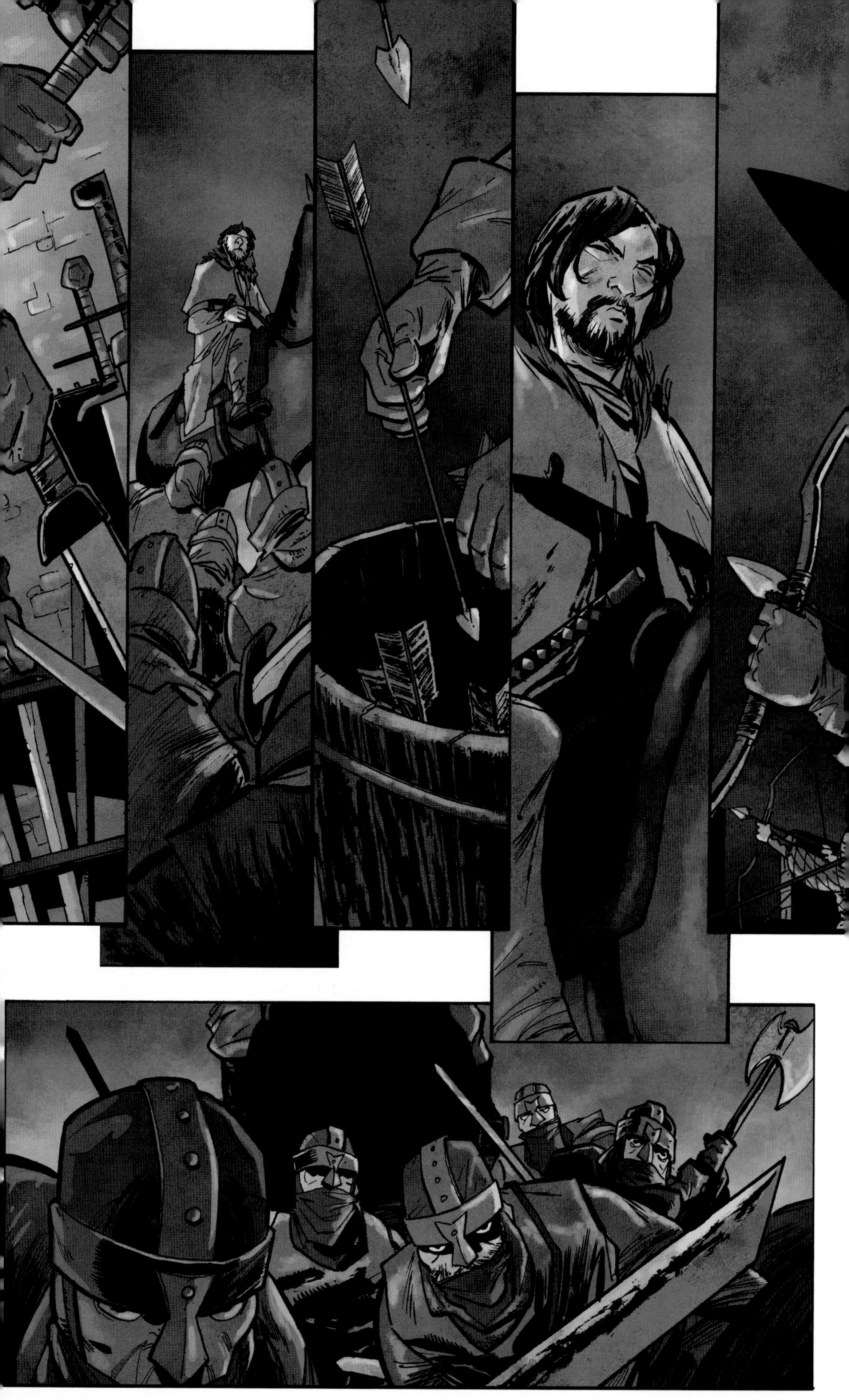

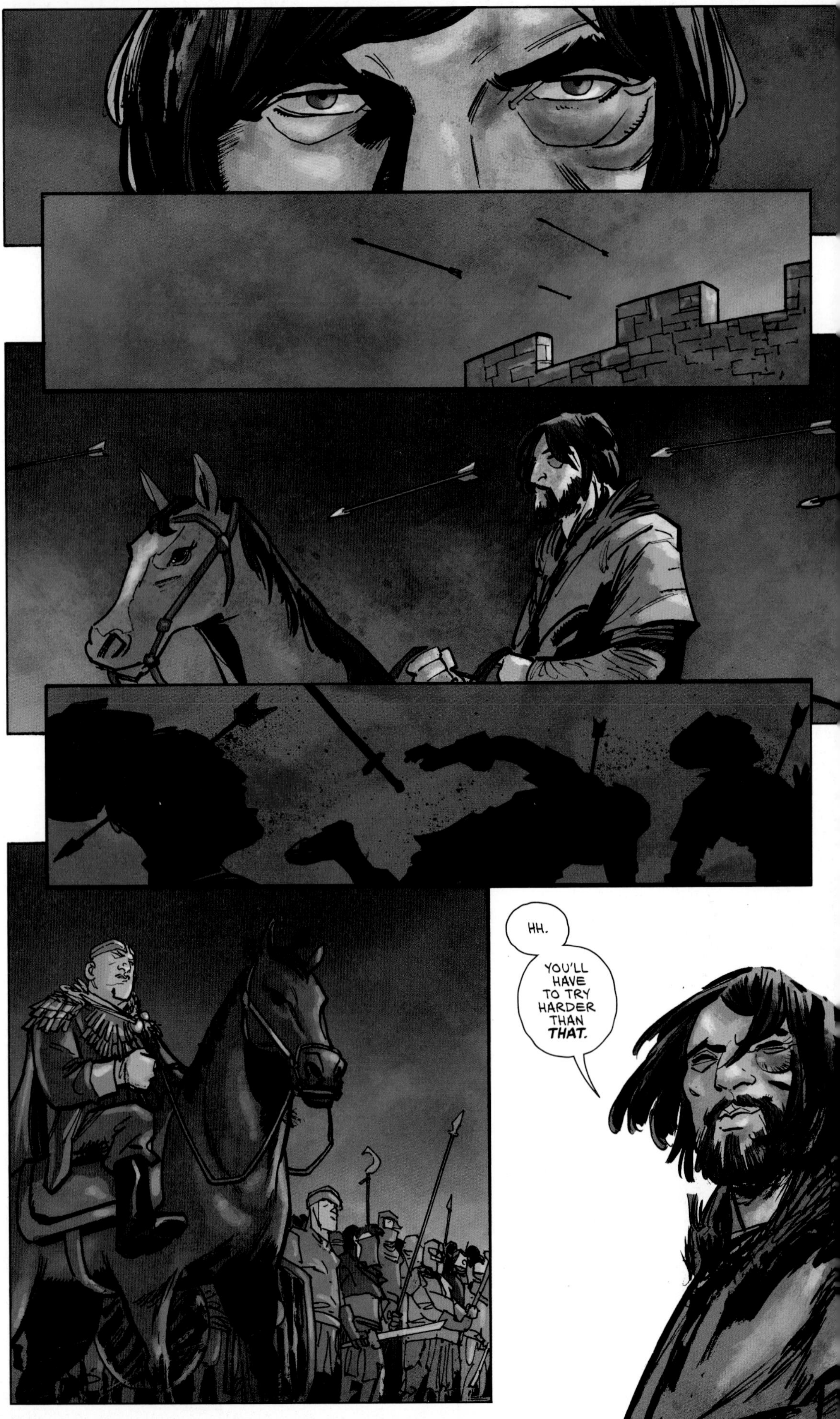
HH.
YOU'LL HAVE TO TRY HARDER THAN *THAT.*

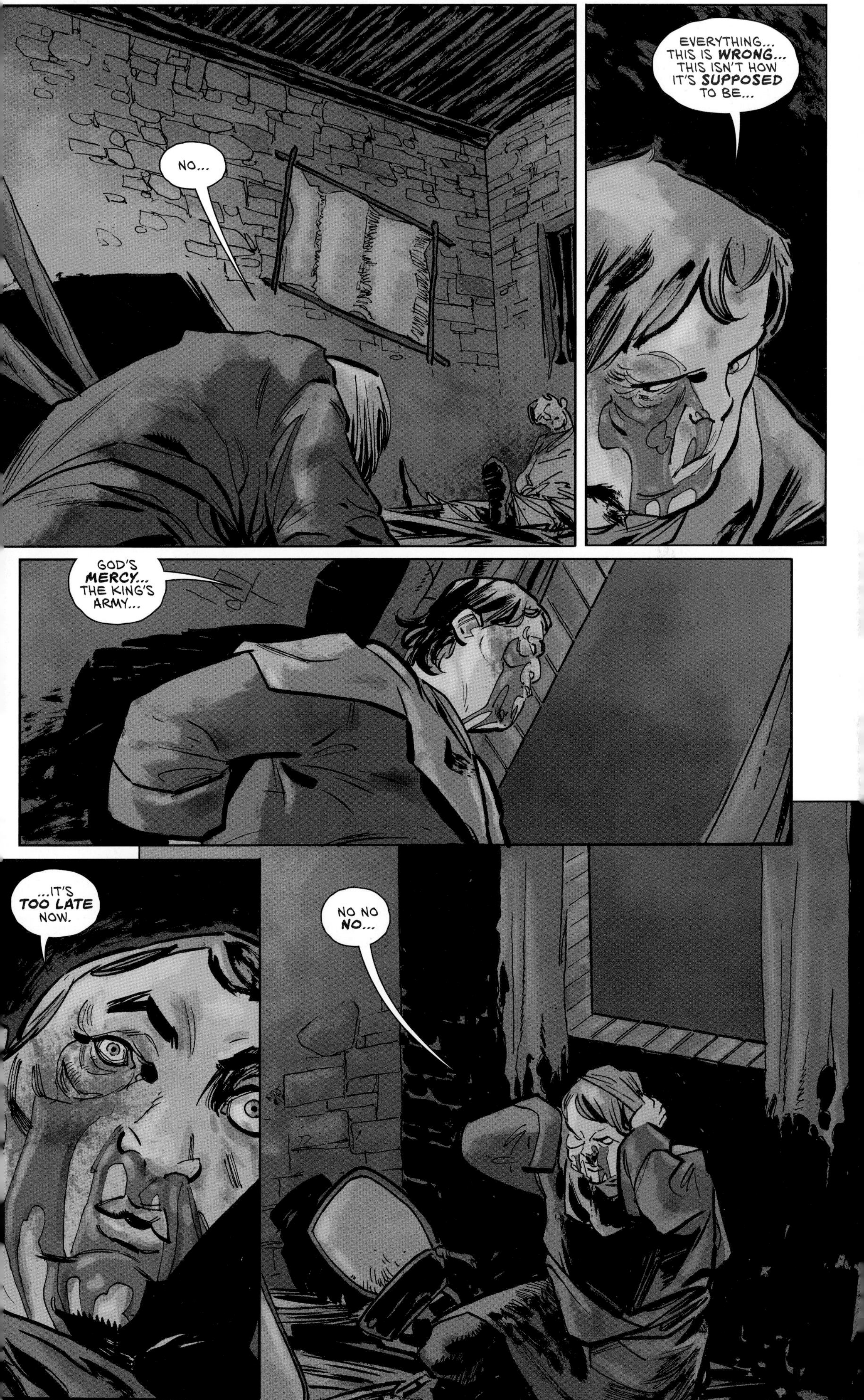
NO...
EVERYTHING... THIS IS WRONG... THIS ISN'T HOW IT'S SUPPOSED TO BE...
GOD'S MERCY... THE KING'S ARMY...
...IT'S TOO LATE NOW.
NO NO NO...

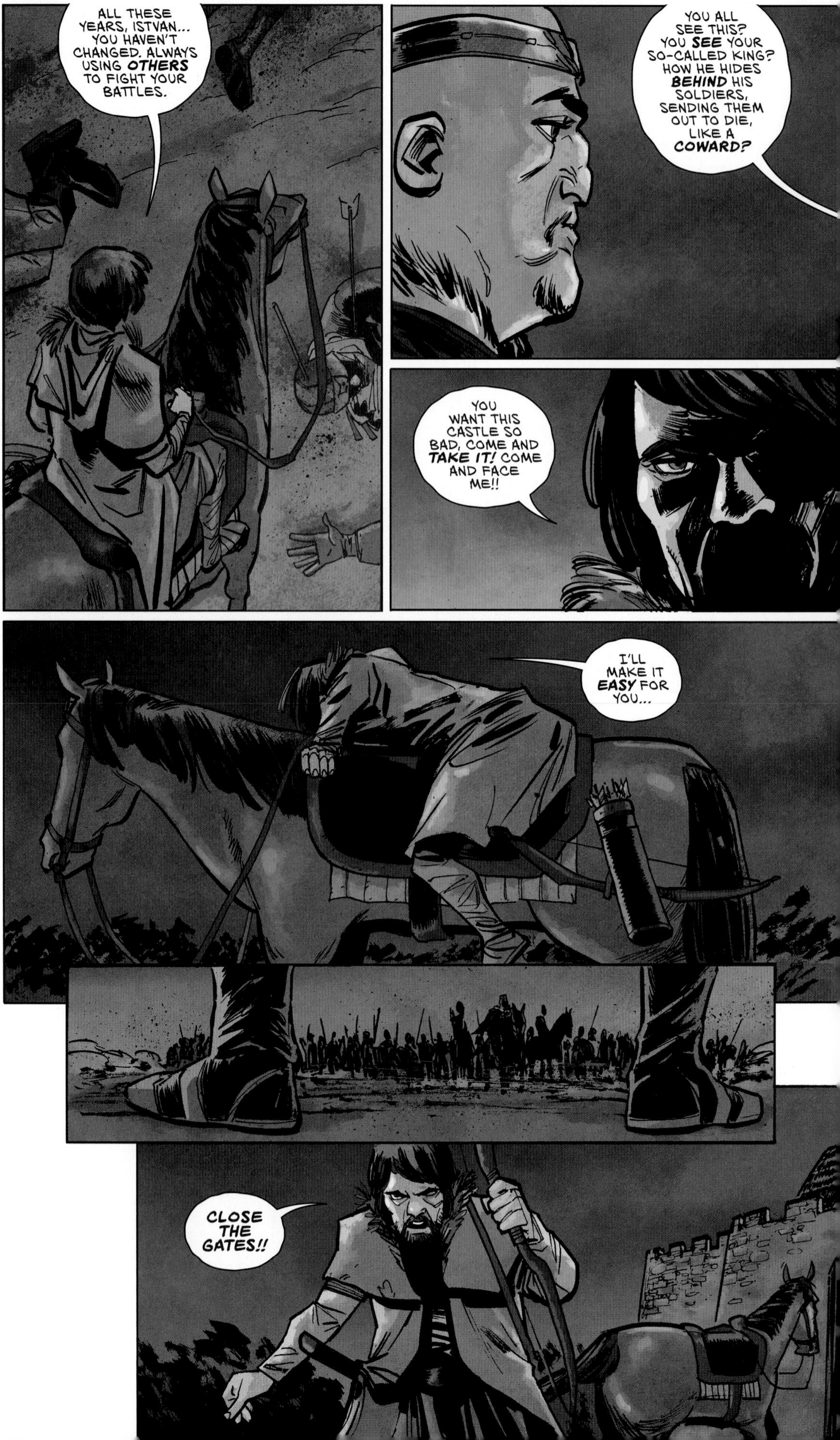
ALL THESE YEARS, ISTVAN... YOU HAVEN'T CHANGED. ALWAYS USING **OTHERS** TO FIGHT YOUR BATTLES.
YOU ALL SEE THIS? YOU **SEE** YOUR SO-CALLED KING? HOW HE HIDES **BEHIND** HIS SOLDIERS, SENDING THEM OUT TO DIE, LIKE A **COWARD?**
YOU WANT THIS CASTLE SO BAD, COME AND ***TAKE IT!*** COME AND FACE ME!!
I'LL MAKE IT ***EASY*** FOR YOU...
CLOSE THE GATES!!

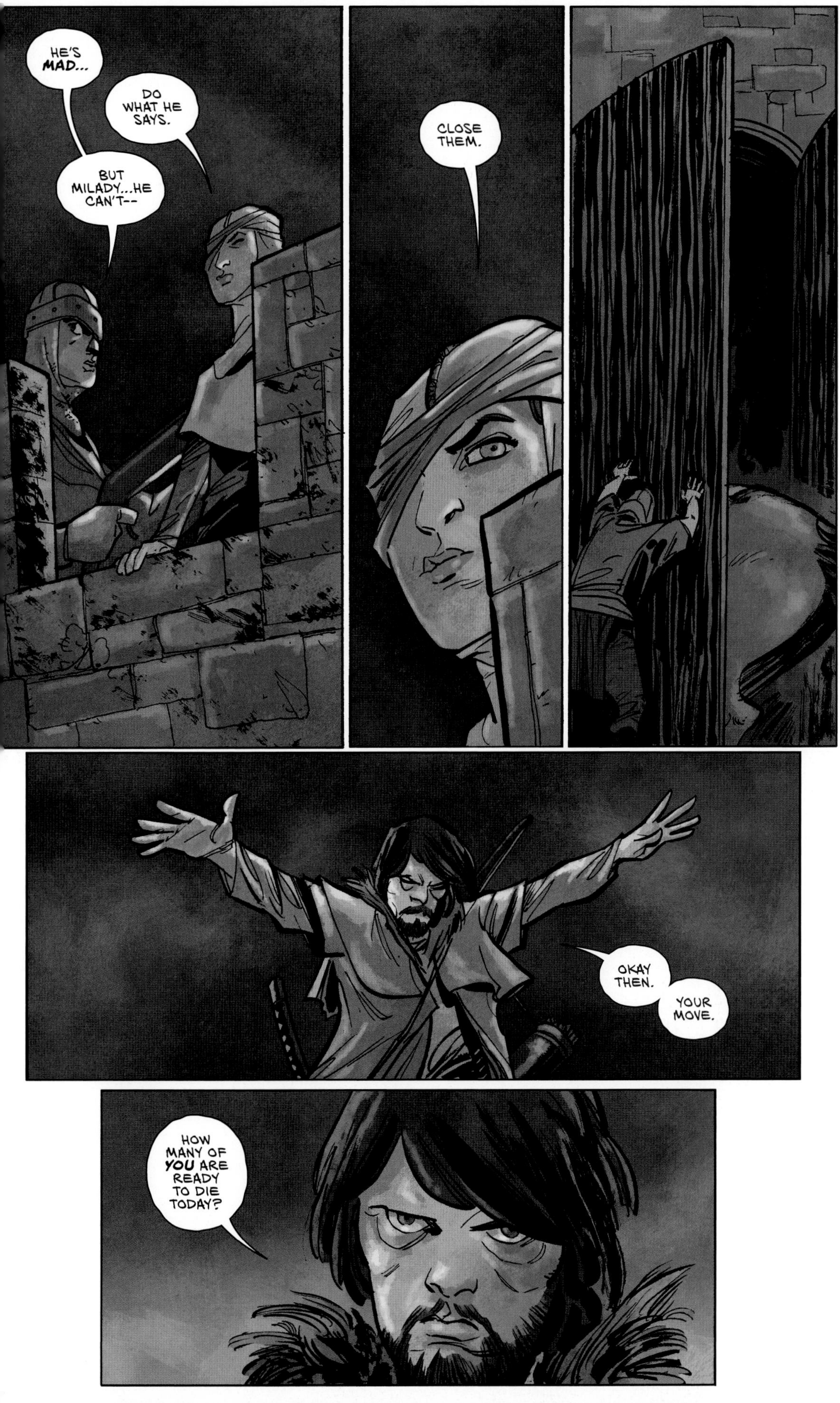
HE'S MAD...
DO WHAT HE SAYS.
BUT MILADY...HE CAN'T--
CLOSE THEM.
OKAY THEN.
YOUR MOVE.
HOW MANY OF YOU ARE READY TO DIE TODAY?

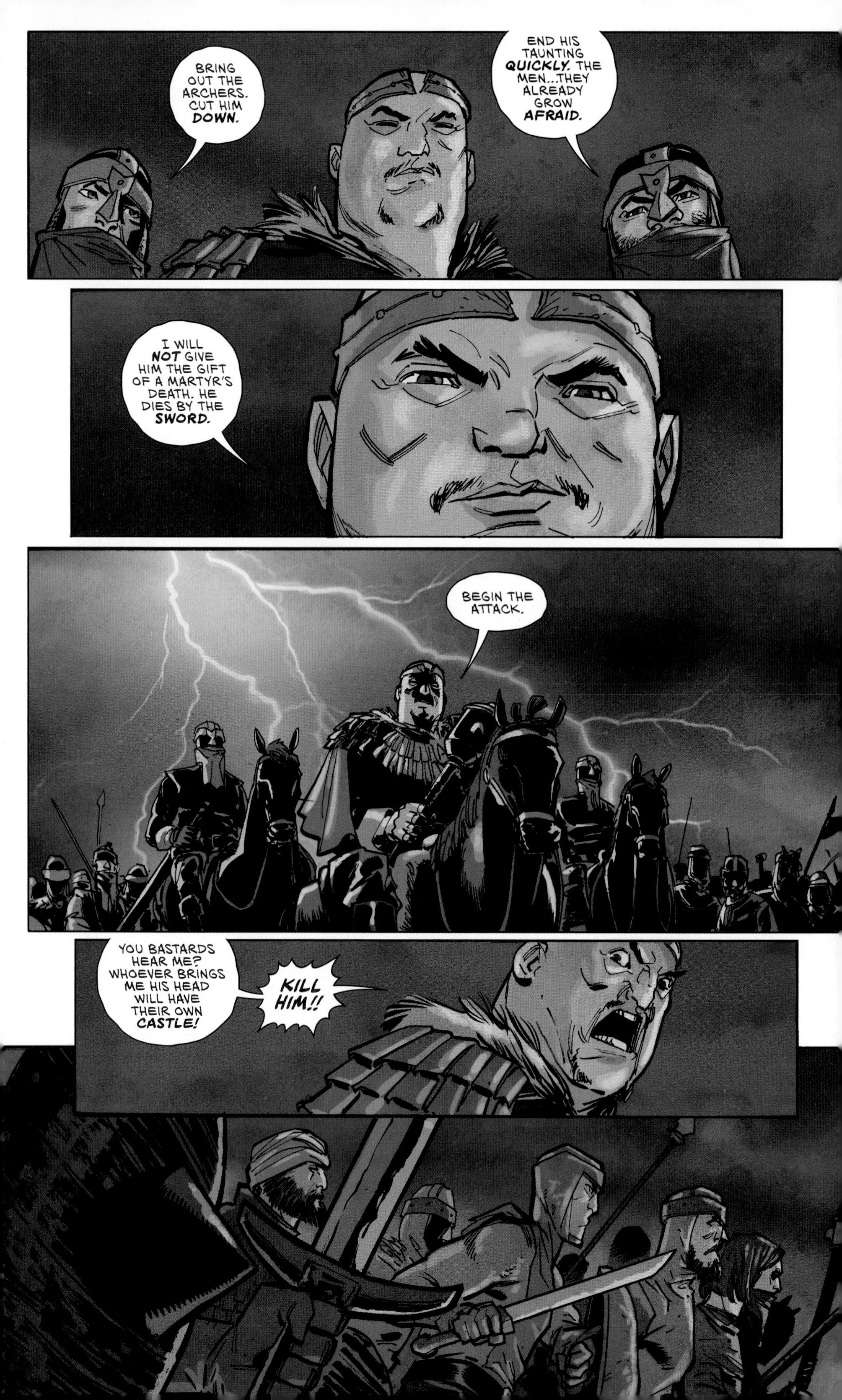
BRING OUT THE ARCHERS. CUT HIM DOWN.
END HIS TAUNTING QUICKLY. THE MEN...THEY ALREADY GROW AFRAID.
I WILL NOT GIVE HIM THE GIFT OF A MARTYR'S DEATH. HE DIES BY THE SWORD.
BEGIN THE ATTACK.
YOU BASTARDS HEAR ME? WHOEVER BRINGS ME HIS HEAD WILL HAVE THEIR OWN CASTLE!
KILL HIM!!

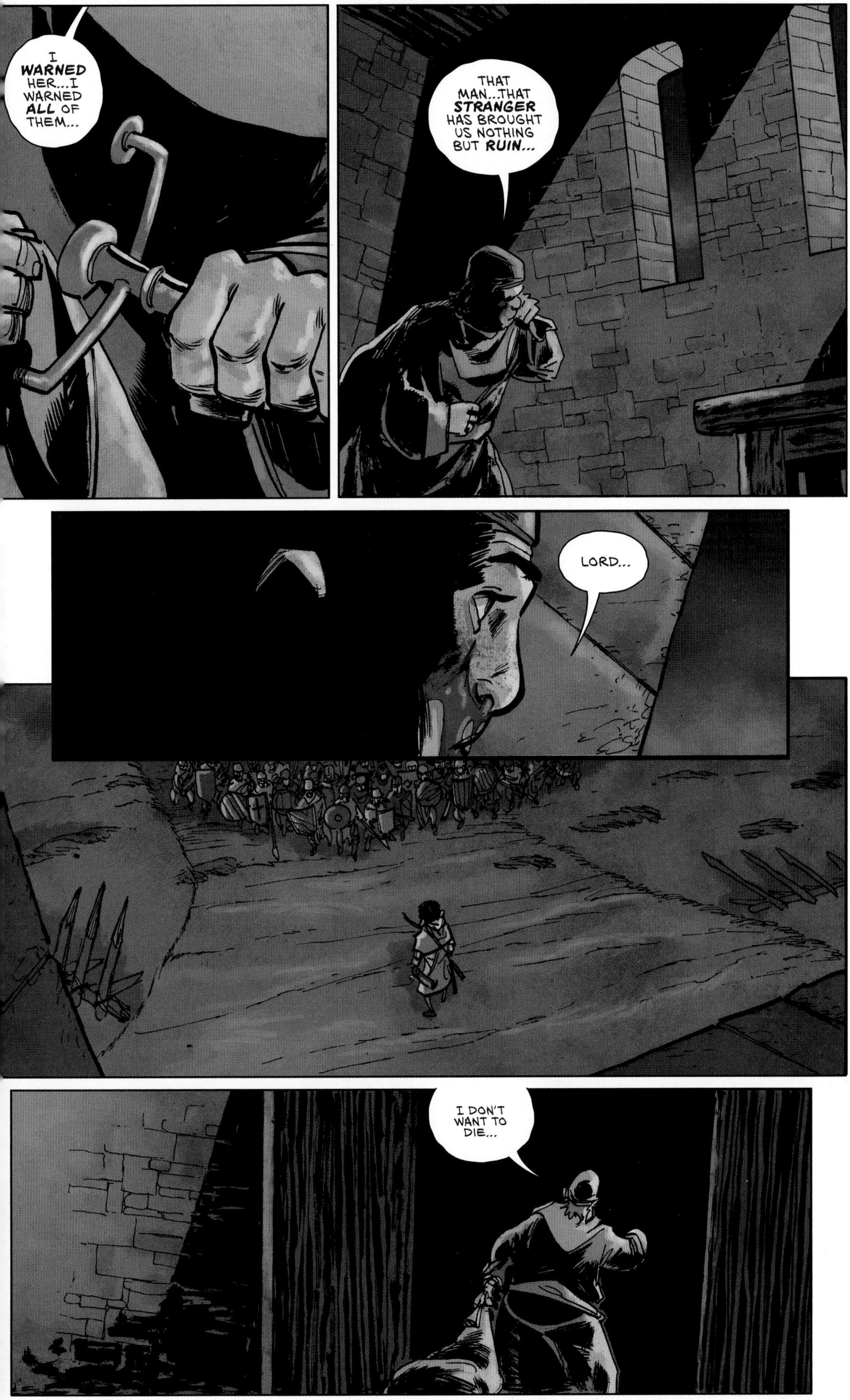
I WARNED HER...I WARNED ALL OF THEM...
THAT MAN...THAT STRANGER HAS BROUGHT US NOTHING BUT RUIN...
LORD...
I DON'T WANT TO DIE...

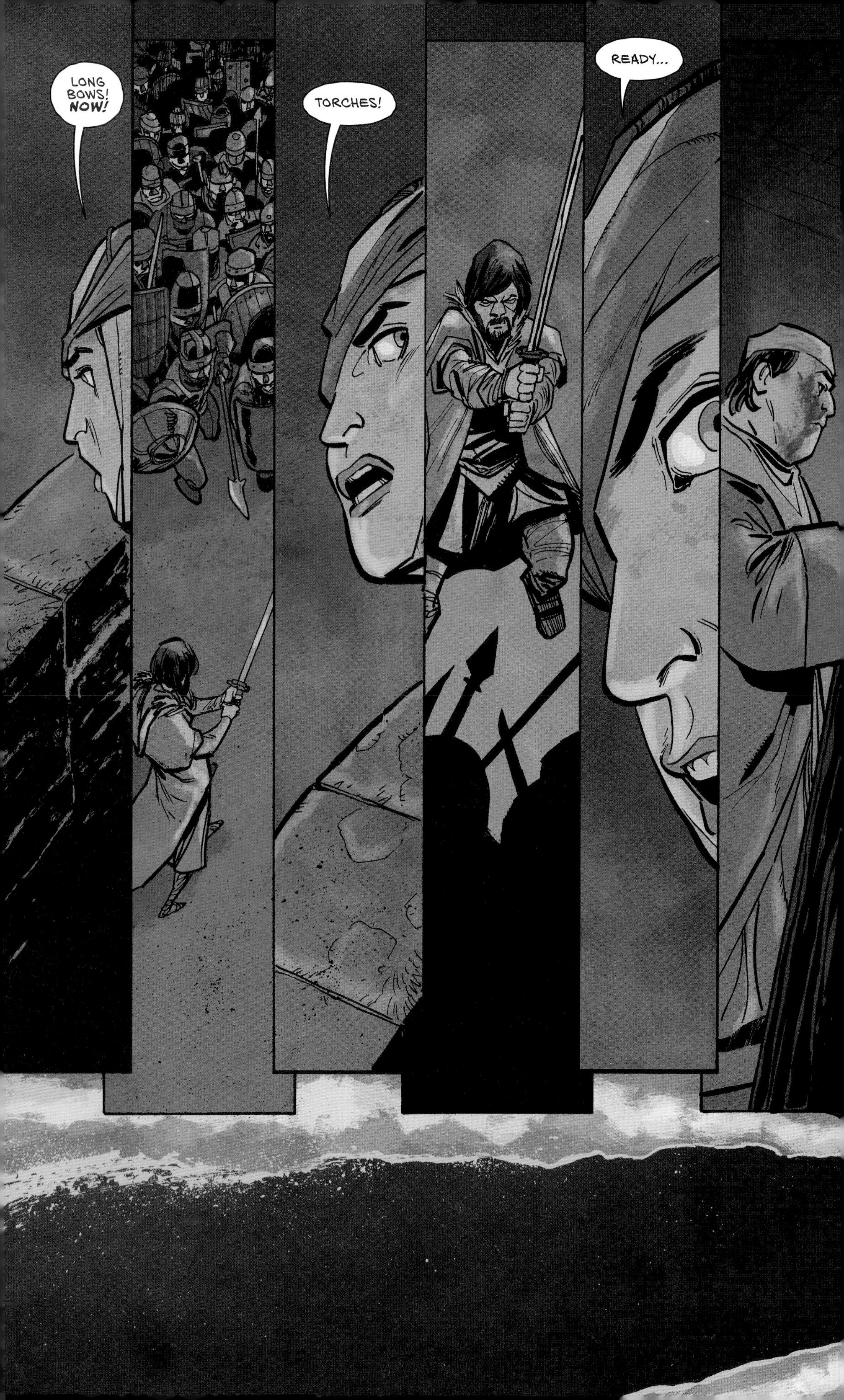
LONG BOWS! NOW!
TORCHES!
READY...

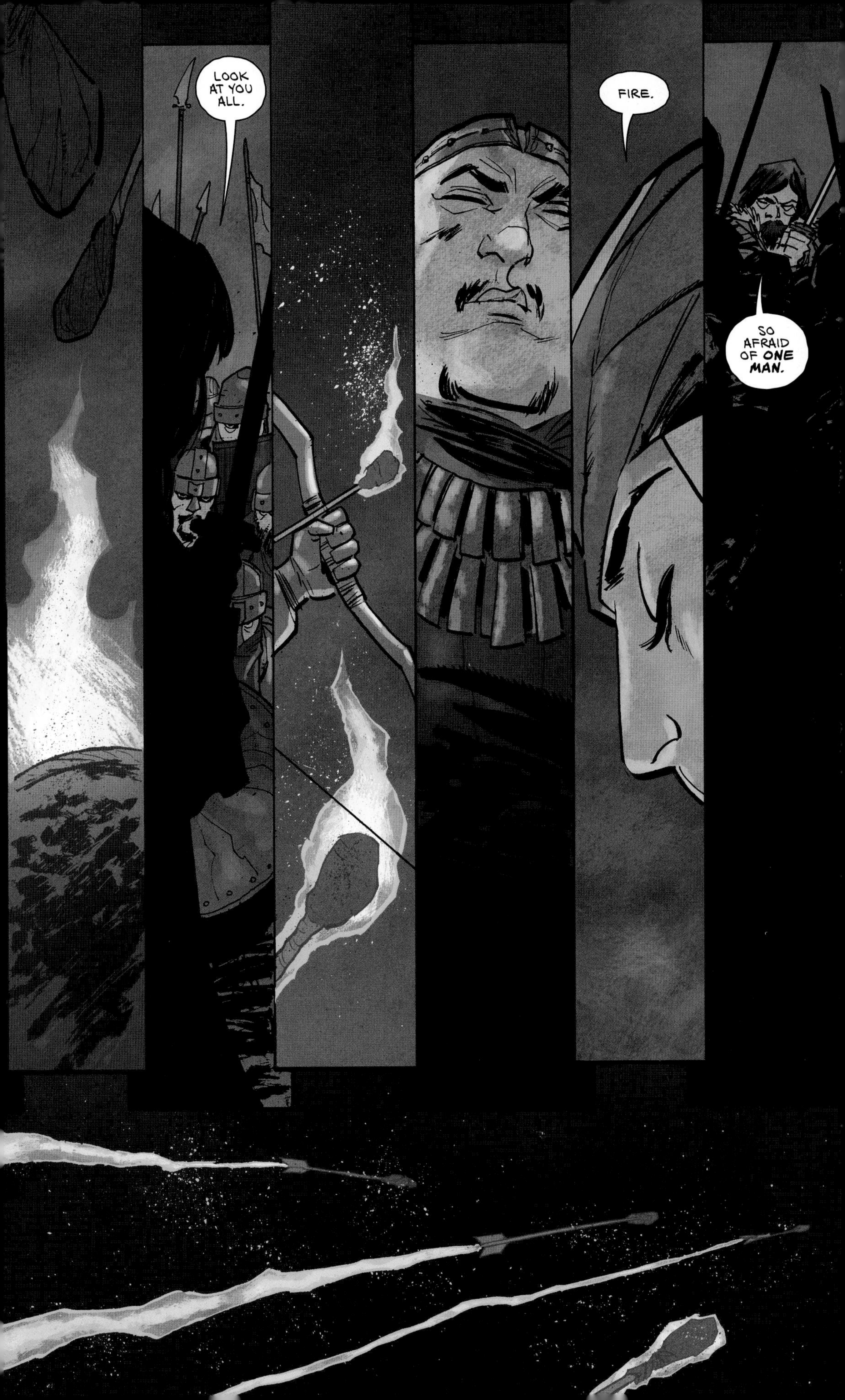
LOOK AT YOU ALL.
FIRE.
SO AFRAID OF ONE MAN.

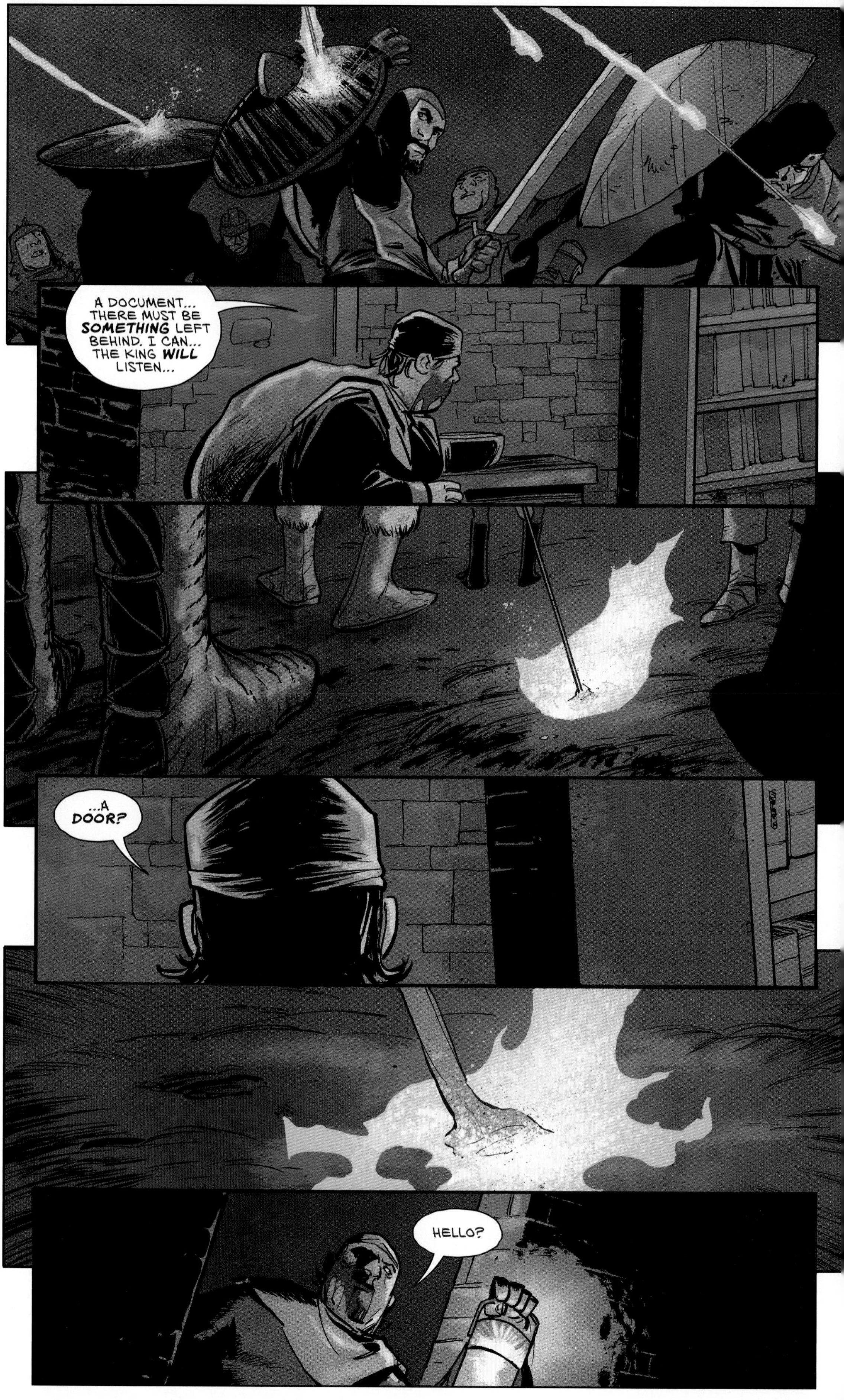
A DOCUMENT... THERE MUST BE SOMETHING LEFT BEHIND. I CAN... THE KING WILL LISTEN...
...A DOOR?
HELLO?

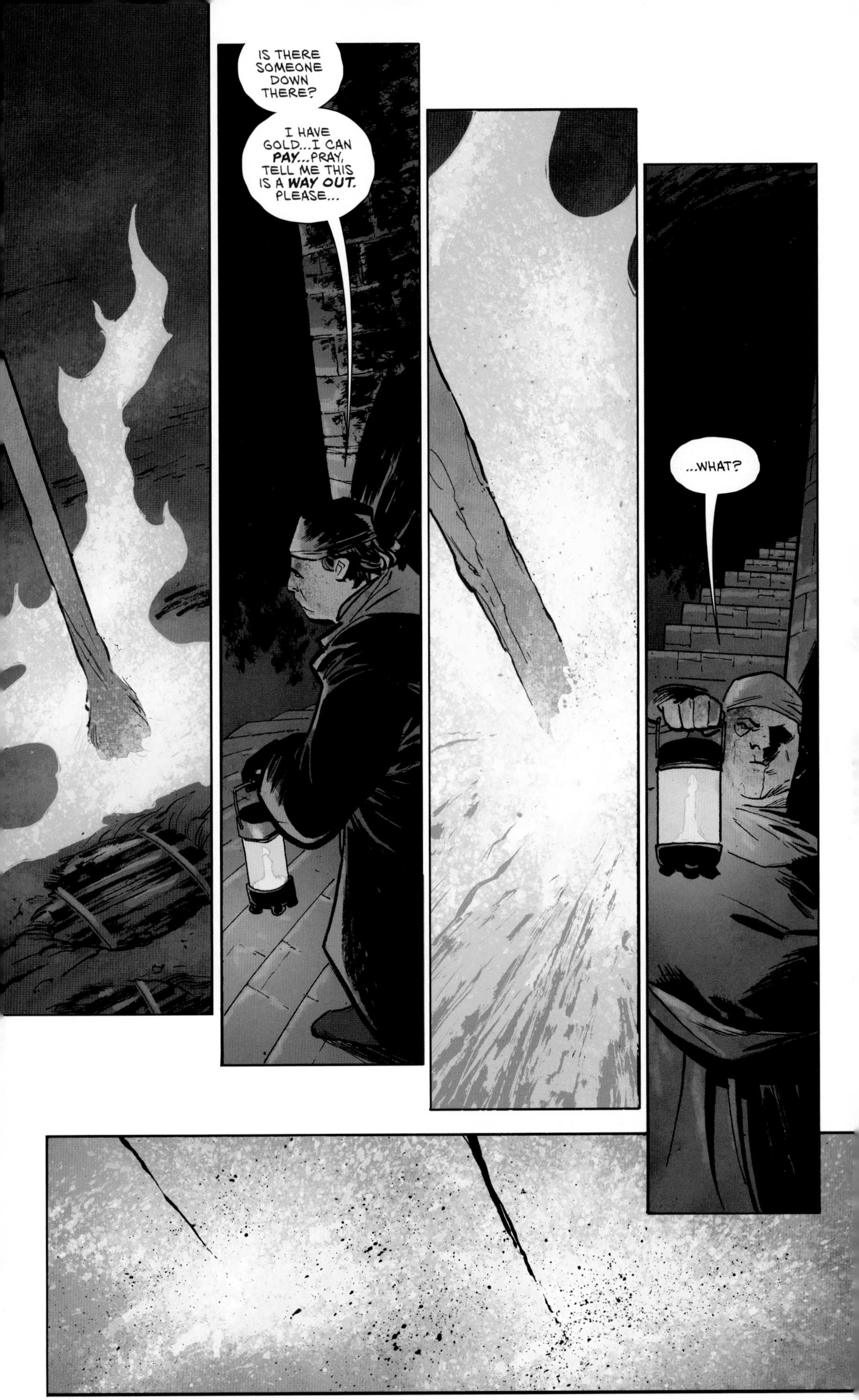
IS THERE SOMEONE DOWN THERE?
I HAVE GOLD...I CAN PAY...PRAY, TELL ME THIS IS A WAY OUT. PLEASE...
...WHAT?

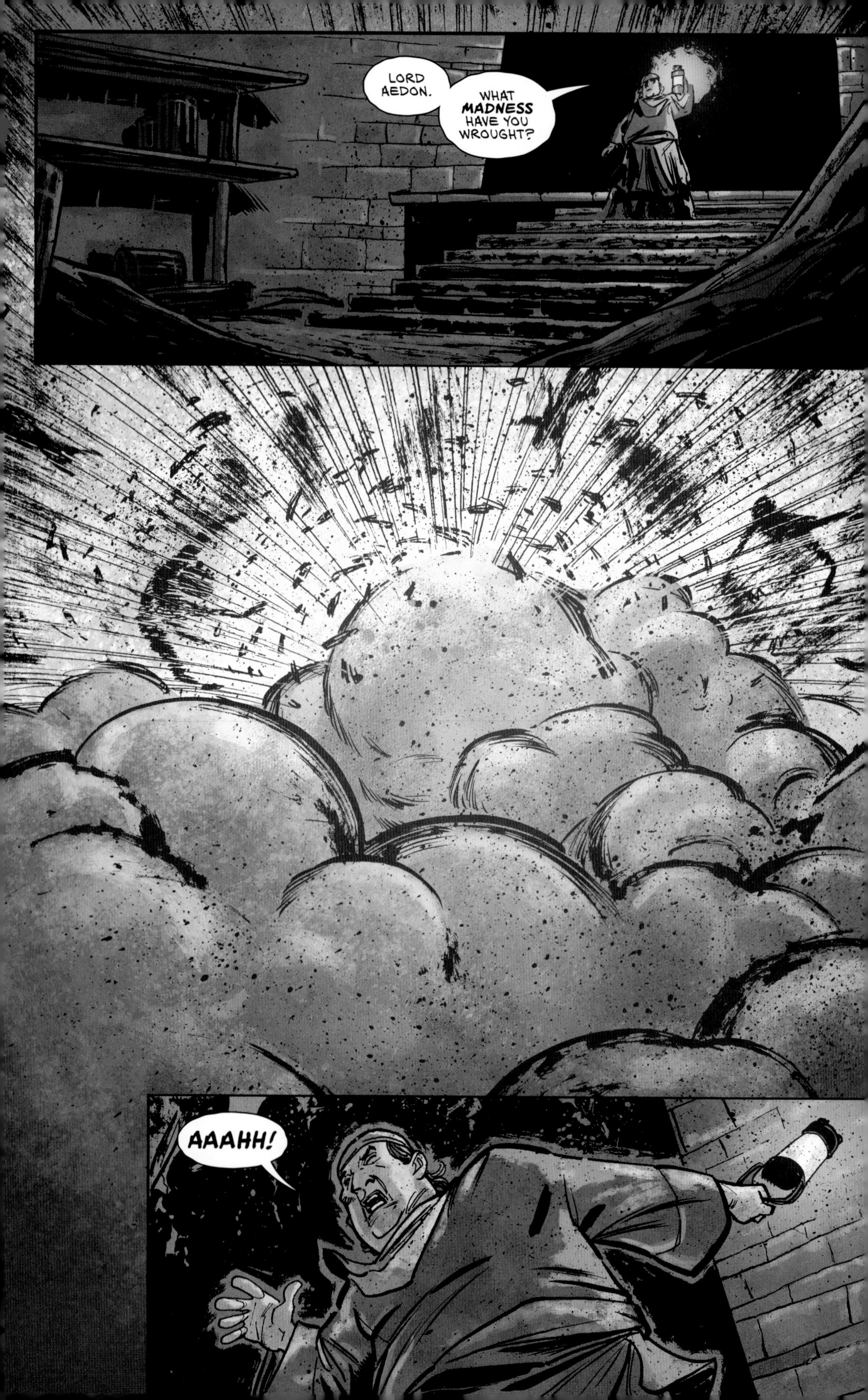
LORD AEDON.
WHAT MADNESS HAVE YOU WROUGHT?
AAAHH!

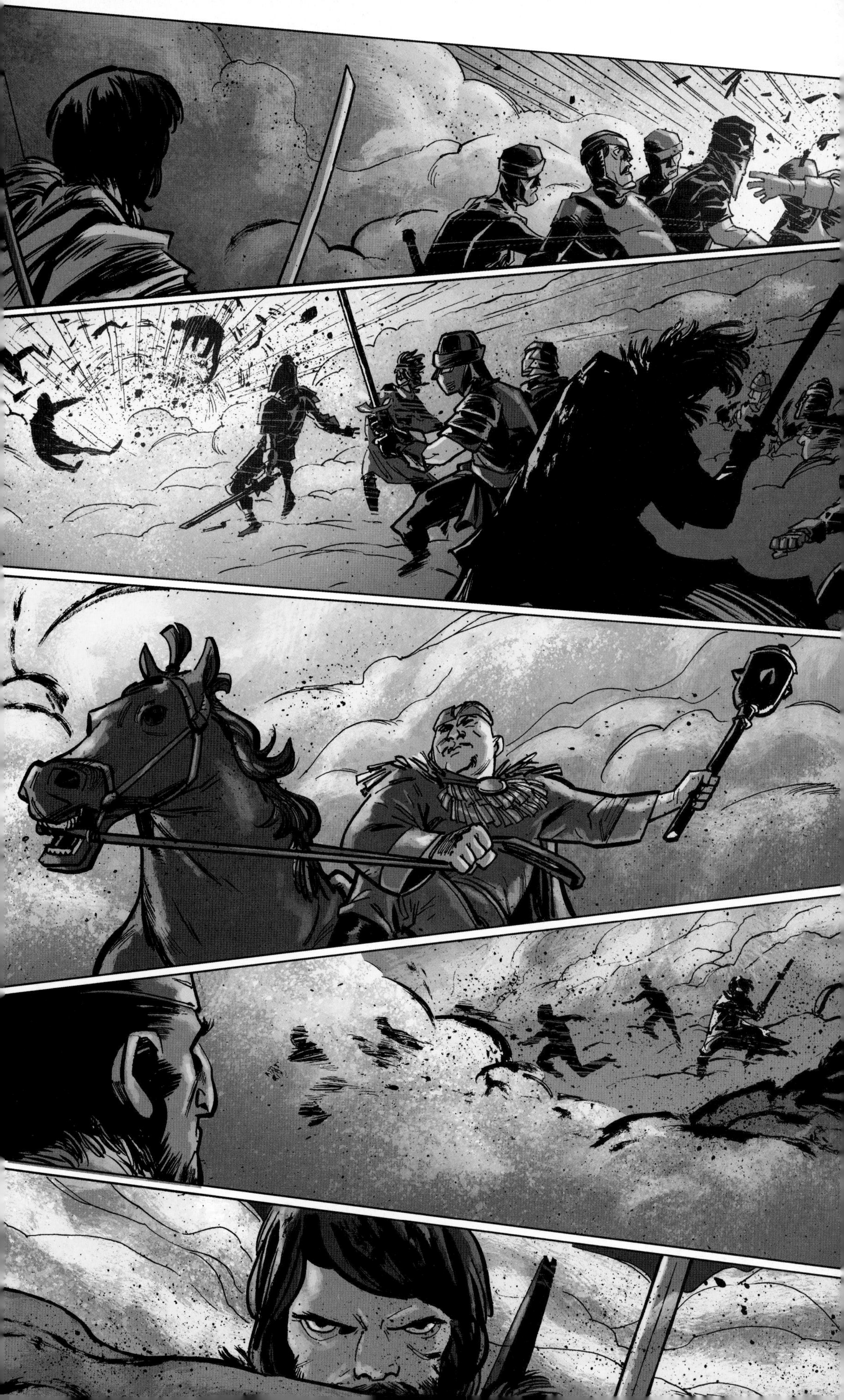

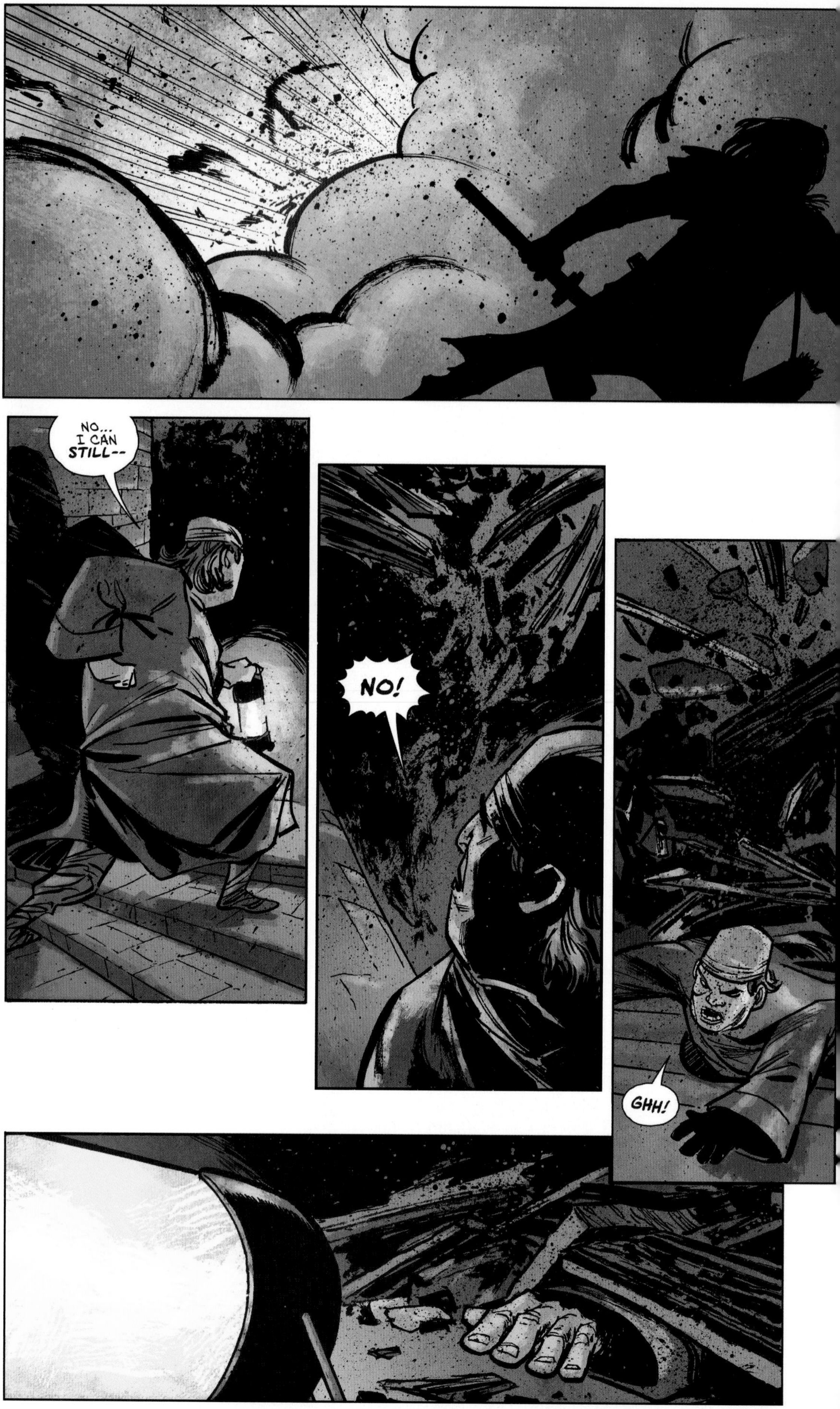
NO... I CAN STILL--
NO!
GHH!

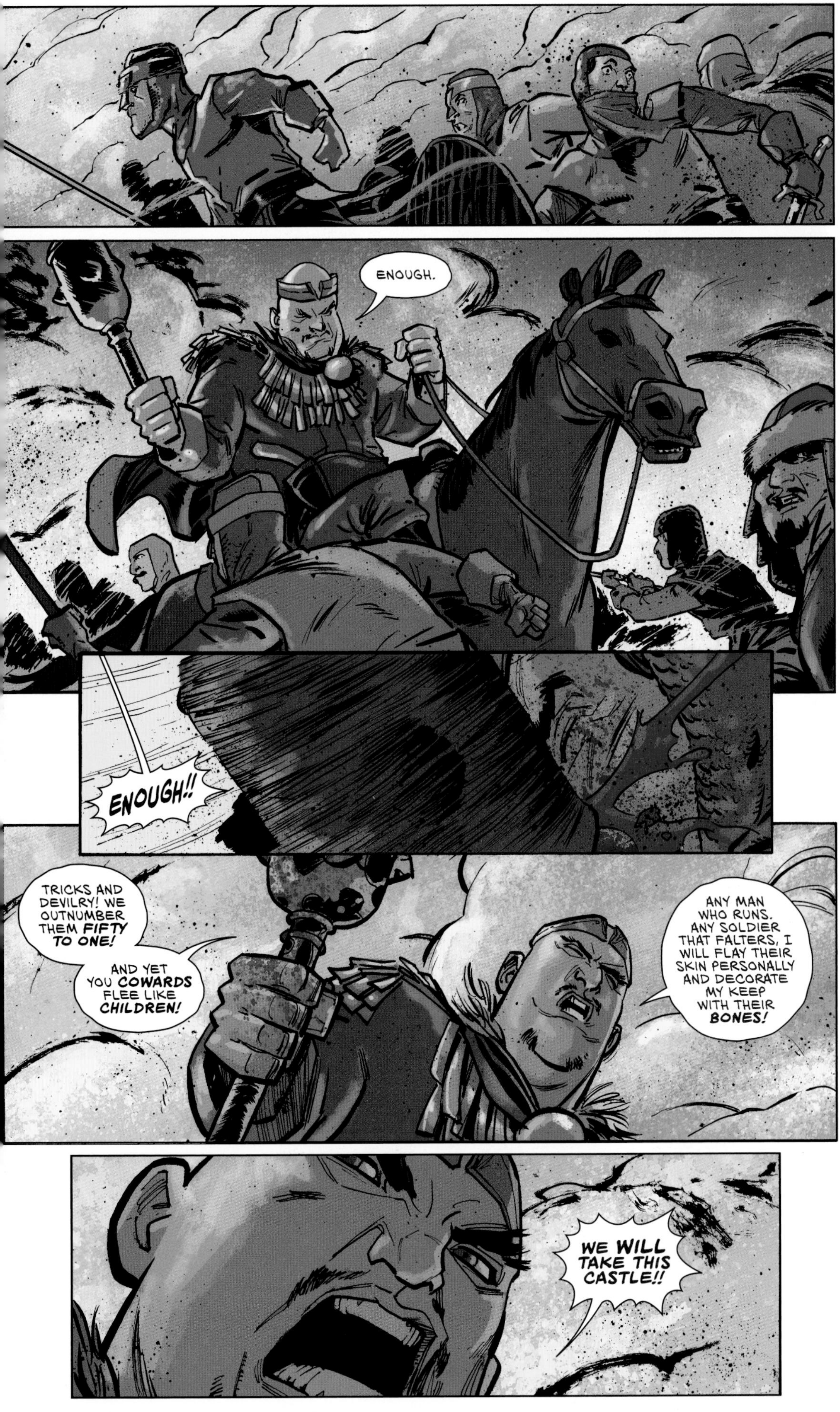
ENOUGH.
ENOUGH!!
TRICKS AND DEVILRY! WE OUTNUMBER THEM FIFTY TO ONE!
AND YET YOU COWARDS FLEE LIKE CHILDREN!
ANY MAN WHO RUNS. ANY SOLDIER THAT FALTERS, I WILL FLAY THEIR SKIN PERSONALLY AND DECORATE MY KEEP WITH THEIR BONES!
WE WILL TAKE THIS CASTLE!!

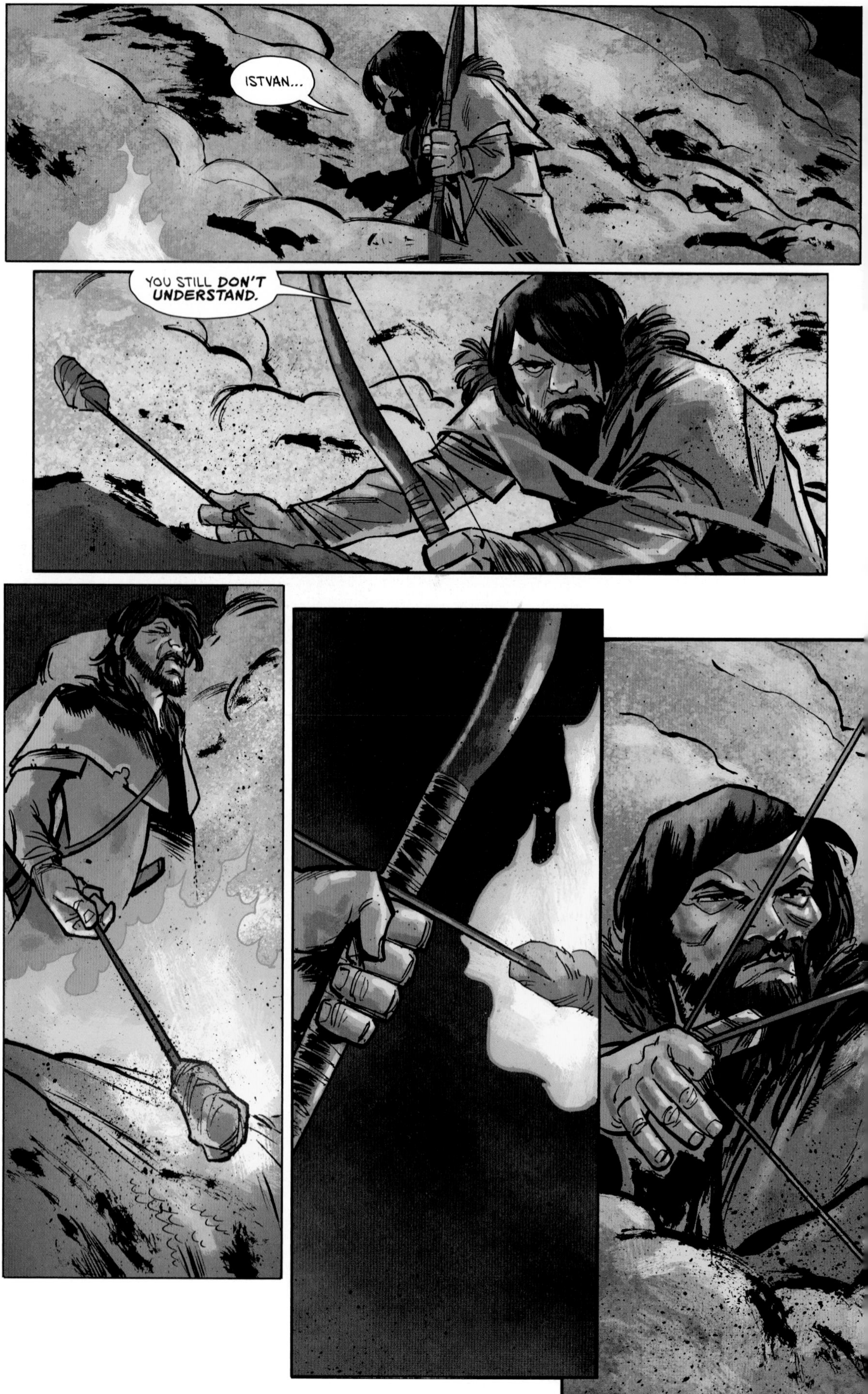
ISTVAN...
YOU STILL **DON'T UNDERSTAND.**

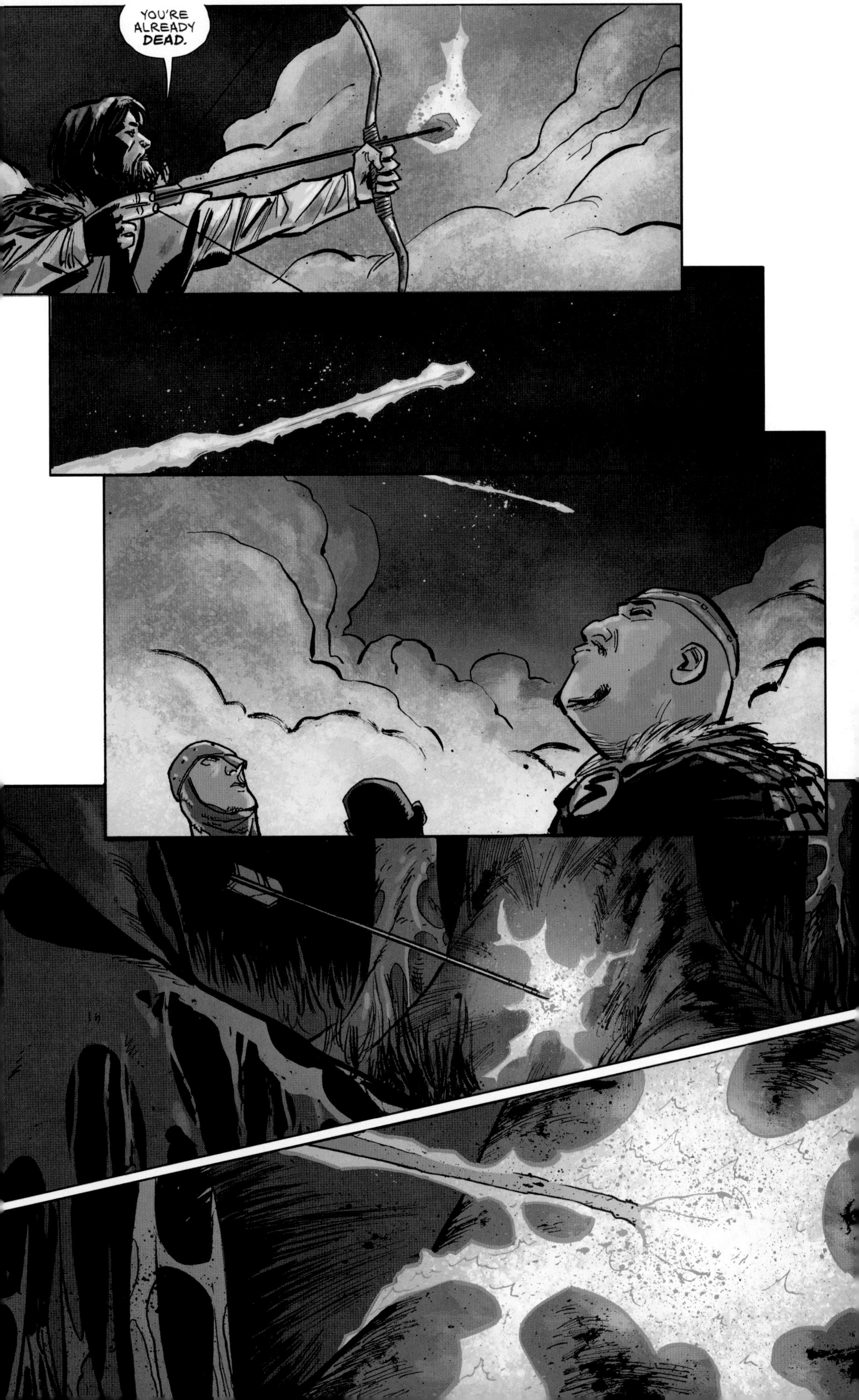
YOU'RE ALREADY DEAD.

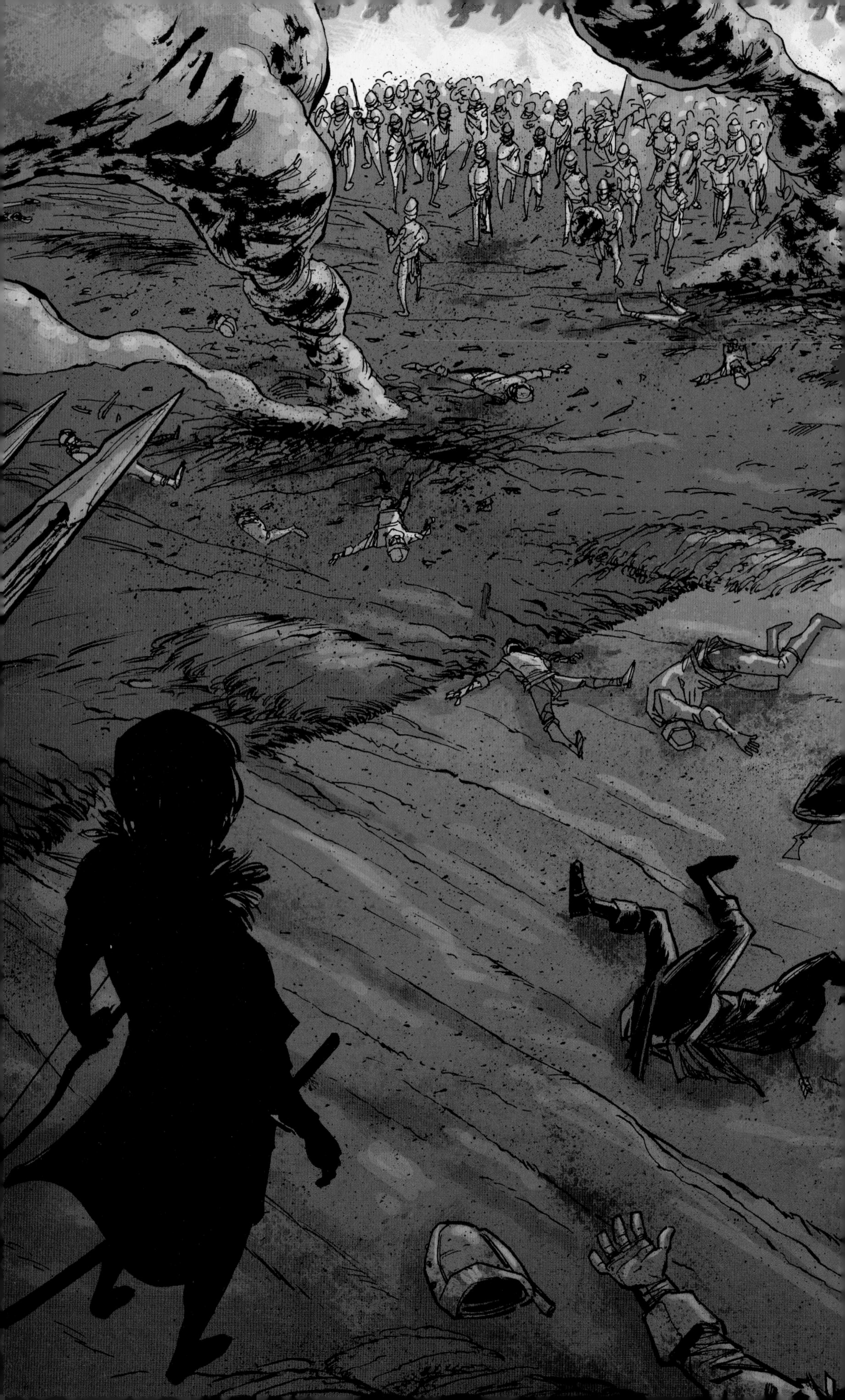

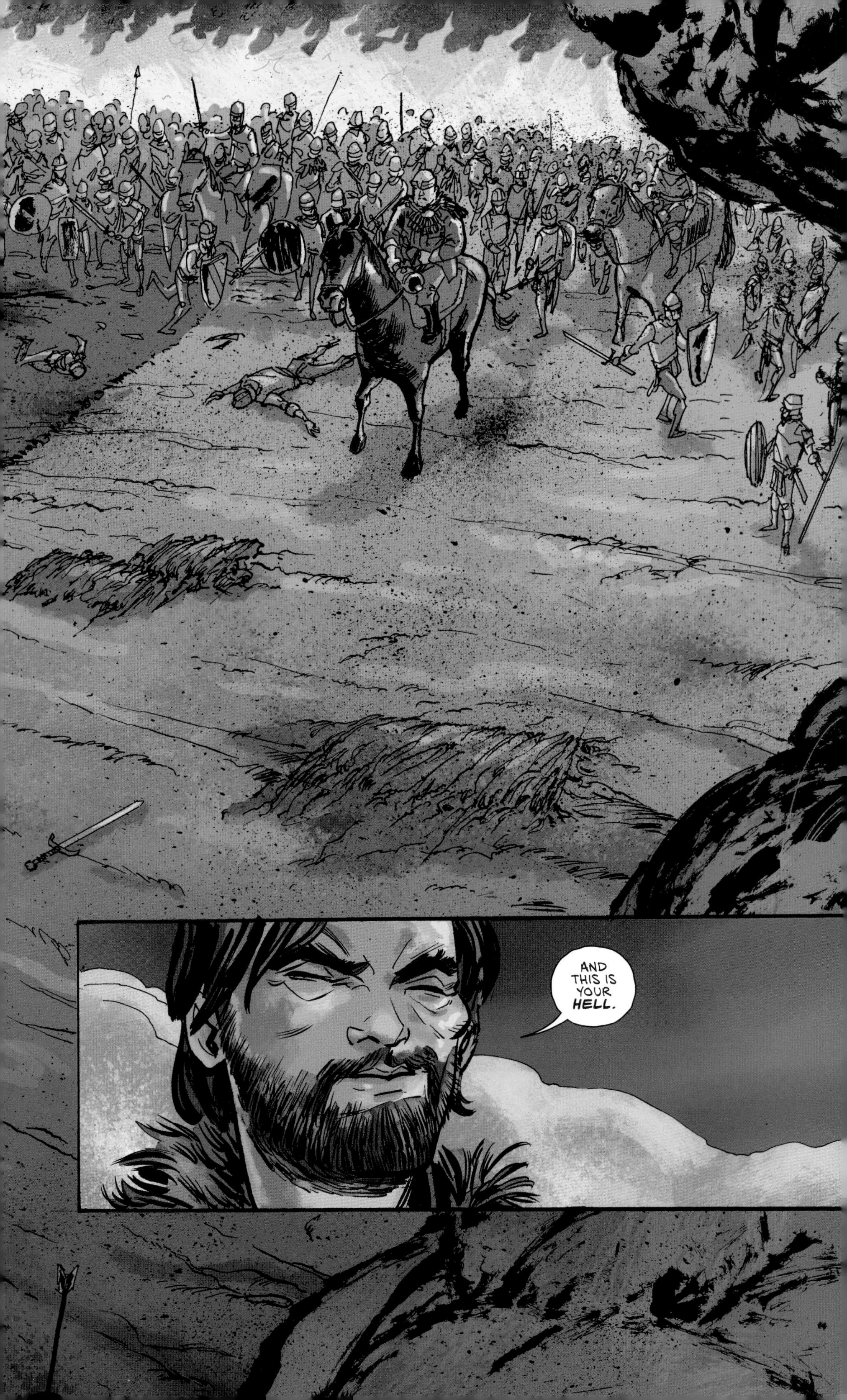
AND THIS IS YOUR HELL.

THE TWO
~ Chapter 2 ~
SWORDS

The city-states had been slow to respond to the rising threat of the Eastern king. It was, Lord Aedon mused, partially understandable. The war had begun on the far side of the continent, separated from the collection of Saxon city-states by a vast sea. And no army in history had ever spread as fast as the one led by this self-proclaimed king, Istvan. But as the warlord began to build his fleet of ships, the Saxon kings finally began to take notice and a council was called.

"He has no claim!" The aging Lord Cyril protested. "And without claim he cannot hold our countries. Not without inciting rebellion!"

"And what concerns would this conqueror have with rebels?" A younger lord by the name of Ryce retorted. "If our armies cannot stop him, then a mob of angry peasants will?"

"His borders would be stretched too thin," Lady Glenna observed quietly.

"My point!" Lord Cyril was increasingly vehement. "Even the largest army imaginable must be sustained. And when they leave the towns that they have pillaged? What happens then?"

There was a cacophony of voices as order fled the room.

"His army cannot be as strong as we have been led to believe," shouted a minor noble. Lord Feist, if Aedon recalled correctly. "Let him build his ships, and when they sail to our coast we will burn them. And those that swim to shore, we'll butcher!"

Feist's men jeered and laughed. It was the same with all of them. They were all kings of their own provinces, and all drunk on the idea of their own invulnerability.

"Istvan's army is not weak," Aedon admonished, stepping forward, "and he holds his lands against the threat of rebellion through fear of his brutality. And moreover, he turns his conquered lords into vassals — those that survive his butchery."

"We must unify our forces," Aedon continued, passionately. "We must be ready, and I fear we do not have long. Istvan's armies will be here soon, and they are hungry for our land and our blood."

"You will have seen the same reports that I have," interrupted Cyril. "I say he is weak. That he will not sail!"

"I have not read the reports," Aedon replied icily. "I have seen Istvan's forces firsthand. I have sailed across the sea and traveled to his home — and my men and I barely escaped with our lives."

Lord Aedon drew his sword and laid it on the table. "I say again, war is coming. I intend to fight. Who is with me?"

✕

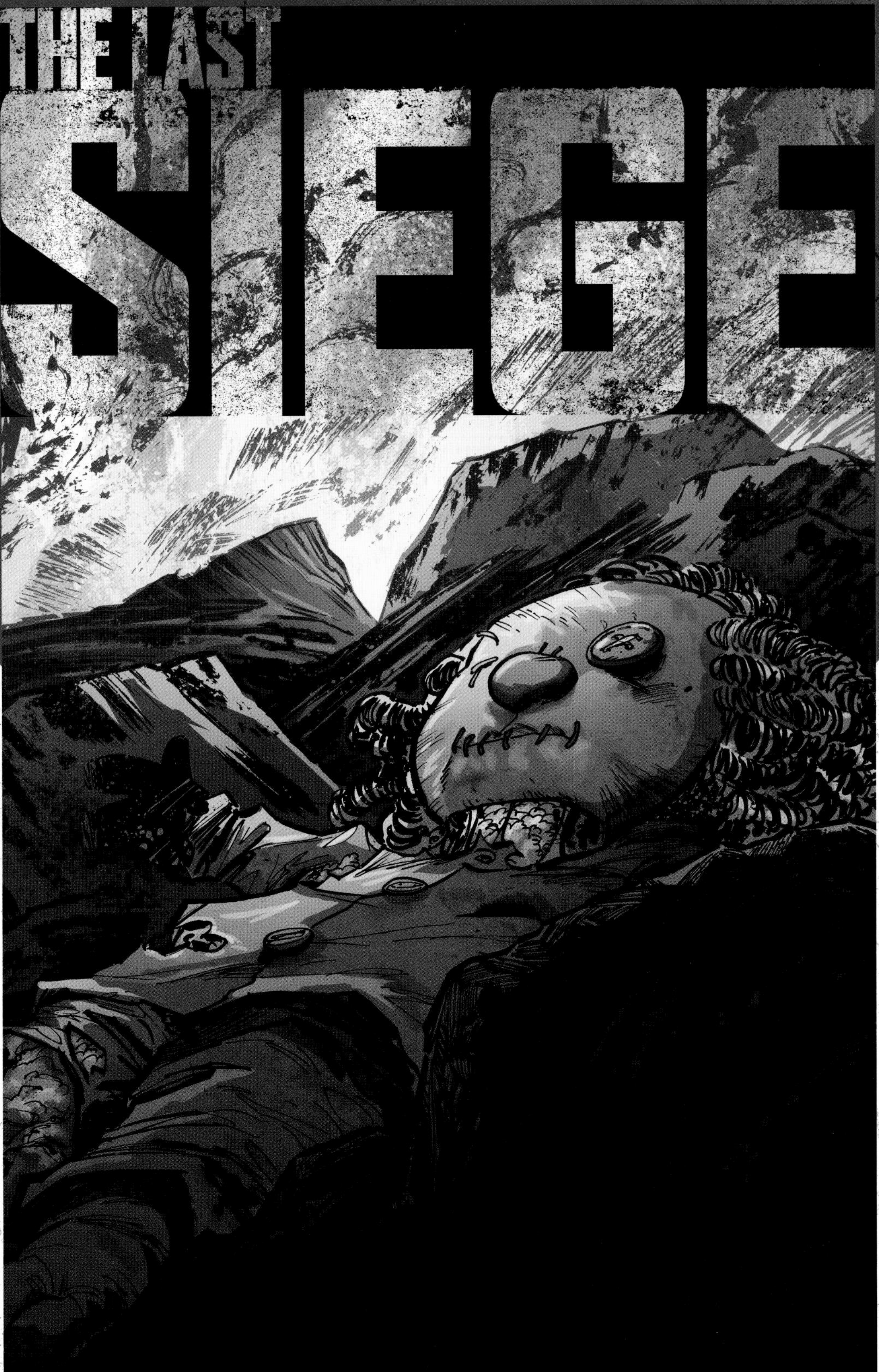
THE LAST
SIEGE

CHAPTER SEVEN

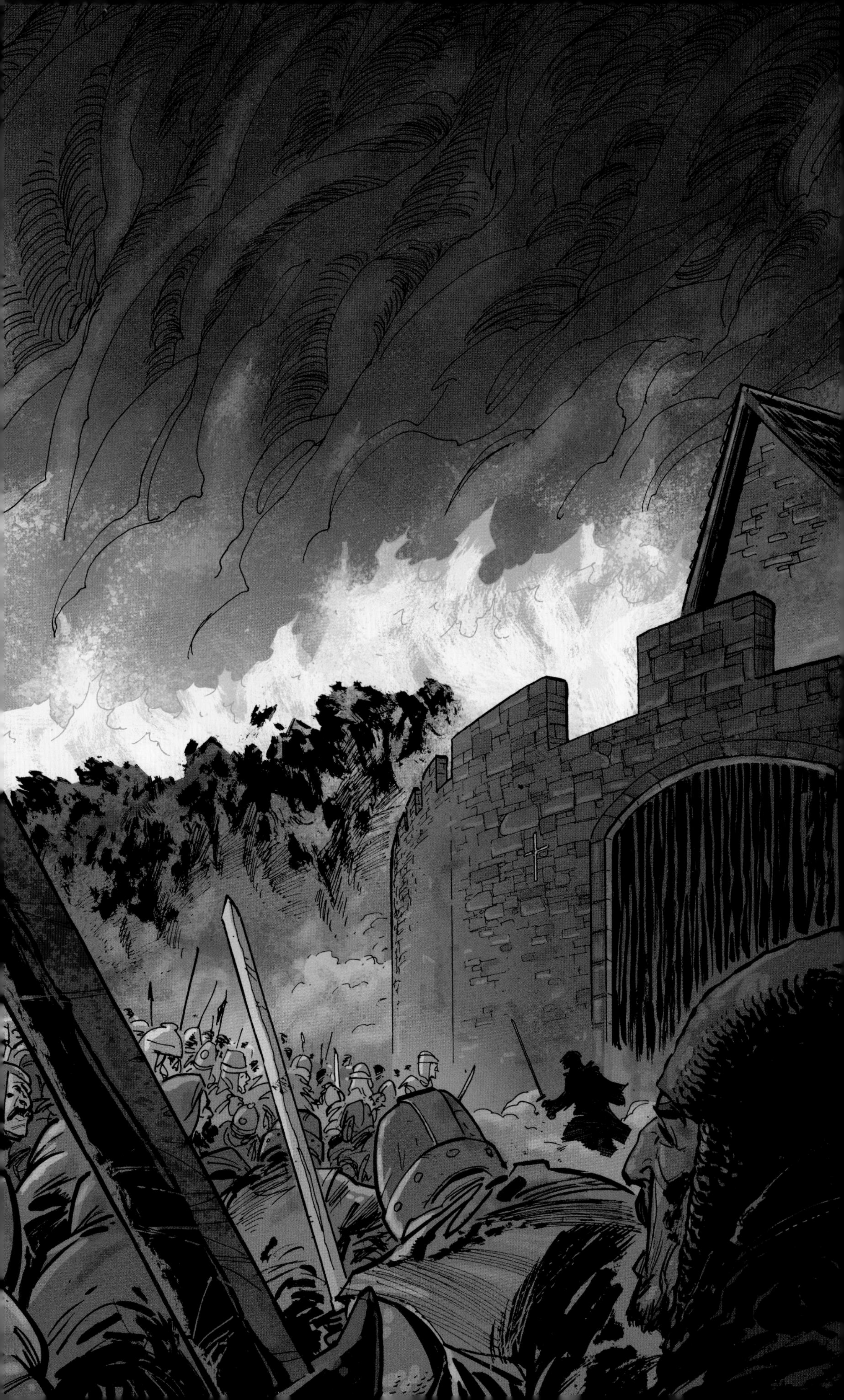

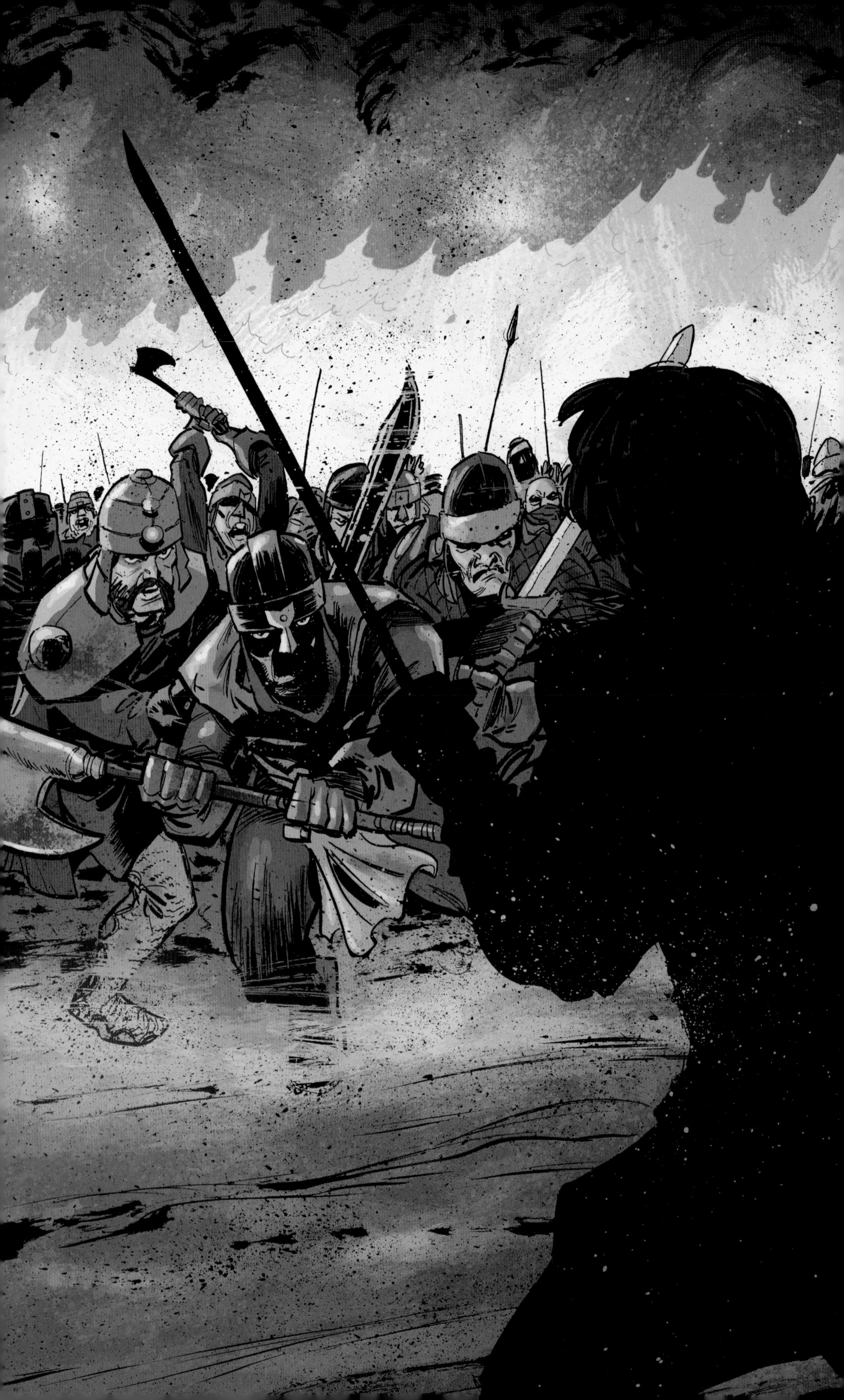

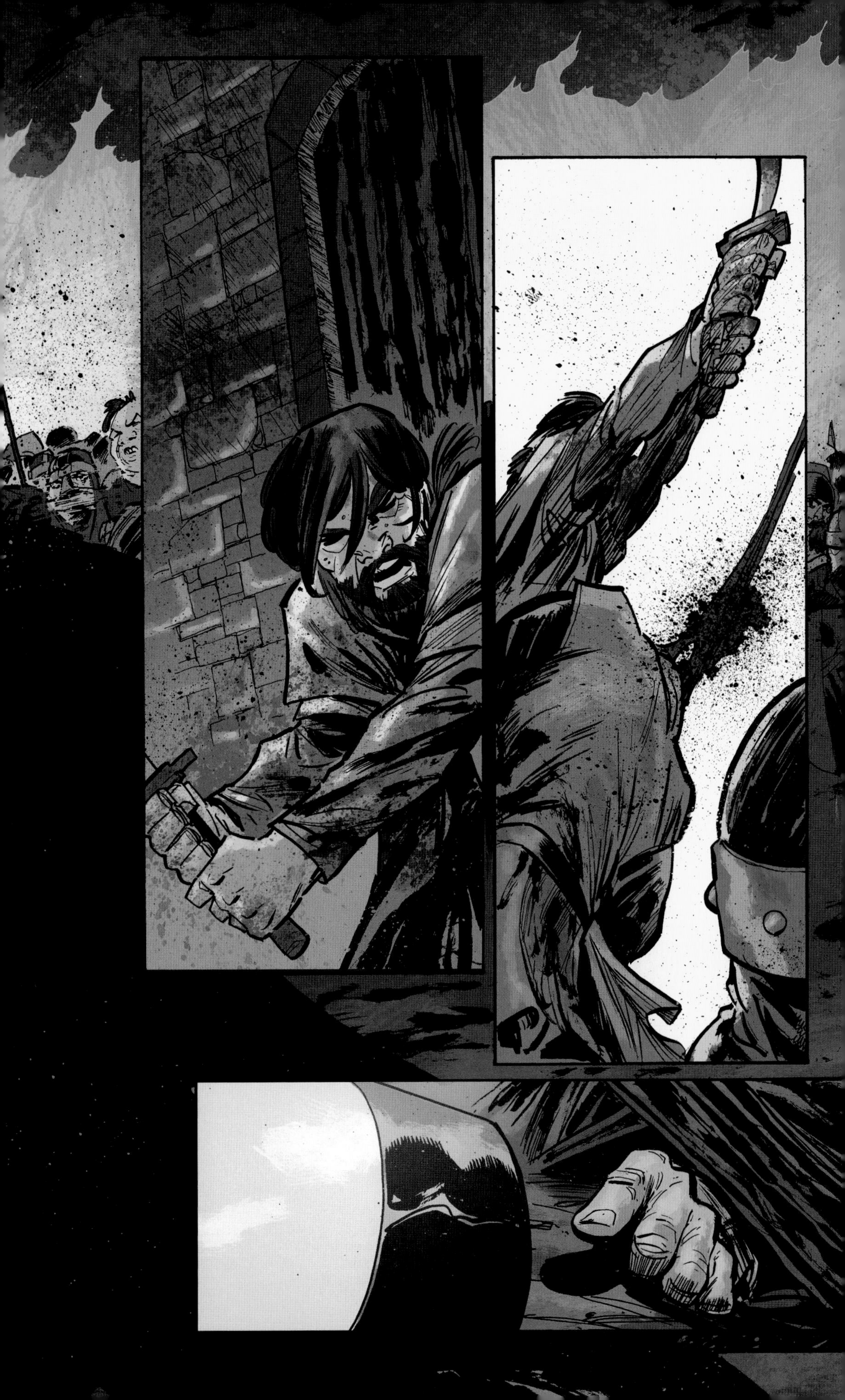

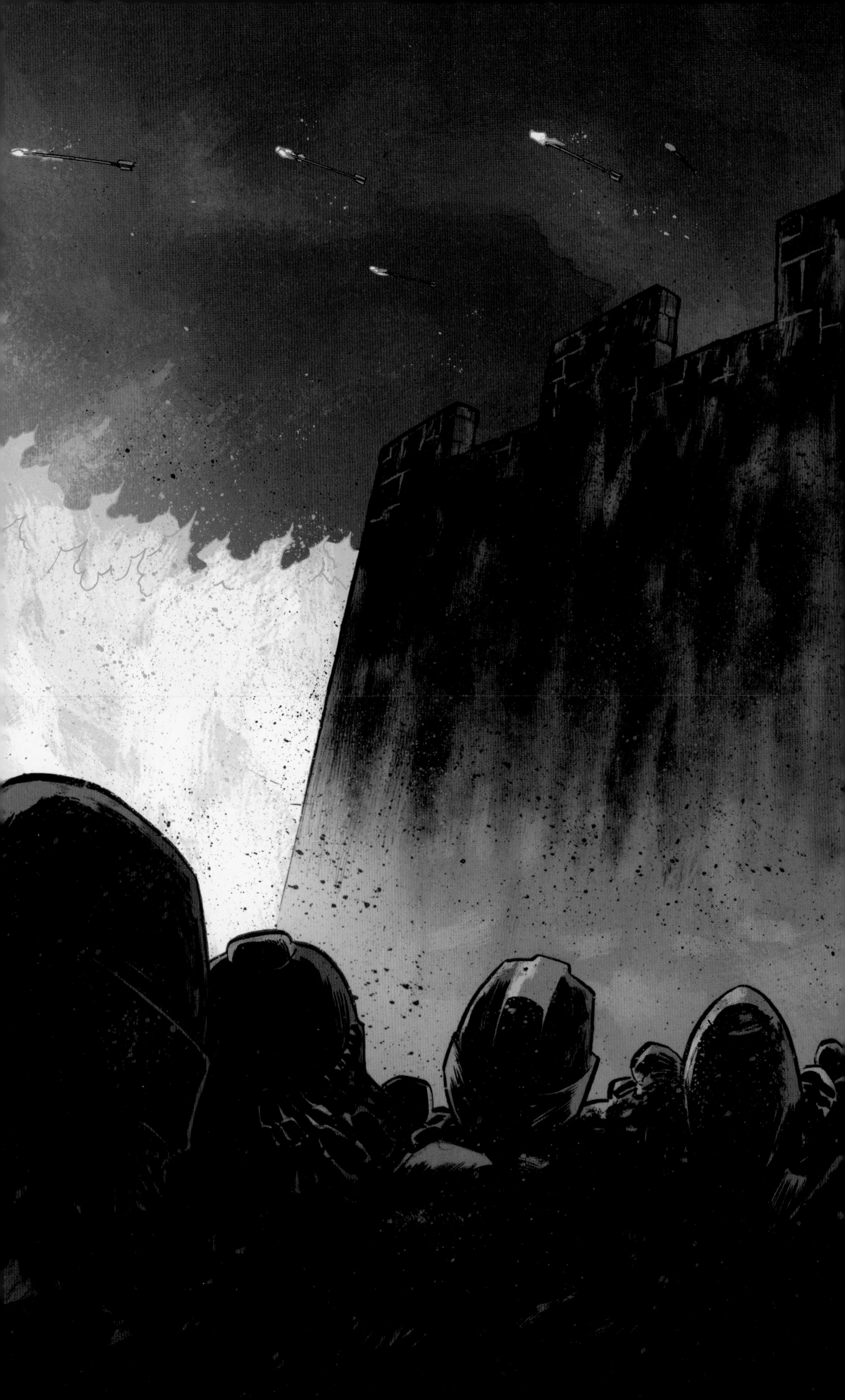

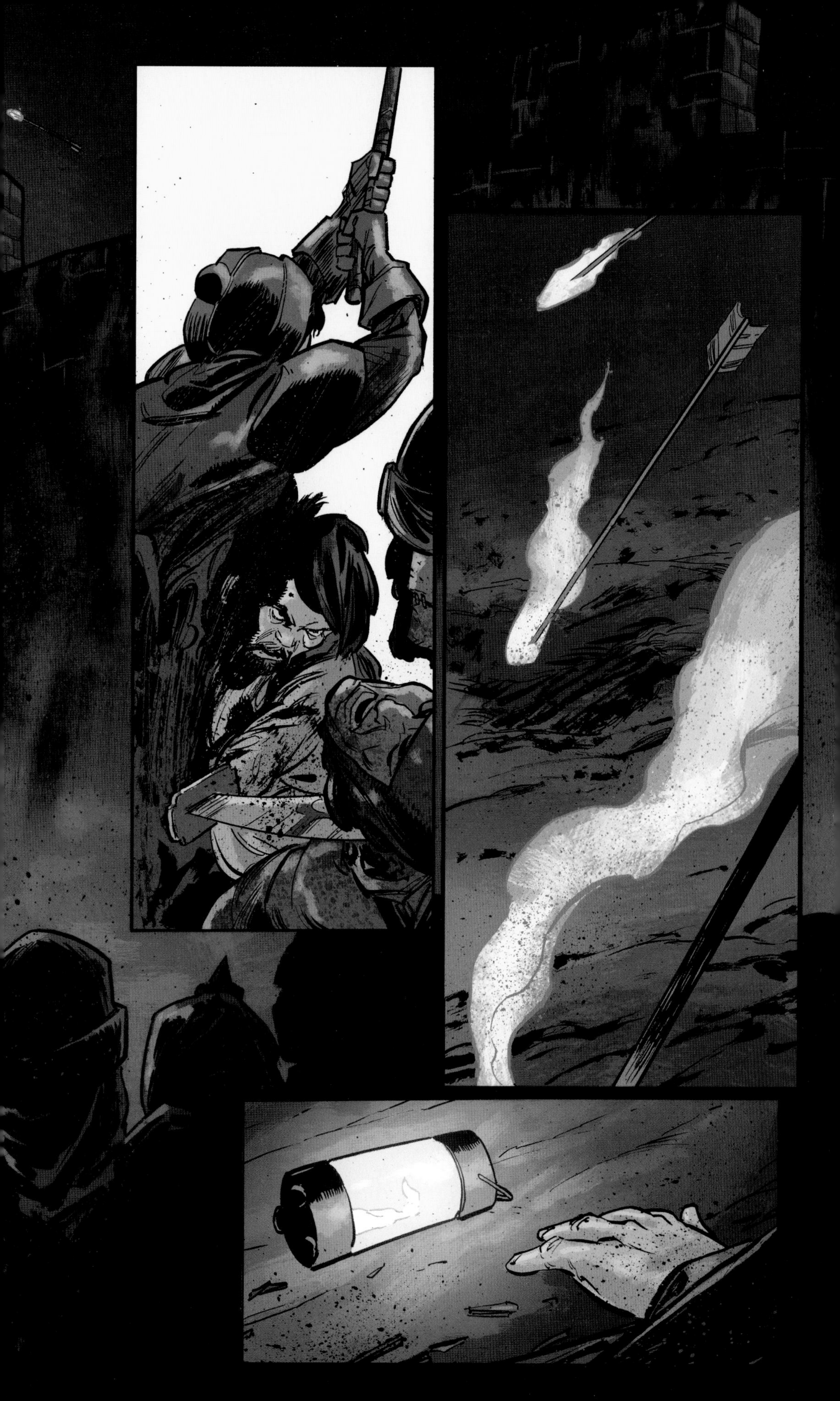

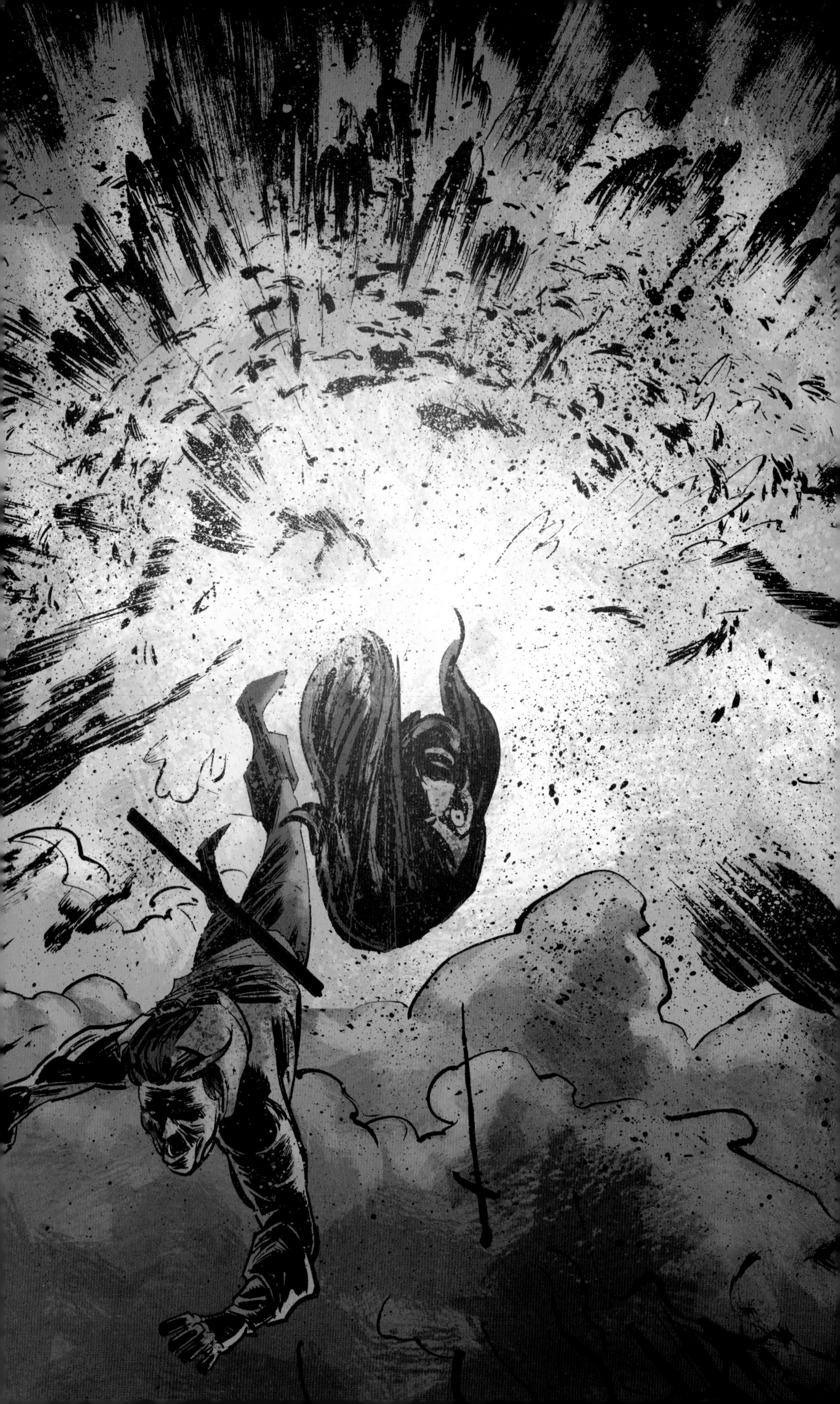

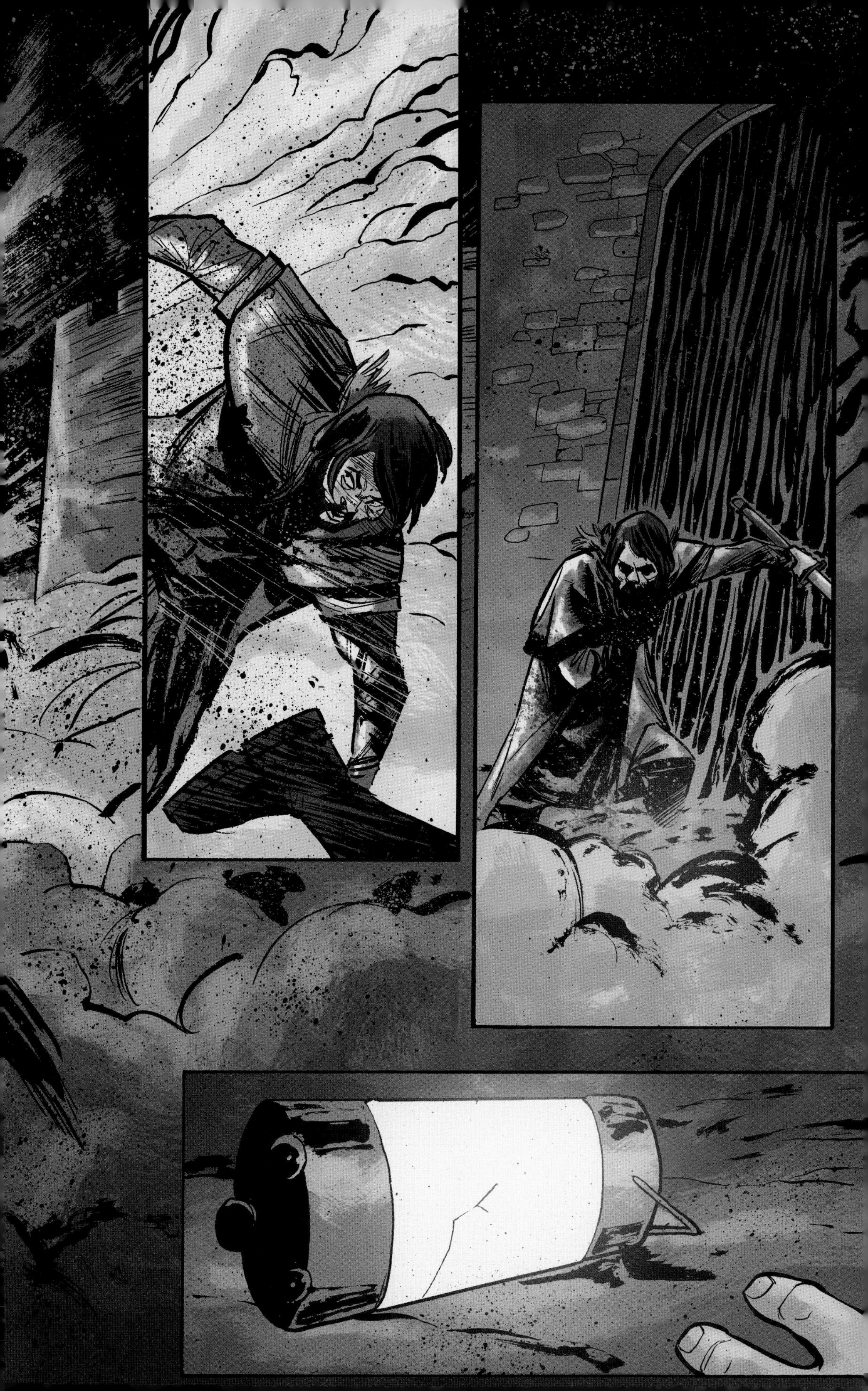

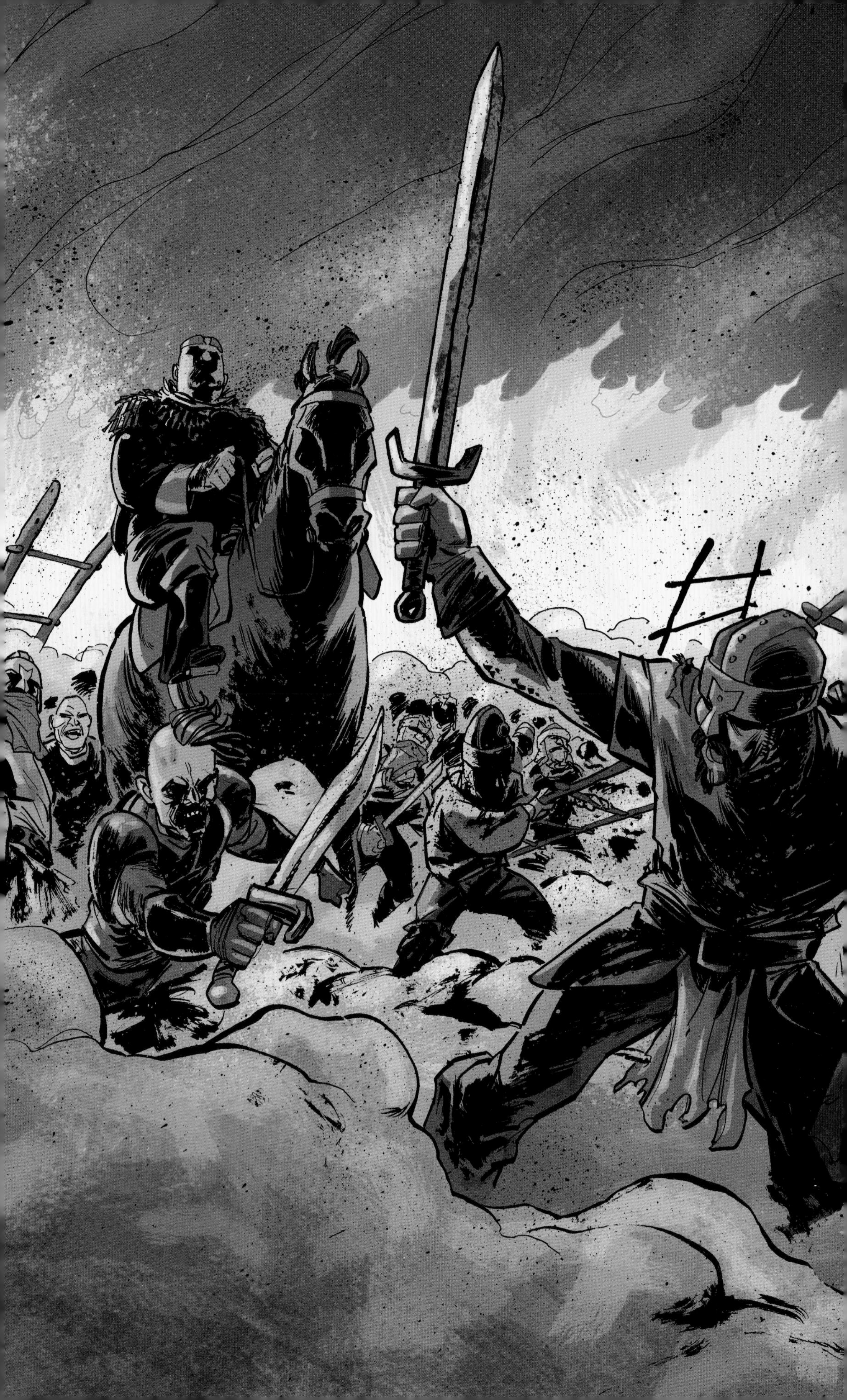

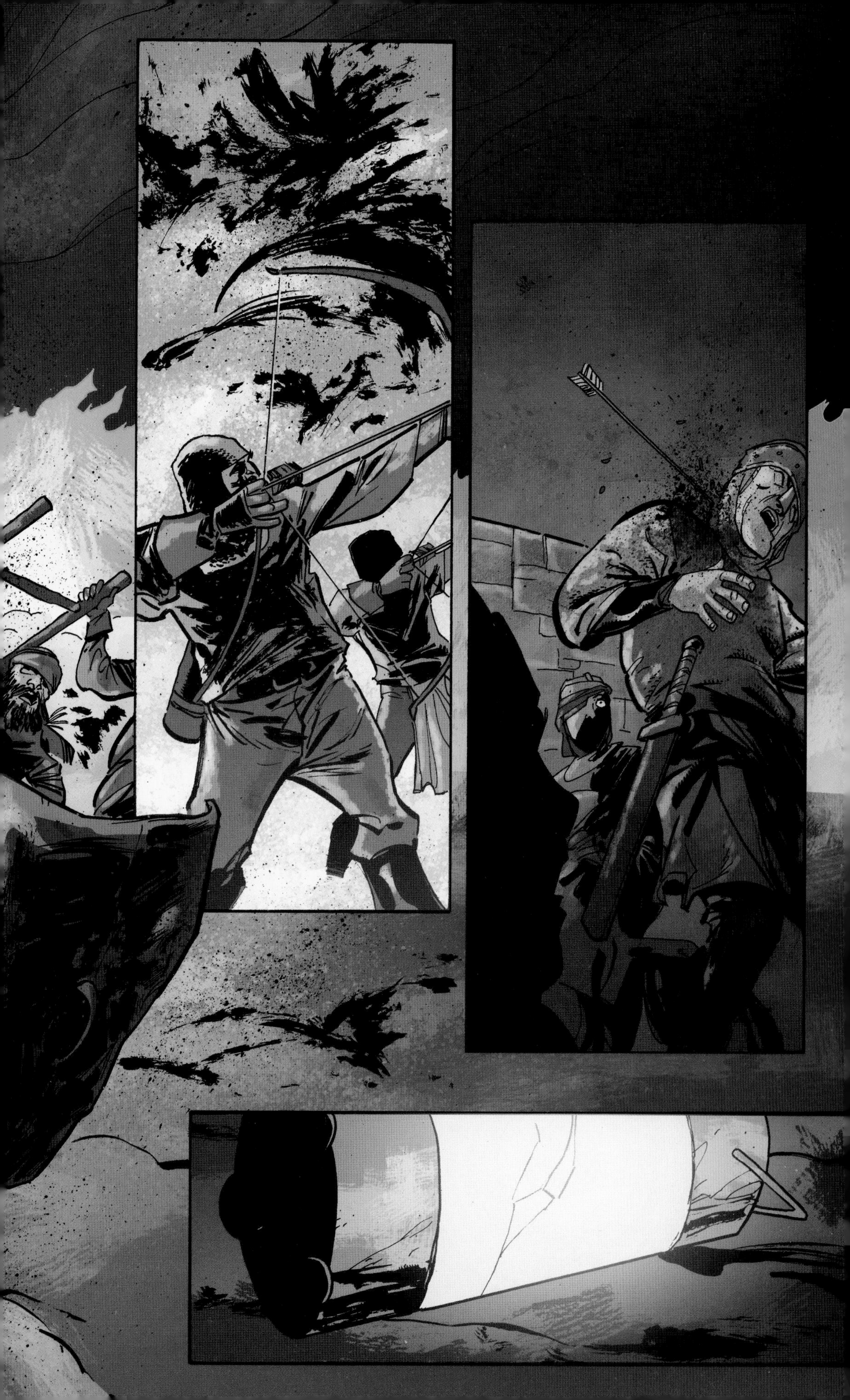

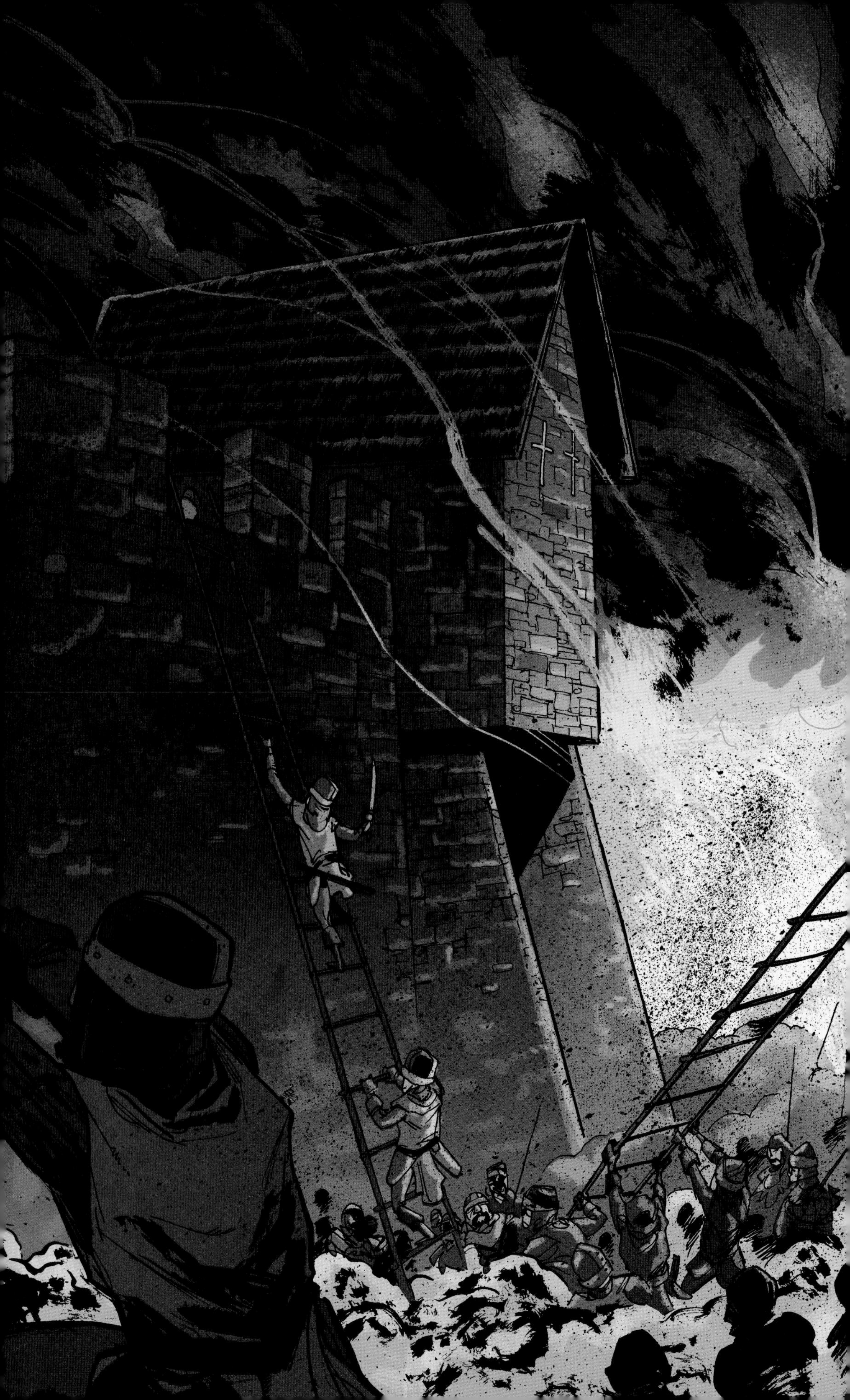

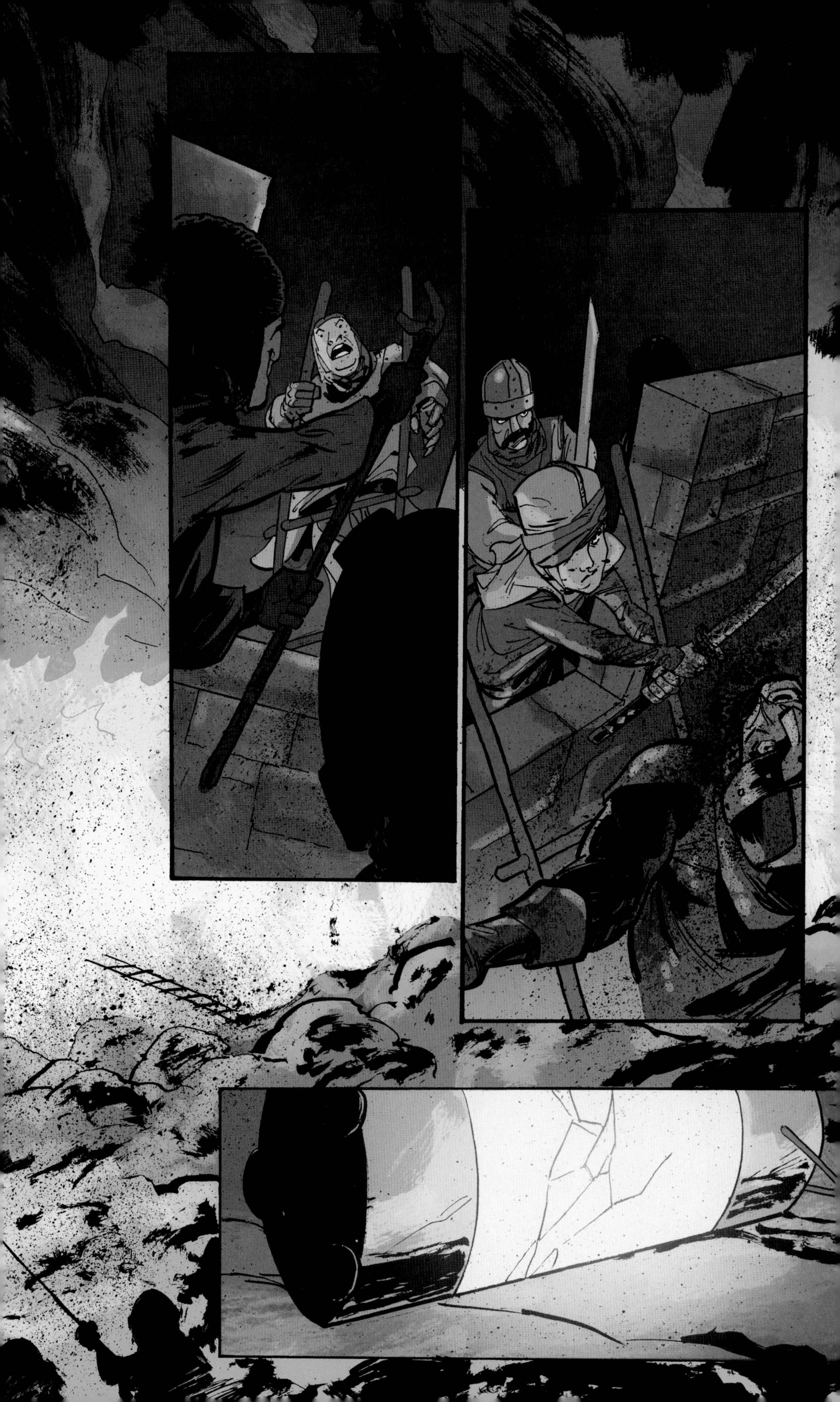

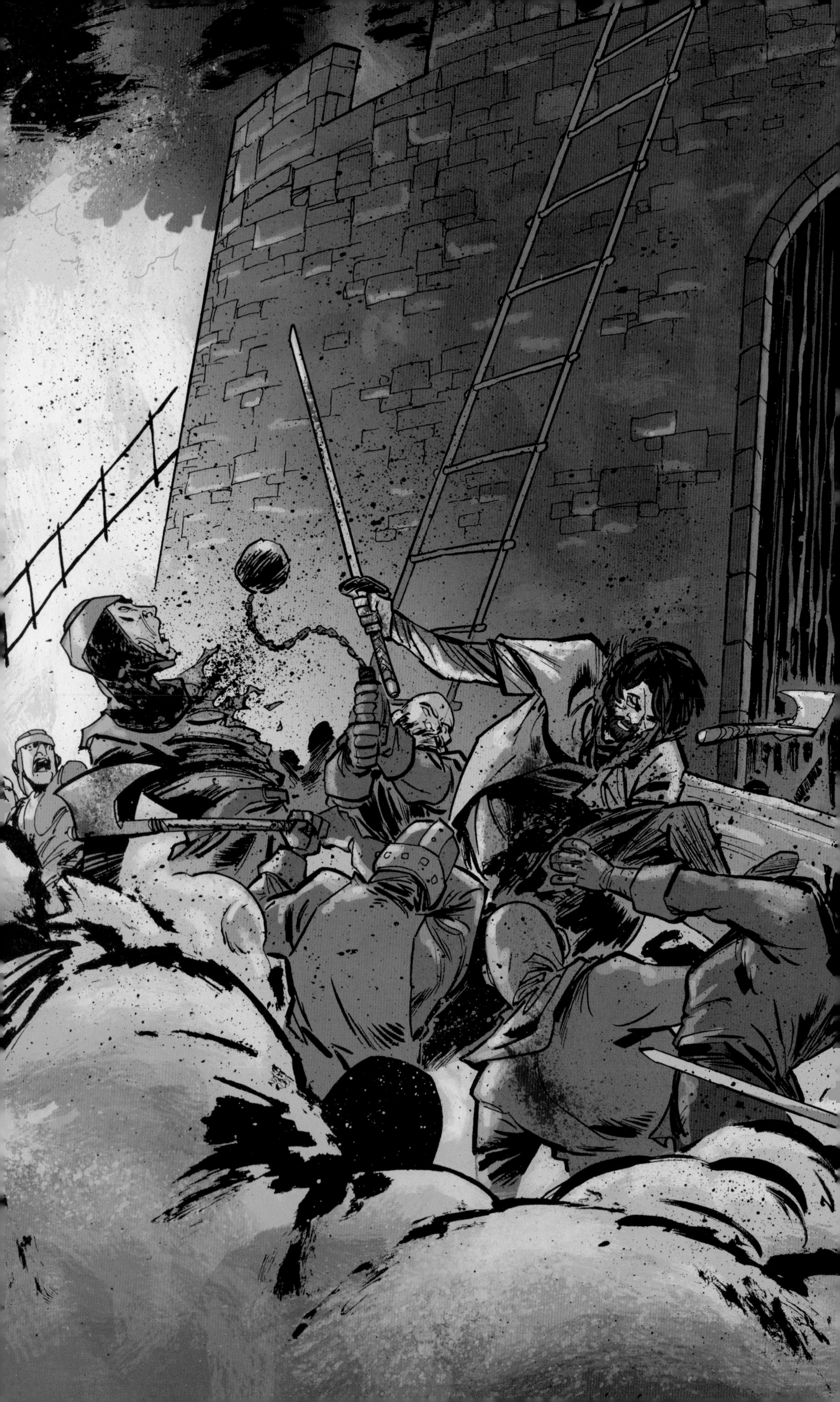

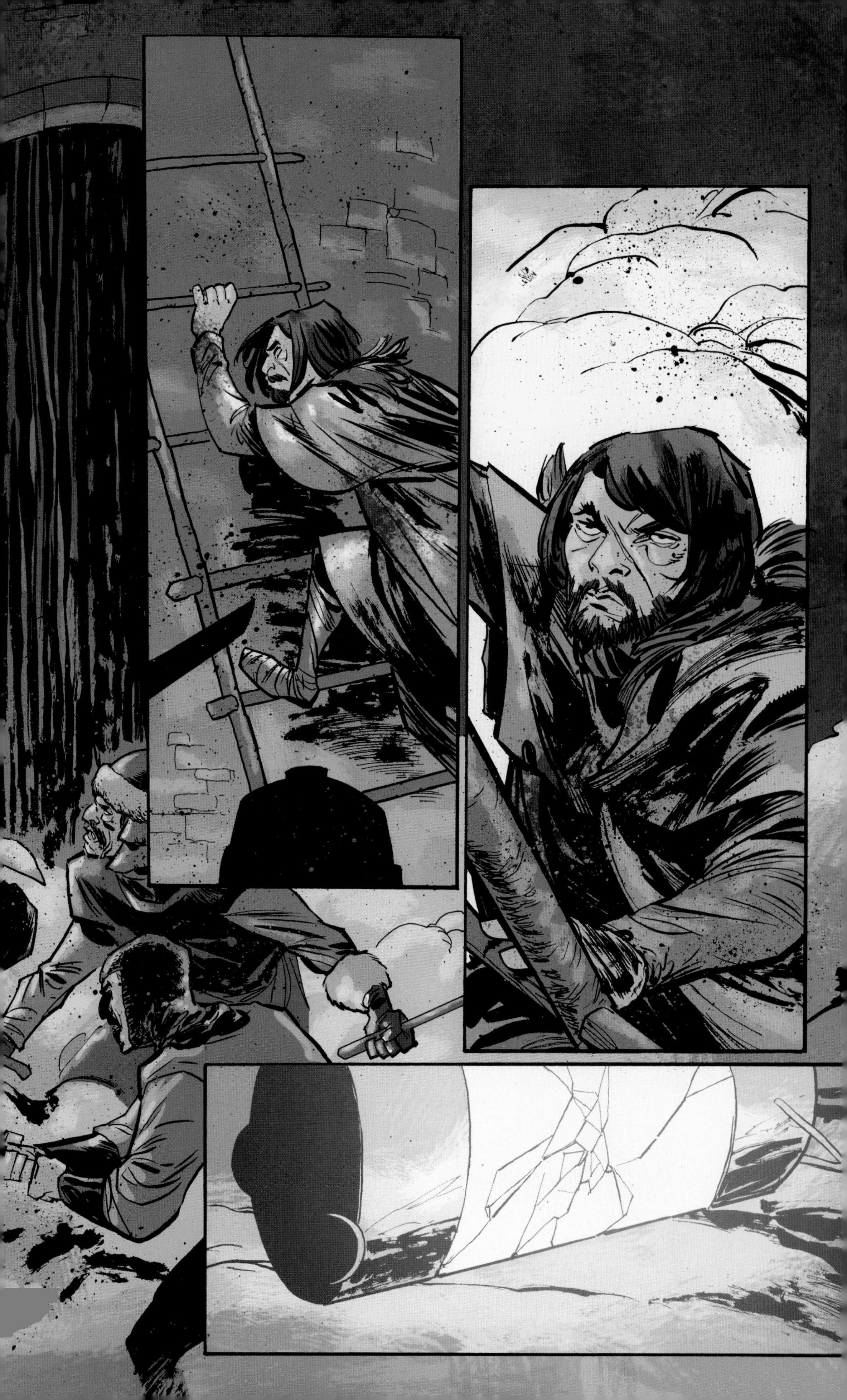

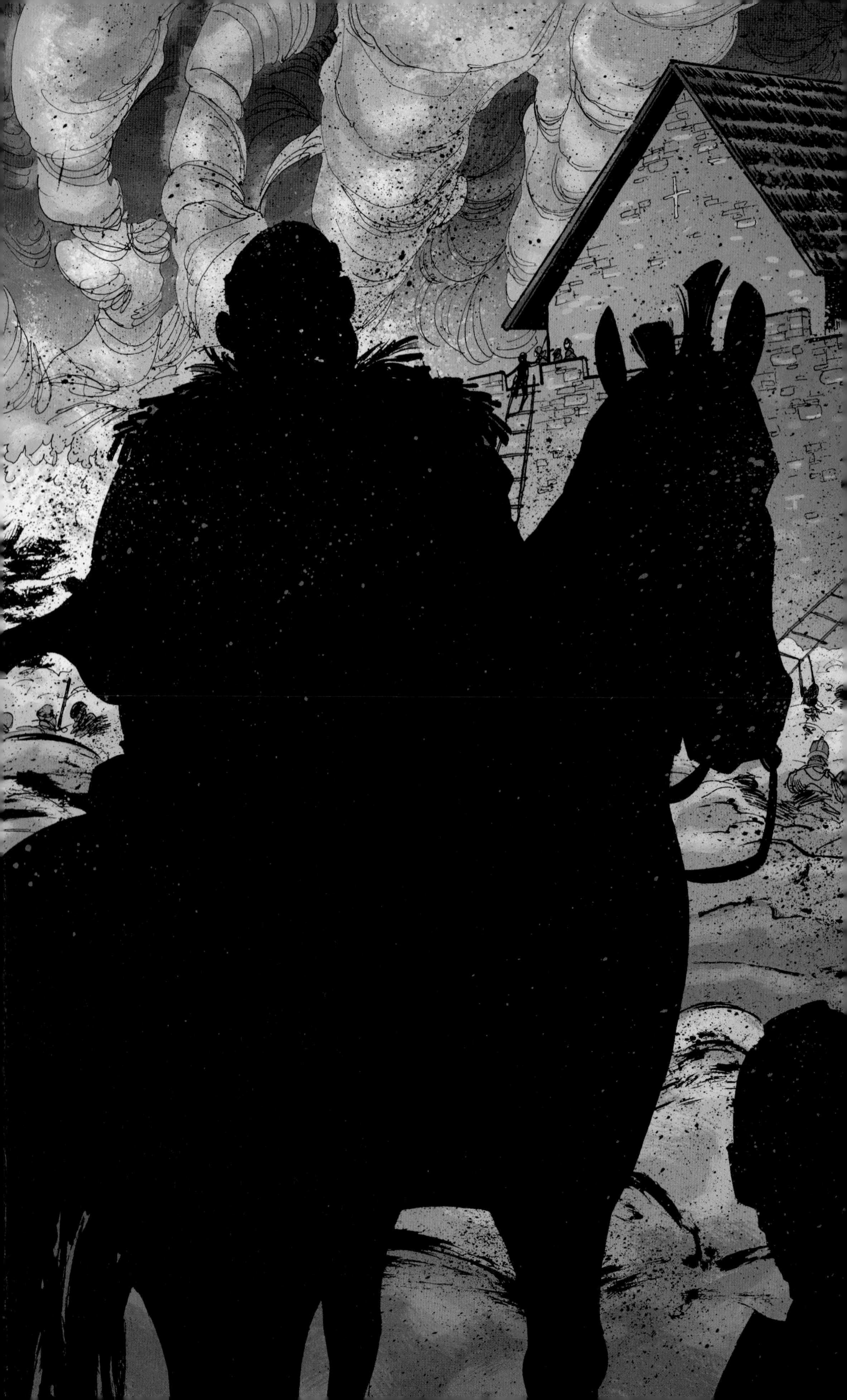

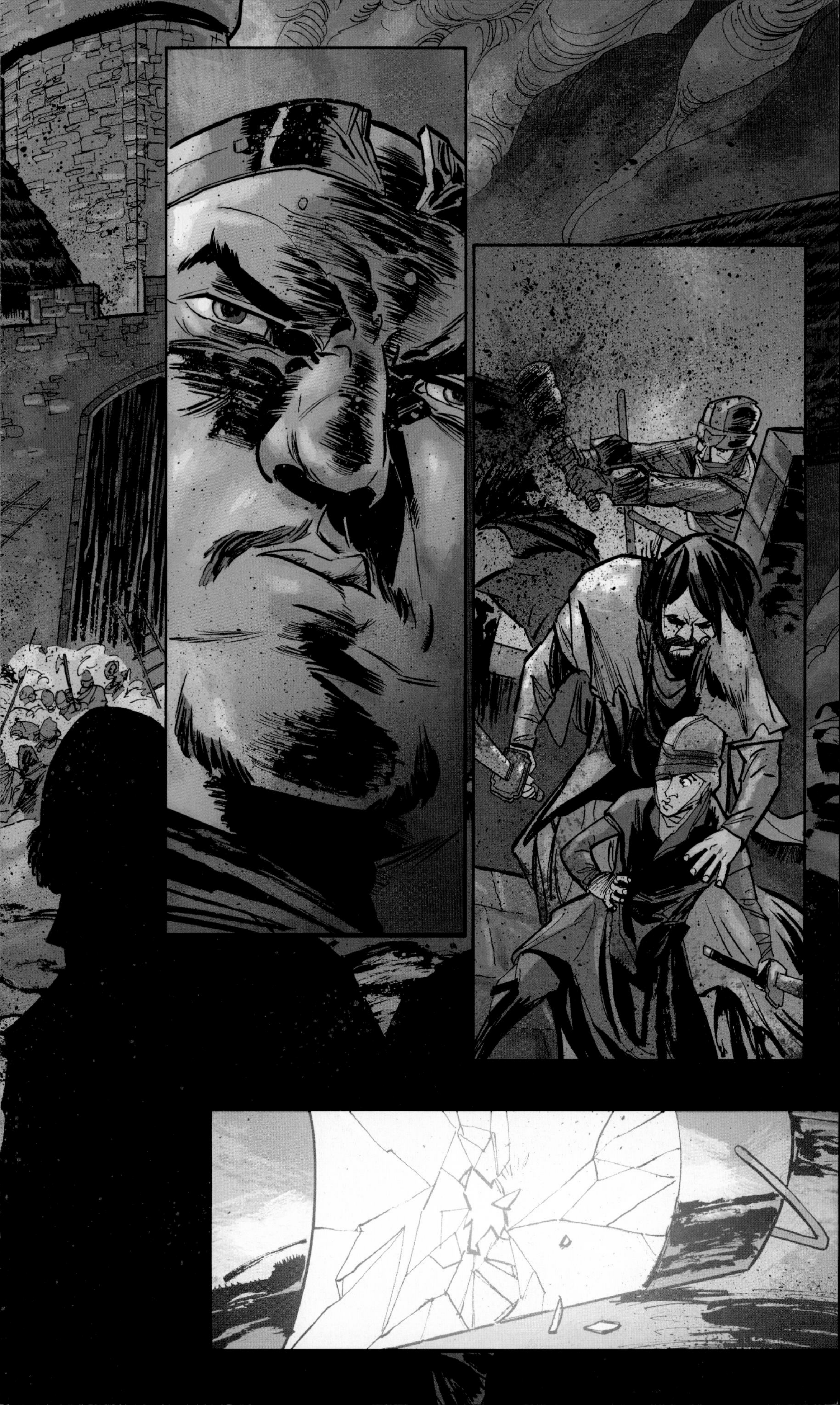

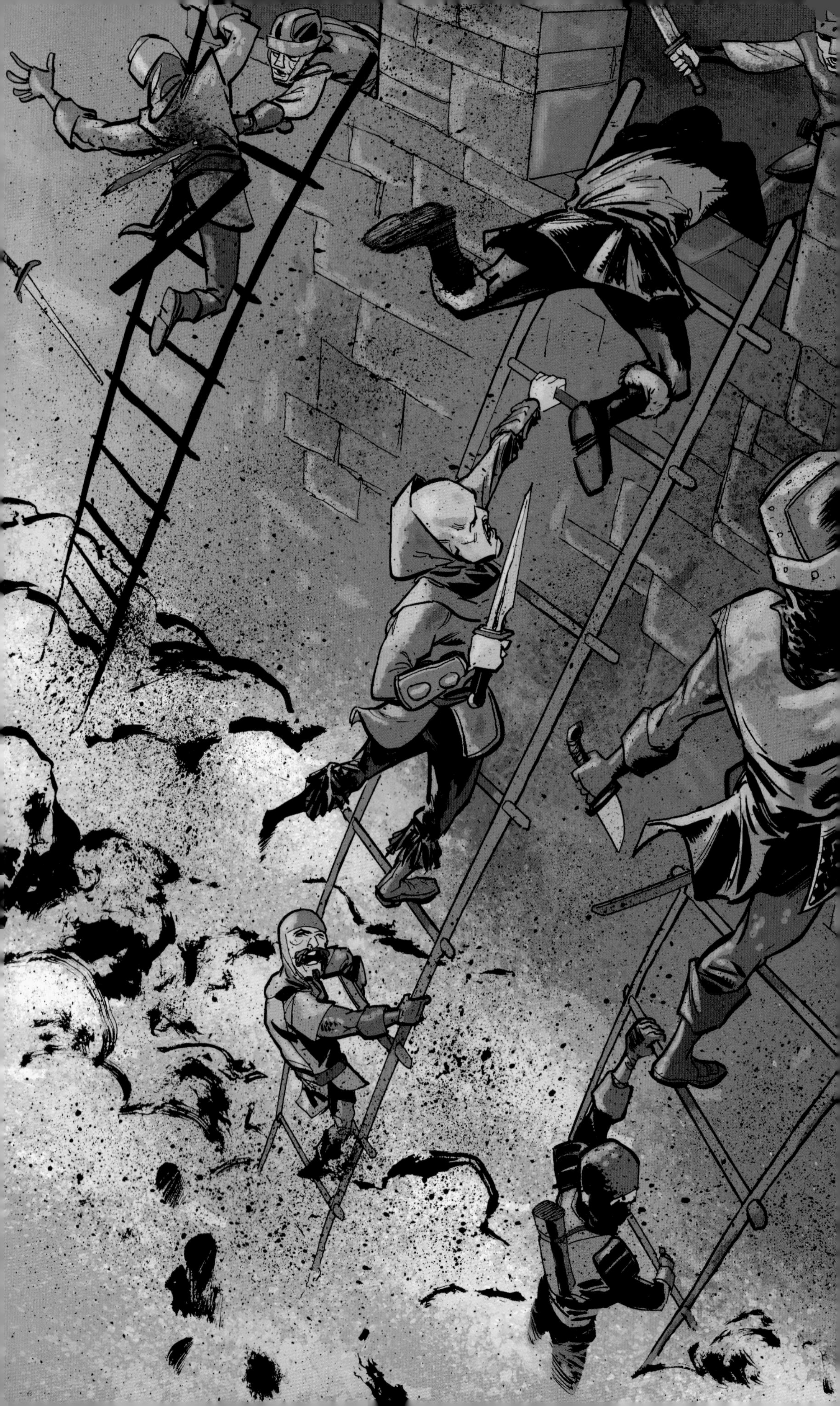

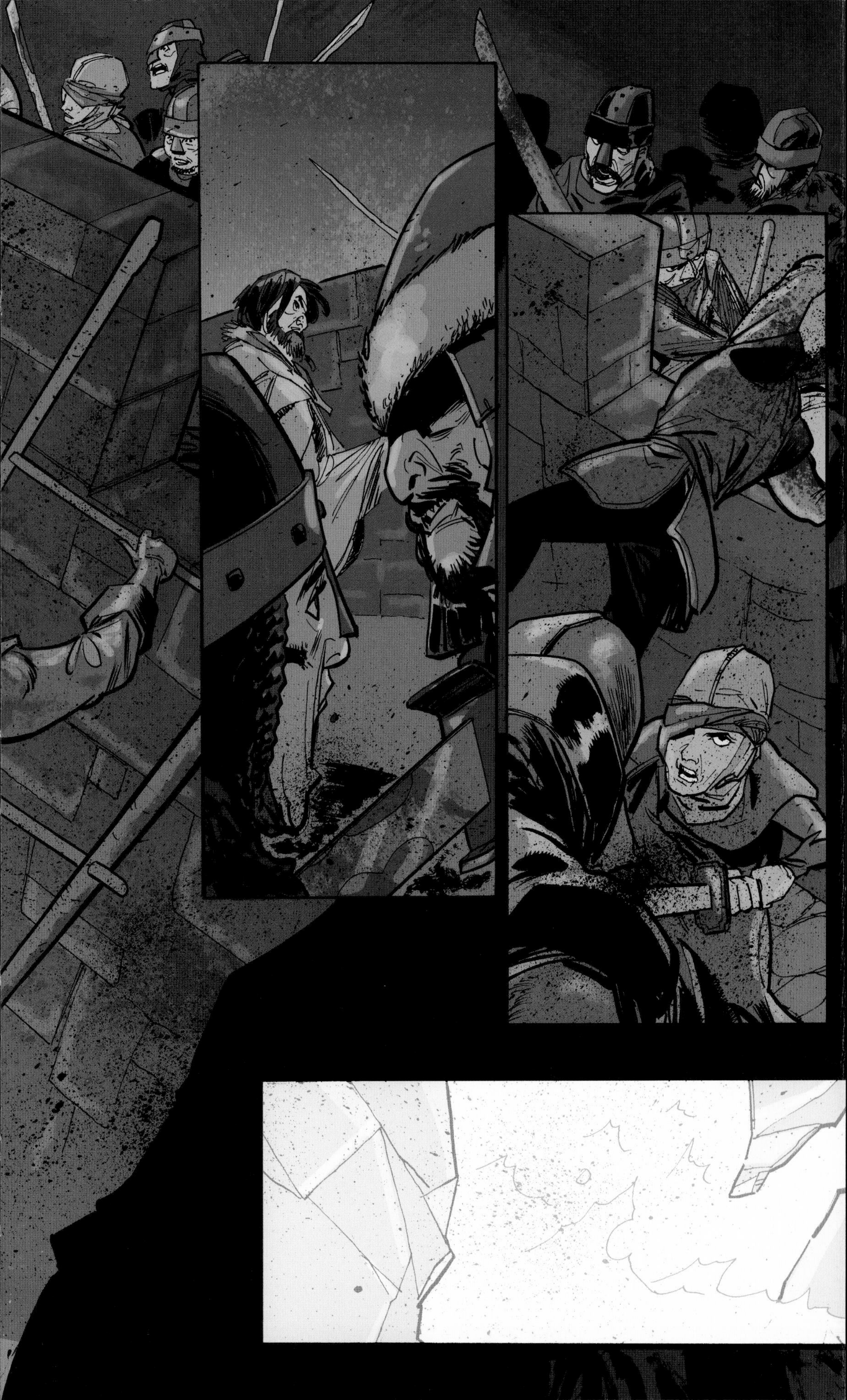

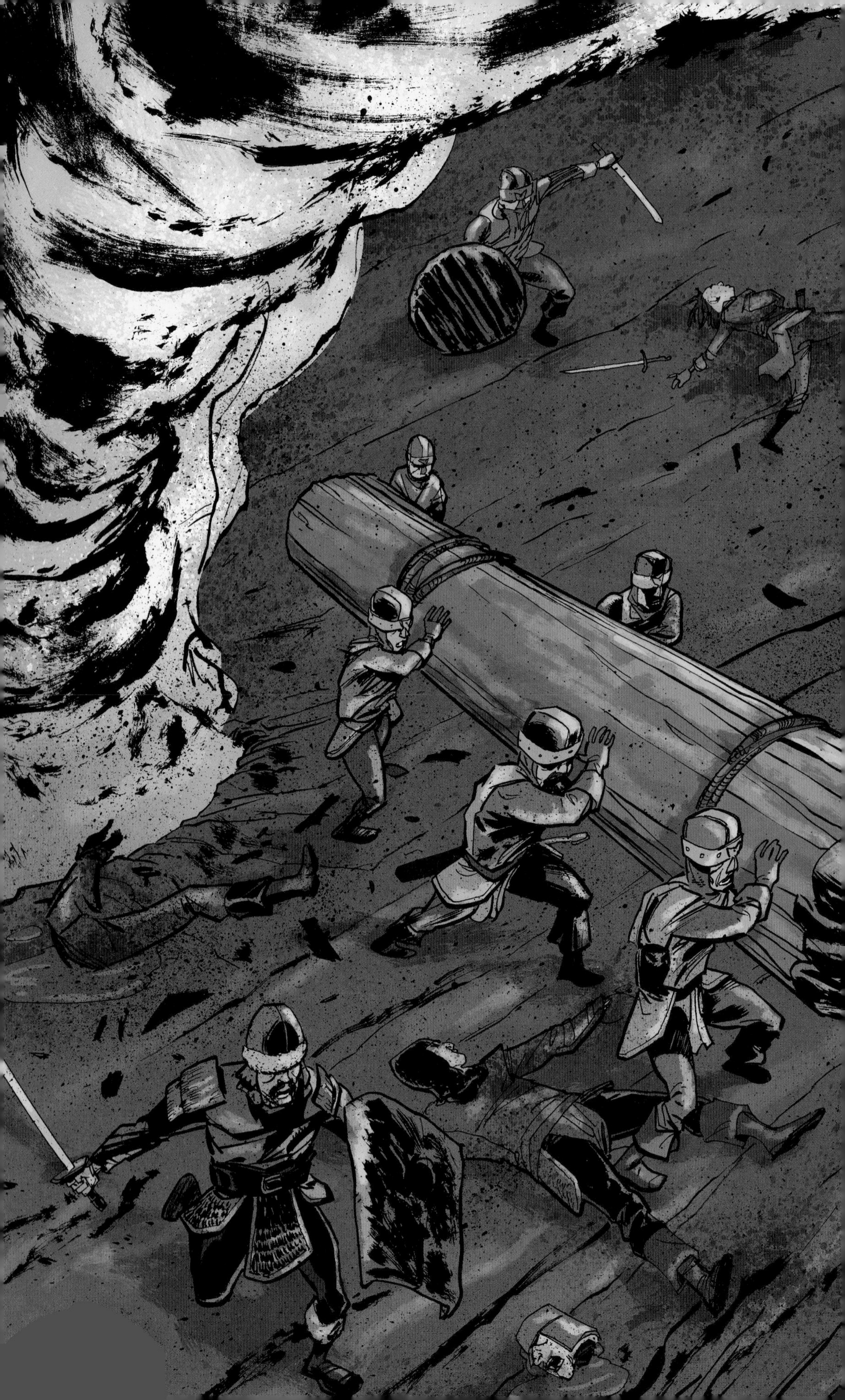

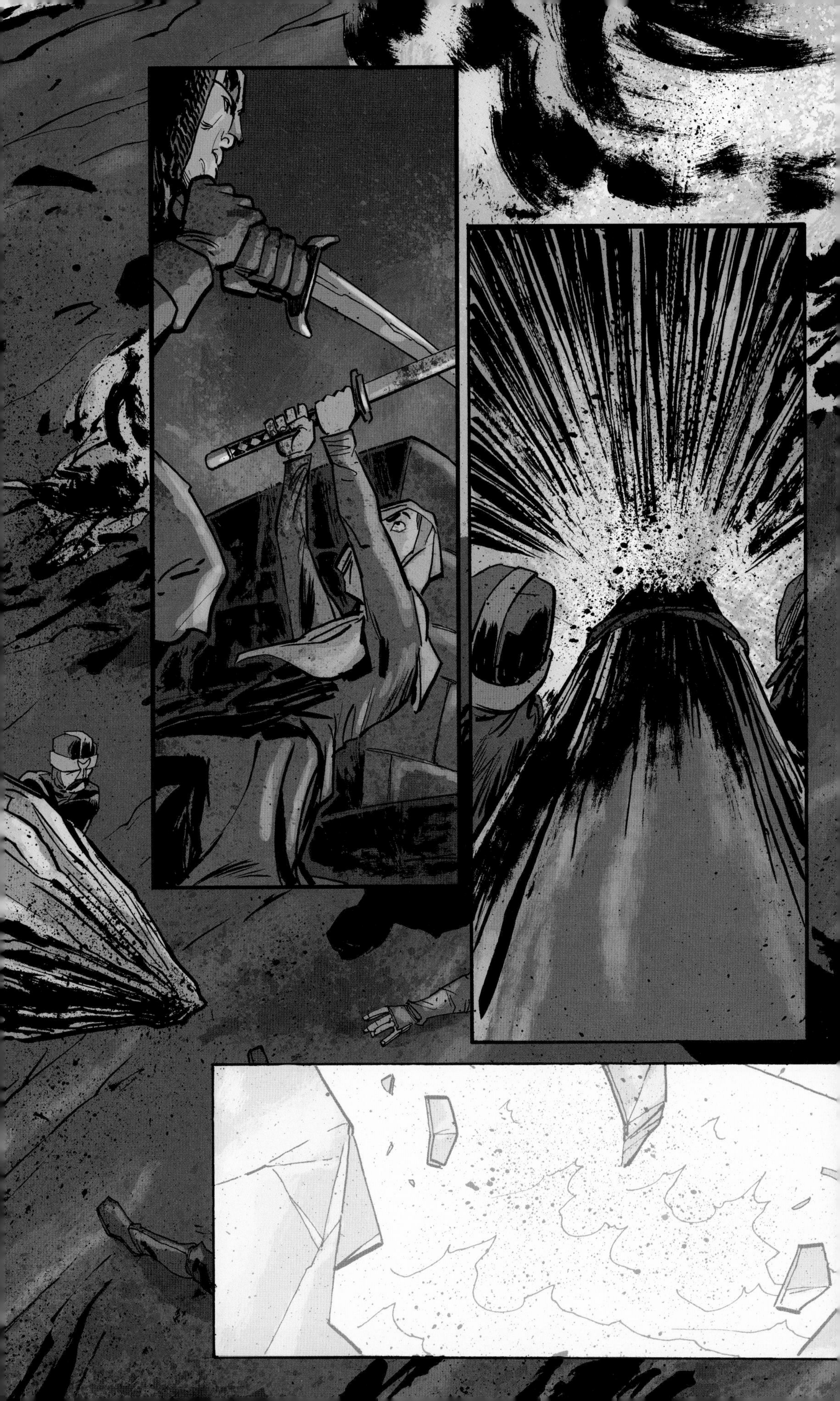

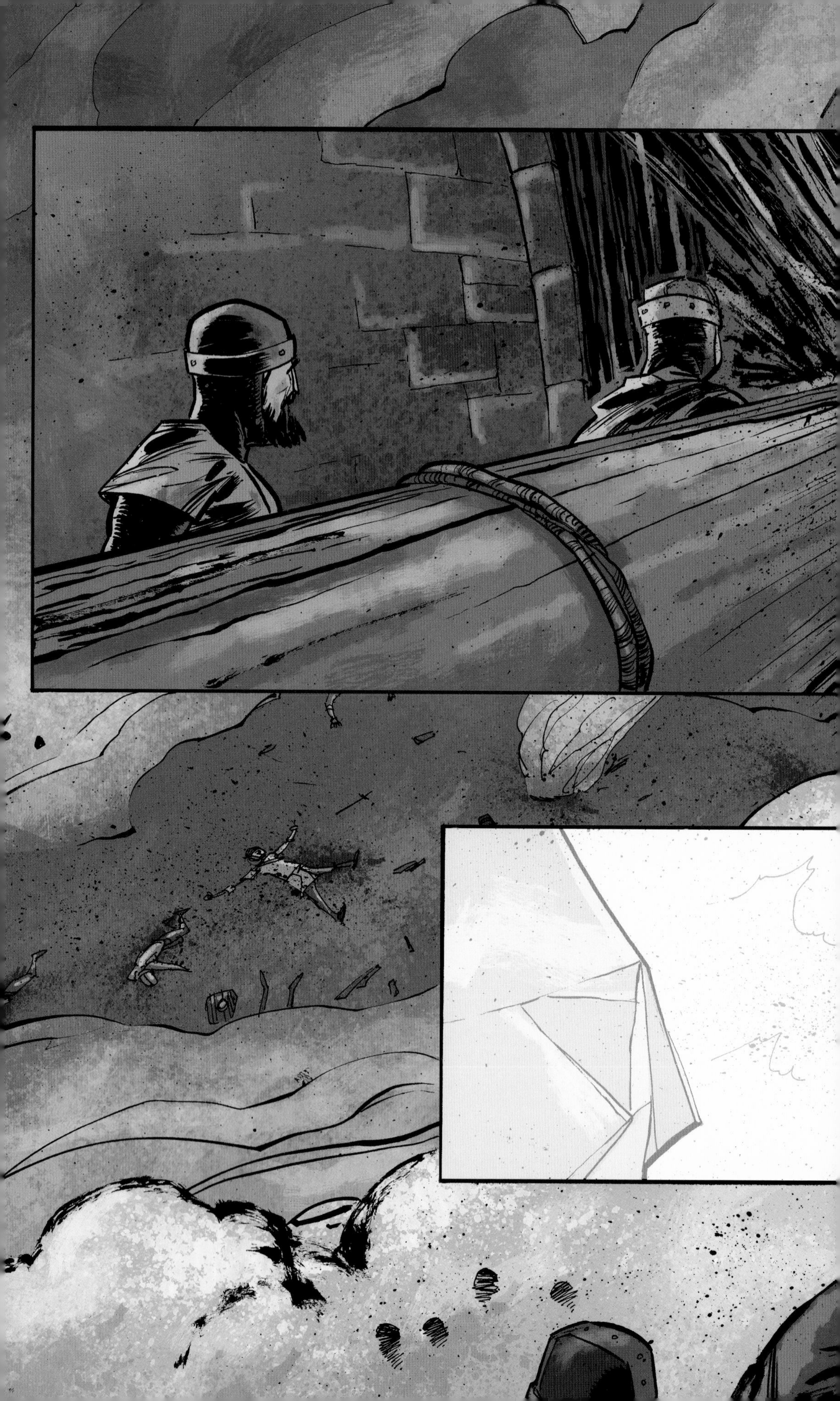

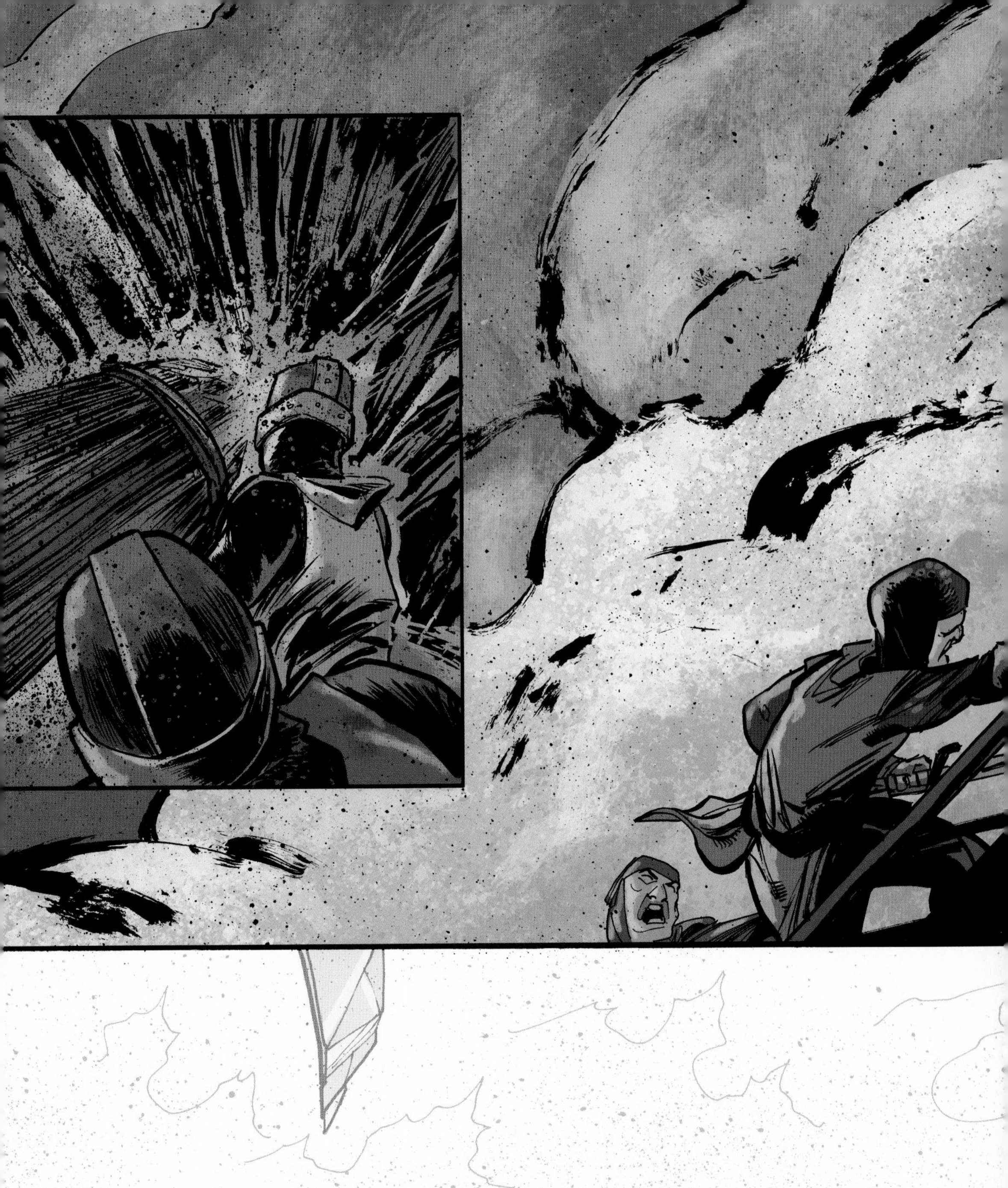

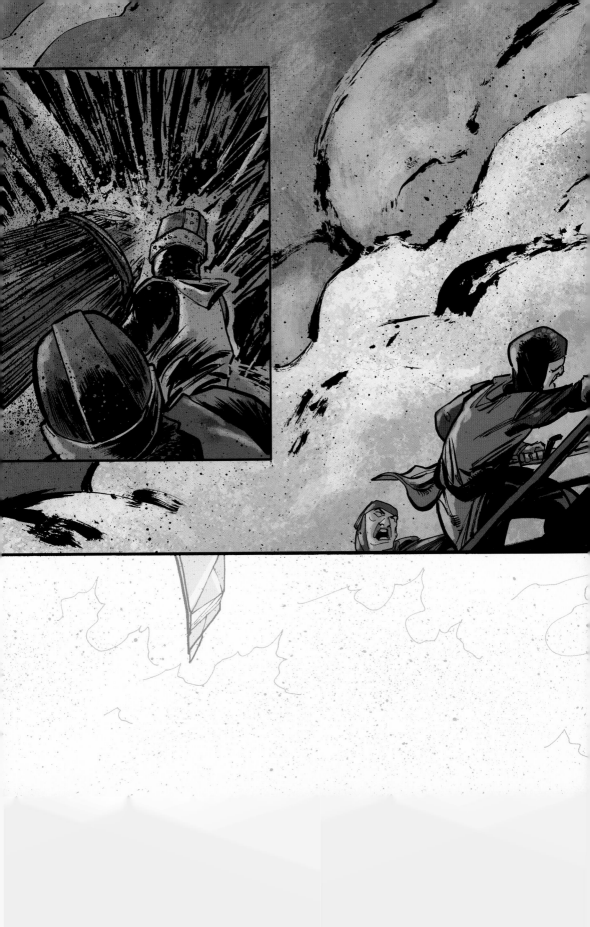

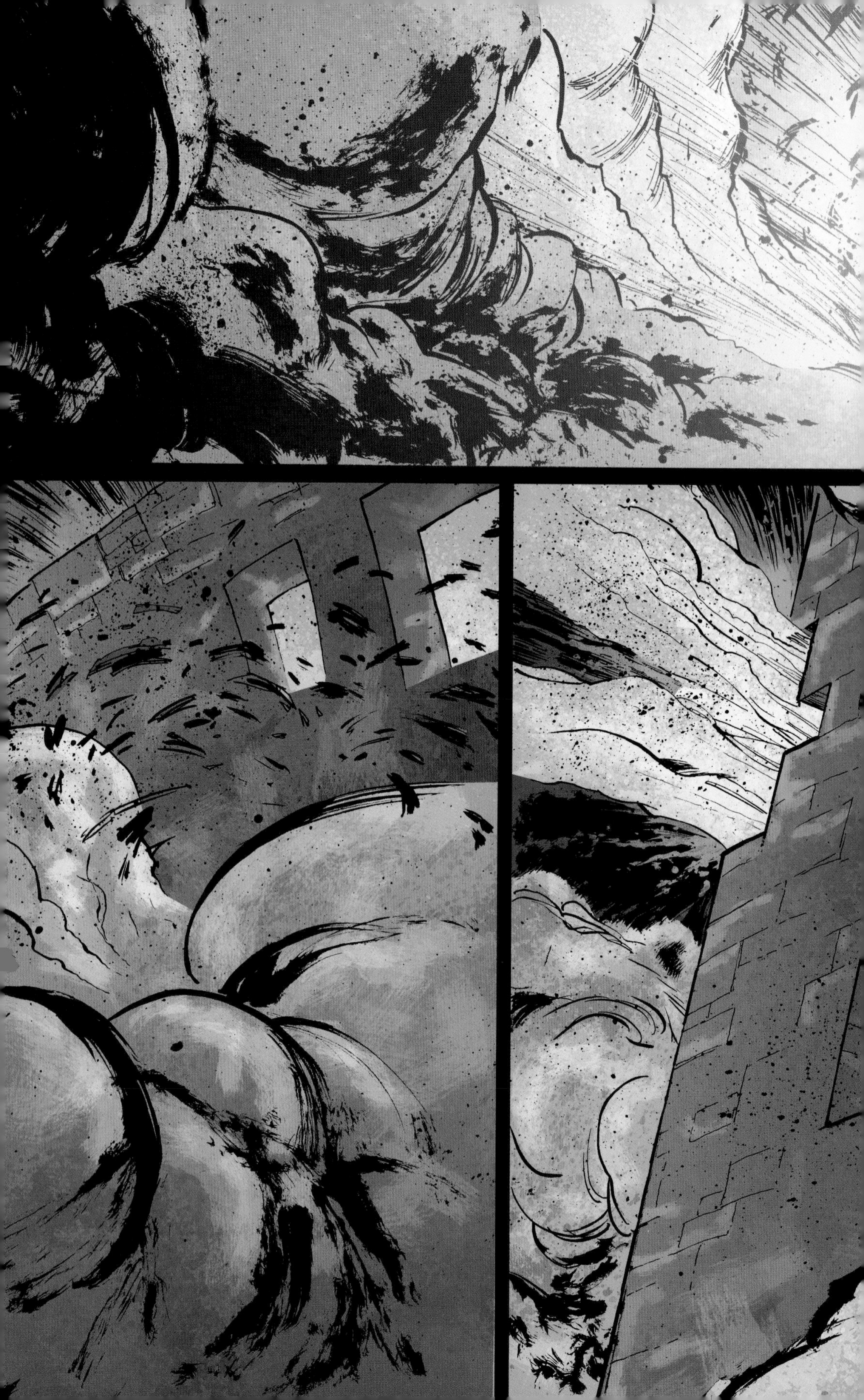

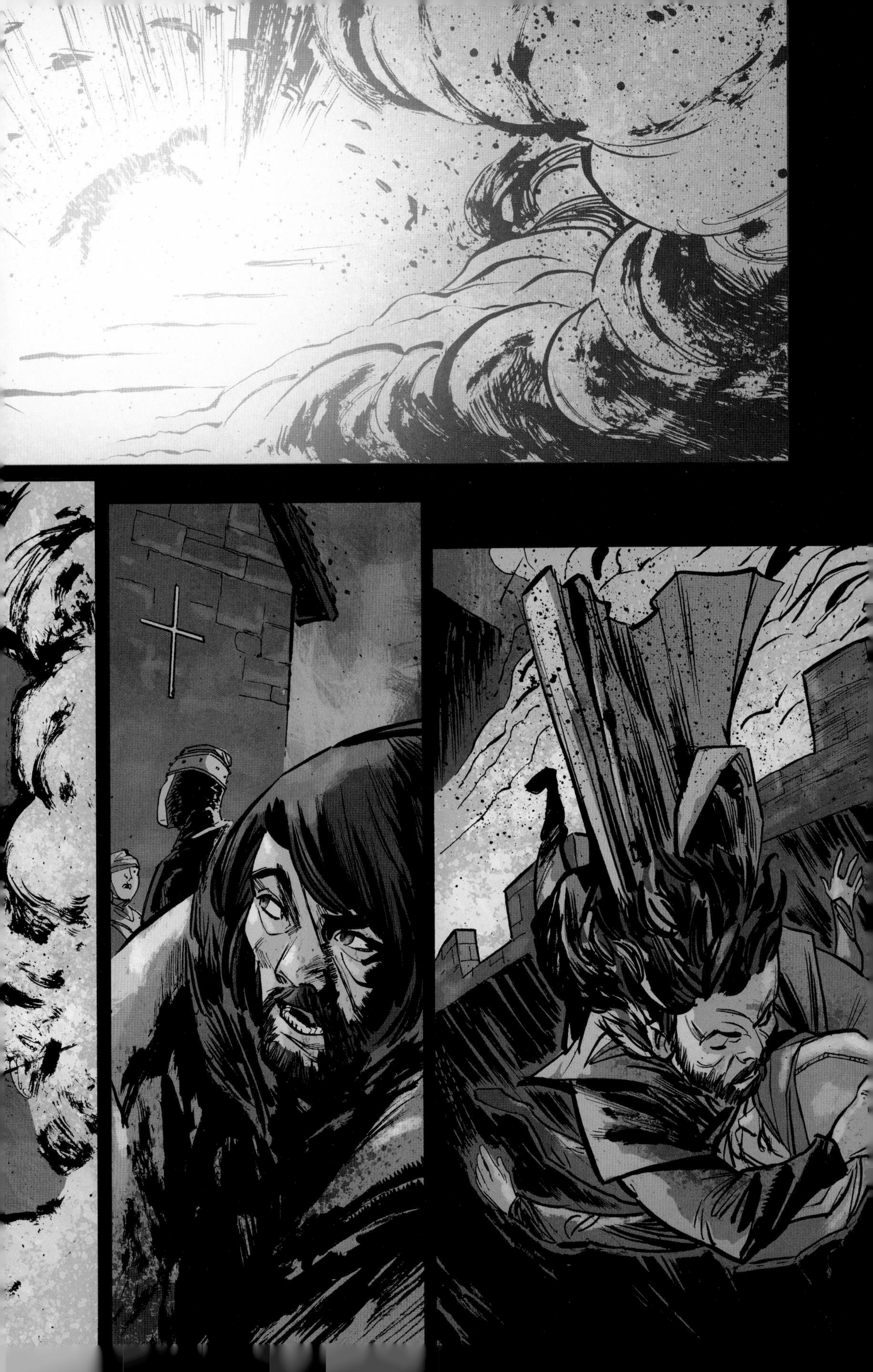

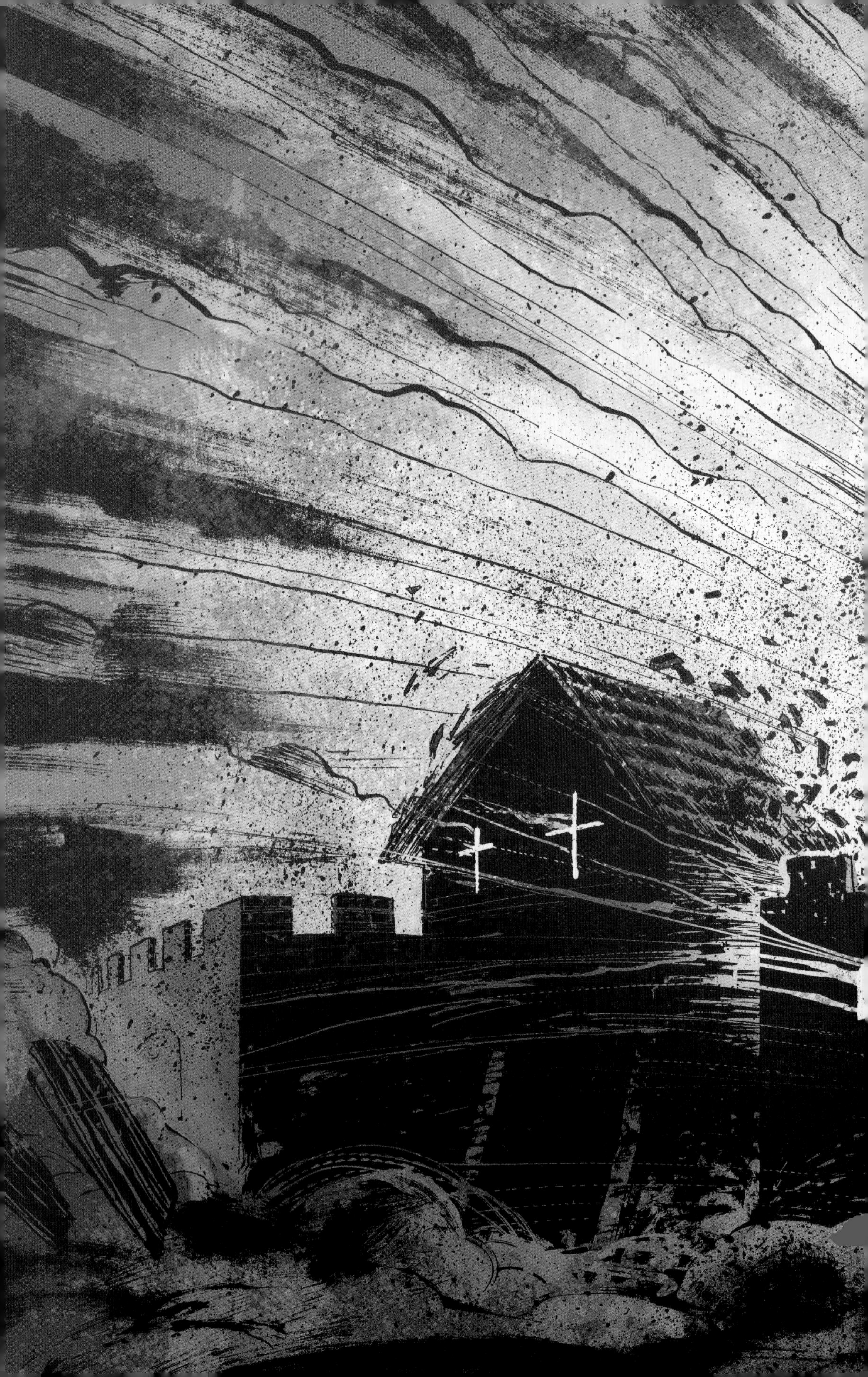

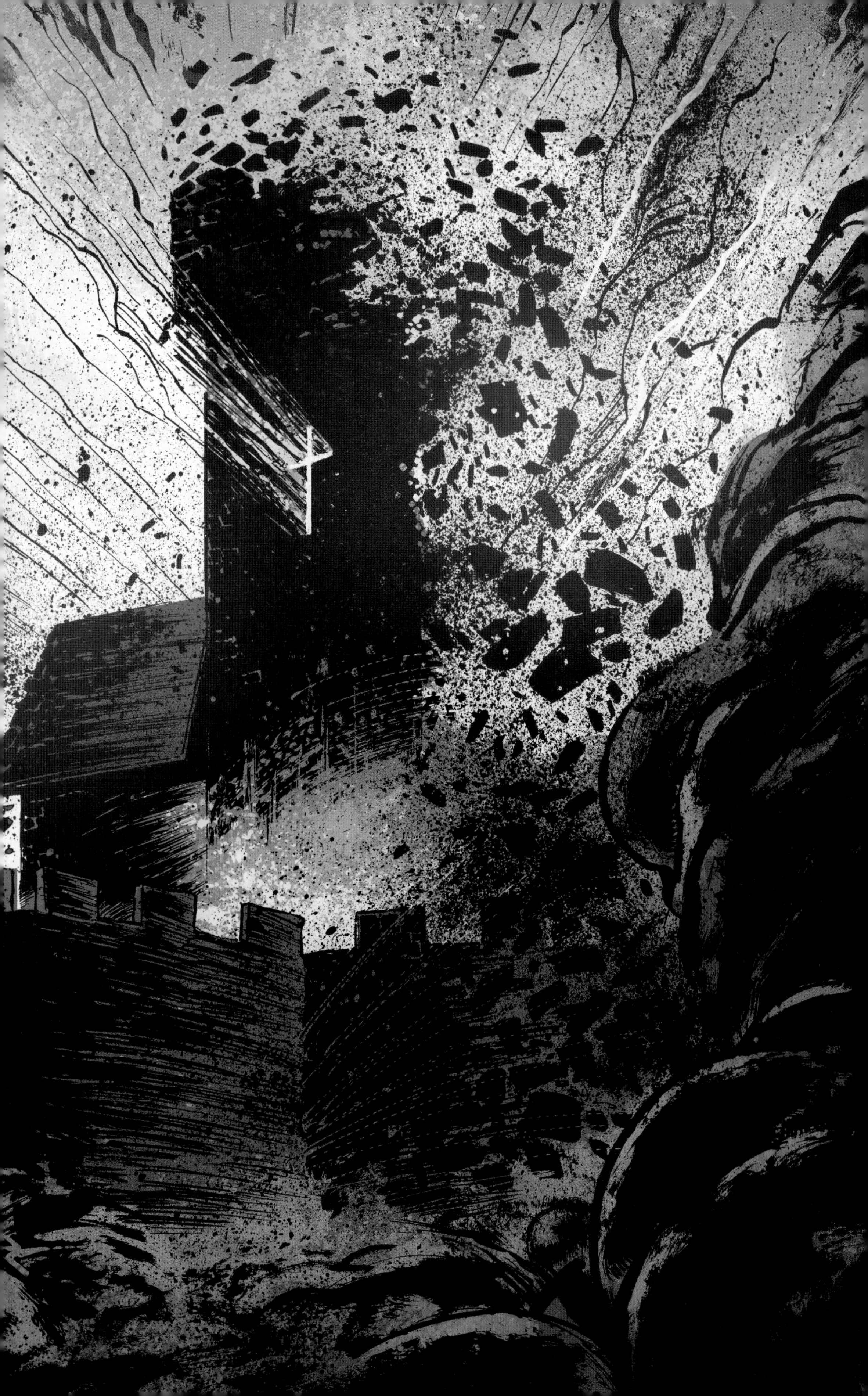

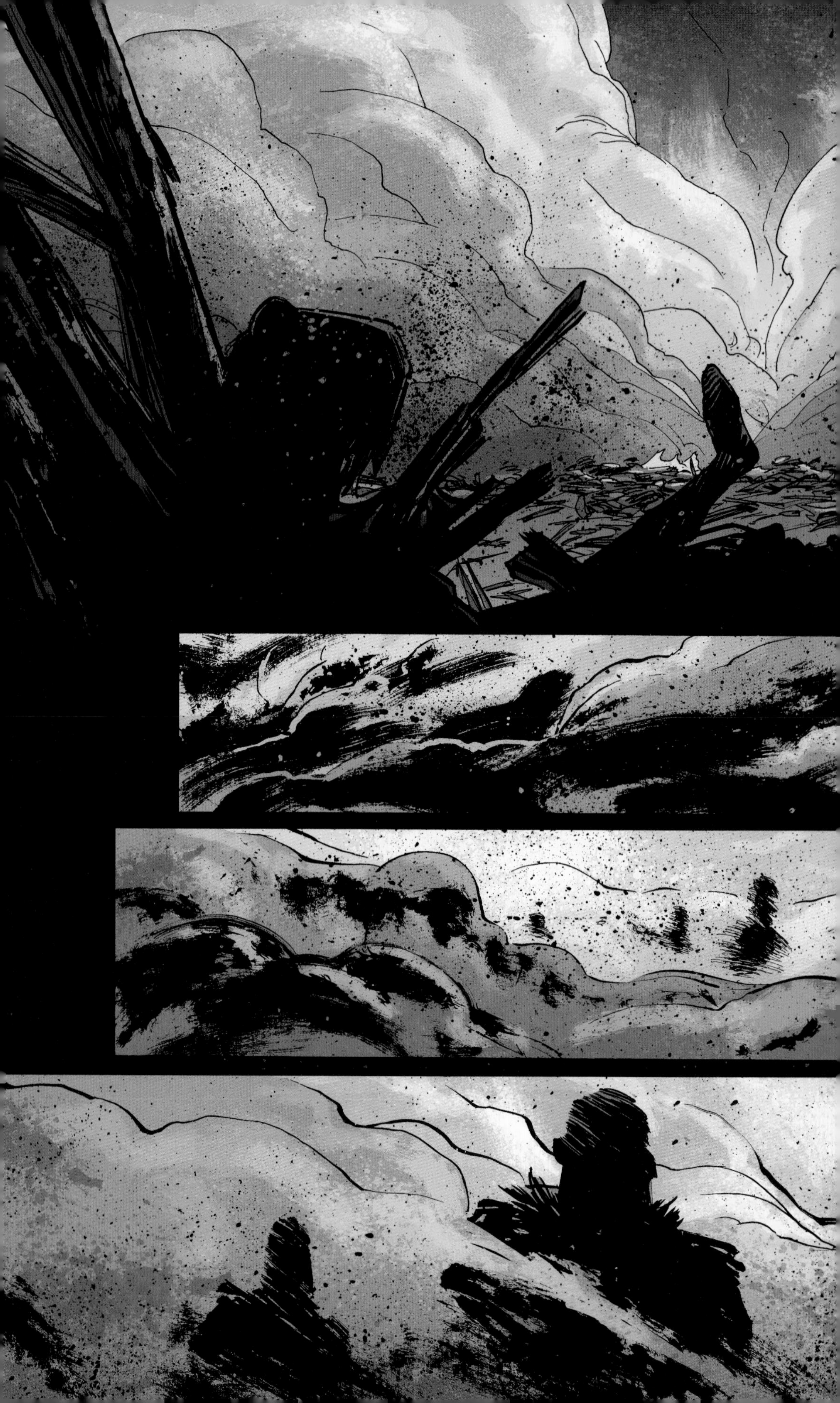

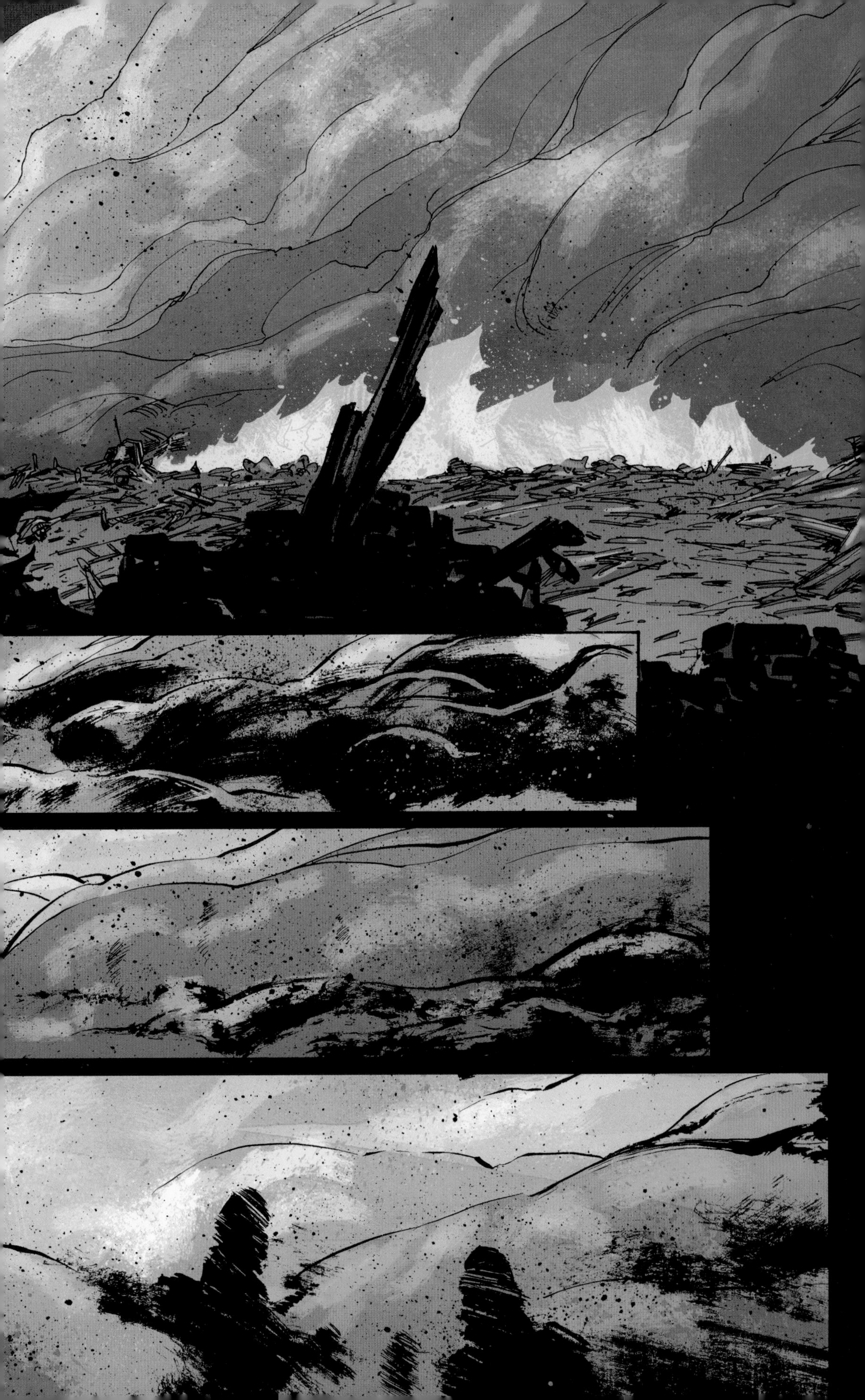

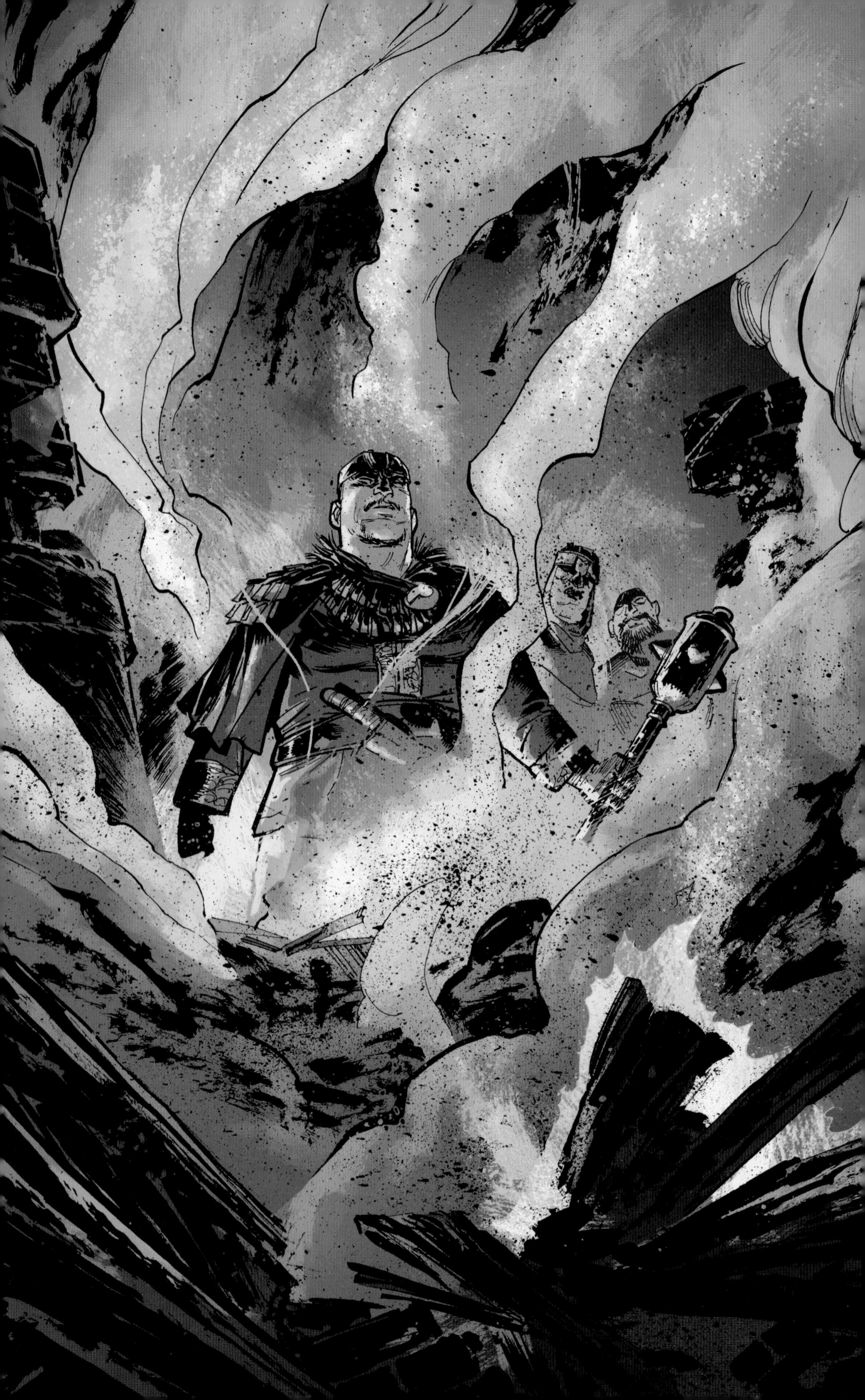

The Two Swords

— Chapter 3 —

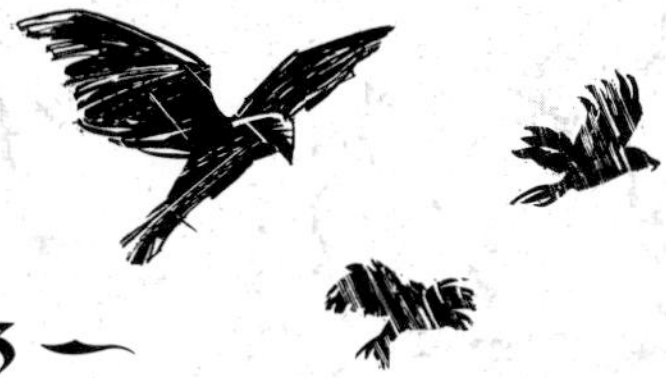

The ship was heavy in the water, and Tomislav would be happy to never sail again.

It had been months since Lord Aedon had rescued him from Istvan's dungeons, months of careful planning and traveling. No one in the world knew the warlord the way Tomislav did, and his years spent as a mercenary at the eastern edge of the world had given this son of a fallen house knowledge of weapons of war that the western lords lacked.

Black powder.

Hundreds of barrels of what looked to be harmless dust. In the lands where Tomislav first encountered it, the material was used mostly for toys or for displays of celebration. Mostly.

The ship could have taken the faster route through the narrow straits — but that would have brought the precious cargo dangerously close to Tomislav's former homeland. No, he told himself. His home was gone, and this mission was too important to risk on sentimentality.

The war between the western lords and Istvan was going poorly. Though the Saxon kings had first shown a united front, the cruel and prolonged slaughter of Lord Cyril and his family had broken the ranks of some of the lesser houses. And as it had gone before, weaker lords quickly turned allegiance in hopes of survival.

Tomislav had witnessed none of this; his mission kept him from the battles. No one else knew the trade routes of the East, no one else spoke the languages needed, nor would they be trusted enough by the mercenaries and pirates that had access to the volatile explosive powder.

Already two ships had sailed ahead. Tomislav's was the last, a vessel bound for the coast near Aedon's castle. From there, Aedon's army would retrieve the powder from its hiding place underneath the castle and move it secretly to the front line. The element of surprise and the advantage of the unknown weapon was their only remaining hope for defeating Istvan and his massive army.

Tomislav's introspection was interrupted by the ship's captain, a dark-skinned pirate hired at a port in the far South. "There was a bird," was all the man said as he handed Tomislav the small scroll, sealed with wax. Tomislav quickly scanned the message.

The news was dire: the king had moved more quickly than any of them had hoped. "Make for shore," he instructed the captain. "I'll find a horse. It will be faster."

With that he picked up his swords, drawing one and testing the edge with his thumb. "Deliver the barrels," he continued. "Speak to no one of your journey. The rest of your payment will be at the port."

"You will ride alone?" the captain asked, his eyebrow raised.

"It's my debt to repay," Tomislav whispered. "If only there's time."

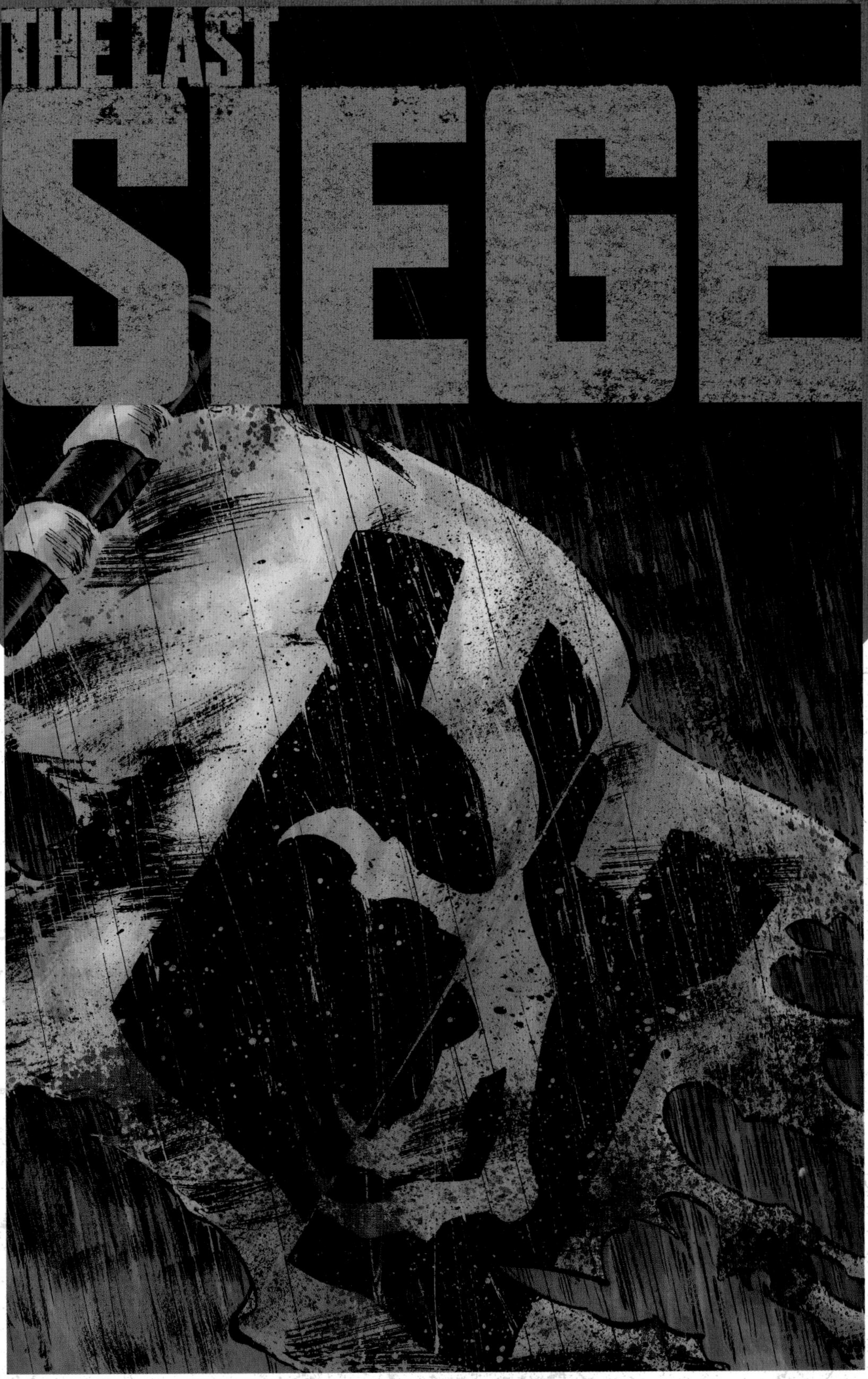
THE LAST
SIEGE

CHAPTER EIGHT

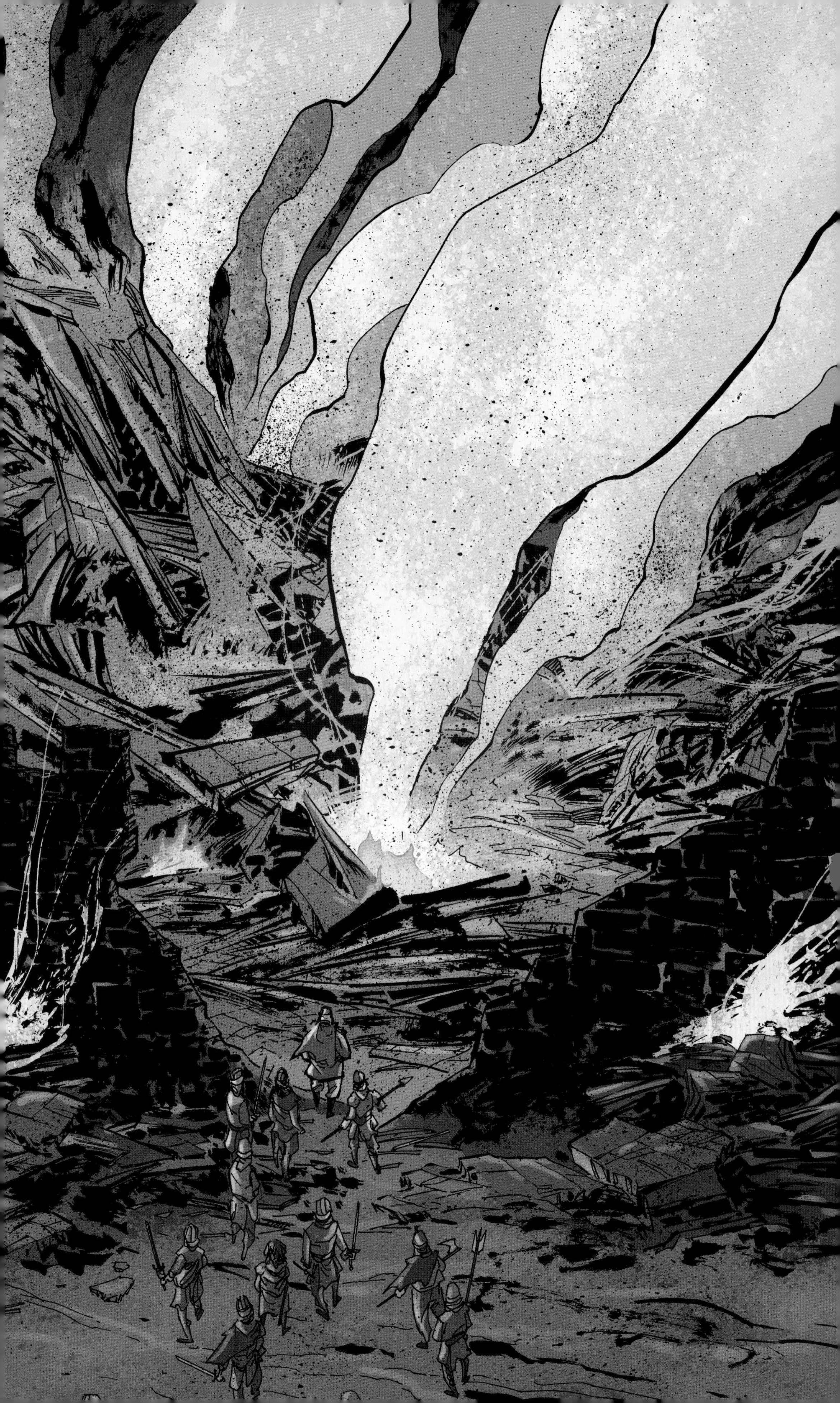

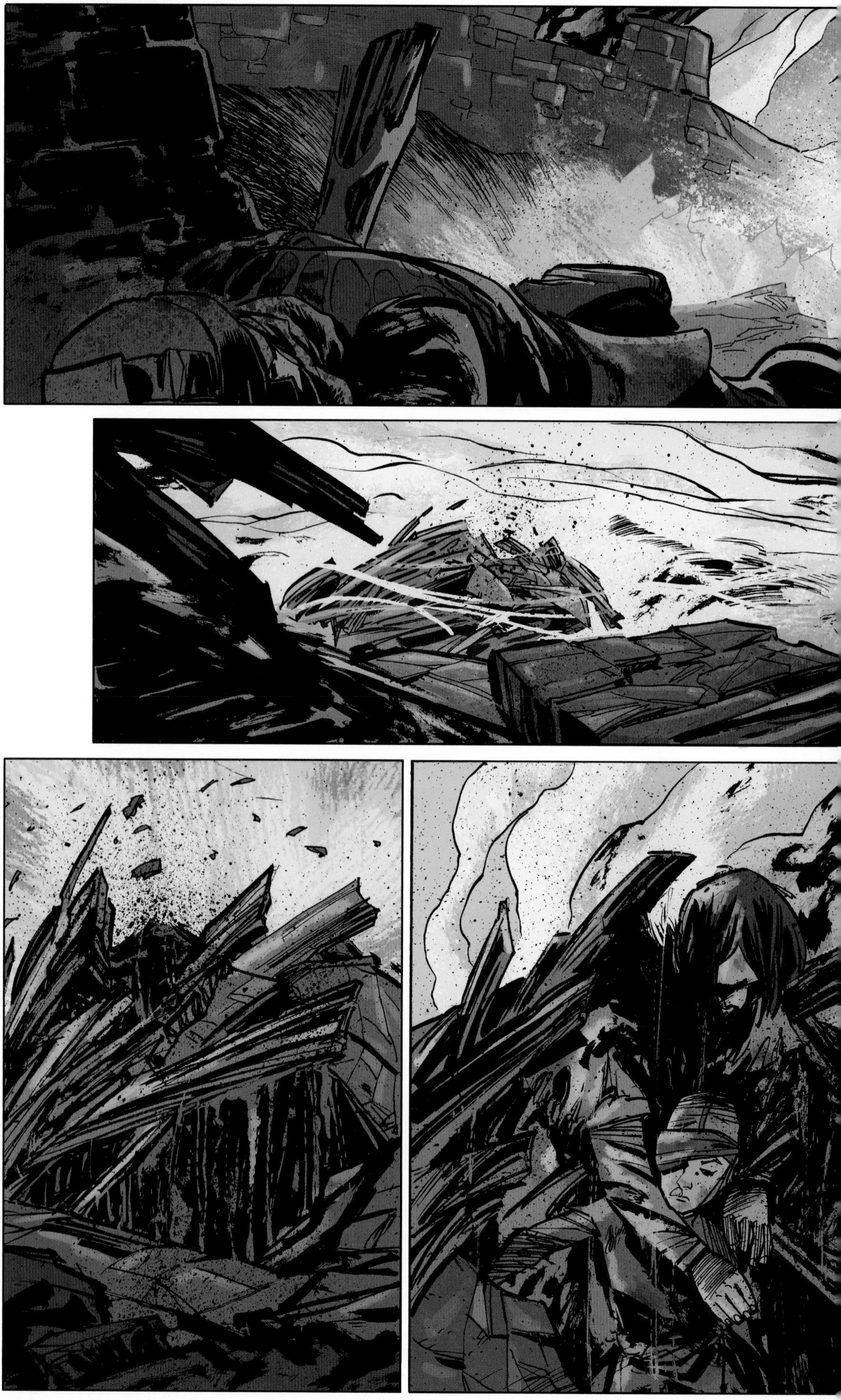

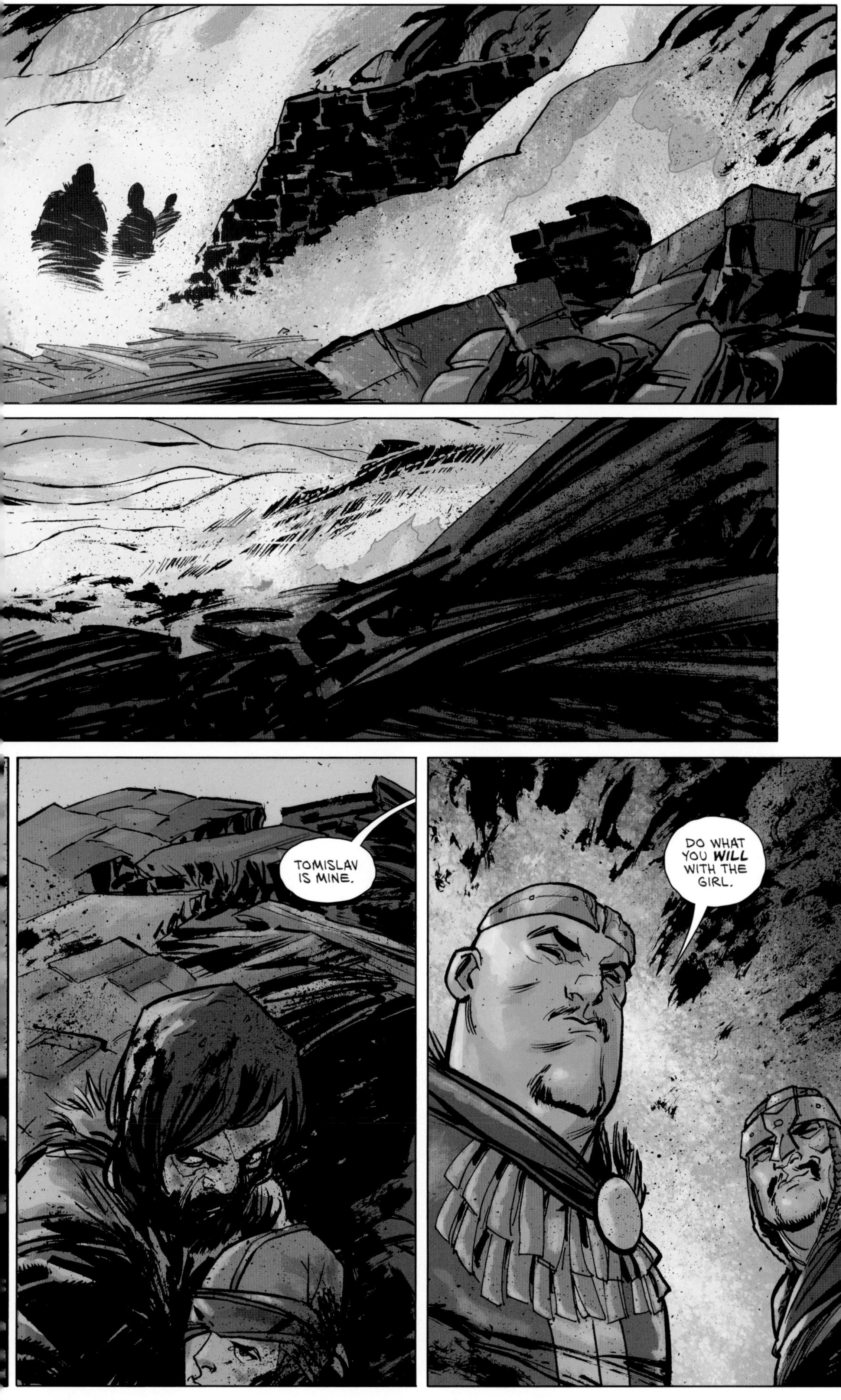
TOMISLAV IS MINE.
DO WHAT YOU WILL WITH THE GIRL.

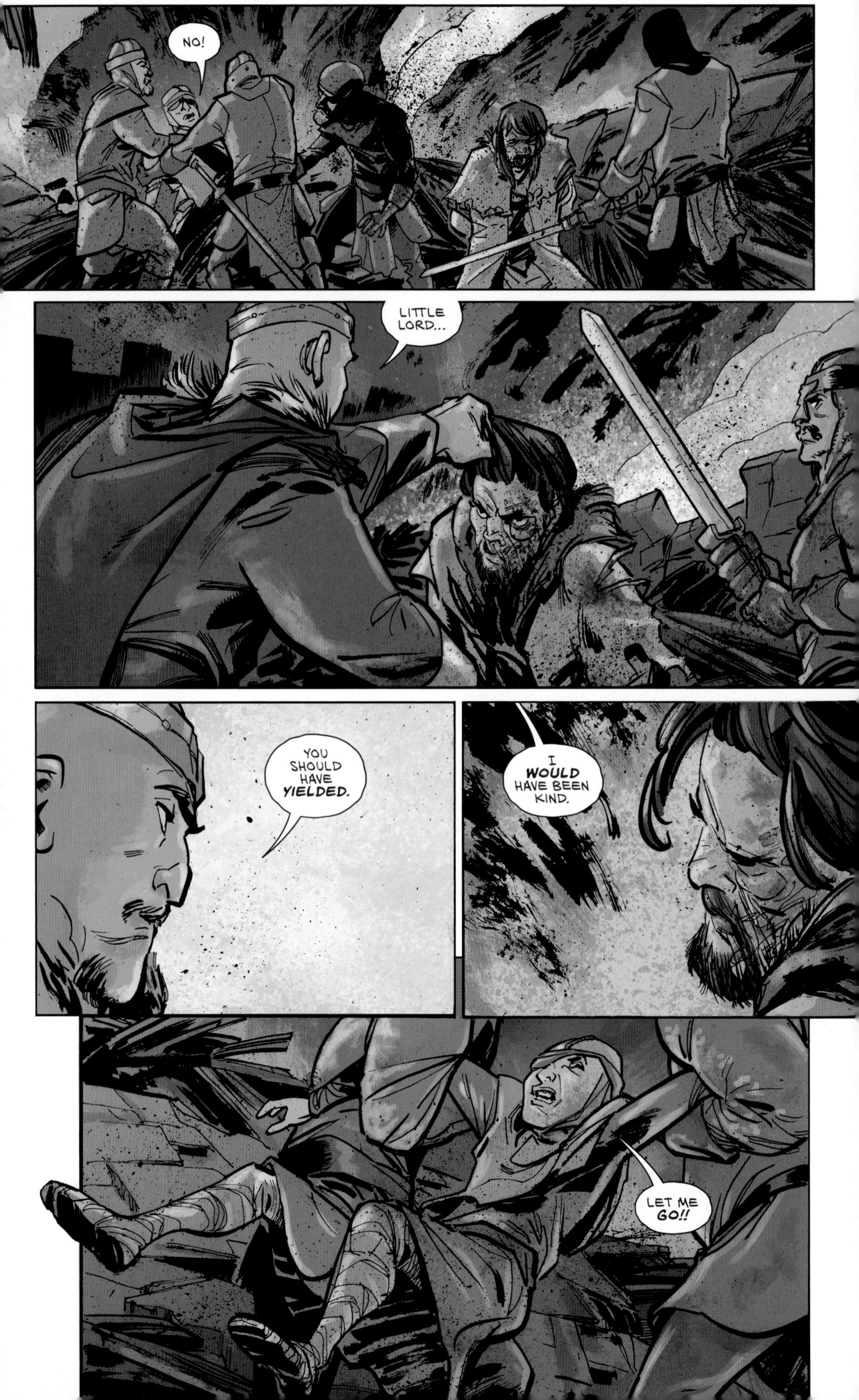
NO!
LITTLE LORD...
YOU SHOULD HAVE YIELDED.
I WOULD HAVE BEEN KIND.
LET ME GO!!

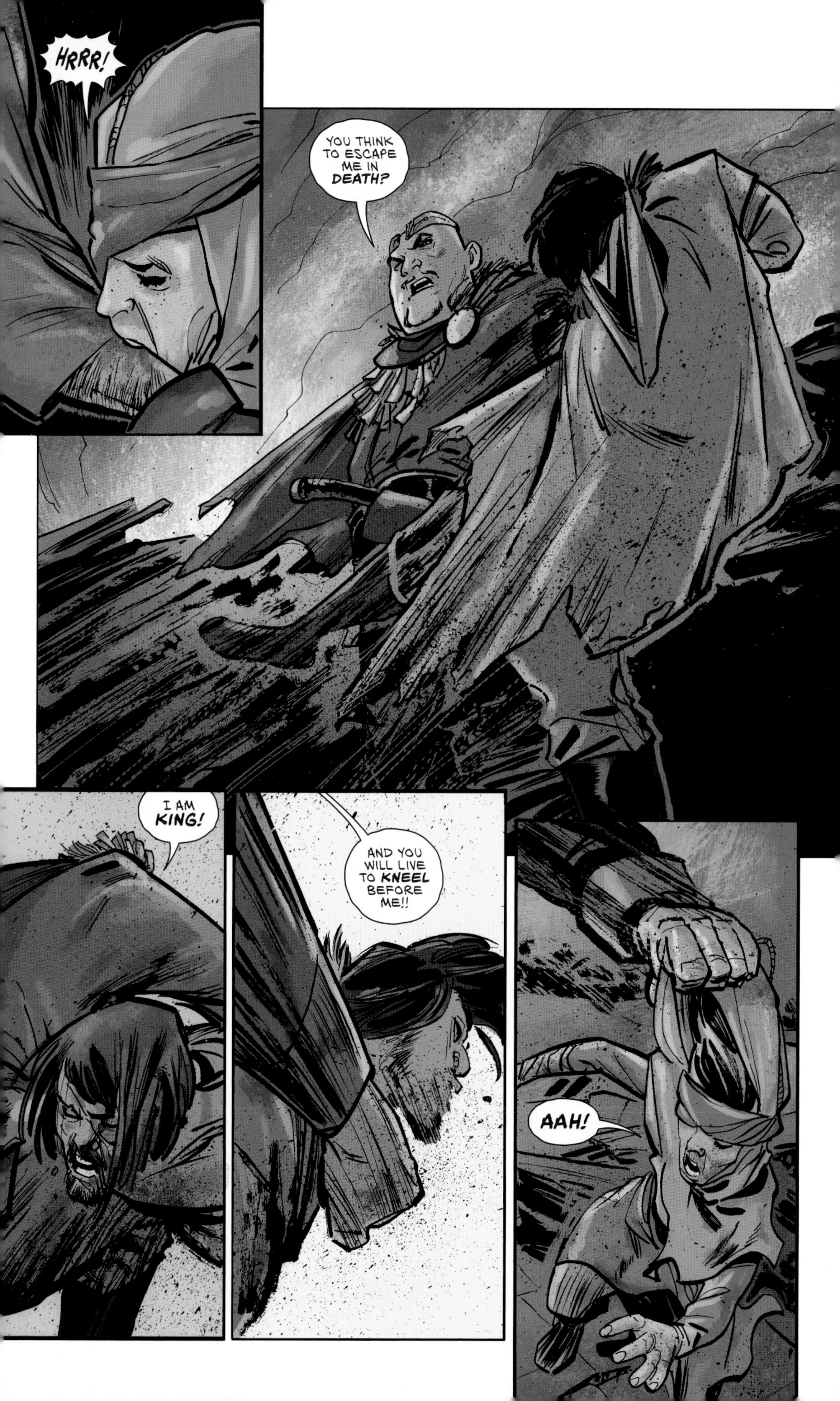
HRRR!
YOU THINK TO ESCAPE ME IN DEATH?
I AM KING!
AND YOU WILL LIVE TO KNEEL BEFORE ME!!
AAH!

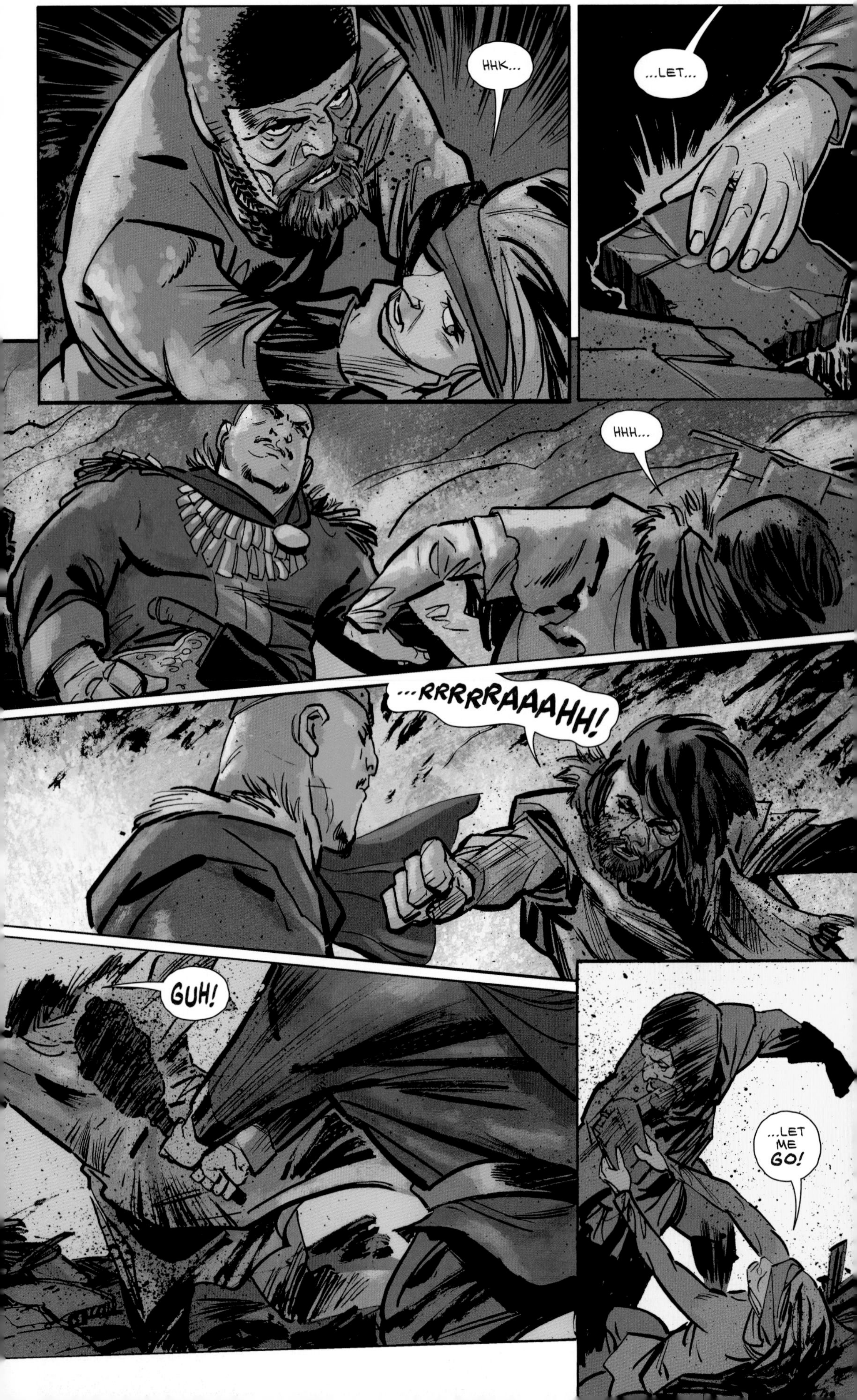
HHK...
...LET...
HHH...
...RRRRRAAAHH!
GUH!
...LET ME GO!

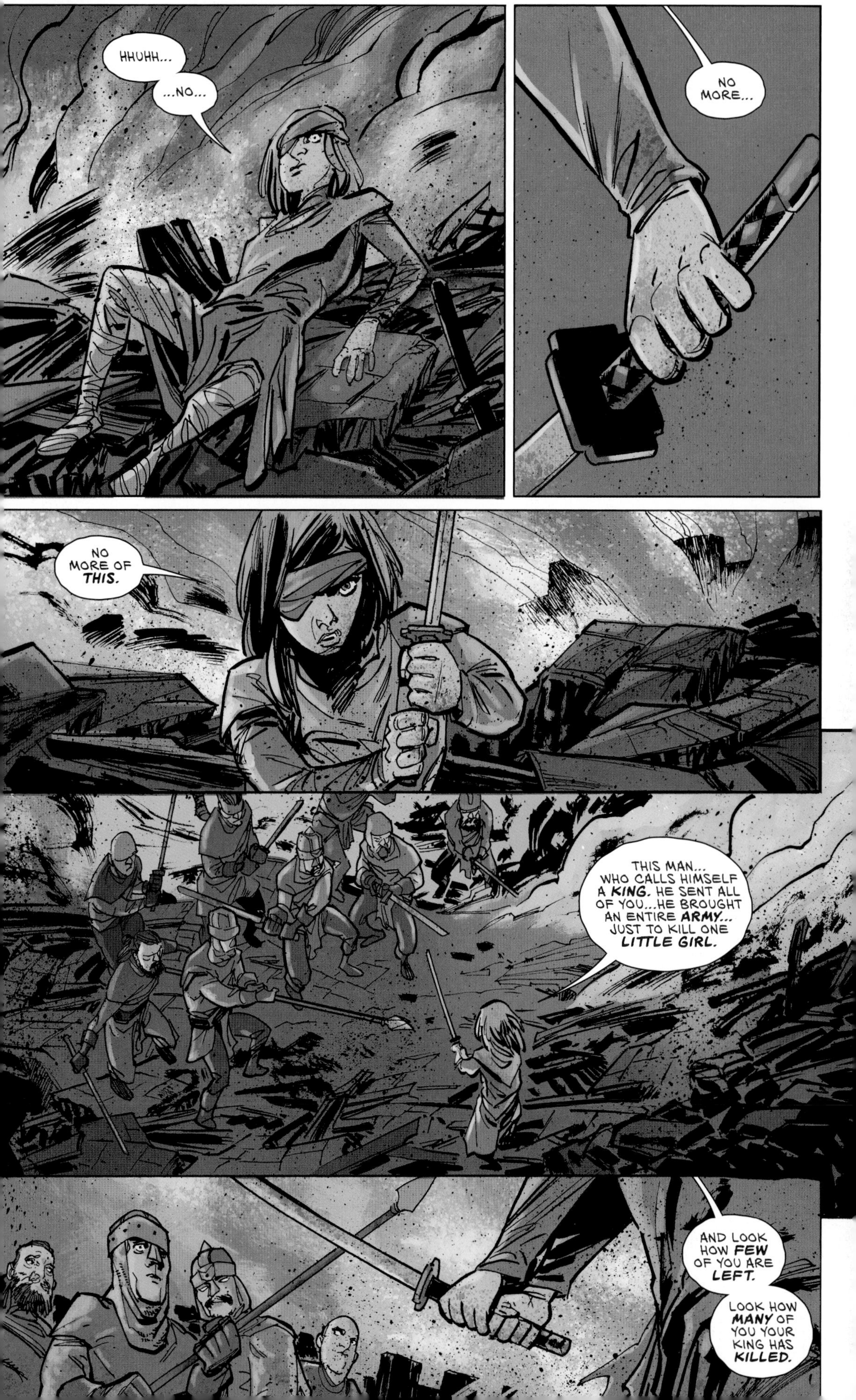

HHUHH...
...NO...
NO MORE...
NO MORE OF **THIS.**
THIS MAN... WHO CALLS HIMSELF A **KING.** HE SENT ALL OF YOU...HE BROUGHT AN ENTIRE **ARMY...** JUST TO KILL ONE **LITTLE GIRL.**
AND LOOK HOW **FEW** OF YOU ARE **LEFT.**
LOOK HOW **MANY** OF YOU YOUR KING HAS **KILLED.**

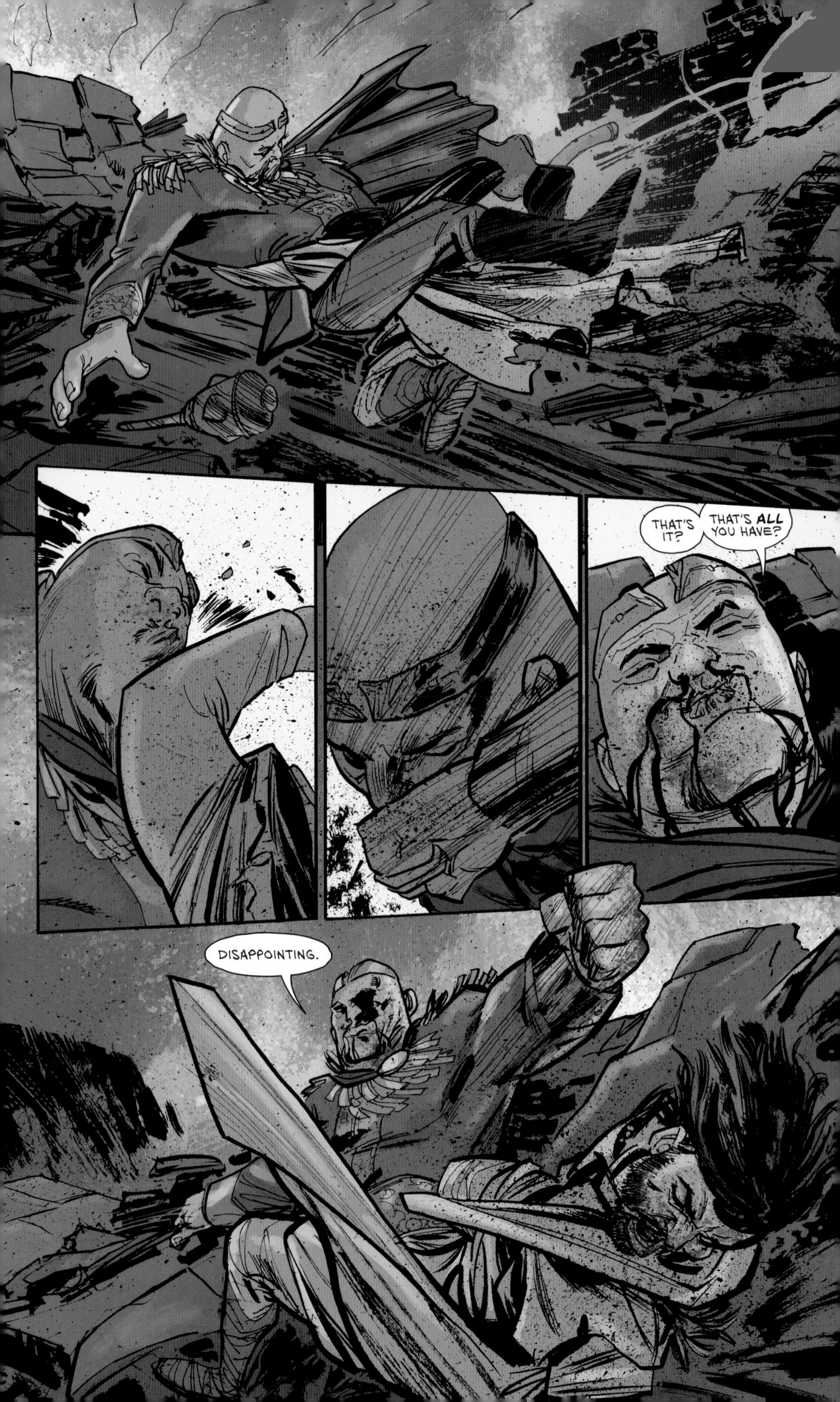
THAT'S IT?
THAT'S **ALL** YOU HAVE?
DISAPPOINTING.

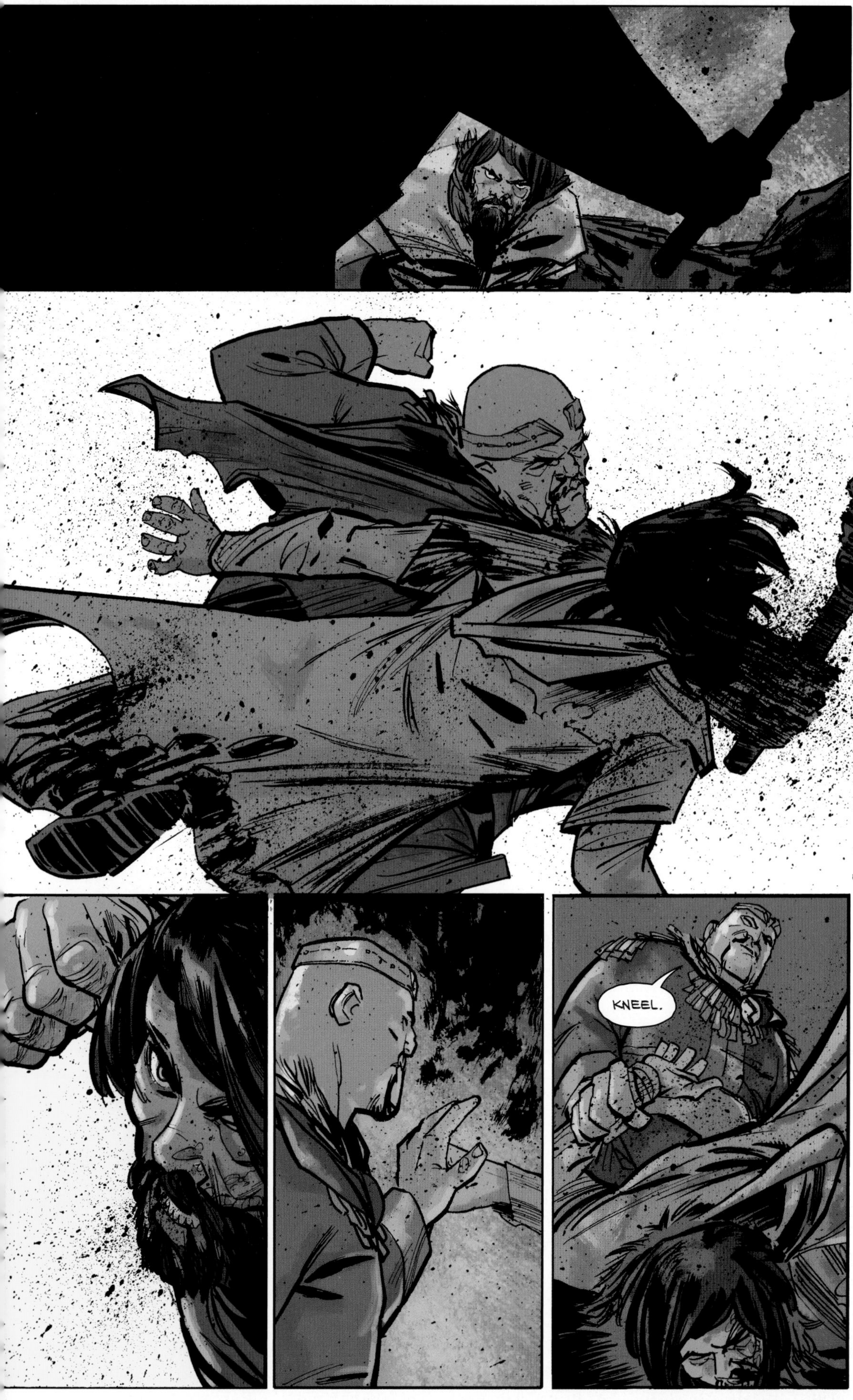
KNEEL.

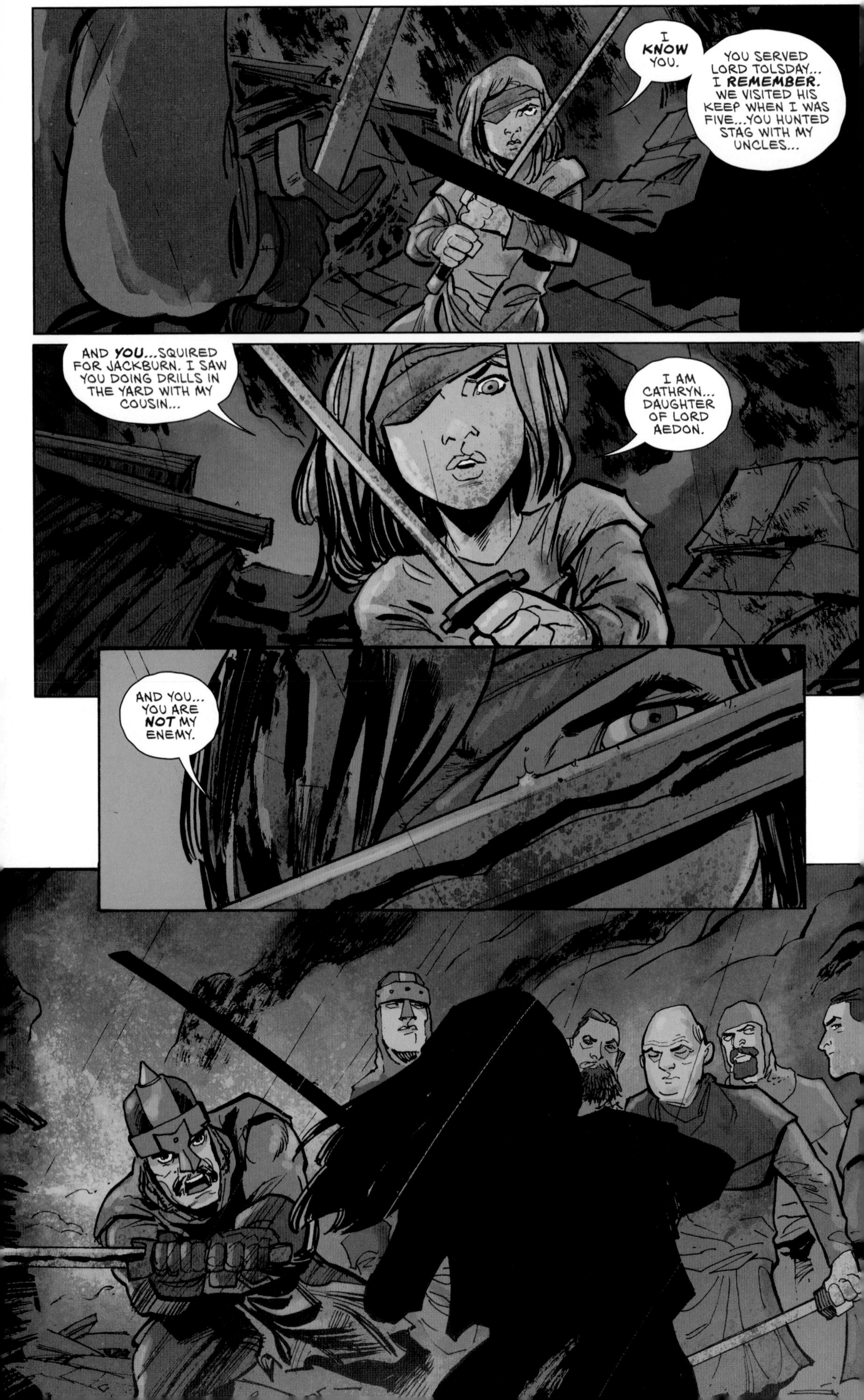

I KNOW YOU.
YOU SERVED LORD TOLSDAY... I REMEMBER. WE VISITED HIS KEEP WHEN I WAS FIVE...YOU HUNTED STAG WITH MY UNCLES...
AND YOU...SQUIRED FOR JACKBURN. I SAW YOU DOING DRILLS IN THE YARD WITH MY COUSIN...
I AM CATHRYN... DAUGHTER OF LORD AEDON.
AND YOU... YOU ARE NOT MY ENEMY.

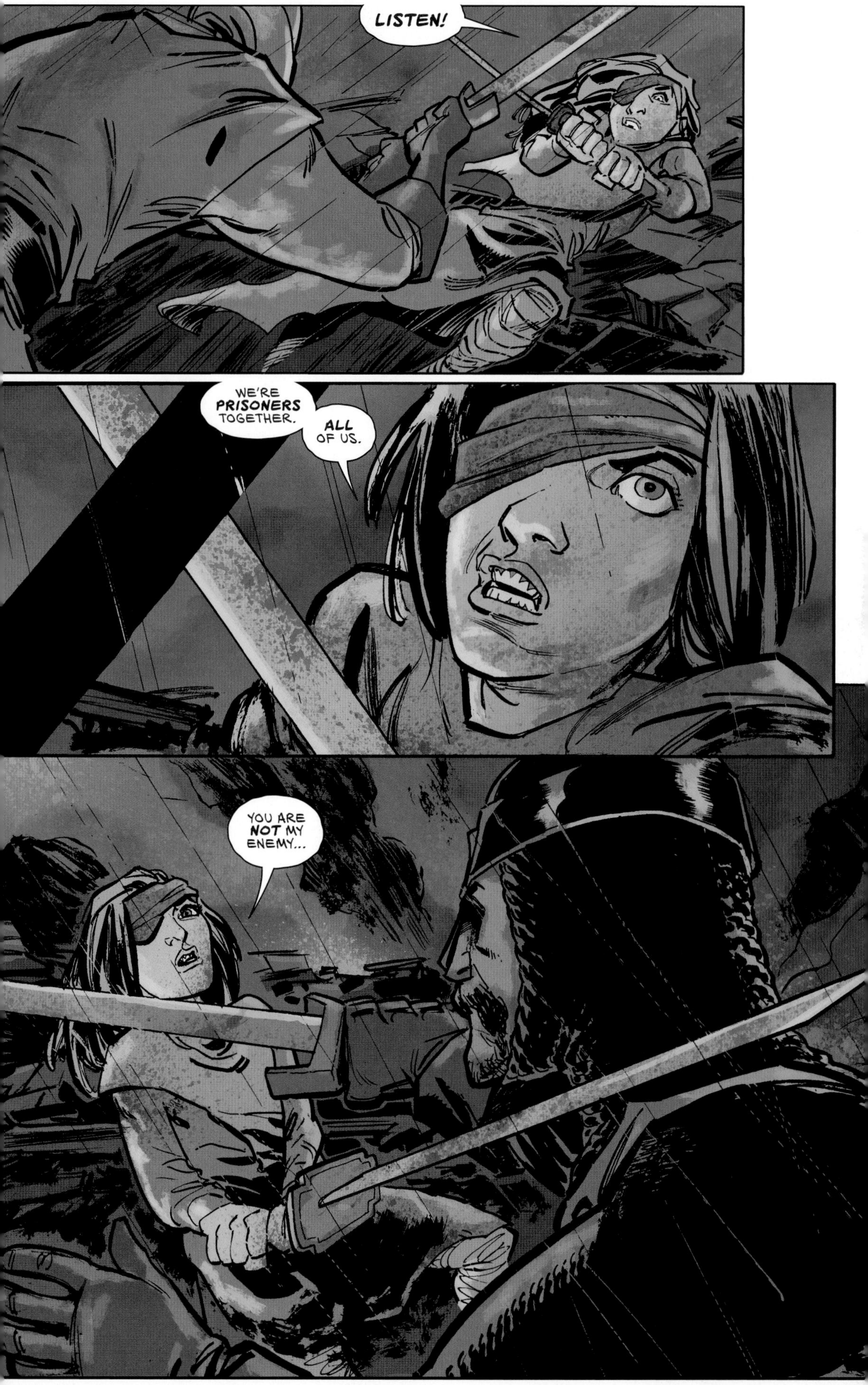
LISTEN!
WE'RE PRISONERS TOGETHER.
ALL OF US.
YOU ARE NOT MY ENEMY...

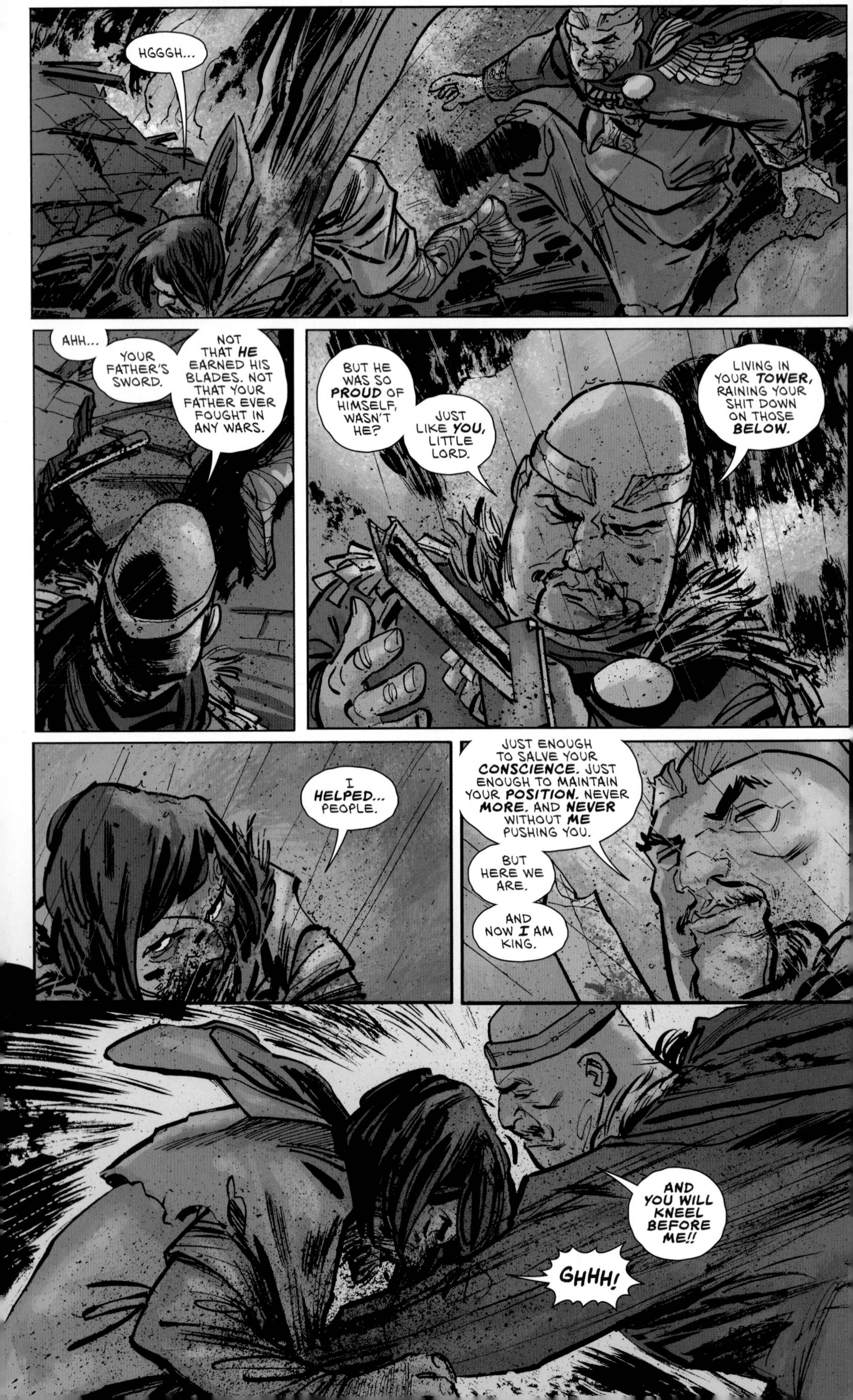
HGGGH...
AHH...
YOUR FATHER'S SWORD.
NOT THAT HE EARNED HIS BLADES. NOT THAT YOUR FATHER EVER FOUGHT IN ANY WARS.
BUT HE WAS SO PROUD OF HIMSELF, WASN'T HE?
JUST LIKE YOU, LITTLE LORD.
LIVING IN YOUR TOWER, RAINING YOUR SHIT DOWN ON THOSE BELOW.
I HELPED... PEOPLE.
JUST ENOUGH TO SALVE YOUR CONSCIENCE. JUST ENOUGH TO MAINTAIN YOUR POSITION. NEVER MORE. AND NEVER WITHOUT ME PUSHING YOU.
BUT HERE WE ARE.
AND NOW I AM KING.
AND YOU WILL KNEEL BEFORE ME!!
GHHH!

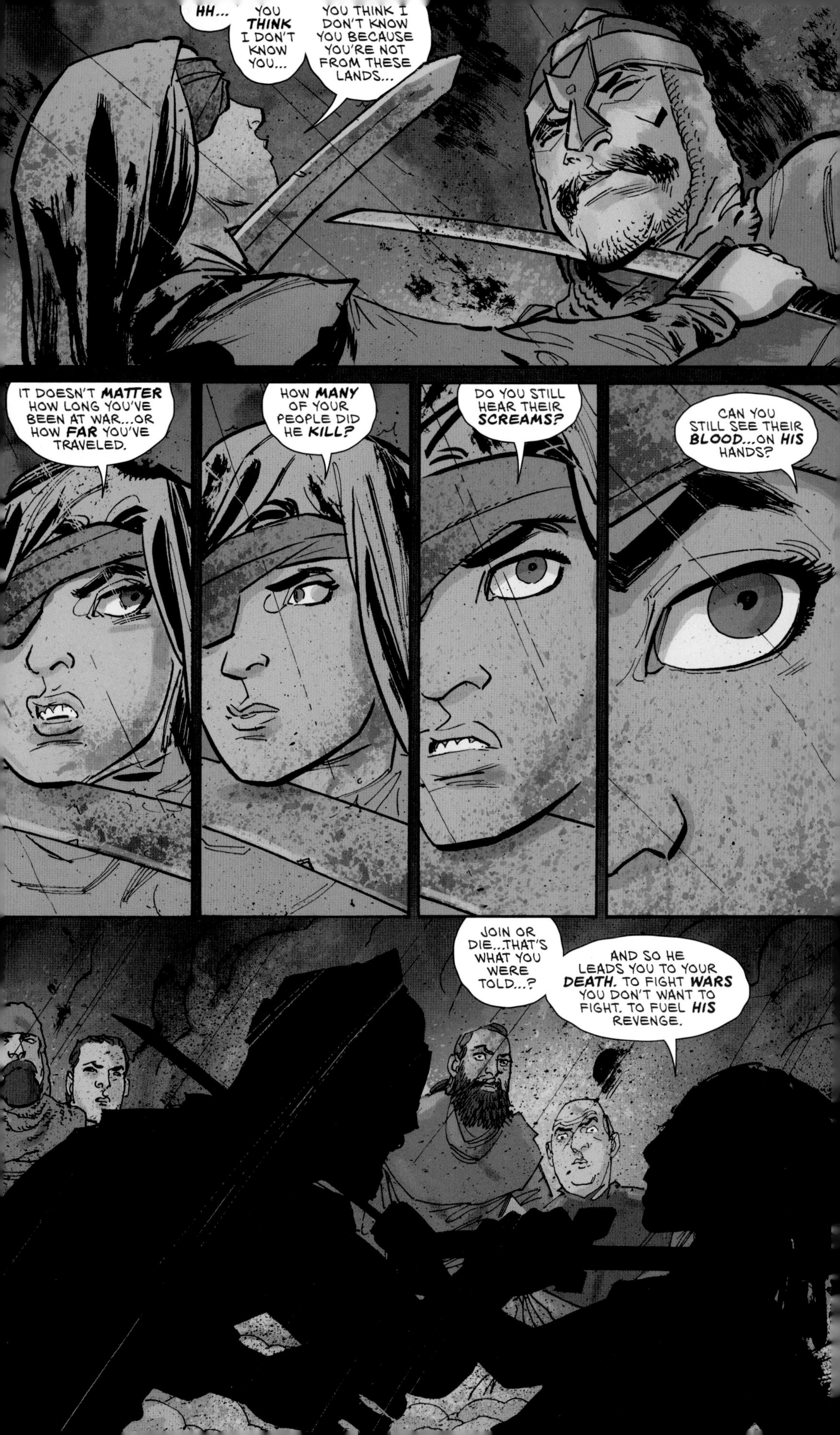
HH...
YOU THINK I DON'T KNOW YOU...
YOU THINK I DON'T KNOW YOU BECAUSE YOU'RE NOT FROM THESE LANDS...
IT DOESN'T MATTER HOW LONG YOU'VE BEEN AT WAR...OR HOW FAR YOU'VE TRAVELED.
HOW MANY OF YOUR PEOPLE DID HE KILL?
DO YOU STILL HEAR THEIR SCREAMS?
CAN YOU STILL SEE THEIR BLOOD...ON HIS HANDS?
JOIN OR DIE...THAT'S WHAT YOU WERE TOLD...?
AND SO HE LEADS YOU TO YOUR DEATH. TO FIGHT WARS YOU DON'T WANT TO FIGHT. TO FUEL HIS REVENGE.

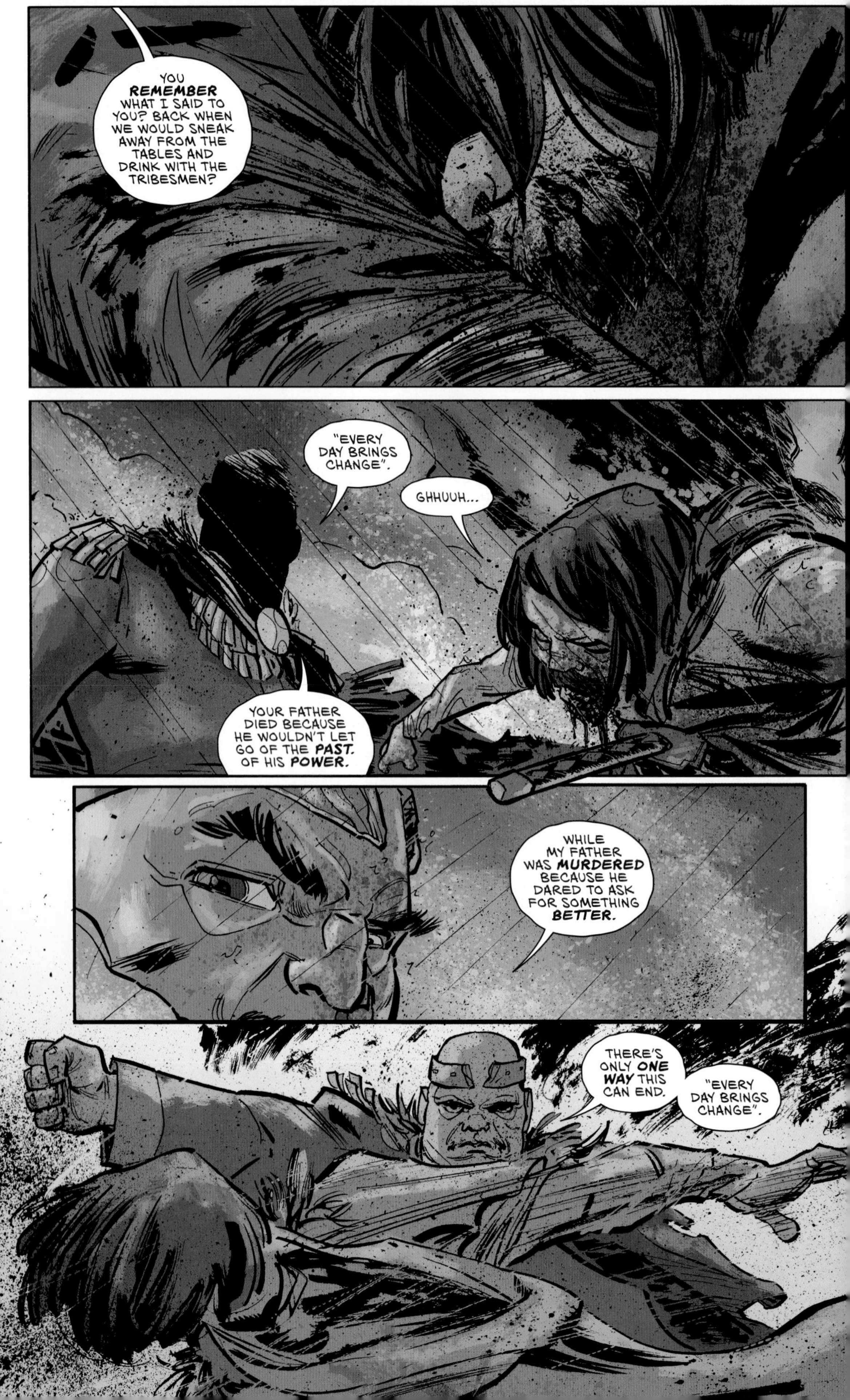
YOU REMEMBER WHAT I SAID TO YOU? BACK WHEN WE WOULD SNEAK AWAY FROM THE TABLES AND DRINK WITH THE TRIBESMEN?
"EVERY DAY BRINGS CHANGE".
GHHUUH...
YOUR FATHER DIED BECAUSE HE WOULDN'T LET GO OF THE PAST. OF HIS POWER.
WHILE MY FATHER WAS MURDERED BECAUSE HE DARED TO ASK FOR SOMETHING BETTER.
THERE'S ONLY ONE WAY THIS CAN END.
"EVERY DAY BRINGS CHANGE".

LISTEN TO ME...

YOU ARE **NOT** MY ENEMY...

...AND I AM **NOT** YOURS.

I AM CATHRYN, RIGHTFUL HEIR TO THIS KINGDOM.

LET ME **HELP** YOU.

LET ME HELP **ALL OF** YOU.

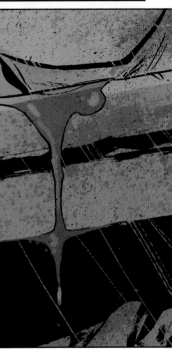

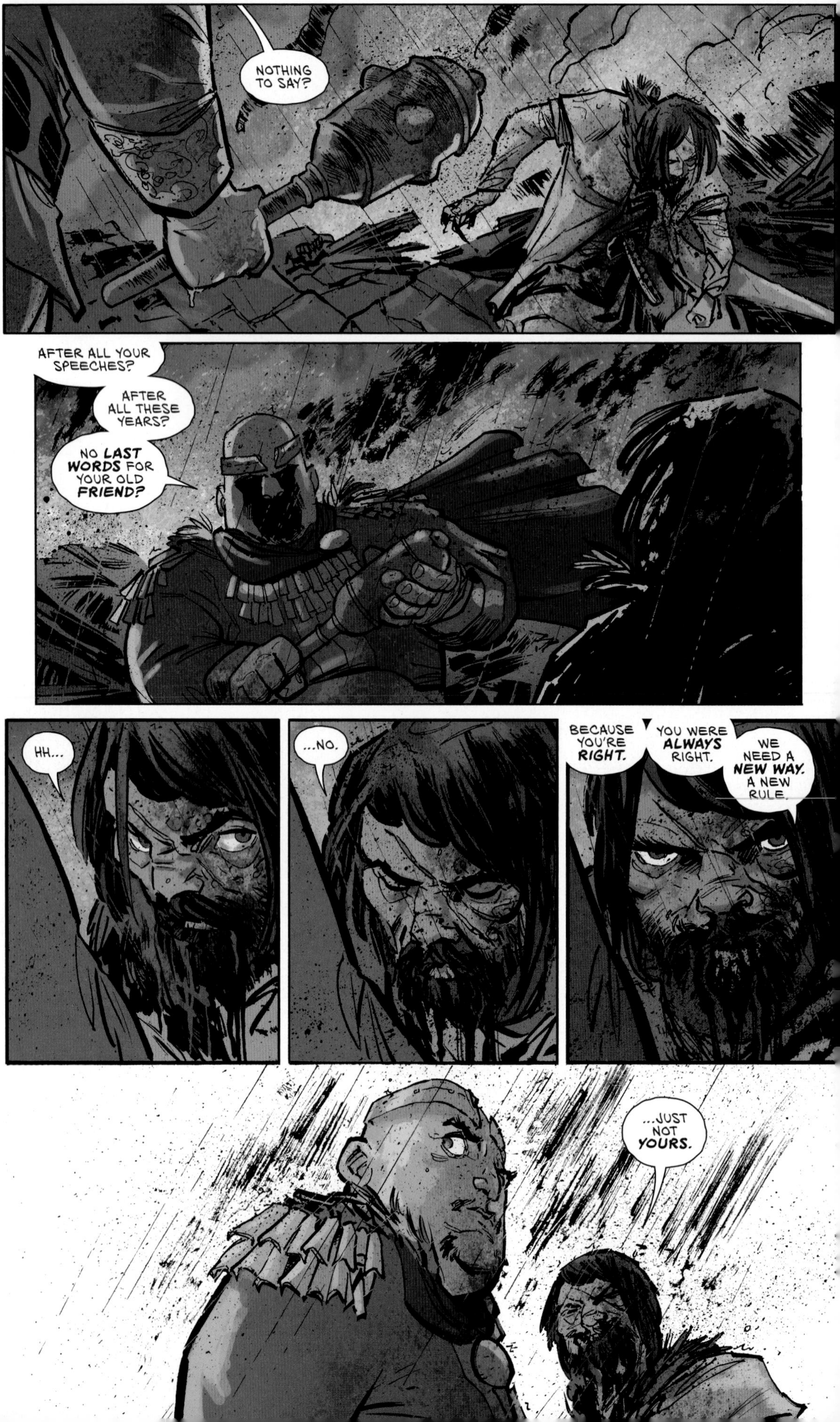
NOTHING TO SAY?
AFTER ALL YOUR SPEECHES?
AFTER ALL THESE YEARS?
NO **LAST WORDS** FOR YOUR OLD **FRIEND?**
HH...
...NO.
BECAUSE YOU'RE **RIGHT.**
YOU WERE **ALWAYS** RIGHT.
WE NEED A **NEW WAY.** A NEW RULE.
...JUST NOT **YOURS.**

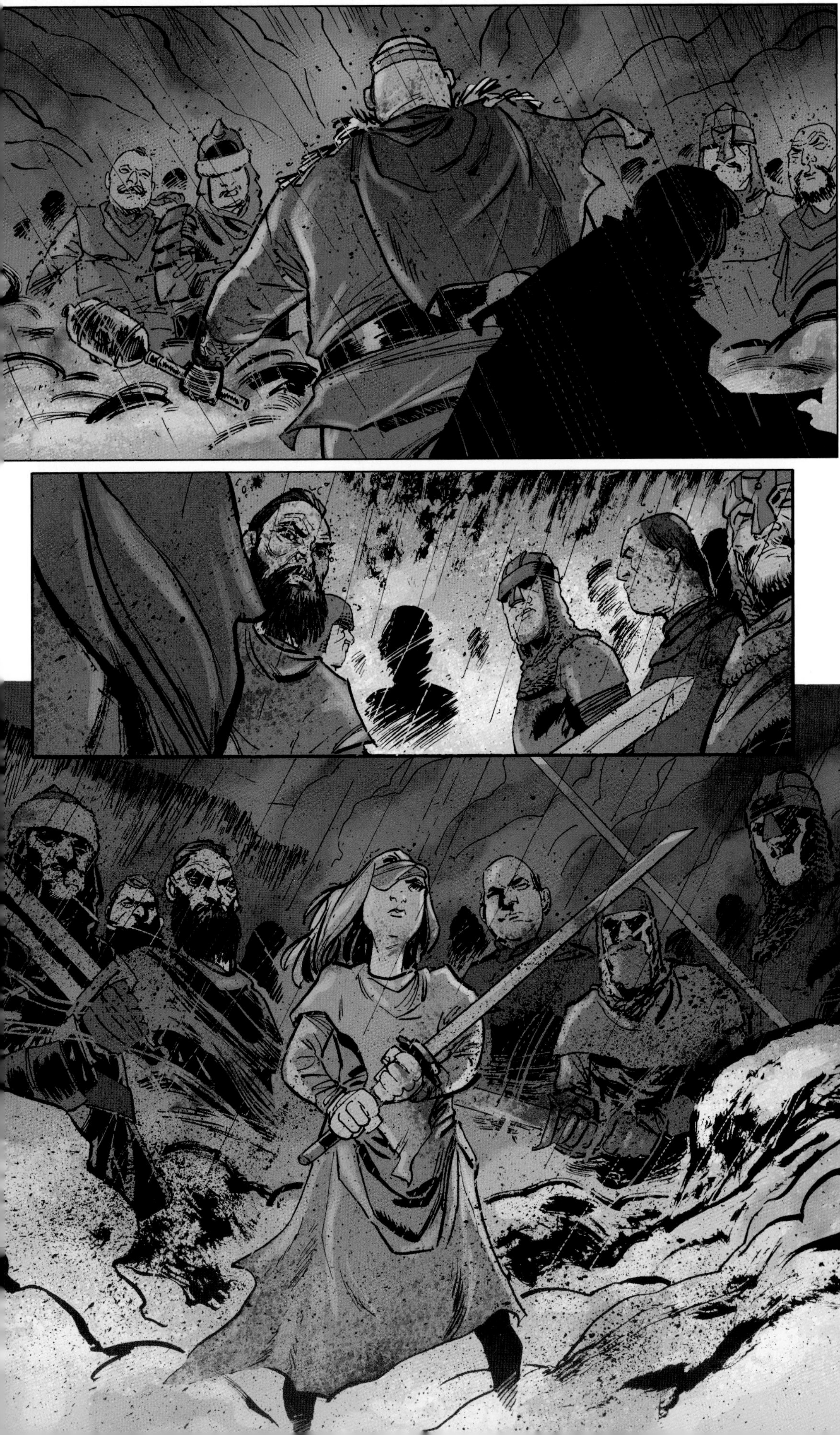

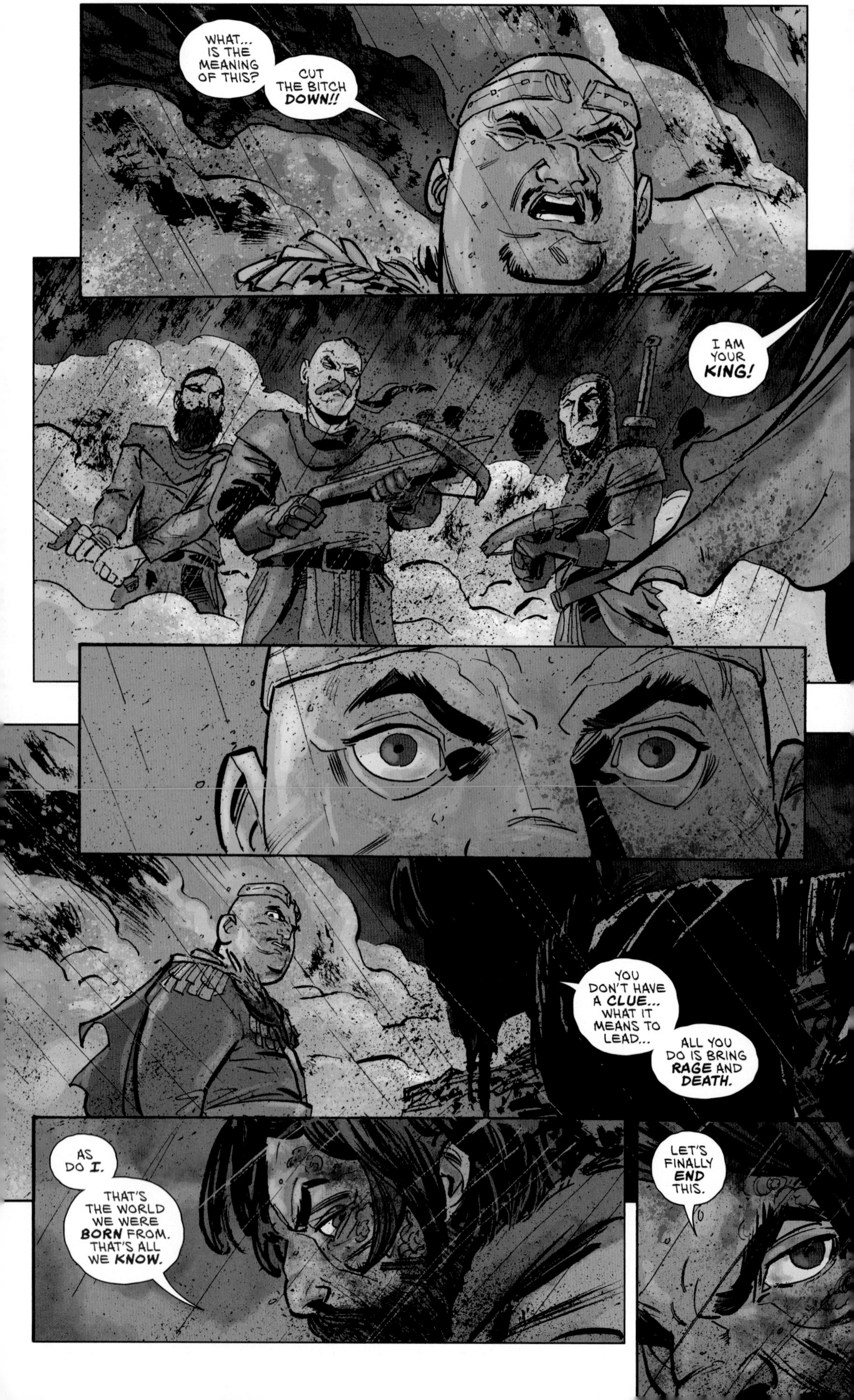
WHAT... IS THE MEANING OF THIS?
CUT THE BITCH DOWN!!
I AM YOUR KING!
YOU DON'T HAVE A CLUE... WHAT IT MEANS TO LEAD...
ALL YOU DO IS BRING RAGE AND DEATH.
AS DO I.
THAT'S THE WORLD WE WERE BORN FROM. THAT'S ALL WE KNOW.
LET'S FINALLY END THIS.

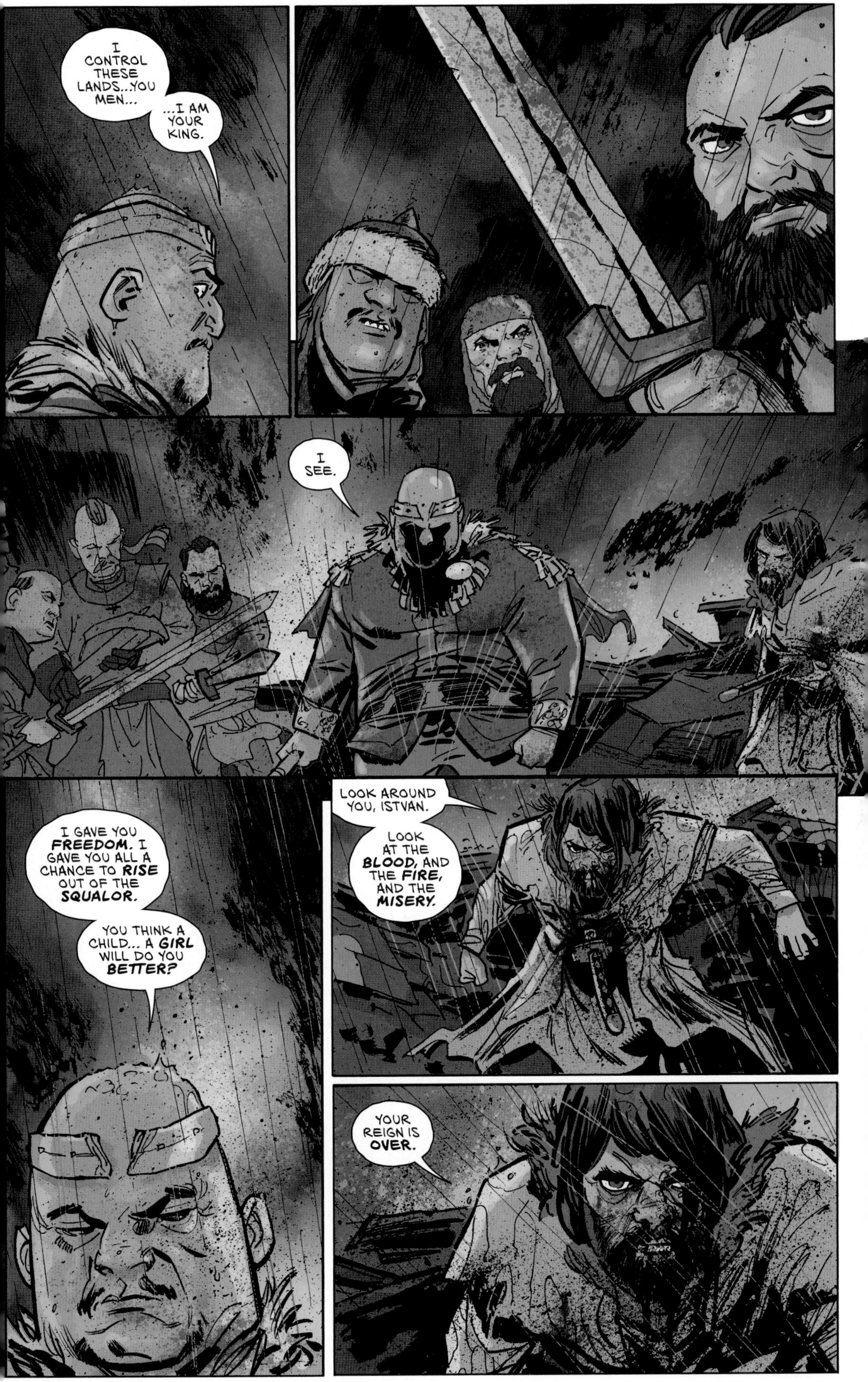

I CONTROL THESE LANDS...YOU MEN...
...I AM YOUR KING.
I SEE.
I GAVE YOU **FREEDOM**. I GAVE YOU ALL A CHANCE TO **RISE** OUT OF THE **SQUALOR**.
YOU THINK A CHILD... A **GIRL** WILL DO YOU **BETTER?**
LOOK AROUND YOU, ISTVAN.
LOOK AT THE **BLOOD**, AND THE **FIRE**, AND THE **MISERY**.
YOUR REIGN IS **OVER**.

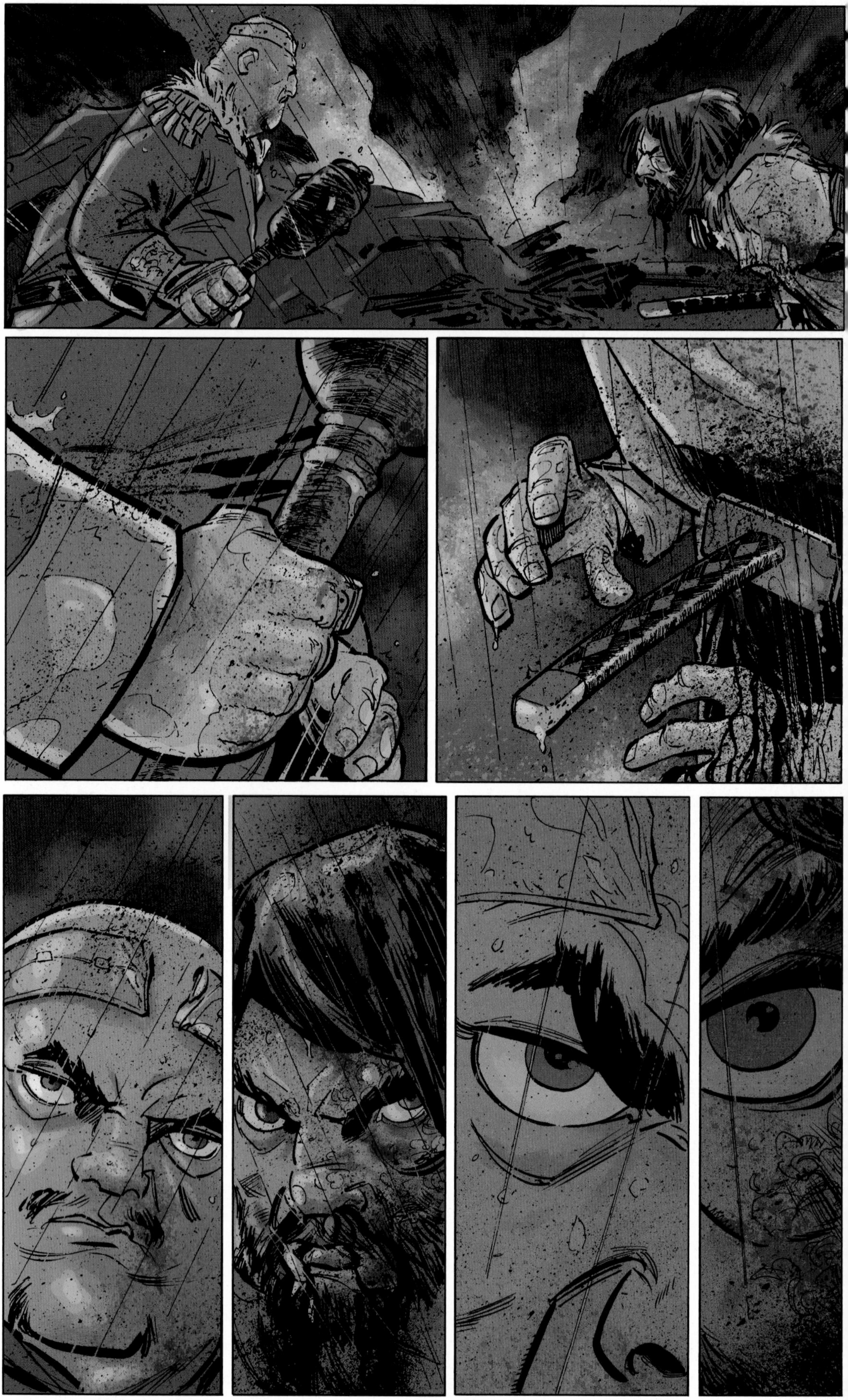

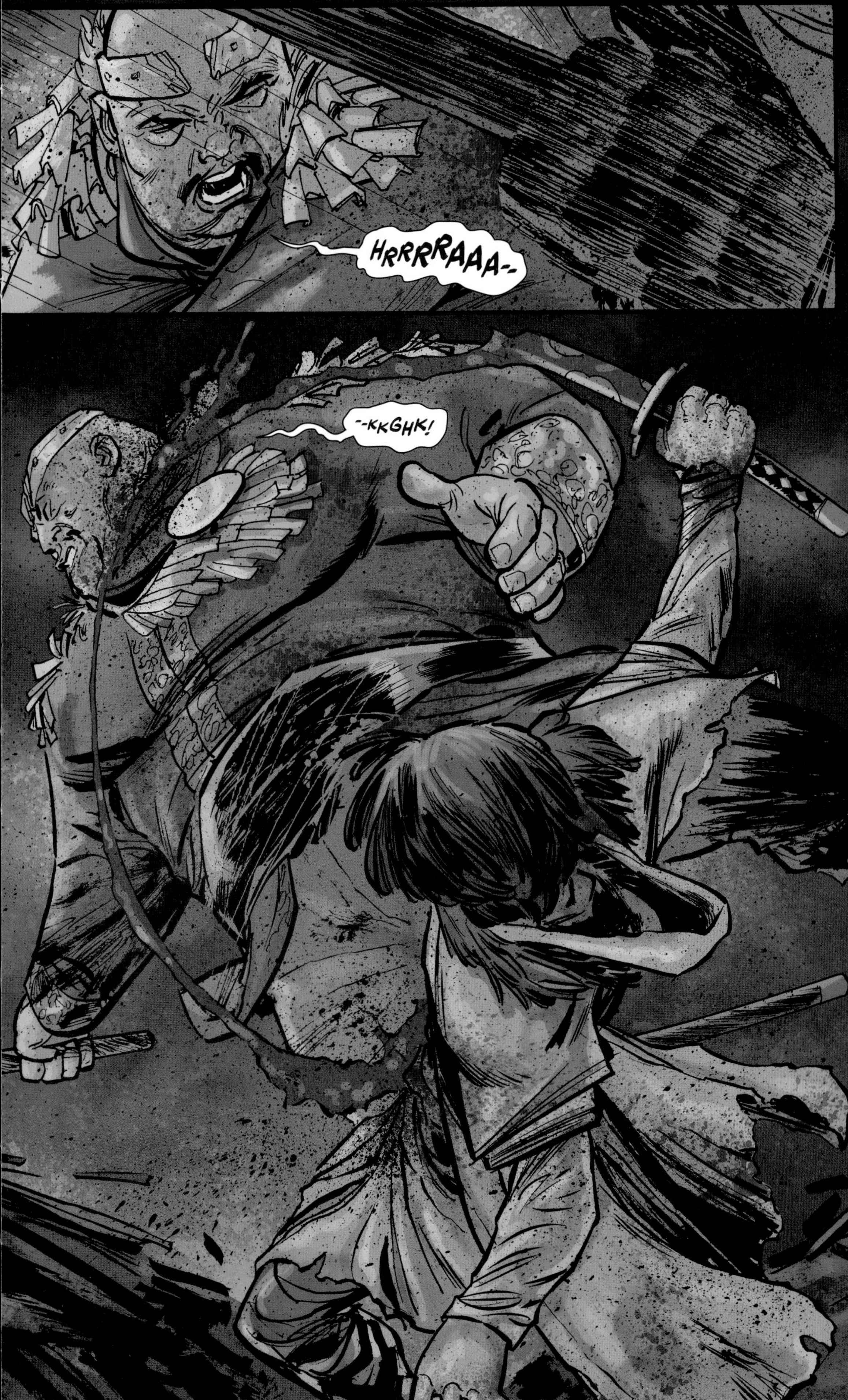
HRRRRAAA--
--KKGHK!

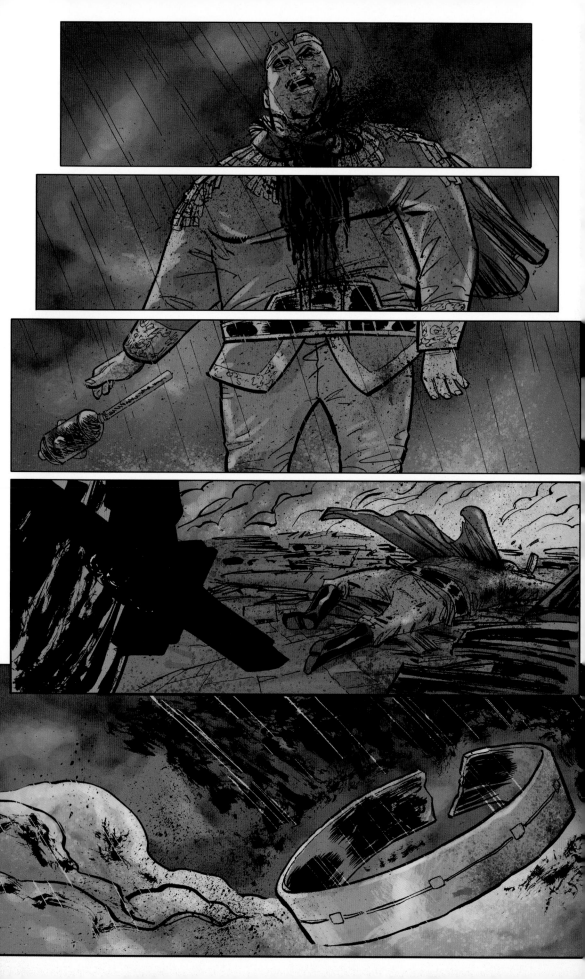

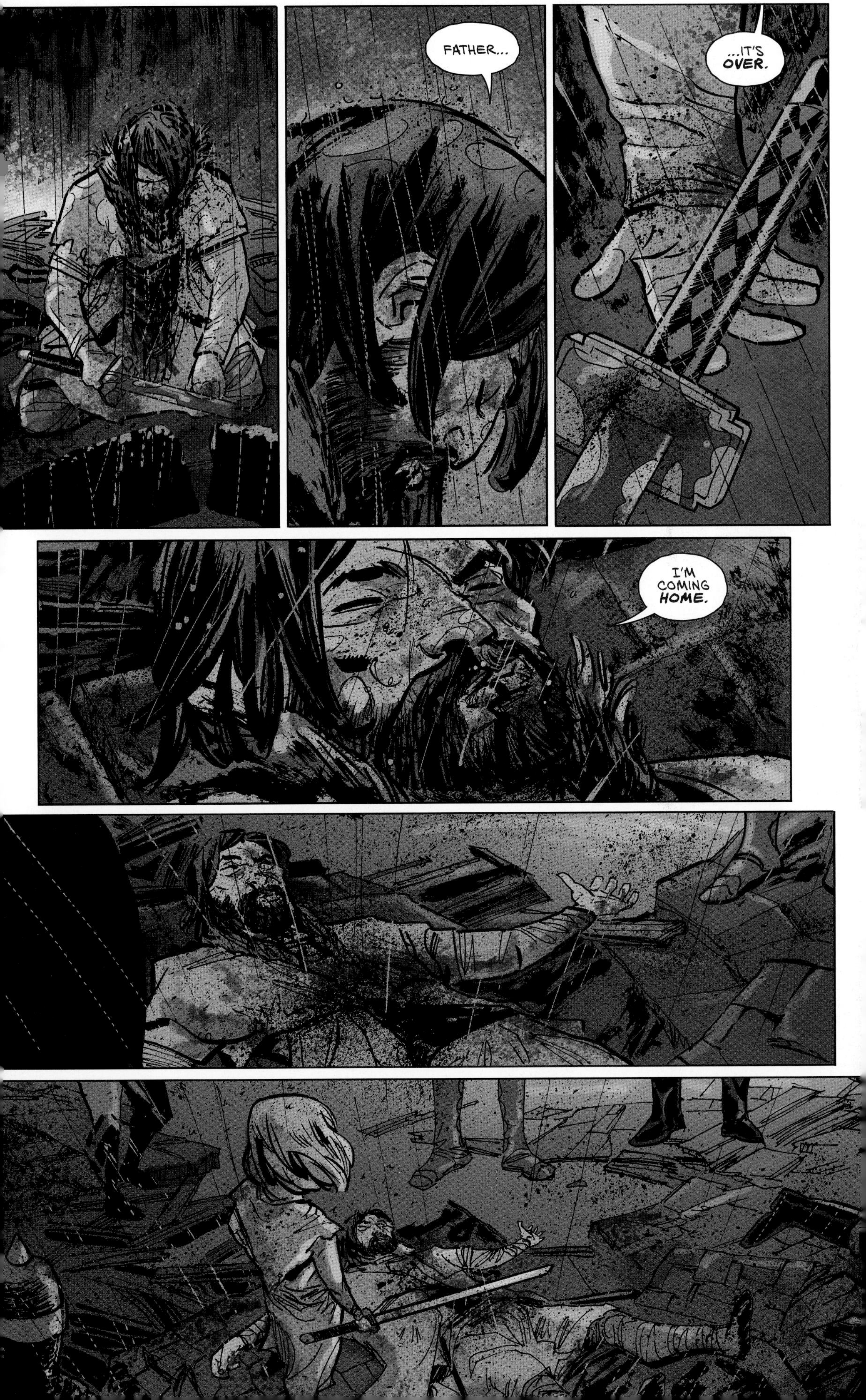
FATHER...
...IT'S OVER.
I'M COMING HOME.

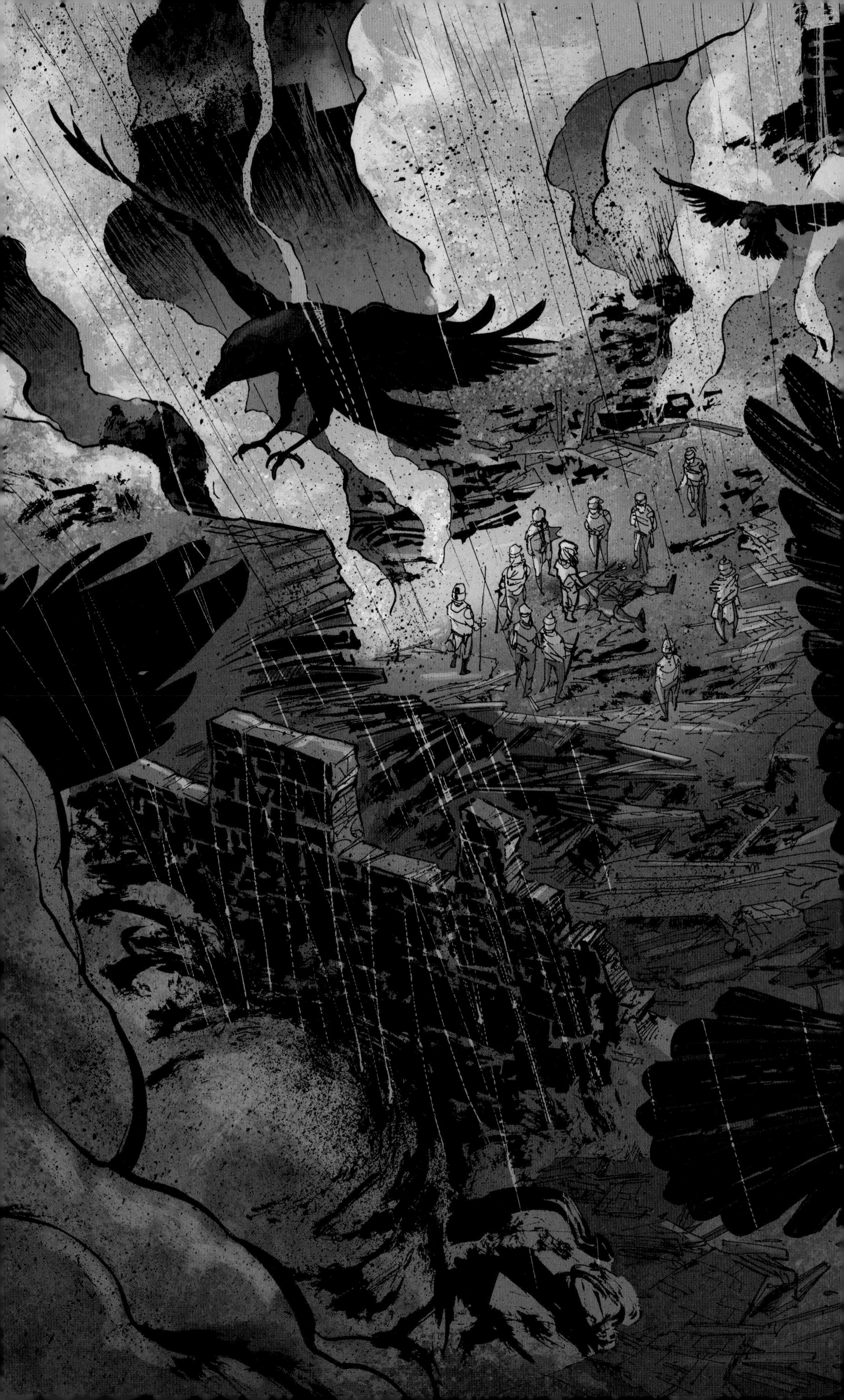

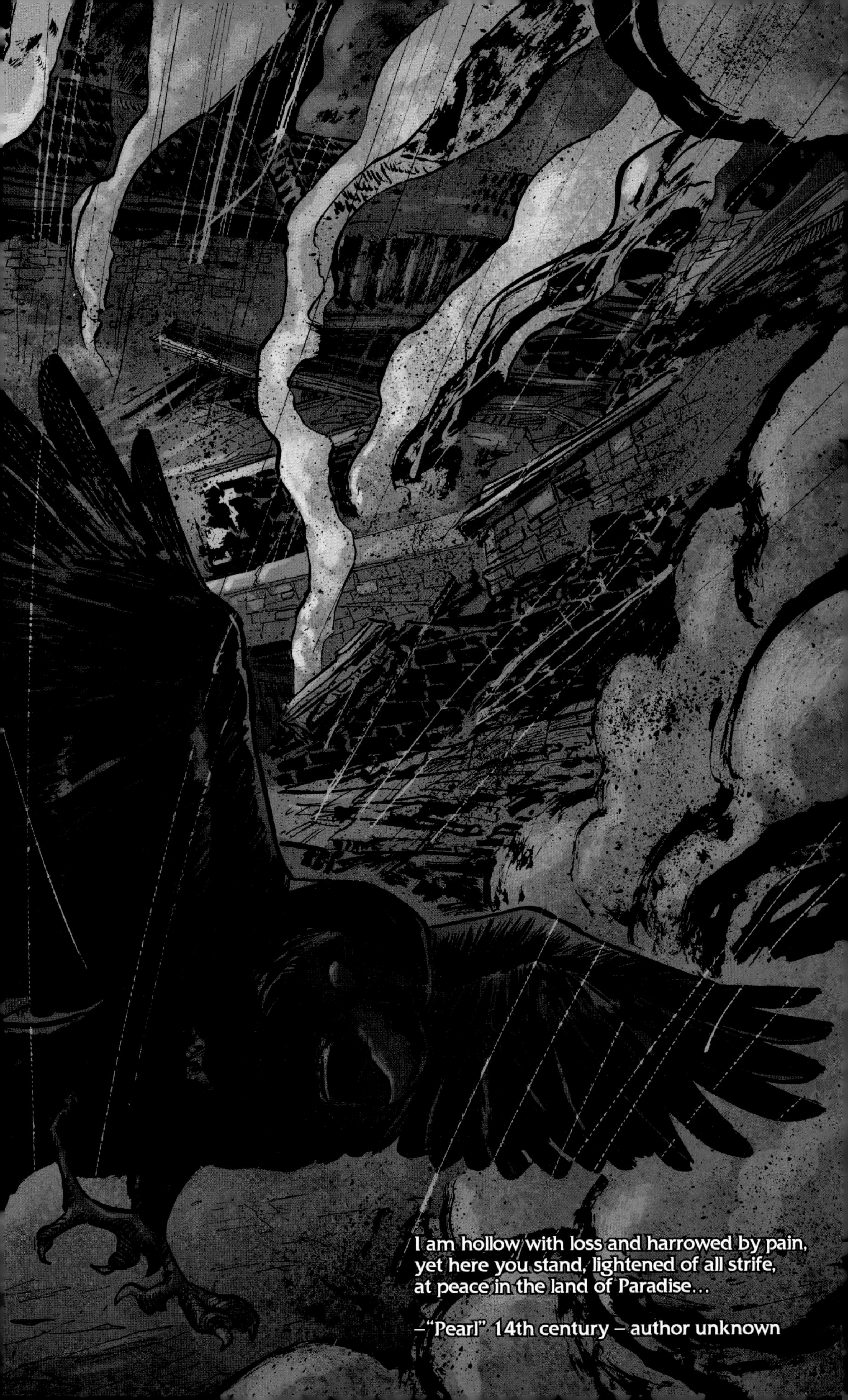
I am hollow with loss and harrowed by pain,
yet here you stand, lightened of all strife,
at peace in the land of Paradise…
–"Pearl" 14th century – author unknown

THE TWO
~ chapter 4 ~
SWORDS

Lord Aedon knew he was dying.

He didn't know whose blade it was that had struck him, but it had belonged to an ally.

Traitors.
Cowards.
His own countrymen, turned to swear fealty to a foreign king out of fear.

The lords of the west had held a strategic point, their phalanx strong enough to stand against the repeated assault of the king's men. The enemy's arrows were wasted against their heavy shields, and their long spears would repel any charge of horses.

It wouldn't last forever. Bit by bit, the king's much larger force would wear the defense down. But that could take the frustrated invaders weeks — and circumventing the pass would take months.

But the ranks of the defenders had been broken through coarse betrayal, and his army had been butchered — leaving only Aedon alive, unable to move due to his wounds, dying slowly on a now-deserted battlefield.

"Cathryn…" he whispered. But he knew it was no use. His daughter would fare no better than he had at the hands of the bastard king and his dogs.

His vision blurred. He held his belly tighter, willing his life not to leak out of him. It was no use. He felt cold…

"Lord Aedon."

Aedon opened his eyes. "Tomislav," he smiled. "You're late."

Tomislav knelt, the pain in his eyes unmistakable. "I came as fast as I could. I'm…"

Aedon shook his head. "No need."

He reached up and gripped Tomislav's tunic. "The weapon…" he whispered hoarsely. "Is it delivered?"

"Under the castle. All of it. And all in secret."

"Then we still have a chance. My horse. Find its body. Bring me my seal and a scroll."

Tomislav blinked, confused.

"My daughter will not die. Not at the hands of those men. Promise me this."

"I swear to you, my lord. You have given me my life back…" Tomislav gripped Aedon's hand tightly.

"…and I will die to protect your daughter."

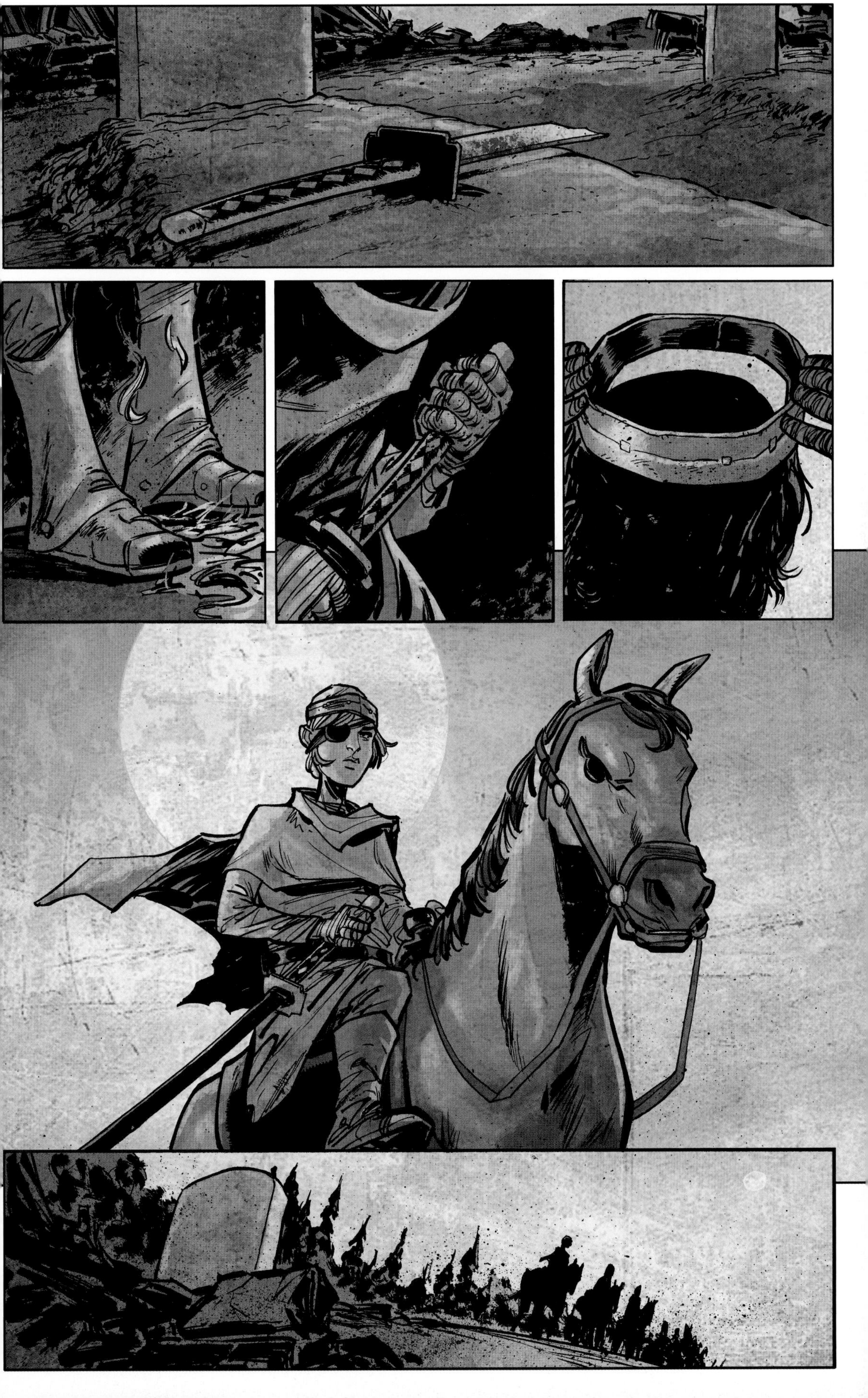

THE LAST SIEGE

VARIANT COVER GALLERY

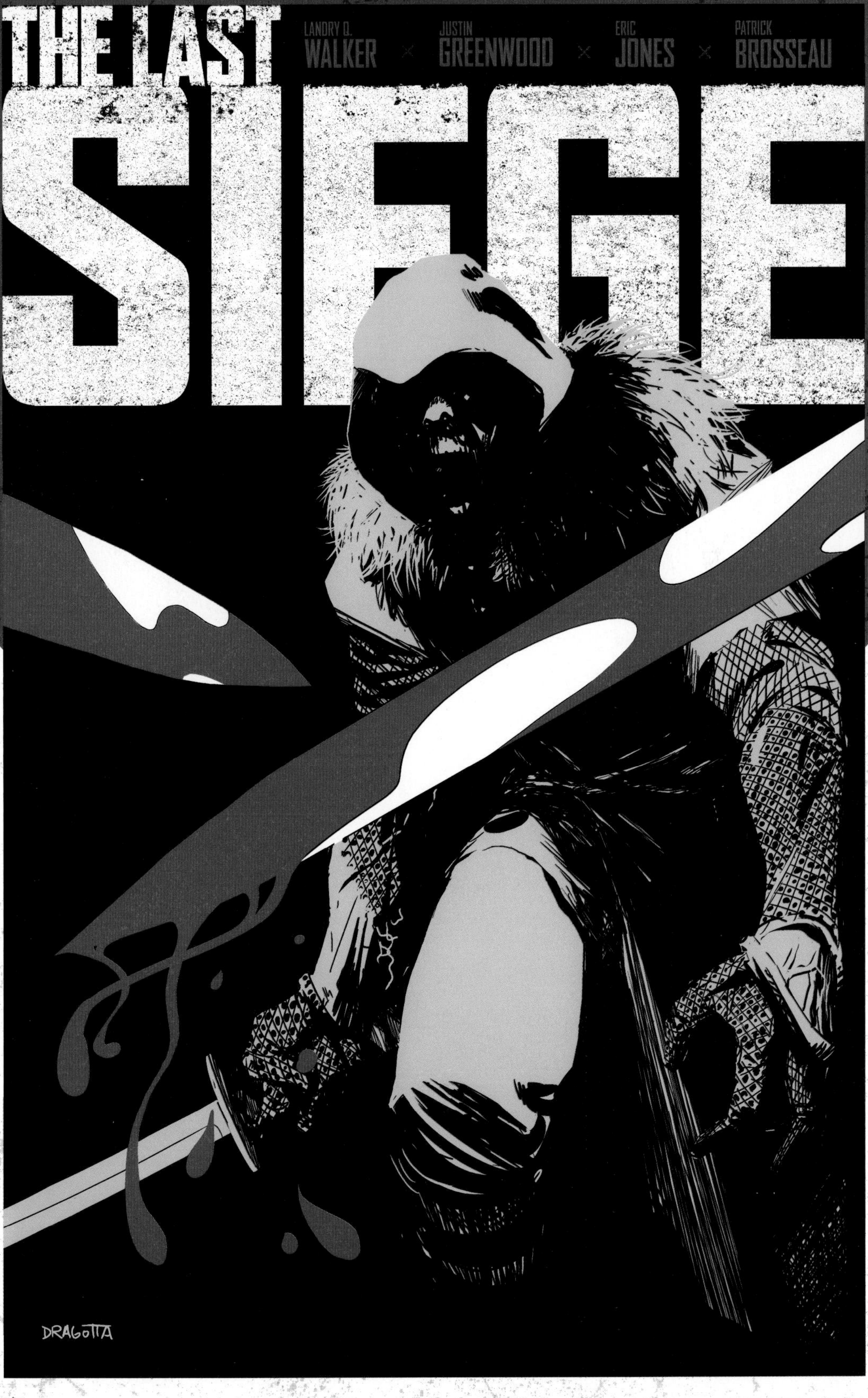

THE LAST
SIEGE
LANDRY Q.
WALKER
JUSTIN
GREENWOOD
ERIC
JONES
PATRICK
BROSSEAU
DRAGOTTA

ISSUE #1 VARIANT COVER BY ×NICK DRAGOTTA

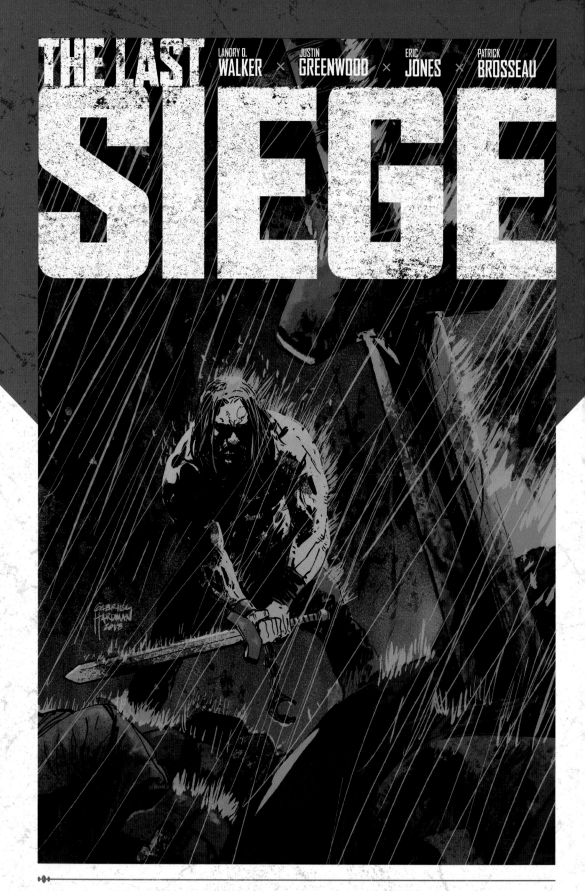

THE LAST SIEGE

LANDRY Q. **WALKER** × JUSTIN **GREENWOOD** × ERIC **JONES** × PATRICK **BROSSEAU**

ISSUE #2 VARIANT COVER BY × GABRIEL HARDMAN

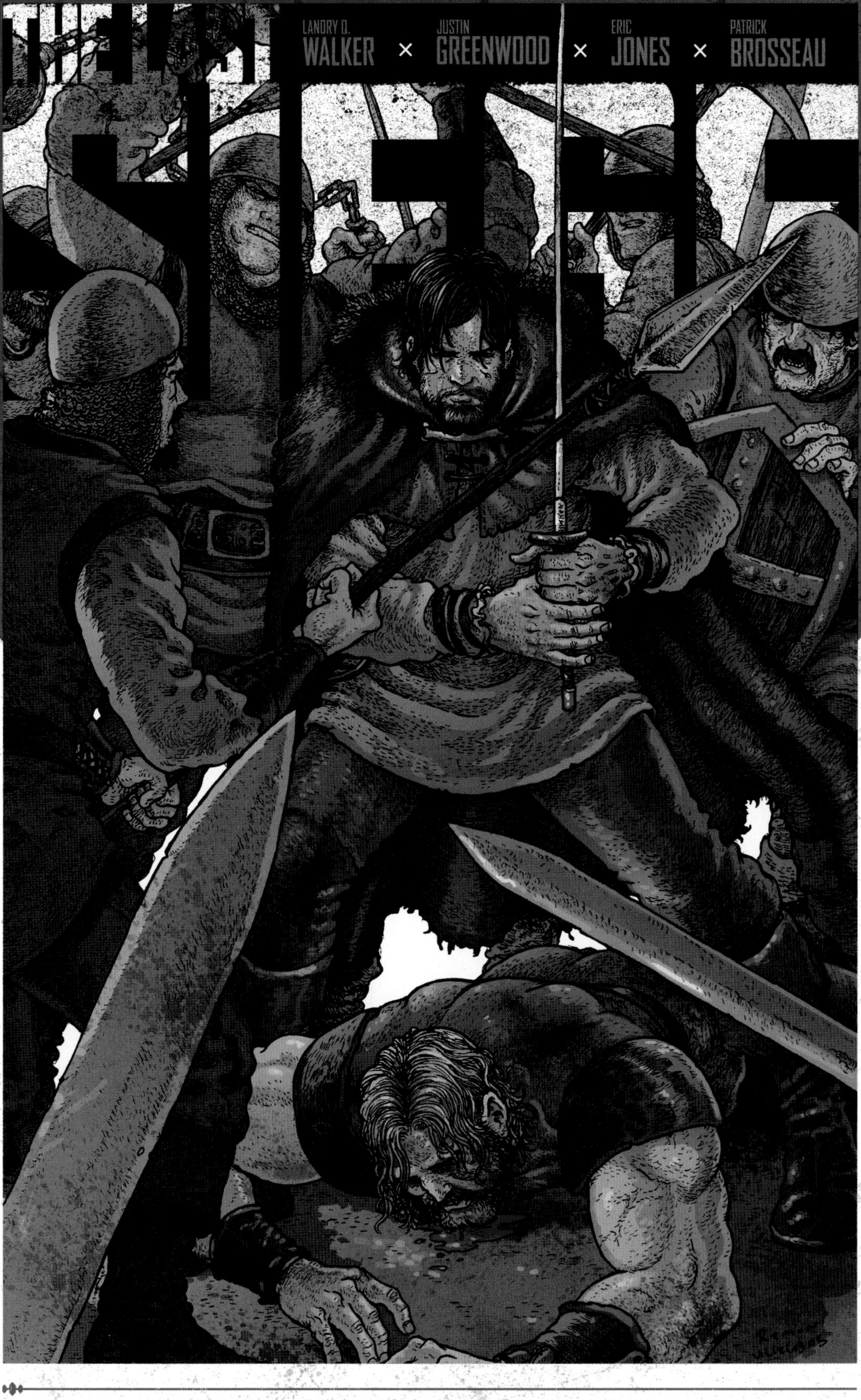
LANDRY Q. WALKER
×
JUSTIN GREENWOOD
×
ERIC JONES
×
PATRICK BROSSEAU

ISSUE #3 VARIANT COVER BY × RAMON VILLALOBOS

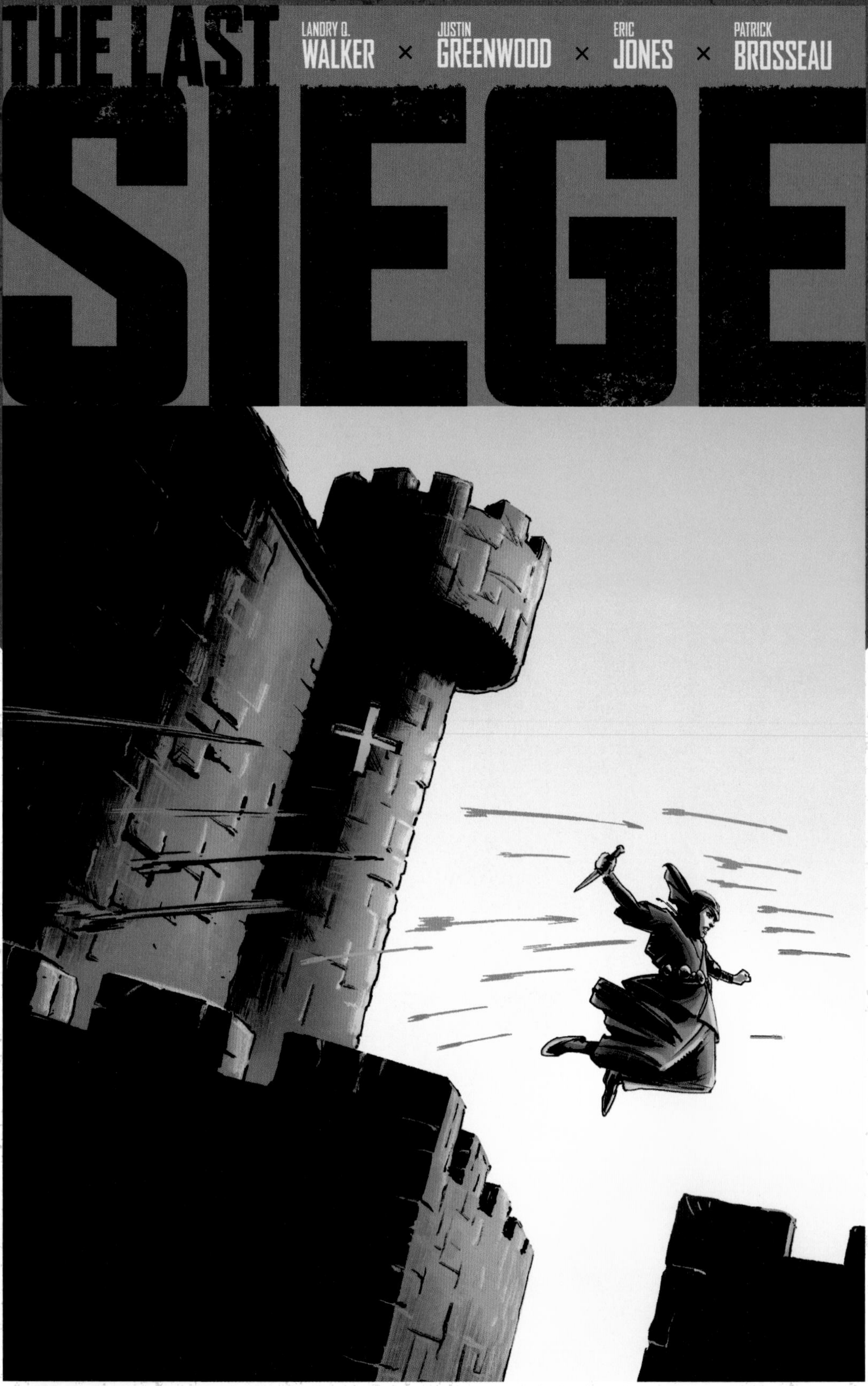
THE LAST
SIEGE
LANDRY Q. WALKER
JUSTIN GREENWOOD
ERIC JONES
PATRICK BROSSEAU

ISSUE #4 VARIANT COVER BY × IBRAHIM MOUSTAFA

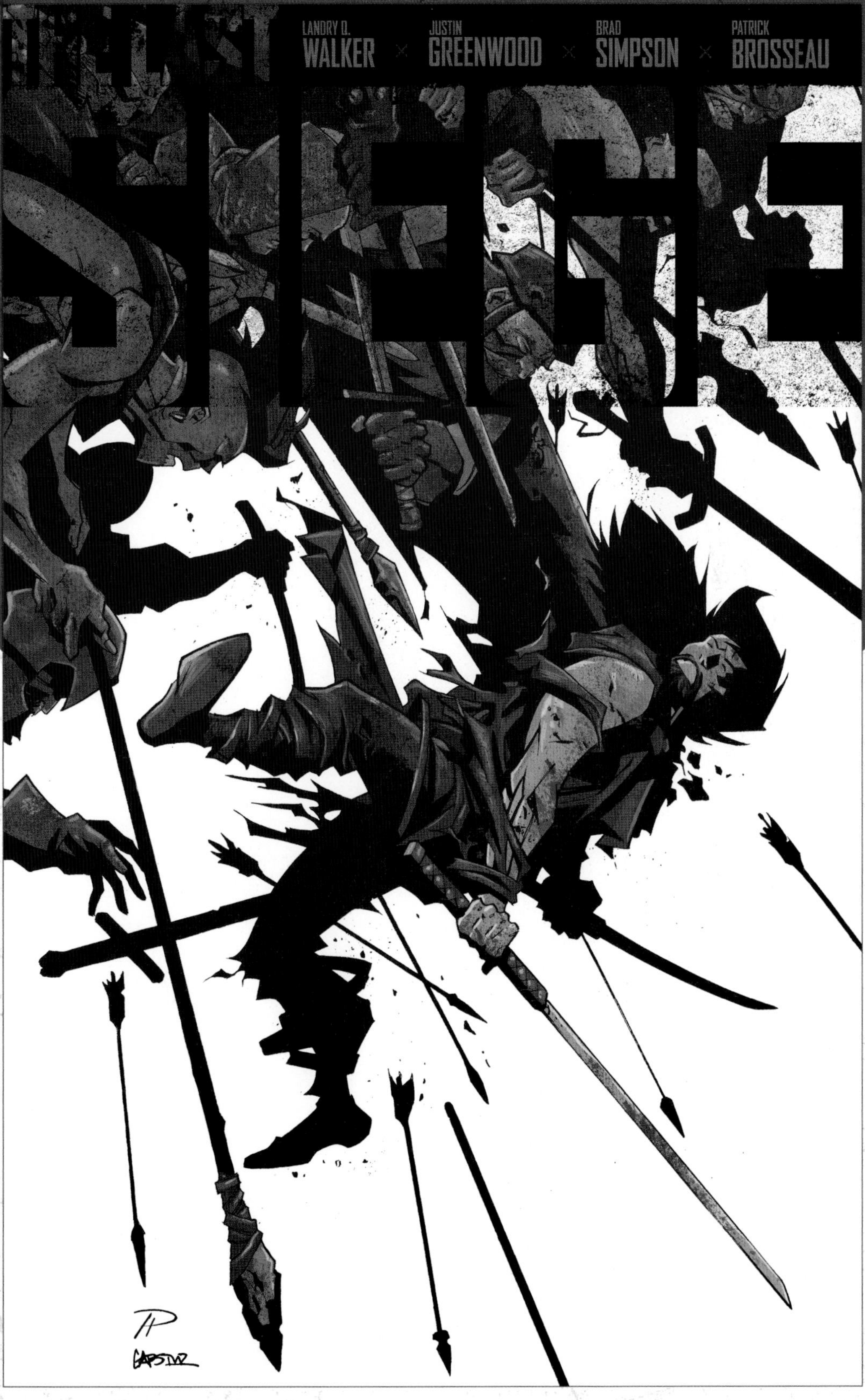
LANDRY Q. WALKER
JUSTIN GREENWOOD
BRAD SIMPSON
PATRICK BROSSEAU

ISSUE #5 VARIANT COVER BY × PHIL HESTER AND × ERIC GAPSTUR

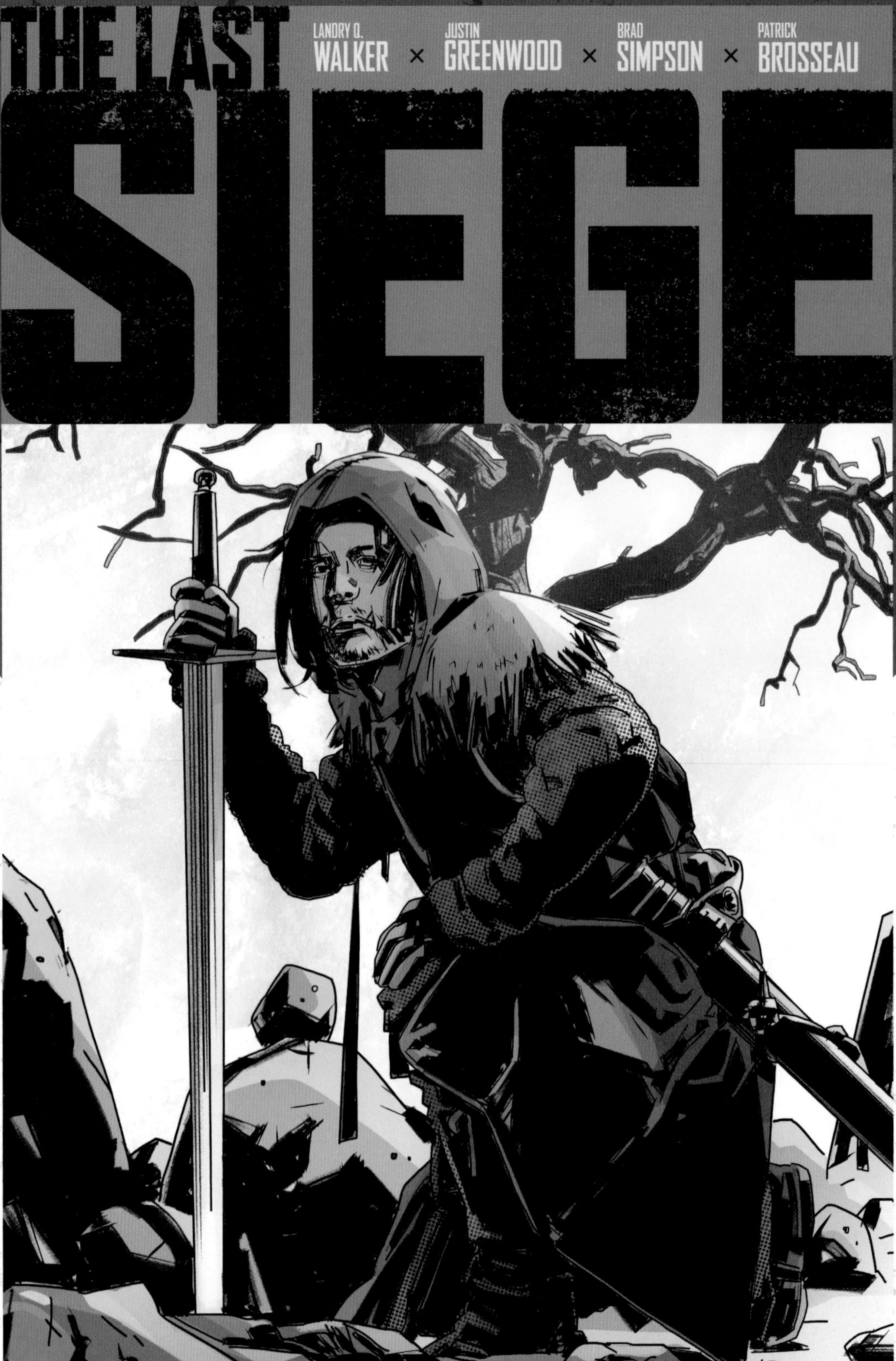
THE LAST
SIEGE
LANDRY Q. WALKER × JUSTIN GREENWOOD × BRAD SIMPSON × PATRICK BROSSEAU

ISSUE #6 VARIANT COVER BY × ANTONIO FUSO

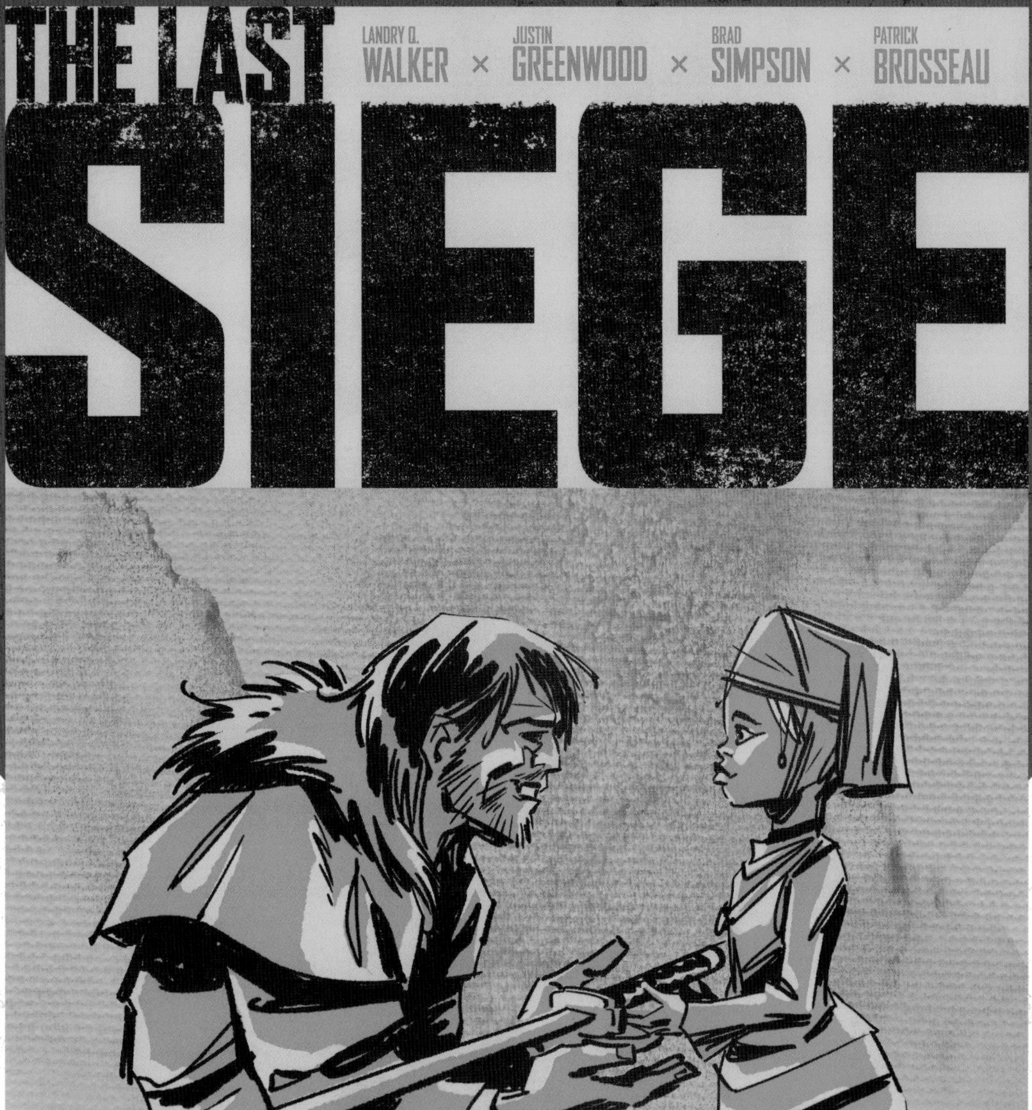

ISSUE #7 VARIANT COVER BY × **ANDY SURIANO**

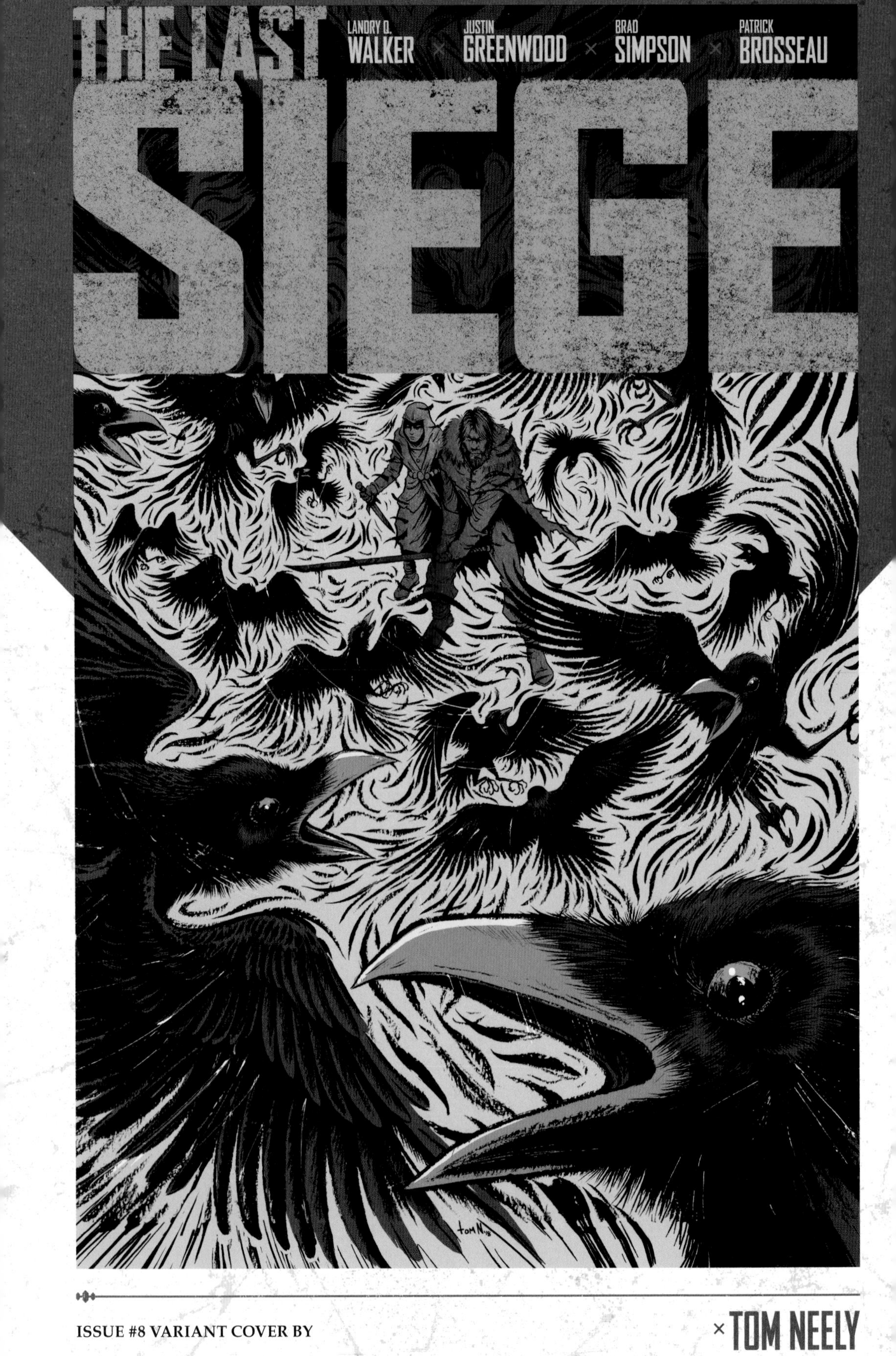
THE LAST
SIEGE
LANDRY Q.
WALKER
JUSTIN
GREENWOOD
BRAD
SIMPSON
PATRICK
BROSSEAU

ISSUE #8 VARIANT COVER BY × TOM NEELY

THE LAST SIEGE

CONCEPT ART BY JUSTIN GREENWOOD

ABOVE: Initial character sketch of The Stranger.

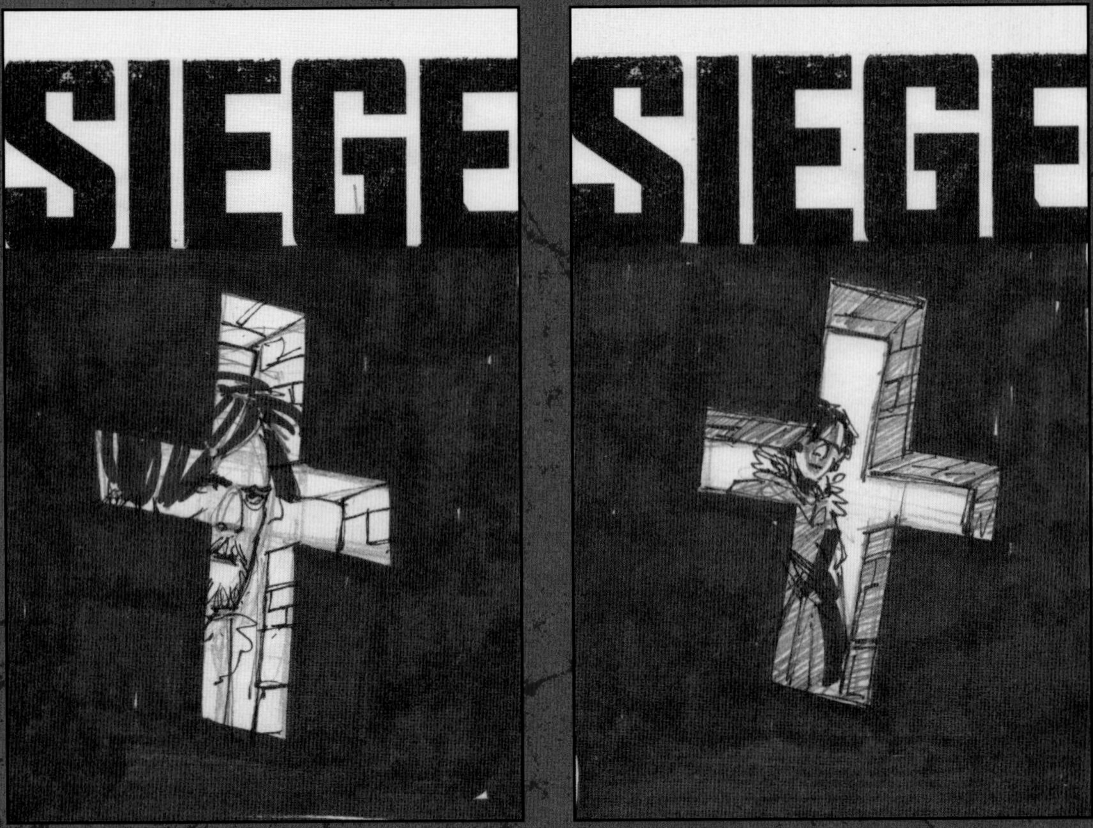
SIEGE
SIEGE

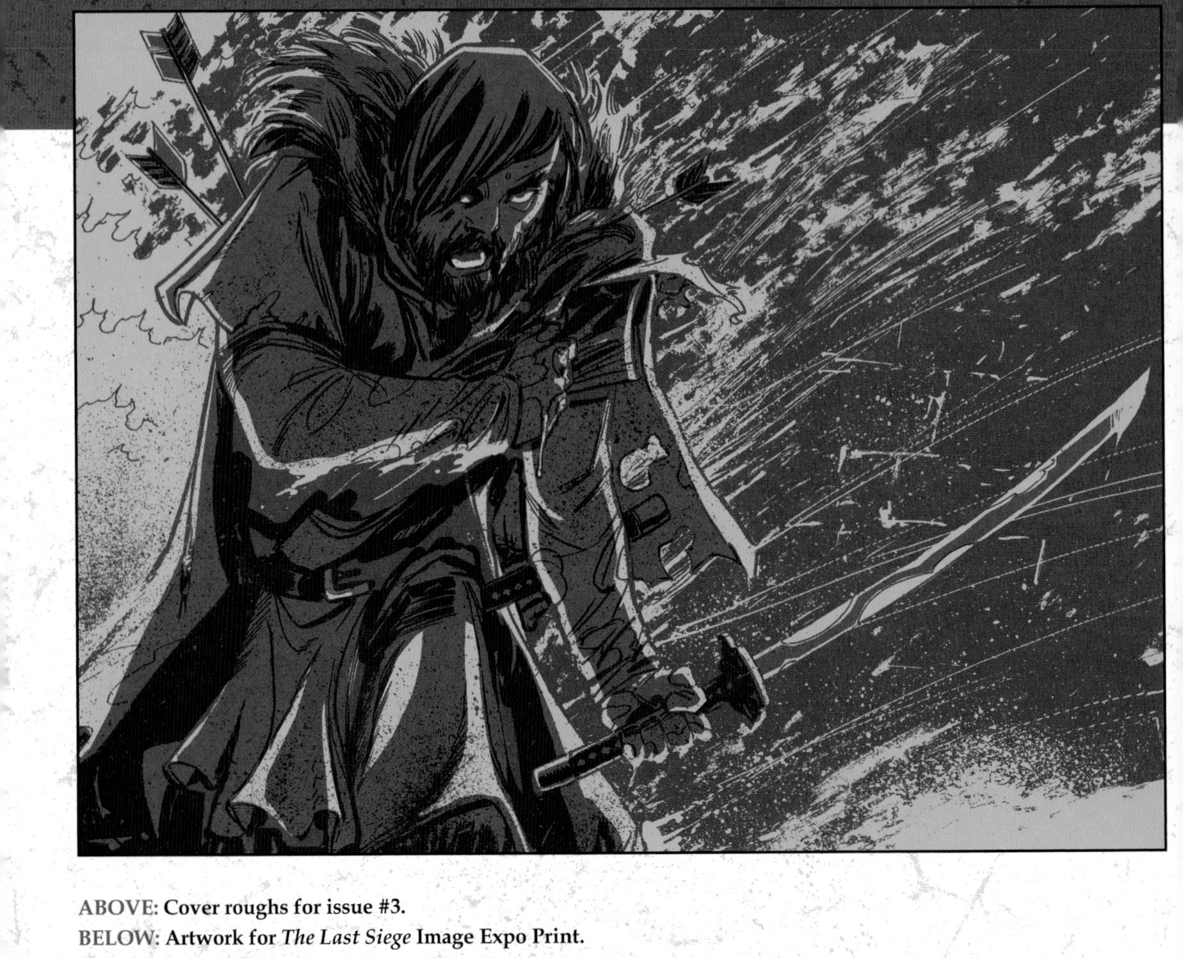

ABOVE: Cover roughs for issue #3.
BELOW: Artwork for *The Last Siege* Image Expo Print.

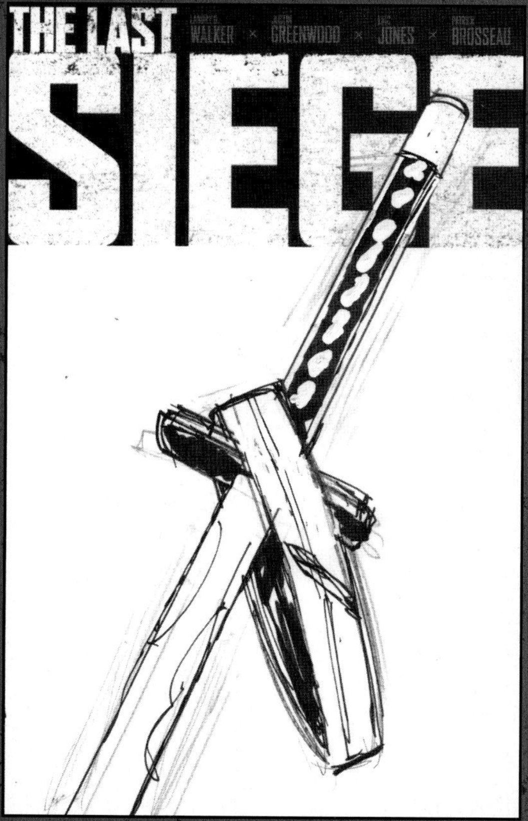
THE LAST
SIEGE
WALKER × GREENWOOD × JONES × BROSSEAU

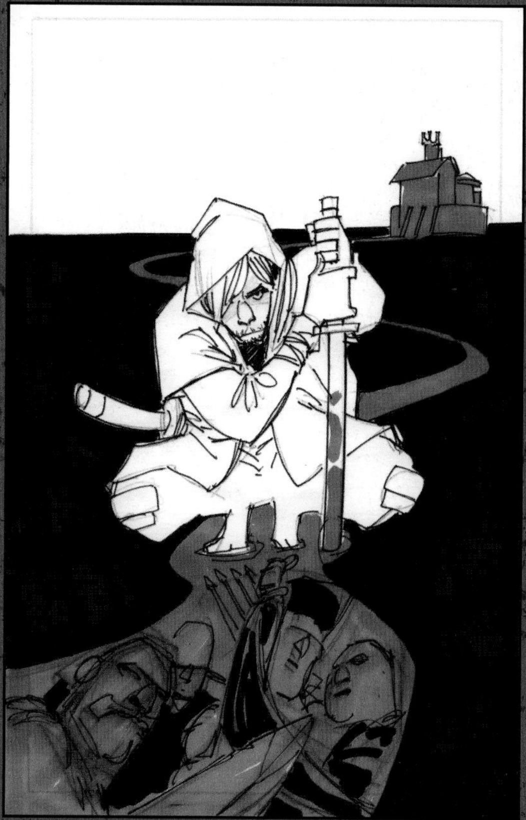

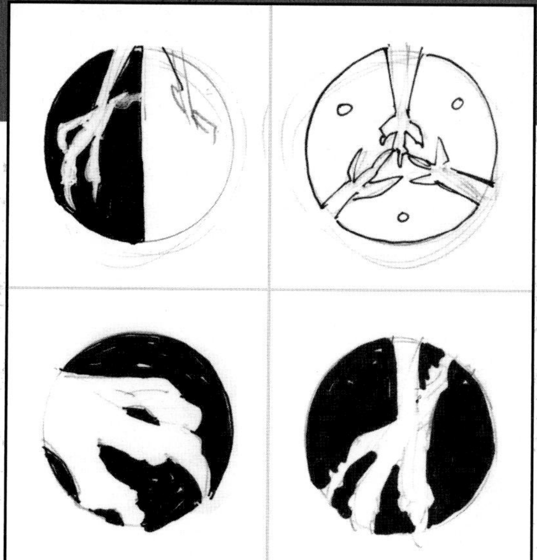

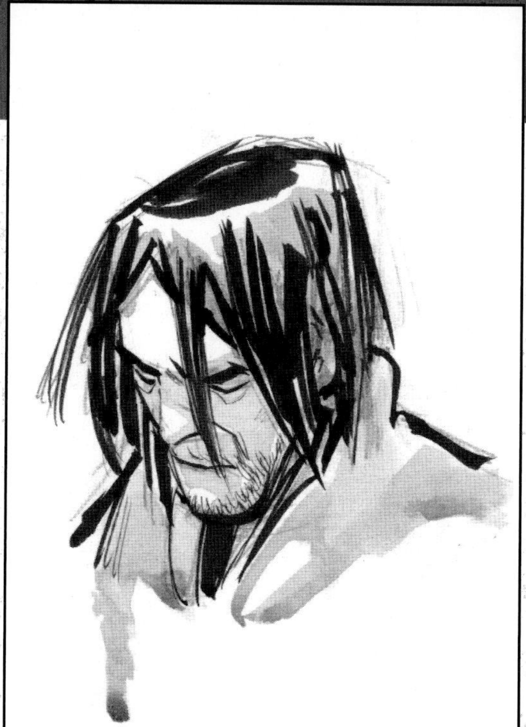

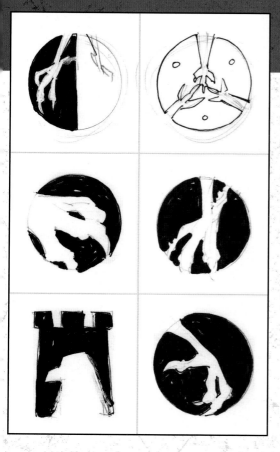

ABOVE: An unused cover layout and the cover sketch to issue #1.
BELOW: Sigil design roughs and a character sketch of The Stranger.

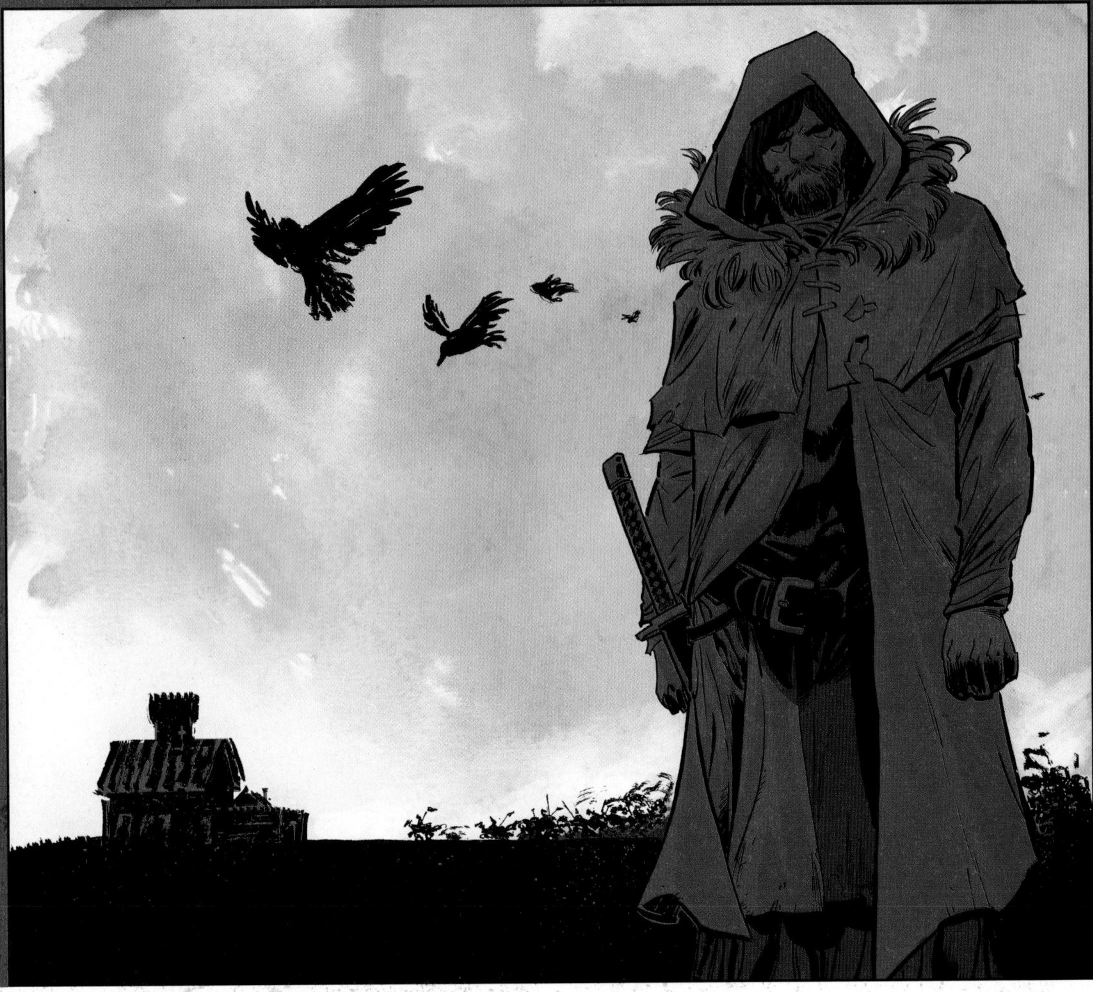

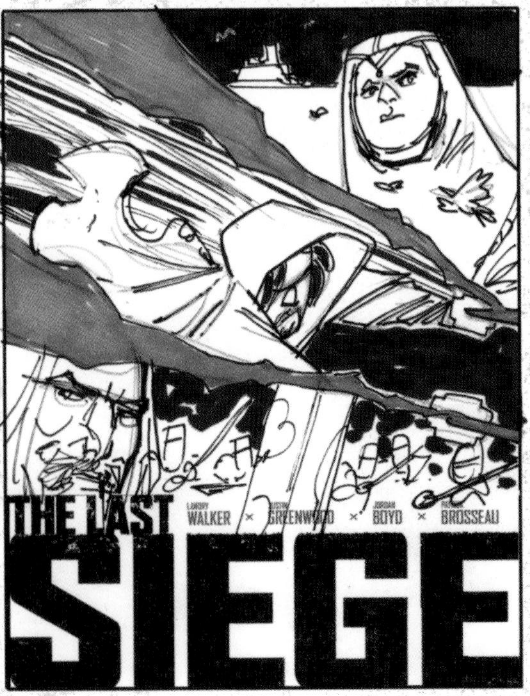
THE LAST
LANDRY WALKER × JUSTIN GREENWOOD × JORDAN BOYD × BROSSEAU
SIEGE

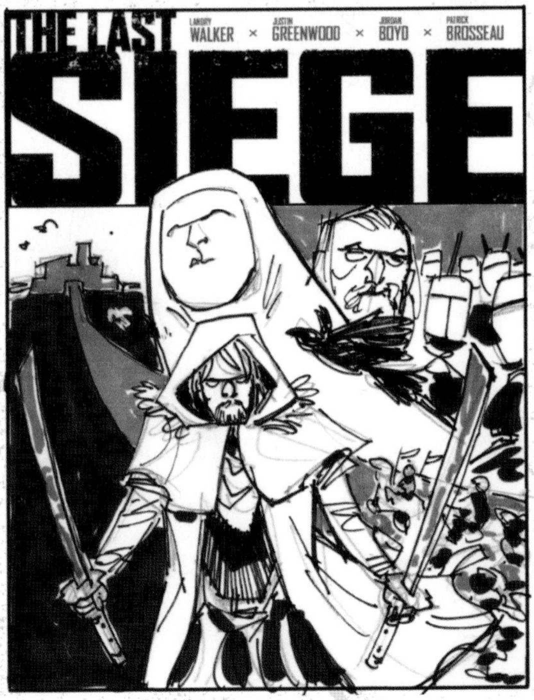
THE LAST
LANDRY WALKER × JUSTIN GREENWOOD × JORDAN BOYD × PATRICK BROSSEAU
SIEGE

ABOVE: **Unused Artwork for** ***The Last Siege*** **Image Expo Print.**
BELOW: **Print Sketches.**

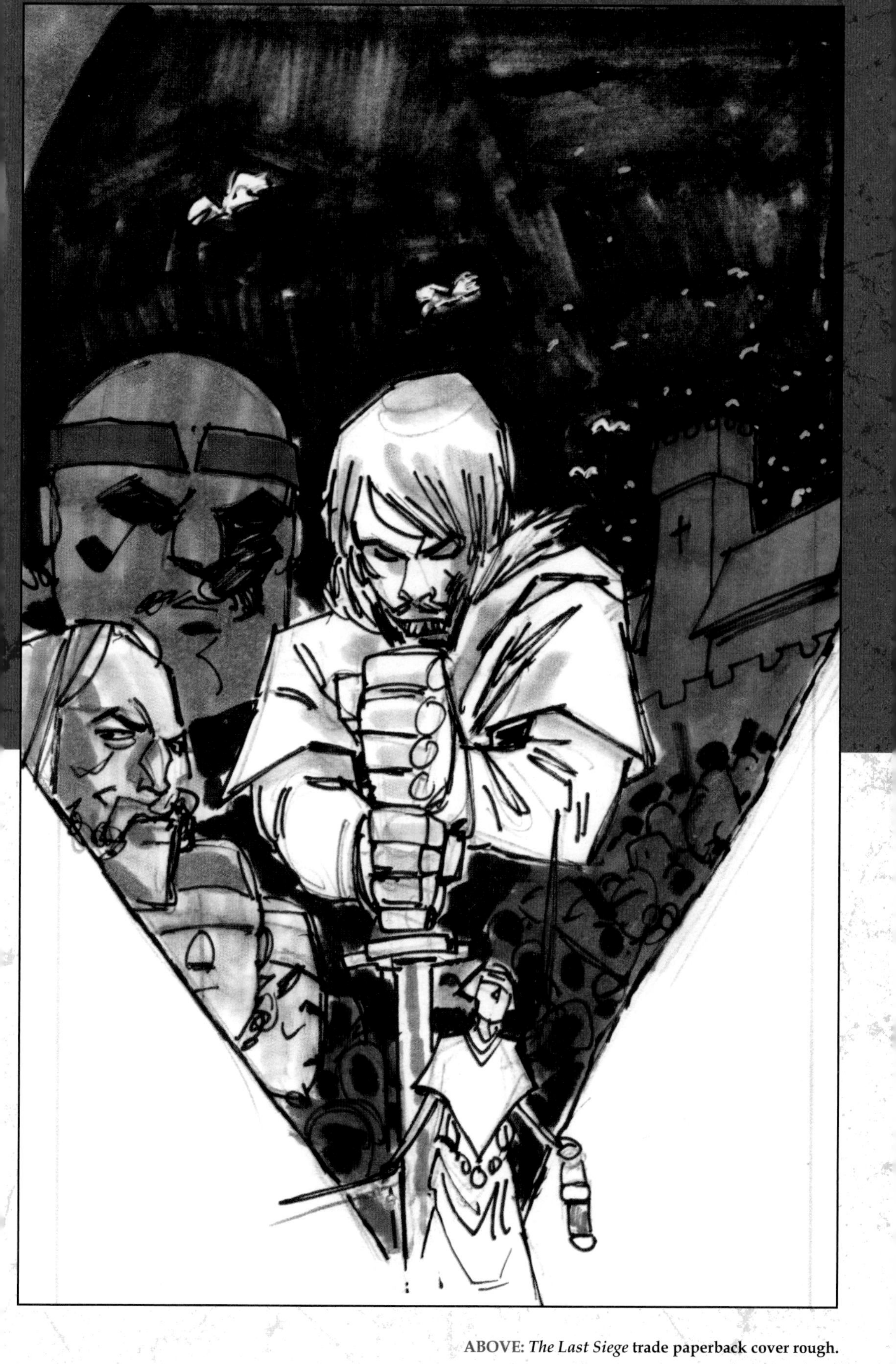

ABOVE: ***The Last Siege*** **trade paperback cover rough.**

ABOUT THE CREATORS

LANDRY Q. WALKER is a *New York Times* bestselling author of comics and books. His work includes the book you are holding in your hands. Also, he writes comics involving *Star Wars, Batman, Supergirl, Teenage Mutant Ninja Turtles*, and a whole bunch of other stuff you've heard of. He even co-created a Saturday morning cartoon called *Scary Larry*. He likes castles and robots and also Pop-Tarts. Most days, he hangs out with his wife and his cats and pushes buttons on a keyboard until stories somehow happen.

landrywalker.com 🐦*@LandryQWalker*

JUSTIN GREENWOOD is an illustrator best known for his work on comic book series like *Stumptown*, THE FUSE, *Stringers*, LAZARUS X+66, *Wasteland*, and *Resurrection*. When not drawing, you can find him hanging with his wife and kids around the foothills of the Sierra Nevadas, pretending to pan for gold while trying to sneak an occasional nap.

justingreenwoodart.com 🐦*@jkgreenwood_art* 📷*justingreenwoodart*

ERIC JONES is an artist, writer, and colorist who has been making comics for 25 years, primarily collaborating with Landry Q. Walker. In that time they've worked on projects as varied as *Supergirl: Cosmic Adventures In The 8th Grade*, *Star Wars Adventures*, and the dark superhero epic DANGER CLUB. He's currently hard at work drawing a new graphic novel he's co-creating with Walker, and he's probably listening to 1970s punk rock right now.

🐦*@cartoonjones* 📷*@cartoonjonesart*

BRAD SIMPSON'S distinct color art has appeared in numerous titles including *The Amazing Spiderman, 30 Days of Night*, and in the current monthly series *Bloodborne*. He resides in Oakland, California, with his wife, Sarah, and sons, Clive and Maddox. When he is not on a deadline, he enjoys anticipating future deadlines.

🐦*@20eyesbrad* 📷*@20eyesbrad*

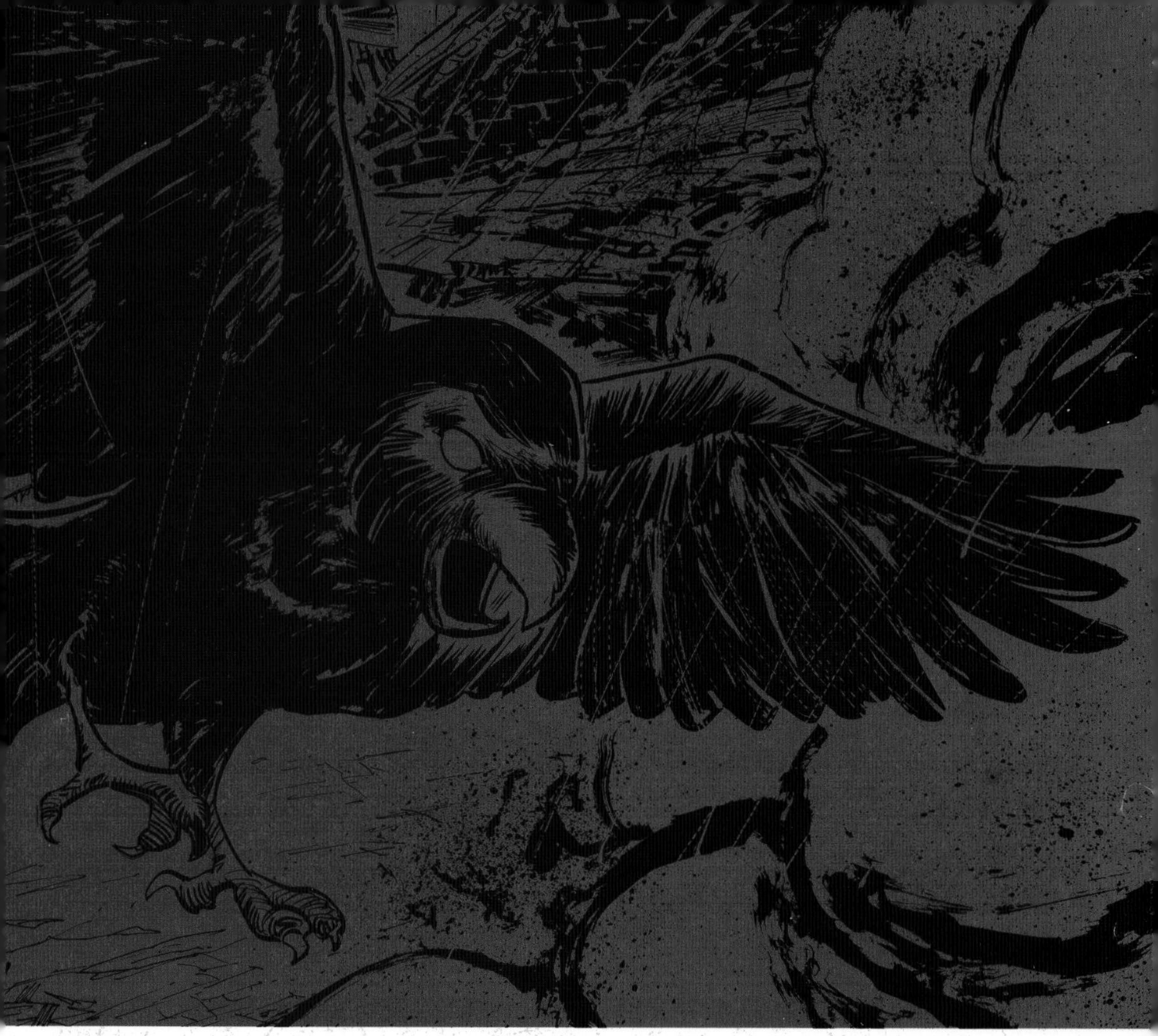

PATRICK BROSSEAU was trained somewhere in the Burmese mountains by Gaspar Saladino worshipping Tibetan monks in the lost art of comic book lettering many moons ago. Patrick quickly rose to the top of the lettering game, only to fall to the bottom after becoming addicted to sniffing felt-tip markers. He now lives in Southern California with his lovely wife and daughter, and letters many fine comic books while daydreaming of lettering the perfect sound effect.

comicbooklettering.tumblr.com *@droog811*

KEITH WOOD is an art director and brand designer specializing in comic books, gaming, and entertainment. He stares at pixels day and night, which is why he wears glasses. He's designed for Darkhorse Comics, Image Comics, Oni Press, ICON, DC Comics, Toonhound Studios, Bandai Namco Entertainment, Microsoft Studios, Electronic Arts, Mojang, Lucas Film Books, 20th Century Fox, Nickelodeon, Konami, Renegade Games, and many comic book creators. He resides in Portland, Oregon with his amazing wife and their two young children. Currently, he's hard at work designing fan-favorite books that will be on sale in approximately 3-6 months.

comicbookdesign.com *@keithawood*

Bay Area native BRANWYN BIGGLESTONE edits comics such as G-MAN, ALPHA GIRL, DANGER CLUB, EXOR-SISTERS, and ME THE PEOPLE, in addition to THE LAST SIEGE. When she's not editing books, you can find her cheering on the Golden State Warriors, walking ten-thousand steps a day around Oakland, reading textbooks with her cats Sheriff Mike and Devil Doll, and acting as CFO for the family game and toy store - Games of Berkeley.

@biggletron